D1544269

FALL GUY

SCOTT MACKAY
FALL GUY

ST. MARTIN'S MINOTAUR ✿ NEW YORK

www.minotaurbooks.com

Designed by Lorelle Graffeo

Library of Congress Cataloging-in-Publication Data

Mackay, Scott.
    Fall guy / Scott Mackay.—1st ed.
      p. cm.
    ISBN 0-312-28155-2
     1. Police—Ontario—Toronto—Fiction. 2. Chinese—
Ontario—Fiction. 3. Toronto (Ont.)—Fiction. I. Title.

  PR9199.3.M3239 F3 2001
  813'.54—dc21

                              2001031948

First Edition: September 2001

10 9 8 7 6 5 4 3 2 1

TO MY DAUGHTER,
JESSICA

ACKNOWLEDGMENTS

I would like to thank James Dubro, and acknowledge his excellent book *Dragons of Crime: Asian Mobs in Canada*.

I must also thank Jeanie Doggett, BSc. (H), MLT, for her expert knowledge on blood-banking procedures and blood phenotyping.

FALL GUY

DETECTIVE BARRY GILBERT STUDIED THE body of Edgar Cheng Lau: his arched back, his bent left knee, and extended right leg. Edgar's big toe pointed with ballet-like grace toward the kitchen door. An elegant corpse, poetic in the positioning of its limbs. His bloodstained shirt, pulled up to his ribs, revealed a flat well-muscled stomach and a ragged gunshot wound. He was about thirty-five. His pale hand clutched a ball of blood-soaked Kleenex; he looked as if he'd been trying to stanch the flow of blood from his wound. His Chinese eyes, partially open, gazed at the French doors, contemplated them in the disturbing dullness of death, as if he found meaning in them—as if beyond their rain-speckled panes he saw things only a dead man could see.

The middle of December, Christmas ten days away, and nothing but rain; no snow, just rain, beating on the old slate shingles of the third-floor dormers, on the tar-and-pebble roof above, on the street outside. Gilbert looked around. Chinese ink drawings hung on the walls. The futon furniture—a sofa and chair—had been slashed, the stuffing pulled out, as if someone had been looking for something inside them. A camera sat on a table. 7-Up cans, crushed to flat little disks, lay piled in a broken bamboo cradle. Books filled the shelves, some Chinese, some English, many on photography, some on Chinese history, a few on Vietnamese history. Dozens of them had been yanked from the shelves and tossed to the floor. Rainwater had been tramped across the hardwood floor in ill-defined footprints. A step ladder stood in the middle of the living room. A torn piece of bloodstained newspaper lay beside it.

Gilbert walked over, had a closer look: a triangular piece of newspaper, ripped from one of the Chinese dailies, stained with small dry smears, slightly crumpled, as if someone had been trying to wipe blood with it, sitting here far from the main pool under Edgar's body. What could it mean?

Gilbert's partner, Detective Joe Lombardo, sixteen years his junior, smart, young, handsome, came out of the bedroom with a photograph album. He also carried a nine-round clip of ammunition. Lombardo flipped through the photograph album as he approached Gilbert, his dark eyes scanning the photographs with Mediterranean intensity.

"What's with the clip?" asked Gilbert.

Lombardo held up the magazine. "Forty-five caliber," he said. "I found it between the mattress and the box spring," he said.

"No gun?" asked Gilbert.

"No gun," said Lombardo. "But take a look at these photos here."

He showed the photograph album to Gilbert, flipped to a page roughly in the middle. The photographs were old, black-and-white, shot on 35-mm film. The deck of a ship. Crowded with men, women, and children, all East Asians, their bodies wasted and thin, their eyes sunken, their expressions hopeless, as if they'd been adrift a long time. The ship, badly pocked with rust, looked barely seaworthy. A few older men stood around the deck with rifles. Some looked out to sea, others stared sullenly at the camera. One of them had a bandoleer of machine-gun ammunition crisscrossed over his chest. Two black pigs tethered to the railing ate what looked like a large snake.

"Boat people?" said Gilbert.

"That's what I thought," said Lombardo.

"He's got Vietnam history books over there," said Gilbert. "A lot of stuff about the war."

The two detectives looked at Edgar Lau. Then back at the photographs. Then at the camera on the table. A Pentax 35-mm. A professional camera. Lombardo turned the page. More photographs, these ones in color, taken with a different camera. Standard Kodak film. The photographs showed the pockmarked ship from the deck of a much larger ship, way down in the well of the blue sea, not so crowded anymore, not as many children. The people on the boat looked up, peering from under the brims of wide straw hats. Another photograph showed sea-worn East Asians climbing aboard the much larger ship, struggling up a rope ladder, all of them skinny; brown stick people with shaggy black hair. Then photographs of white people on the bigger ship, some in uniform, two or three in regular clothes, one man wearing a shirt with a large collar, a garment identifiably from 1970s.

"That's a Dutch flag up there," said Lombardo, pointing to the ship's mast.

Gilbert glanced at their victim. Had the man been on that boat, he wondered, maybe as a child a long time ago? Why else would he have this photograph album? He gave the album back to Joe.

"We voucher the clip," he said.

"I agree," said Lombardo.

Gilbert turned to the victim. He took a few distracted steps toward Edgar Lau.

"Barry?" said Lombardo.

Gilbert didn't answer. He knelt beside Edgar. A handsome face. Skin the color of ripe wheat, a strong jaw, wide cheekbones, black hair, but with a streak of turquoise dye in it, like his nineteen-year-old daughter Jennifer had. The detail stuck, Edgar connecting to Jennifer, Jennifer connecting to Edgar, each saying something with a bit of blue dye. A rebel? Perhaps. A small earring pierced his left ear. He had a striking nose, a nose not often seen on a Chinese, strong, with a Roman bridge. He wore Levi's and a black leather belt studded with hobnails.

"Poor bugger," said Gilbert.

Lombardo turned, pointed to the French doors. "The killer came in the back," he postulated.

Was that why Edgar stared at the French doors with a look of such perplexity on his face? Gilbert gazed at the French doors, twelve panes of glass in each, the white paint flaking from the frames, showing older green paint underneath, the corners of each frame darkened with mildew. Beyond the windows the rain came down like a deluge—black, inky, rattling against the metal fire escape like inmates rattling their bars before a prison riot.

"No sign of forced entry," said Gilbert.

"And the victim has an ammunition clip," said Lombardo.

"Which means there's got to be a gun. Only we just haven't found it yet." The clip an undeniable signpost, an intimation of a problematic investigation. "A man who owns a gun wouldn't leave his back door unlocked."

Here was the mystery. Not only the clip, but the French doors, unlocked, the water tracked onto the floor, no splintered latches or broken locks, just Edgar Lau opening the door for his killer, maybe talking to his killer, but ultimately succumbing to his killer. What did that say about the relationship between the victim and his attacker? Gilbert got up. Edgar knew his murderer. His killer had entered without protest or resistance. Perhaps words had been exchanged. Then the murder weapon had been fired. And the apartment had been searched.

"I'd like to talk to the first officer again," said Gilbert. "What'd he say his name was?"

Lombardo took out a damp notebook and consulted the second page. "Kennedy," said Lombardo. He looked up. "Donald Kennedy. From the 52 Division. Your old division."

Gilbert nodded, thinking of 52 Division down on Dundas, a big white building, his home during his years in patrol, a squat building with as much Chinese writing on the big glass doors as English writing.

"Was there anything else in the bedroom?" he asked.

"Lots," said Lombardo. Gilbert caught a whiff of Lombardo's musky cologne. "Luggage packed on the floor and several quotes for plane tickets to San Francisco."

The two detectives walked to the bedroom, the soles of their wet shoes squeaking against the floor. As they crossed the hall, Gilbert spotted scratch marks on the hardwood floor. He knelt and had a look at them: four scratch marks configured into the corner points of a rough rectangle. He remembered the ladder. He looked up and saw an access panel recessed into the ceiling leading to the attic, a dirty handprint visible on the white paint, and a sticker of the Rolling Stones's famous mouth-and-tongue logo in the corner.

"We'll check the attic later," he said.

They continued into the bedroom.

Two Samsonite suitcases stood packed on the floor beside the bed. A small writing table, badly scarred, with some green paint splattered in the left top corner, stood next to the bed. Ink and brushes rested on the desk. Several samples of skilled Chinese calligraphy lay on top of the blotter, the scimitar-like strokes constructed delicately one against the other like a fragile house of cards. Gilbert moved these samples aside and found quotes for airline tickets—the price for two fares, Toronto to San Francisco.

"I wonder who he was taking?" asked Gilbert.

Lombardo looked around. "He's a bachelor," he said. "It takes one to know one."

Gilbert scanned the wall. "Look at this photograph," he said. Edgar loved his photography, that was for sure.

A framed photograph hung on the wall: a man and a boy sitting on a small yellow motorcycle with a wide eucalyptus-lined boulevard in the background; street and shop signs not in Chinese but in Vietnamese, U.S. soldiers in battle fatigues and helmets standing on street corners. The man and the boy smiled, their teeth broad and white in their brown faces. Both were wiry, strong, resembled each other. The boy carried a bamboo cage full of pigeons.

"Is that him?" asked Lombardo, pointing to the boy. "Is that our victim?"

From out in the hall Gilbert heard heavy footsteps coming up the stairs. He looked at the street scene closely. A boy in that far-away time in that faraway place, smiling happily on the back of this yellow Honda motorcycle. Was this smiling boy Edgar Lau? The ceaseless December rain on the tar-and-pebble roof sang a soft song overhead. The boy wore an orange windbreaker. The man wore thin, much-washed clothing, as if he were too poor to afford anything new to wear. Yet, incongruously, he had a glittering gold watch on his wrist. Gilbert looked at the boy again. He definitely thought he detected a resemblance to the man lying out in the dining room.

"I think it might be," he said.

"Joe?" a voice called.

"We're in here," answered Lombardo.

The two detectives left the bedroom and went out to the hall where they found Constable Donald Kennedy of 52 Division, first officer on the scene. Despite the unusually mild December weather, Kennedy wore a navy-blue police parka, a fur cap, and standard-issue winter boots. He was a large, ruddy-faced man, a drinker by the look of him, with a rust-red mustache and sharply focused blue eyes, eyes that looked wide and surprised and chiseled out of azure marble. His lower lip sagged, as if he had a deficit in his muscles there, hung pink and moist above his chin, as pendulous as a piece of uncooked liver.

"The CSU is here," said Kennedy. Kennedy had a challenging manner. He seemed to think he owned the scene, and that he might have to defend it at any moment, even against Gilbert and Lombardo. "They're coming up with their equipment."

"I just want to ask you," said Gilbert, "is the victim known to you at all?"

"I'm having the 52 run a check," said Kennedy.

"How long have you worked Chinatown?" asked Gilbert.

"Fifteen years," said Kennedy. "I was out in 41 Division before."

"Because I doubt he has a permit for that . . . that clip," said Gilbert, nodding toward the magazine on the dining room table. "Or the gun that goes with it."

"I doubt it too," said Kennedy.

"He was still warm when we got here," said Gilbert. Gilbert raised his eyebrows and looked at Constable Kennedy. "Any sign of life when you got here?"

"Barely. But he went ten-fifty-five on me two minutes after I got here." The officer turned to Gilbert, serious, professional, his face as hard as a piece of frozen meat. "I told the paramedics not to touch him." He nodded, glanced around the apartment. "I didn't want them to wreck your scene."

"And his mother lives downstairs?" asked Gilbert.

Kennedy nodded, then gestured toward the apartment door with nicotine-stained fingers. "She's with Mr. Sung right now," he said. He looked at Gilbert questioningly. "Foster Sung." Kennedy gave the name a moment. "Know him?"

"Sure," said Gilbert. Gilbert recalled an article in the pages of *Toronto Life,* a picture of an impeccably dressed middle-aged Chinese man standing over an architectural model of a proposed condominium development near the old Greenwood Racetrack. "He's in real estate," said Gilbert. He recalled a map of Toronto East, the Sung-owned buildings marked with little gold stars. "He's a millionaire developer."

"That's the one," said Kennedy, as if to Kennedy's mind Sung had committed a felony by being so rich.

"And a friend of the Laus?" said Gilbert.

"Yeah," said Kennedy. "He was down in the restaurant when the shooting occurred."

"And he's the one who called?" asked Gilbert.

"He's the one," said Kennedy.

When the two Crime Scene Unit officers reached the apartment, both out of breath from two flights of stairs, both wet from the rain, Gilbert pointed to the water on the floor as well as to the torn piece of newspaper with blood on it, and asked them to get pictures of both.

"I think I'm going to check the fire escape," Gilbert told Lombardo.

"Okay," said Lombardo. "I'm going to continue with the bedroom."

The French doors opened onto a small balcony with a steel-slat floor and steel railings painted black, scourged by scabs of rust. Down below, a paved yard backed onto an alley. The alley ran north from Baldwin Street, curved left, then ran west toward Kensington Market. Gilbert took out his flashlight and turned it on. Rain streaked past the beam like a swarm of bugs. The smell of Chinese food drifted up from below. Gilbert descended the metal steps, stopping on the second-floor landing.

He peered into Mrs. Lau's apartment. He couldn't see the victim's mother. He couldn't see Foster Sung either. Just a neatly furnished living room, a dining room, and the kitchen beyond. A black Chinese folding screen with mother-of-pearl inlay depicting a landscape of mountains, pagodas, and willow trees partially hid a tailor's mannequin.

Gilbert continued down the metal stairs until he reached the bottom. Clumps of mud dotted the pavement, amoeba-like in the rain. The kitchen door of the Champion Gardens Chinese Restaurant was open. He saw a chef in a chef's hat, a slight but dapper man who glanced continually toward the front of the serve-through. He cooked at a large stove, tossed food—chunks of beef, bean sprouts, and snow peas—expertly in a battered old wok. Gilbert glanced to the top of the stairs, then through the kitchen door, and wondered if any kitchen staff had heard the gunshot over the heavy rain. The cook took a meat cleaver and whacked something on his cutting board. Then a timer went and he hurried from view.

Gilbert stepped off the landing into the yard. To the right lay a small garden, no more than a patch of mud, with a few stakes for plants, a wheelbarrow on its side, an empty fertilizer bag, a crude scarecrow with a baseball hat, an empty can of motor oil, and a stack of Chinese newspapers tied in a bundle, now a solid wet brick of newsprint. Gilbert walked across the yard to the alley. He looked up and down the alley. Turn left or right? he wondered. Rain trickled down his collar. Left went south to Baldwin Street, a few doors down, a broad residential street leading directly to, and in full view of, the bus-choked and car-clogged Spadina Avenue, not a place a killer would likely flee after his crime. So. To the right, then.

Gilbert followed the secluded curve past the back of Gwartzman's Art Supplies, then turned west toward Kensington Market. Garages. Garbage cans. Litter. Tall grass grew around telephone poles and fences. Fences leaned this way and that. A dim streetlight near the end of the alley cast black shadows. Puddles stood in the potholes along the pavement. He shone his flashlight from side to side, hating the rain because the rain was destroying any possible evidence he might find out here—a footprint, a blood trail, tire tracks. When was the rain going to stop? He hadn't seen rain like this in years. The jet stream blew far to the north these days, sucking up damp weather from the Gulf of Mexico, dumping it on southern Ontario and western New York. Only two dry days so far this month. No snow. Rain obliterating any and all evidence along his killer's getaway route.

Then he saw the glove.

A glove up in a tree. In a backyard. Beyond a fence.

Anybody could lose a glove, but how many people lost a glove in a tree? It dangled from a low branch. Caught. Like a severed hand. Not lost. Thrown. Jettisoned. As if somebody had tried to get rid of it in a hurry. Gilbert walked over and had a look.

Here was a glove, looked like a brand-new one, up in a tree, and it was as if this glove had an invisible thread connecting it all the way back to the corpse of Edgar Lau, a thread tugging at Gilbert's sensibility, forcing his pale blue eyes to squint in speculation, making him forget the rain as it peppered his cheek with small close drops. He opened the gate and went into the backyard. He reached up and took the glove down. A brand-new beige Isotoner. For the right hand. A man's glove? Soaking wet on the outside, yes, definitely drenched on the outside, the beige darkened like a damp tea leaf. But was it wet on the inside? He looked around the backyard, thinking he might see the other glove, then looked up at the house, a crumbling red brick row house, narrow, built in the 1890s, sagging to the left, a crooked house. But was there a crooked man inside? He felt the inside of the Isotoner with his fingers.

Dry.

He smelled the glove, thought he detected a faint whiff of gunpowder, a wayward hint of a discharged weapon.

He spent some time searching for the other glove but couldn't find it anywhere.

He walked up the narrow path and banged on the back door. A minute later an elderly Chinese man answered. The man had something wrong with his left eye; it bulged strangely, was red around the rim, and in the dim light of the mudroom looked faintly reptilian. Gilbert presented his badge and identification.

"Anybody in this house lose a glove?" he asked.

The Chinese man looked at him without answering, as if Gilbert had just recited some arcane bit of liturgy from an unknown religion. Then the man called down the hall in Cantonese, his voice squeezed and nasal, sounding more like a woman's voice. A much younger man, Chinese, came to the door in a white undershirt, jeans, and muddy construction boots, his mouth open in inquiry, holding three spark plugs in his hand.

"Yes?" he said.

"Anybody lose a glove?" Gilbert asked again. The question, to Gilbert's ears, sounded sadly comical, especially against the enormity of that pool of blood back at the apartment. Gilbert saw the man needed an explanation. "I'm police."

The man looked at the glove. The situation was bizarre, a page out of absurdist theater, a homicide detective going door to door asking about lost gloves, as if the problem of that pool of blood back at the apartment could be solved only if he settled the question of this glove first. The young Chinese man looked scared, as if he might have a half dozen illegal immigrants hiding in the house.

"No," he said, looking at the glove nervously. "Nobody lose glove."

Eliminating possibilities. "Thanks," he said. "Sorry to bother you."

Wet on the outside, dry on the inside, and up in a tree. Bizarre. Gilbert shook his head. Too bizarre.

CHAPTER
TWO

GILBERT WALKED BACK TO EDGAR Lau's apartment. He climbed the metal stairs slowly, his knees bothering him. Was it really arthritis? Forty-nine, and he had arthritis? He didn't like to think about it. He didn't want to take big enteric-coated aspirins for the rest of his life. He had a pair of lungs, still had the lungs, did twenty lengths at Leaside Pool three days a week, but his long legs were starting to creak, and he finally had to admit that maybe he was mortal after all, that he was going to have to accept the constant dull ache as an unwanted guest, and that maybe he was going to have to give up playing inter-squad baseball this summer.

The CSU recorded the crime scene—tape measures out, cameras flashing, dusting unshelved books for prints. Edgar looked paler, colder, and his eyes stared like dull gray stones, still gazing at the French doors, but no longer interested in them, as if such earthly portals could never mean anything to him again. Gilbert opened his briefcase, the scarred soldier of countless homicides, took out an evidence bag, and slipped the glove inside. He held the glove up to the light and had a closer look. No blood. But what about gunshot residue? Had he really smelled something on the glove? The lab techs on the sixth floor would definitely have to check for it.

"What have we got here?" asked Lombardo, coming out of the bedroom.

Gilbert looked at his young partner, deadpan, thinking he was going to get a hard time about it. "A glove," he said.

"From where?"

"From the alley."

"Are we desperate, then?" asked Lombardo, tilting his head to one side, hoisting that smile of his to his face.

"I don't know," said Gilbert. "You're the one who hasn't had a date in three months."

Lombardo lifted his chin. "I've got my standards."

"I know," said Gilbert. "Anything in panty hose."

"Speaking of panty hose, you should see what I found."

Gilbert held up the glove. "Maybe the other glove?"

Lombardo shook his head. "There's nothing sadder than a desperate detective." He gave Gilbert an elaborate cuff on the shoulder. "Next you'll be asking me for a witness."

Gilbert raised his eyebrows, as if Lombardo were a lost cause. "Celibacy has made you mean, Joe," he said.

"Believe me, it's a habit I'm trying to break," said Lombardo.

He followed Lombardo into the bedroom.

Lombardo walked over to the writing desk. "Look at these," he said.

Lombardo lifted yet more photographs and handed them to Gilbert. Eight-by-ten color photographs of a woman. Most probably taken by the Pentax out on the table? Photographs of a young woman. A pretty woman. A woman he recognized. She lay on the futon in the living room wearing a Chinese silk cheongsam, nothing else—a white woman, blond, with strikingly intelligent eyes, a high forehead, and the pedigree cheekbones of someone with fortunate genes. The photographs enticed. The enthralling mix of feminine vulnerability and intellectual brilliance startled.

"Rosalyn Surrey?" said Gilbert, looking up.

Lombardo nodded, his eyes filled with admiration, his heart melting even as he shook his head at the complicating and potentially nettlesome discovery of these photographs.

"What a babe," he said.

Surrey was a hardheaded ambitious city councillor, a woman whom a lot of people loved to hate. But in these photos she looked more like a geisha girl. Lombardo flipped to the next photograph: sitting, her knees up, the silk gown sliding away, revealing a shapely bit of thigh. Startling photographs, perplexing photographs, disconcerting images of a woman who was often characterized in the press as a hellcat and an unrelenting climber, a woman with a tongue as barbed as accordion wire and with mayoral aspirations as poisonous as machine politics could make them. Now looking like the Playmate-of-the-Month. With the roundest, greenest eyes Gilbert had ever seen. Damaging photographs. With lips as full and pink as a midsummer's rose. Photographs that resonated with motive. With a smile so tender, so relinquishing, Gilbert now sensed yet another thread, woven from more dangerous emotions, and derived from much higher stakes. Photographs like these could easily ruin an ambitious city councillor's career. Photographs like these could easily get a man like Edgar Lau into trouble.

Photographs like these were photographs to kill for.

* * *

The CSU finished their preliminary work.

"You want us to vacuum now?" asked Hutchison, a harried bald man with a circular wind-up tape measure on his belt. "Get a couple bags for the lab?"

Gilbert surveyed the scene one more time. He knew that sooner or later the technicians would have to vacuum, but once they did, the scene would be gone, forever disturbed, and the living breathing snapshot of Edgar's murder would be obliterated. He heard an agonized wail from downstairs, Mrs. Lau clutched by her first frantic grief, the wail modulating into a tangle of muffled Cantonese words. Was there a father in Edgar's life? He stared at Edgar. He couldn't help thinking of the man on the yellow Honda in the bedroom photograph. Was that Edgar's father? That man with the brown face and all the teeth?

"Not yet," he said. "Go get a coffee. If you see the guys from the Coroner's office, tell them to wait. Joe and me are going to pick this place apart."

They were going to pick this place apart because he knew that in this apartment there had to be a clue, a shred, some item that might later turn out to be of consequence, something he had to find before the crime scene was dismantled by the creep of time and the carelessness of well-meaning techs. He had a chance with this one. A real chance. This wasn't some crack dealer shot in a back alley with no clues anywhere. This was inside. An interior. These rooms could yield a wealth of raw information.

The CSU techs left. Gilbert continued to stare at Edgar Lau. Murdered in his own dining room. But did Rosalyn Surrey have anything to do with it?

"How soon can we move him?" asked Lombardo. "I'm sure Mrs. Lau is upset with him here like this."

Gilbert's eyes narrowed. He hardened himself against Mrs. Lau's grief.

"He stays like that until we're through with him," he said:

"Foster Sung wants to go," said Lombardo.

Foster Sung puzzled Gilbert. The man owned millions in real estate, yet consorted with the Laus? Immigrant Chinese, presumably from Vietnam, who lived in impoverished and decrepit apartments downtown? "Get a statement from him," he said. "Tell him I'll call him tomorrow."

"What about Mrs. Lau?"

He listened, could hear her weeping. "See if she has any friends she can stay with," said Gilbert. Her weeping was upsetting him. "Get what you can out of her, but I don't think she's in any shape to talk." He turned to Edgar, looked at Edgar's belt buckle: crossed silver cobras with fake rubies for eyes, the silver smeared with blood. "We'll give her a day or two before we have a real go at her."

While Lombardo took statements from Foster Sung and May Lau, Gilbert went back to the living room, carefully sidestepping the blood. He looked at Edgar's clip sitting on the dining room table. The clip was starting to bother him. Where was the gun? Would the gun remain unfound? He looked around the living room. The man had books on Chinese and Vietnamese history, possessed skill as a photographer, and practiced ink-and-brush Chinese calligraphy. Evidence of a cultivated man. A civilized man. But he also had a gun.

Somewhere. Why did he own a gun? The question gnawed at Gilbert. To protect himself? Why did he have to protect himself? And from whom? The clip posed many questions. Was Edgar's life in danger? Did that danger have anything to do with Metro Councillor Rosalyn Surrey? The clip was like a signpost to Gilbert, evidence that overwhelmingly suggested Edgar's involvement in criminal activity, and, most likely, criminal activity within the ethnic framework of the Toronto Chinese. Was Edgar's murder gang-related? Was this about tongs and triads, something that would complicate the murder a hundredfold? The ransacked apartment suggested Edgar had been hiding something. Had gang members come to find whatever he had been trying to hide? Or was this just a plain and simple robbery?

Gilbert looked around the apartment. No dust anywhere, not even in the accordion folds of the lampshade. A large set of pan-pipes hung on the wall. A brass elephant two feet tall stood next to the slashed futon. An impoverished apartment, not the best real estate in the city, but a neat apartment, and, despite the obvious ransacking, the apartment of a man who cared enough to keep it clean and organized.

But what of the ladder? Simply a tool for obtaining a higher camera angle, or a means of getting into the attic?

Gilbert got the ladder and carried it to the front hall. The spacing between the ladder's feet matched exactly the spacing between the four scratch marks on the floor. He climbed. He pushed the access panel aside and pulled himself up into the attic, his nostrils flaring at the damp musty smell, his ears adjusting to the rattle of the rain against the roof. He got to his feet, clenching his jaw as the dull ache in his knees came back, and turned on his flashlight.

Pink insulation lay scattered between the joists. The rain susurrated, crescendoed, like a million tiny snare drums, a lulling but disorienting sound, driven by the wind into oscillating and chaotic phrases, a gray melody without a tune. Several planks had been laid over the joists to form a walkway, old planks splattered with old paint, tossed-away pieces, maybe scavenged in side streets, one with a decorative design of beer bottle caps hammered into it, another with rusty nails battered flat. As Gilbert shone his flashlight along this walkway he saw a rat scurry away into the gloom, gray fur matted with rain, pink tail covered with fine translucent hairs. He heard a drip somewhere, and, turning, saw a leak, the drops falling like diamonds past the beam of his flashlight, dripping at an angle from one of the roof joists.

Gilbert was a tall man, six feet three, had to stoop. The attic was chilly and damp, and his breath steamed over in the cold. A dismal place, as if he'd taken a wrong turn in somebody else's nightmare.

He advanced three steps along the walkway and stopped. He heard pigeons cooing, the beating of wings, but, scanning the attic, couldn't see them anywhere. Why was it so empty up here? No boxes of junk, no exercise bicycles, no cans of old paint, just an uninterrupted expanse of pink insulation, all of it sprinkled with old attic dust, like a big polluted rose-colored cloud.

He continued along the walkway, inspecting the insulation as he went. It looked undisturbed. He heard the pigeons cooing more loudly, swung his flashlight upward. Where could they be? Somewhere behind the roof planks? He smelled them in the overpowering damp, the gagging smell of dirty birds crowded together in their own excrement.

That roof plank up there looked new. He stopped, shone his flashlight at the plank. A new section of roofing plank, fixed with wing nuts, not nails.

How to get over there? The floor planks stopped just a few feet ahead. He pondered the unexpected obstacle. He would have to balance on the joists. One misstep and he might fall through the ceiling.

He tested the first joist with his left foot, then placed his right hand against the slope of the roof for support. He brought his right foot forward to the same joist and balanced, the cartilage inside his knees grinding uncomfortably. Once sure of his balance, he moved to the next joist, paused again, and so on, until he came to the wing-nut plank.

The plank was cut to size, no more than three feet long, flush with the contiguous planks, but white, fresh, unsullied by the last hundred years of dirt, dust, and mildew. As he unscrewed the first wing nut, he heard the cafuffle of pigeons nearby. Placing his left hand against the plank to keep it in place, he unscrewed the remaining wing nut and removed the plank. The plank was heavier than expected, with something attached to the other side.

He turned the plank over and saw an old leather knapsack, scuffed and worn, the straps with silver buckles, a small knapsack, a child's knapsack, with the faded crest of a boys' private school—Victoria College in Hong Kong—pressed into the leather of the fold-down flap. The knapsack was screwed into the plank with half-inch screws. Gilbert held the plank under his right arm and negotiated his way back to the walkway. He lowered the plank to the walkway. He opened the leather knapsack and pulled out an IGA grocery bag. He untaped the grocery bag and withdrew its contents.

He instantly recognized the contents, still had an eye for such things, like riding a bicycle, or learning the Australian crawl. He never forgot, had a knee-jerk instinct for it, even though he hadn't worked in Narcotics for seventeen years. What the Chinese gangs called a "piece"—three of them. Eight hundred grams each. Wrapped and sealed in heavy-duty clear plastic, fashioned into hard bricks, stamped with a few rough Chinese characters. Glowing like the first snow of Christmas. Like mother-of-pearl. Like ivory. Like the white of the whitest lily. Not brown, such as the Iranian gangs sold. Not the yellow of the Indian gangs. But white. China White. From the Golden Triangle, that mountainous jungle land where the opium poppies grew fat, where stems swelled with sticky goiters, where peasants scarred bulbs with special knives so they bled with the thick tarry gold that the jungle labs turned into heroin. Three "pieces," twenty-four hundred grams in all, eighty percent pure. The most potent heroin anywhere. Estimated street value, once turned into caps for the average junkie, three-point-five million dollars.

He knelt beside Edgar, rolled up the dead man's sleeves, checked for track marks, found none. Just bloodstains. He knew how destructive heroin could be, remembered several sad cases from his years in Narcotics. A mother so strung out she forgot to feed her baby and found the infant dead in its crib. A fire in a shooting gallery, the junkies too spaced out to escape. That tragic night when undercover officer Carolyn Yano had been gunned down while buying 150 caps from a Turkish street dealer. Edgar Lau wasn't just another street dealer. He was a player. This man was a dangerous victim, and this murder was a dangerous murder, and Gilbert knew he might be looking for dangerous suspects, suspects who might possibly have a stake in the multimillion dollar stash of drugs on the table, a stash with such a dizzying value that even the most cautious trafficker would take a chance, would count any number of homicides simply as the cost of doing business.

He heard footsteps on the metal fire escape, saw the French doors open, reached for his gun, racked one into the chamber, and aimed. Lombardo. In his off-white London Fog trench coat, his hair roguishly tossed by the wind, his square jaw showing its usual late-in-the-day shadow of whiskers. Just Lombardo. Eyes glittering in the lamplight, uncertain, sensitive, accepting. Joe looked first at Gilbert, then at Gilbert's gun, then raised his hands.

"Okay, okay," he said. "I'll pay my parking tickets."

Gilbert holstered his gun, the weapon sliding snugly against his ribs with reassuring smoothness. "Sorry, Joe," he said.

"Too much caffeine?" asked Lombardo.

Gilbert nodded toward the table. "Look what I found in the attic."

Lombardo looked, grew still, eyed the bricks of product with quick comprehension, then turned to Gilbert. "Shit," he said.

Gilbert stared at Lombardo. "No, Joe," he said. "It's heroin."

The two detectives gazed at each other. Then smiled. Then laughed. Laughed the way shipmates on a sinking ship laugh, the way miners trapped in a cave-in laugh, laughed because they understood what the illegal narcotics on the desk meant to their investigation. It meant that the people they had to investigate might take lethal measures to stop them. It meant they couldn't work this one alone, that they were going to have all kinds of interference; the Ontario Provincial Police, the Royal Canadian Mounted Police, and not only the OPP and the Horsemen but also some of the American agencies; way too many pilots to steer the plane. Laughed to the point of tears because they were working a dozen murders already, and Christmas was two weeks away, and neither of them had done their Christmas shopping, and the rain was never going to stop. Laughed because they now had to watch their backs. Both men just wanted to go home and forget about the glove in the tree, about Playmate-of-the-Month Rosalyn Surrey, and the multimillion-dollar dose of China White on the desk. But at last their laughter died, and Gilbert felt empty, spent, like a junkie coming down, as if the joke hadn't been worth it after all.

They sat quietly for a few seconds. Gilbert again listened to the rain, then looked at Edgar. The rain was this man's requiem. Soft and mournful. The rain lulled Gilbert into a few seconds of introspection, an examination of how easily he had pulled his gun. Had the product on the table really changed the complexion of this murder so quickly?

"What did Foster Sung say?" he asked.

Lombardo slid his hands into the pockets of his coat. "He said he was in the restaurant downstairs having coffee with his associates—that's the word he used—when May Lau came in and told him her son had been shot."

Associates. Had Sung been having a business meeting then? This late at night? "Were you able to talk to Mrs. Lau at all, or was she too upset?" asked Gilbert.

"Some," said Lombardo. "But she was shaky."

"How's her English?"

"Her English is good."

"What did she say?"

Lombardo took a deep breath, rubbed his nose, an Italianate nose, strong, forthright, handsome. "She said she wasn't sure if she heard the shot or not," he said. "She was sitting in the front room. You have a lot of trucks on Spadina Avenue. She heard something. But . . . you know . . . with this rain . . . she thought it was a truck backfiring. Not only that, she's deaf in one ear. Sung says she lost her hearing when an artillery shell exploded ten yards from her in Saigon. That's where they're from. Ethnic Chinese from Saigon. Ho Chi Minh City."

"So she came up here?"

"Not at first."

"What did she do?"

"She finished hemming the skirt she was working on," said Lombardo. "She used to work as a seamstress. She still does piece-work. Sung has her working as a receptionist out in Agincourt. A firm called New Asian Solutions. They have a branch office out there but they also have an office down here, on University Avenue."

"So why did she come up here if she wasn't sure about the gunshot?" asked Gilbert.

"She had a feeling."

"A feeling?"

"She's the man's mother, Barry." Lombardo shrugged. "I don't know."

"Okay," said Gilbert. "She had a feeling."

"And she came up," said Lombardo.

Gilbert glanced at Edgar. "And saw him lying there on the floor," he said. He scratched his head. "And was he still alive?" he asked.

Lombardo peered at the heroin, had a closer look. "That's the story," he said. "She came up here, saw him lying on the floor, and ran down to get Sung because she thought Sung might be able to save him."

"So she knew Sung was downstairs?"

"Sung always says hello whenever he comes to the restaurant. He said hello before he sat down with his friends. She knew he was there."

"And when she came up here and saw her son lying on the floor, was he alive and conscious?" asked Gilbert.

"That's the story."

"Still alive, still conscious." Gilbert thought there might be hope after all. But his partner just as quickly destroyed his hope.

"I know what you're thinking, Barry," said Lombardo. "But no, he didn't tell her who shot him."

Gilbert tried not to be disappointed. "What's with Foster Sung?" he asked. "Is he a relative? A friend?"

"A friend," said Lombardo. "A close family friend."

"How close?"

Lombardo picked up on the implication. "I'm not sure," he said. "But Edgar's father is dead, if that's what you mean." Lombardo pointed to the photograph album. "Sung said he died on that refugee boat fleeing Vietnam twenty-four years ago."

"So we're right about boat people?"

"I guess so."

"Did Sung come up here?" asked Gilbert.

"After May Lau came and got him," said Lombardo.

"You know," said Gilbert, feeling angry, "it's lucky we didn't get a double homicide here, or even a triple homicide. The killer could have still been in the apartment."

"I know," said Lombardo. "But you know how people get when they see someone they love bleeding to death on the floor." Lombardo looked at Gilbert solemnly. "They forget about procedure. They don't go in with guns and make sure the place is clear before rushing to aid the victim."

Gilbert's face settled, and he felt at once irked and grateful. "Okay," he said, "I'm sorry. But I just wish people would think."

Distant lightning flashed beyond the rain-speckled panes of the French doors. Both detectives looked. Lightning in December. Bizarre. Lombardo continued.

"Edgar was still breathing when Sung came up here," he said.

"And conscious?" asked Gilbert.

"No."

"So Sung phoned nine-one-one," said Gilbert.

"He did. Officer Kennedy got here before the fire trucks and paramedics."

"And by the time Officer Kennedy got here, Edgar was nearly gone."

"That's right," he said. Lombardo consulted his notebook again, as if he had just remembered something. "Kennedy's partner, Paul Szoldra, said he took a statement from a waiter downstairs. The waiter said he saw a woman exit the downstairs door around the time of the murder. The waiter actually knew her. I talked to the waiter."

Gilbert gazed at his young partner, astonished by the small offerings Lombardo eked out of the most unlikely places, how he could produce, seemingly out of thin air, a woman, adding substance and depth to their cloudy first impressions, filling in with one bold stroke a disconnected but undoubtedly valuable piece of the puzzle. A woman walking down the stairs and leaving the building around the time of the murder.

"Did you get the woman's name?"

"Pearl Wu."

Gilbert let the name settle, searched his memory to see whether he knew it, wondered why so many Chinese, when choosing English first names for their kids, chose old-fashioned ones, nineteenth-century names.

"That's great, Joe."

"I asked Mrs. Lau about Pearl Wu," said Lombardo. "She says she's a friend of Edgar's."

"A girlfriend?" he asked.

"I think it's a hot-and-cold thing," said Lombardo.

"Did May Lau see Pearl?"

"No."

Gilbert nodded. "So we go after Pearl Wu," he said. He conceded a smile to Lombardo. "Who knows, maybe she has the other glove."

Lombardo shook his head. "Like I say, there's nothing sadder than a desperate detective."

CHAPTER
THREE

ON MONDAY, GILBERT SAT IN the autopsy room in the Coroner's Building on
Grenville Street. Hot, bright surgical lights shone overhead. Drains pit-
ted the floor. Edgar Lau lay on a steel table, a tag tied around his big
toe. Dr. Blackstein, a short, comfortable-looking man in his late
fifties, examined Edgar's naked body. Gilbert and Blackstein were waiting for the X rays to come down. The wrong ones had been delivered
by mistake and the porter had gone upstairs to get the right ones.

"Look at this here," said the coroner, pointing to a dull purple
spot an inch in diameter on Edgar's right shoulder. "Another gunshot
wound. A fairly recent one."

Gilbert examined the circular scar, the color of his favorite
mauve columbines in Regina's garden at home, puckered and
uneven, like a giant vaccination scar. "How recent?" he asked.

Blackstein had a closer look, like a jeweler examining an
equivocal gem. "I'd say three or four months," he said.

Three or four months. A gunshot wound received late last summer. Another attempt on Edgar's life. They had no record of this gunshot wound on file; he remembered all the assault-with-a-deadly-weapon files going back to January, and this wasn't one of them. Which meant this one had gone unreported or had happened in another jurisdiction. The prospect teased him. Maybe there was another bullet somewhere, tweezered from Edgar's shoulder last summer, put in a bag by some unknown officer, delivered to an evidence repository, labeled neatly, a piece of the puzzle all set to be snapped snugly into place. If their own bullet matched the bullet from this other shooting, if the people who had killed him last night were the same people who had been after him in August, if he could take this previous gunshot wound and the bullet that went with it as another signpost . . . was he going to get lucky on this after all?

"Anything else?" he asked, struggling to check the tenor of optimism in his voice.

Blackstein gazed up and down the length of Edgar's body. "He worked out," he said. "Look at those muscles. I've never seen such a physically fit victim before. The man's perfect. I wish I had my students here. He's a great cadaver as far as musculature's concerned."

Gilbert had to agree. In death, Edgar's body bulked with muscles—muscles as sculpted and lithe as a cougar's, carved from his flesh as unerringly as Michelangelo had carved David.

Blackstein glanced at the door. "I wonder what's taking the X rays so long?" he said. "I'm getting behind." He turned back to the corpse and pondered Edgar's body, reached up, twisted the thick hairs coming out of his own ear, examined his fingers for any exudate, then pulled a pair of latex gloves from the box of one hundred on the instruments table. "I might as well cut him open." He snapped on the gloves. "We might as well dig out the bullet while we're waiting."

Gilbert nodded. "Sure," he said.

Gilbert walked back to his chair and sat down. He emptied his mind, became a receptacle for whatever secrets Edgar's body might yield.

The initial Y incision, that which opened Edgar Lau's chest and abdomen, acted like an anesthetic on Gilbert, numbed his body, sharpened his mind, prepared him for a good two-hour sit, a limbo of postmortem carnage mixed with equal parts of hope and boredom. From that point on he felt nothing but a stolid determination to learn. Edgar's body became nothing more than an interesting puzzle, a piece of meat from which a helpful sketch of murder might emerge.

With the Y incision complete, Dr. Blackstein removed Lau's lungs, heart, esophagus, and trachea, and placed them to one side. "He didn't smoke," he commented to Gilbert. Blackstein had a closer look at the victim's abdominal organs, picking and pulling with a long pair of surgical tweezers at the gunshot wound, working the traumatized tissue with a quick, practiced hand, as if the nature of its texture, friability, and resilience were so well known to Blackstein, the ragged mapwork of bullet wounds so well-traveled, his tweezers might as well have been a divining rod for lead.

He spoke into the voice-activated dictation microphone above his head. "Cause of death was a gunshot wound of unknown caliber to the abdomen." He picked at Lau's intestine more vigorously. "The mechanism of death was exsanguination and presumably shock secondary to traumatic hemorrhage of the stomach and duodenum." Dr. Blackstein bent lower to the body, stopped poking around, and looked more closely. He went in dexterously with the tweezers and pulled out a bullet. He held it up to Gilbert. Gilbert nodded, encouraged by the find. "Correction," said Dr. Blackstein, dictating into the microphone. "Cause of death was a *thirty-eight-caliber* gunshot wound to the abdomen." He put the bullet on a steel tray, where it shone like a dark ruby. "The officer's warrant indicates the manner of death was homicide, occurring in and around the hour of ten P.M., on December fifteenth, in the municipality of the City of Toronto, and that the—"

Dr. Blackstein stopped dictating, his brow knitting. His face showed a flicker of perplexity, something Gilbert hardly ever saw on the coroner's face. Blackstein stuck his hand into Edgar's body, oblivious to the goriness of its gaping incision, and squeezed. He turned to Gilbert.

"What the hell is this?" he asked.

"What?" asked Gilbert.

"There's a hard spot in his intestine." He squeezed again, testing, eyes pondering. "I wish the porter would hurry up with those X rays. This might turn out to be interesting."

"What is it?" asked Gilbert, forcing himself not to get too excited.

"I don't know," said Blackstein. "It's not a bullet or a bone fragment, that's for sure. It's too far down from the wound to be either of those things, and there's no trauma around this particular area. We've got nothing but fresh meat down here."

Gilbert came over and had a look. "Where?" he asked.

"Right here," said Blackstein, pointing. "In his large intestine." Blackstein squeezed yet again, as if he were now angry at Edgar's intestine. "You see how there's a lump inside there?"

Gilbert peered at the lump. "Maybe it's cancer," he suggested.

"No," said Blackstein. "He's the wrong age group, for one thing. And from a clinical standpoint, it's inconsistent with cancer." Blackstein turned to him. "You said you found drugs in his apartment?"

"We did," said Gilbert.

Blackstein shrugged. "Maybe he swallowed some drugs."

Gilbert thought of the three football-sized pieces. "No," he said, "he didn't."

"Because I think he swallowed something, like drugs in a condom. Something like that. Only it feels really hard."

The porter entered the autopsy room with the X rays. Blackstein took off his gloves, rinsed his hands, and dried them. The porter handed the large brown envelope to Dr. Blackstein, had the doctor initial for them, then quickly retreated, keeping his eyes averted from the corpse.

"Let's have a look," said Blackstein, taking the stiff films from the envelope and pinning them to the panel lights.

Both men just stared . . . stared in perplexity, in surprise, and with a keen sense of cynical wonder when they saw what was inside Edgar's intestine. The image was sharp, clear, and unmistakable: a tied-off balloon with a key inside, a key such as might be used for a public locker at a swimming pool, a library, or a subway station. Gilbert remembered a suicide he worked once, where the victim had swallowed seven safety pins and two razor blades, how he had seen the safety pins and razor blades as clear as day, sharp and defined on the X-ray film. The key in the balloon appeared just as clearly. The wonders of the spectrum beyond the visible range. Farther up, the bullet wound showed up white and luminescent, star-shaped and ragged, with the bullet a solid block, hot and overt, just above Edgar's duodenum.

The door opened and Joe Lombardo walked in, his notebook in one hand, double-tall skinnies for all in the other.

"Funny place to keep a key," said Gilbert to Blackstein.

Blackstein shook his head. "Did he never think of under the doormat?"

Blackstein stared at the X ray with neutral professionalism. Lombardo settled with the coffees at a table across the room.

"We'll have to get it out," said Gilbert. "We'll have to have a look."

Blackstein nodded distractedly. "Sure," he said. He stared at the X ray. "I'm going to lift his intestine onto the small-parts dissection table and make an incision," he said. "You might as well go back to your chair. You know what a mess this makes."

"Thanks."

Gilbert went back to his chair and sat next to Lombardo. Blackstein put on fresh latex gloves.

"Still raining?" Gilbert asked Lombardo.

"In piss-pots." Lombardo looked at the disemboweled body of Edgar Lau. "Anything interesting?"

"An earlier gunshot wound."

"Really?"

"Three or four months old. And Blackstein's found something in Edgar's intestine."

Lombardo's eyebrows arched. "The other glove?" he asked.

Gilbert raised his hands in a monk-like gesture of prayer. "You scoff, my son," he said. "But let the wisdom of my years guide you." Gilbert lifted his coffee. "He found a key inside a balloon." Gilbert raised his coffee toward the panel lights. "You can see it up there on the X ray. Go have a look."

Lombardo got up and had a look. He came back. He was smiling in that winsome way he had sometimes. "If I get hungry," he said, "I stick to glass and nails. I hear keys give you indigestion."

The two detectives watched the coroner remove Edgar's liver, spleen, kidneys and adrenals, stomach and intestines and put them on the small-parts dissection table. Gilbert turned to Lombardo.

"Any luck with Pearl Wu?" he asked.

Lombardo flipped to a fresh page in his notebook. "She lives in a condominium on Murray Street. You know the one? With the big fountain in the courtyard? One Park Lane. Only there's no Park Lane anywhere around, they just call it that. Right behind the National Life Building. I drove by. She's not there right now. And I phoned. She's got her voice mail on."

"Is Telford checking priors on everybody?"

"On everybody," said Lombardo.

Blackstein turned to the two detectives. "I got it," he said. "Come have a look."

Gilbert and Lombardo walked over to the small-parts dissection table. Gilbert looked through the incision Blackstein had made in Edgar's small intestine. In and among the products of digestion, snug in the whitish blue tissue, Gilbert saw a yellow balloon. Blackstein went in with his tweezers and pulled it out, an uninflated yellow balloon, messy with blood, tied tightly at its neck. He held it up to the light. The balloon had some black writing on it. Blackstein wiped the balloon with an alcohol swab. "New Asian Solutions," the writing read.

"Let's see the key," said Gilbert.

The coroner lifted a scalpel from his tray and sliced the balloon open.

A key for a public locker. The key had an orange plastic handle. Why would Edgar swallow a key? And how many public lockers could there be in Toronto? Gilbert grew suddenly dismayed. Who even said the locker had to be in Toronto?

"Does it have a number?" asked Lombardo.

Blackstein turned it around. "Forty-three," he said.

Locker 43, thought Gilbert. But locker 43 where?

After the autopsy, Gilbert drove to New City Hall to see Metro Councillor Rosalyn Surrey. Having spent two years in architectural school back in the 1970s, Gilbert had some interest in the municipal seat of government, a building which still looked futuristic even after thirty years. Two glass-faced office towers, both curved, embraced the saucer-shaped council chamber. The architectural array was modernist and sculptural, a design by Finnish architect Viljo Revell, submitted in competition against other designs from all over the world back in 1958. Gilbert entered the podium block, the two-story office block at ground level. He followed the broad winding stairs to the second level, glanced at the council chamber's supporting column as it rose and spread like a giant toadstool from a sunken carpeted amphitheater down below.

On the second floor he walked along a corridor until he came to Rosalyn Surrey's office. Out the window at the end of the corridor he saw Old City Hall, a Romanesque pile of red brick which had served as Toronto's seat of government as far back as Queen Victoria's reign. He opened the door and went inside, the photographs in his briefcase, unhappy that he should have to trample upon the obvious tenderness he saw in them, but compelled as if by an internal command to follow up on this most obvious lead.

Rosalyn Surrey's secretary looked up from her computer and smiled brightly, her lips glossed with a crisp shade of red, her gold earrings discreet but suggestive. The nameplate on her desk said Ms. Cindy Cheng. She was a pretty Chinese woman of thirty, wore a brown two-piece outfit, had her hair cut shoulder-length, styled with a hint of curl, and wore peacock-blue eye shadow. Her smile broadened. She smiled with as much cheerfulness as Gilbert could stand.

"Can I help you?" she asked.

Gilbert took out his badge and ID and showed them to Ms. Cheng. "I have an appointment to see Rosalyn Surrey."

Ms. Cheng looked at his shield. "She's not back from council yet." Cindy Cheng looked at him questioningly. "Is this about the Police Services Board meeting?" she asked. "Are you delivering the agenda?"

Gilbert didn't know whether to be flattered or insulted. Did she really think he looked young enough to be a messenger boy?

"No," he said. "This is an unrelated matter."

"Oh," said Ms. Cheng, surprised. "And she knows you're coming?" She glanced at her Compaq PC. "Because I don't have you marked down here in the computer."

"It's last-minute," said Gilbert, "but she knows I'm coming. I gather she didn't tell you. I called early this morning."

"She's been in Council since nine," said Ms. Cheng.

"Is she due back soon?" Gilbert had to meet Lombardo at the Champion Gardens Restaurant in an hour. Donald Kennedy's report said the cook had seen a man prowling near the back of the restaurant around the time of the murder, but the cook had gone off duty before they'd had a chance to question him about it. "Can you not page her?"

"If she knows you're coming, I'm sure she'll be back." Ms. Cheng smiled brightly again. "I wouldn't want to take her out of Council. Have a seat over there if you like."

Gilbert glanced at the waiting area. "Thanks," he said.

He sat down. Magazines lay fanned out over the table. Also some Chinese newspapers—Rosalyn Surrey knew who her constituents were. Up on the wall Gilbert saw framed photographs of Rosalyn Surrey at various public functions. One showed Surrey opening the Annual Dragon Boat Race on Toronto Island, dressed in a red tracksuit, a paddle in one hand, a starting pistol in the other, her smile so genuine it looked as if it might jump out and hit Gilbert over the head. Another showed her shaking hands with a visiting Chinese dignitary at the black-tie gala celebrating recent Royal Ontario Museum acquisitions from Zhejiang Province; she was dressed in a simple black evening gown stitched with subtle black beading, and, in this incarnation, looked like a sophisticated and cosmopolitan woman who knew how to handle her duties as a functionary well. Another captured her with a smudged face on a hot August night serving bottles of Gatorade to brawny police officers—like a cheerleader among football players—during the subway-crash rescue effort a few summers ago. Poignant public service photographs. Vanity photographs. Photographs meant to show visiting constituents that she was the right woman for the job.

A few minutes later Councillor Surrey walked into the office. She was tall, wore a pale green blazer with a matching skirt, had her blond hair up and off her neck with a spring-clasp comb, and wore jade earrings, ones that offset her cat-green eyes. She gave Gilbert a pleasant and helpful smile, perhaps thinking he was a constituent. He got to his feet, his knees bothering him again.

"Ms. Surrey?" he said.

"It's Mrs. Surrey," she said, correcting him politely.

He extended his hand. "I'm Detective-Sergeant Barry Gilbert, of Metro Homicide. We spoke earlier on the phone."

Though her smile stayed in place, he detected a change in her eyes, a dimming of their brightness. "How do you do," she said. She shook Gilbert's hand, a firm handshake for such a feminine hand. "Perhaps we can talk in my office," she suggested. He understood; Ms. Cheng eyed them curiously.

Gilbert nodded. "Whatever you prefer," he said.

He followed her into her office and they sat down. From up here on the second floor of the podium block he saw the reflecting pool in Nathan Phillips Square, now converted into a skating rink despite the constant drizzle. He saw the big bronze sculpture by Henry Moore, *The Archer,* the brown metal dark and slick in the rain. He saw hot dog vendors, streetcars on Queen Street, and the towers of the financial district farther down. He turned to Rosalyn Surrey. He was surprised by the anxiety he saw in her face. She leaned forward, her green eyes intent.

"It's about Garth, isn't it?" she said.

Gilbert's brow rose. "Garth?" he said, caught off-guard by this unexpected inquiry. "Who's Garth?"

She stared at Gilbert. Her expression changed. She made an instant retreat. He expected some explanation but none came. Garth, whoever he might be, was none of his business. She leaned back in her chair, tapped the space bar on her keyboard, watched

the screen saver disappear, scrutinized the e-mail prompt as it flickered to the monitor, and turned back to Gilbert. The look on her
face, blank yet challenging, made Gilbert feel as if he had just inadvertently been rude to her.

"I'm sorry," she said, her voice now bland, unapologetic. "You
weren't specific on the phone."

He opened his briefcase and took out the manila folder. He
saw no reason to delay her embarrassment. He opened the envelope
and withdrew Edgar's compromising photographs. She looked at
the photographs—her own lithe body sheathed in the crimson
cheongsam—with unsurprised eyes. She wasn't going to tip her
hand this time.

"Where did you get those?" she asked.

"In Edgar Lau's apartment," he said.

He let that sit. He was a homicide detective. He was here
because of a homicide. He knew she had to know that. He watched
her closely. He admired her self-control. Yet for all her miraculous
calm, she was too calm. Her face was too still. Too placid. She
waited. But Gilbert waited longer. Stared at her. Waited for her emotional reflexes to betray her.

"Is he all right?" she asked at last.

He continued to stare. Was that a lover's anxiety he saw in her
eyes? "Mrs. Surrey," he said, "you're on the Police Services Board.
You have some knowledge of the way we work."

"Those photographs," she said. "They were my idea. I wanted
to give them to my husband." Denying guilt, denying blame. "As a
Christmas gift."

Gilbert looked at the photographs. "You're lovely," he said.
"But I'm afraid I'm going to have to keep these photographs. You've
got a few shopping days left. You better get your husband some-

thing else." He looked at her. "I'm afraid Edgar Lau was murdered last night in his apartment." He let it out of the box, the dark little fact of another human being's violent death, like releasing a predator into the wild, not sure of the reaction he would get. "Shot to death around ten o'clock." Saying it as if he believed even she were capable of shooting someone. "When we searched his apartment we found these photographs. You understand that because of the intimate nature of these photographs . . . we have to investigate."

He studied her reaction. She stared at him with wide eyes. Her lips tightened, then pursed. Her eyes moistened and she looked away, the soft rainy light of the overcast sky blanching her face. The corners of her lips hardened.

"What do you want?" she asked softly, but with enough force to make him understand that she considered his intrusion ill-advised.

"Anything you can tell us," he said.

He observed a slight sag in her shoulders.

"Edgar was one of my volunteers," she said. Gilbert was disappointed. She was retreating again. "Half the photographs you see on the wall outside were taken by Edgar." Doctoring the damage, spinning the evidence, hiding what he so plainly saw was a lover's woe. "Many of the photos in my campaign literature were taken by Edgar." Emphasizing a professional side to their relationship. "He was a friend, Detective Gilbert. Nothing more." She looked at her hands. "Your innuendo is in bad taste."

"What innuendo?"

"I'm a happily married woman, Detective Gilbert. My constituents know that."

He looked outside where he saw a handful of soggy skaters make their way around the civic rink. "Mrs. Surrey, I don't want to wreck your day," he said. "I'm just eliminating possibilities. And I want to do that as quietly as I can. I understand your position."

"Thank you," she said.

He felt sorry for her, having to hide like this when she was so upset. But he had to get on with it. "Were you anywhere near Edgar's apartment last night?" he asked.

She shook her head. She knew how it worked. "I was here until eight o'clock last night. Then I went home. You can ask Cindy."

"Is there anyone who can confirm that you actually went home at eight o'clock?" he asked. "Your husband, perhaps?"

"No," she said. "My husband is away on business."

"Okay," he said. "Don't look so worried."

"I'm not worried."

"I think it'll be all right." He couldn't ignore her pain, even if she resolutely denied it. He felt he had to offer her something. Condolences, at least. "I'm sorry about Edgar," he said. "I'll double-check the things you've told me, and I'll be in touch with you." He looked at her inquiringly. "There's nothing else you want to add?"

"There's nothing else I can add," she said. "He was an acquaintance. A friend. A volunteer. That's all."

Gilbert sensed the lie behind her brittle poise. She fabricated the most obvious smoke screen, out-and-out denial, the most tired tale he had ever heard. "Okay," he said, deciding to give her time to think about it. "I promise this will all be done with a lot of discretion." Deciding to make her feel safe. For now.

She looked out the window. "Thank you, detective," she said.

But she didn't sound thankful in the least.

GILBERT MET LOMBARDO AT THE Champion Gardens Chinese Restaurant, the restaurant immediately below the two apartments where the Laus lived, at three o'clock. December 18th, and Christmas shoppers filled the streets. He parked in front of Gwartzman's Art Supplies and Lombardo ran from the doorway of the art store through the rain, a leather zip-up folder under his arm, and got into Gilbert's unmarked Lumina. The rain splashed against the roof of the car in a soothing manner, blurred the windshield, and peppered the hood.

"Where'd you park?" he asked Lombardo.

"I'm around back," said his young partner. "I wanted to look at the alley and the fire escape again. I'm not so convinced our killer came in the back door anymore. Maybe Edgar went out to the balcony before the killer arrived and tracked water over the floor. He's got some stuff out there. Garbage cans and so forth. A blue box."

"It's possible," said Gilbert. "How did Telford make out? Anything on Edgar?"

Lombardo nodded. "He's got a fairly extensive sheet," he said. "Why doesn't that surprise me?" said Gilbert. "Narcotics?"

"No."

"No?" said Gilbert.

"Mainly assault charges," said Lombardo. "Three old ones going back ten years. Then a much later one. It's the later one we have to concern ourselves with."

"Why?"

Lombardo looked at his lap, squinting, his mouth going slack, as if he were bothered by this later assault charge. "He attacked Pearl Wu," he said. He looked at Gilbert, oddly shamefaced, as if he felt he had to apologize for Edgar. "He slashed her face with a knife." Here was a sad little discovery, one that deadened the air inside the car with a chill malice. Lombardo shook his head. "I guess it's more of a hot-and-cold thing than I thought." Lombardo glanced out at the rain. So did Gilbert. The nature of the assault needed a moment or two. "He was convicted and sentenced," said Lombardo. Lombardo turned to Gilbert. "He served two years of a six-year sentence." A sad little discovery that proclaimed motive, and, in the most lurid way, implicated Pearl as their strongest suspect. "He must have had top-flight legal talent to get him out so early. I phoned the sentencing judge. Justice Martin Raff. Ever heard of him?"

"No."

"He said he went hard on Edgar because Pearl Wu had been a fashion model. Raff says she's one of the most beautiful women he's ever seen." Lombardo shook his head, his eyes growing solemn. "To slash her face like that was to take away her livelihood. Even with a lot of plastic surgery, Raff says she still has a highly visible scar. He was surprised to learn Edgar got out so early."

Gilbert watched a Spadina Avenue bus splash through a large pothole. He knew what needed to be said. "So we have a beautiful woman with her face slashed. She wants revenge. She's had enough of looking at herself in the mirror every day. She's got to make Edgar pay. She goes to his apartment and shoots him. She's seen leaving the apartment by the waiter downstairs."

Lombardo nodded. "And then she disappears," he said. Lombardo's words were like lead now, his voice dropping into a well of disappointment.

Gilbert looked at his partner with questioning eyes. "Disappears?" he said.

"I still haven't found her yet," said Lombardo. As if the small miracles he had already worked this morning amounted to nothing.

Gilbert went over one of the more likely scenarios. "She searches his apartment because she knows he has a ton of heroin."

"Only I don't think she would be interested in a ton of heroin," said Lombardo.

"Why not?" asked Gilbert.

"Because she's rich."

"How do you know that?"

"Raff told me," he said. "And Benny Eng confirmed it."

"Benny says she's rich?" said Gilbert. Gilbert thought of the small smiling detective from the Asian Investigative Unit.

"She's married to Bing Wu," said Lombardo.

The name struck a chord in Gilbert's mind. "Why does that name sound familiar?" he asked.

Lombardo perked up. "He's one of the richest men in Hong Kong and an alleged 14K Triad member."

This information made Gilbert feel as if he had just stepped off a tall building. "Shit," he said. "I knew it."

Lombardo steamrollered ahead with the rest of his facts. "Benny says Pearl had a highly successful career as a fashion model in Hong Kong," he said. "As for Edgar Lau . . ." Lombardo's brow knitted doubtfully. "He's really not much of a criminal. Other than the assaults, he's never been charged with anything. He was a floorman at a few Chinese gaming houses here in town for a while, but the officers of 52 Division never got around to charging him with anything related to illegal gambling. Benny says we should talk to a Constable Jeremy Austin at 52 Division if we want more information on the illegal gambling, and where Edgar might have worked."

Gilbert tapped the steering wheel a few times, thinking. "Did Benny have anything to say about Foster Sung? What's this New Asian Solutions he owns?"

"It's a property management and development company. But also an import-export company."

"Christ."

"I know. Benny's had his eye on the import-export division for a long time. But so far nothing. They've had dogs into the warehouse. And when the container ships come in, they get dogs down there too. But everything Sung brings into the country is innocuous. Jade jewelry. Brass trinkets. Incense. A lot of stuff comes from a company Bing Wu owns in Hong Kong, tourist-trade stuff, but also textiles and Chinese fashions. Benny's been probing the Wu-Sung connection for a decade. He's had his sights on Sung for a long time. But it's been hit-and-miss. Remember the immigration scam case a few years back?"

"Benny worked that?" asked Gilbert.

"Yes. Foster Sung was indicted on that. And get this: he was indicted with two members of Toronto's Kung Lok Triad, Sid Yuen Pan and Leslie Lee." Lombardo pulled out a mimeographed copy of a newspaper story about the scam, with pictures of the three men. "Sung was acquitted, but the other two went to jail." Lombardo's lips stiffened, like a boxer who had lost a few rounds but who was now determined to win the match. "Benny's convinced of a connection, he just hasn't been able to prove it in court yet."

Gilbert shook his head, wondering how long he could keep Edgar Lau's murder away from the press.

"Anything else on Foster?"

"He was stabbed by an unknown assailant seven years ago while walking to his car in an underground parking lot late at night."

"Really?"

"Telford found the original assault report on our database using that new search program. Sung nearly died. He managed to drag himself to the attendant's booth and the attendant called an ambulance. The ambulance took him to Mount Joseph, where they gave him an emergency O-positive blood transfusion, but something went wrong with the transfusion, his body had a delayed transfusion reaction a couple days later, and before they could give him another transfusion they had to have their blood bank run a battery of matching tests. He almost died waiting for the results, but they finally found him some blood he could use."

"Did they ever find his assailant?"

"No."

"Did Telford dig up anything on our other suspects?" asked Gilbert. "What about Mrs. Lau?" he asked.

"She came up clean," said Lombardo. "Not even a parking ticket."

"What about Pearl?"

"She has a gun charge."

"A gun charge?" he said. "Maybe the revenge angle works after all. Tell me about the gun charge."

"A two-shot Derringer fell out of her purse at a dance club. The bouncer saw it and called the police. A Derringer. Can you believe it? They stopped manufacturing those things in 1935, so she must have had it custom-made. And she must have her loads custom-made too."

"Why?" asked Gilbert. "What's it take?"

"A forty-one-caliber."

"Forty-one-caliber?"

"She was acquitted. She's rich. Her lawyers argued successfully that the gun didn't belong to her, and that the bouncer was wrong about it falling out of her purse. The bouncer didn't show up to testify." Lombardo shook his head. "I'm sure he was threatened."

Gilbert considered everything Lombardo had told him. Connections. He knew they had to be there, but he had no idea how they joined up yet. The name Bing Wu was indeed familiar. And what about Pearl Wu? He now wanted to see Pearl Wu. Beautiful but scarred. Was it a crime of passion? He tried to reconstruct it. Pearl Wu goes up to Edgar's apartment and shoots him to avenge herself. But does she then search the apartment for the heroin? For the key in the yellow balloon? For something that incriminates her in another crime?

He opened the door of the Lumina. "Let's talk to the cook," he said.

Gilbert and Lombardo hurried through the rain to the Champion Gardens Chinese Restaurant. A door next to the restaurant led to the upper apartments—Mrs. Lau's on the second floor, and Edgar's on the third. Gilbert glanced at the dirty plate-glass windows of the restaurant: dusty snake plants thrust upward in a profusion of blade-like points from a long narrow planter attached to the low-slung sill. He pushed his way into the restaurant.

The restaurant had red carpeting, red wallpaper, red velveteen chairs, and tables with white tablecloths. Bamboo lanterns, lit with candles, glowed here and there. Decorative pagoda-style roofs hung over some of the tables at the back. Small Chinese gongs dangled from hooks overhead. The lights were dim and the air smelled of shark soup and chop suey. A bar stood to the left. A Coors Light sign in red and blue neon tubing hung above the bar.

A waiter in a white shirt and black bow tie approached the detectives and asked them if they wanted a table.

"No," said Gilbert. "We're here to see Dock Wen. We understand he comes on duty at one o'clock."

The man's welcoming smile faded. "Wait right here," he said.

The waiter walked to the kitchen, looking put out by the task of fetching the cook.

"Is he the waiter you talked to last night?" asked Gilbert.

"No," said Lombardo. "He's a different one."

"And the one you talked to last night had no idea who was sitting at Foster Sung's table?"

"No."

"But saw Pearl Wu."

"Yes."

Gilbert bent his right knee a few times, easing the stiffness. "I don't think your waiter's giving it to us straight," he said.

Lombardo glanced around at the scattered patrons. "Neither do I," he said.

The waiter came back, stopped halfway up the aisle, and beckoned. "You come," he said. "He see you now."

Gilbert and Lombardo followed the waiter through the tables.

As they reached the back, Dock Wen emerged from the kitchen wiping his hands on a white dish towel. He was a thin man of forty, tall for a Chinese, with a narrow face which tapered to a small chin. His eyes possessed little of the usual epicanthic folds, were round, dark, and bulged from the general flatness of his face. He gazed at the detectives with marked suspicion, not something Gilbert liked to see in a potential witness.

Gilbert showed his shield and ID. Joe did the same. The three men sat under one of the pagoda-like overhangs. Wen immediately lit a cigarette with a brown Bic throwaway lighter.

"We're just following up on the statement you gave Officer Kennedy last night," said Gilbert.

The cook took a ravenous pull on his cigarette, wolfing a solid block of smoke into his lungs. "Sure, go ahead," he said.

"You saw a man last night," said Gilbert.

"That's right," said Wen.

"Out back," said Gilbert.

"A big man," said Wen. "A big, big man."

"And he was Chinese."

Wen cocked his head to one side, glanced at Lombardo, then at Gilbert, looking confused. "He wasn't Chinese," he said. "He was a white man, like you. Very, very big."

Gilbert paused to think through this discrepancy in the facts. "Didn't you tell Officer Kennedy the man you saw was Chinese?" he said. He opened the case folder and found the appropriate report. "That's what we have right here, in your statement."

But Wen was emphatic. "No," he said. "He was a big white man. Not Chinese."

Was Wen changing his story then? Or had Officer Kennedy made an error in taking the statement? Gilbert decided to move on.

"Okay," he said. "Forget the man out back. Did you see Foster Sung last night?" he asked. "He was sitting at a table right up there."

"Foster Sung?" said Wen, looking up at the ceiling, his eyes narrowing. "Foster Sung? Who's Foster Sung?"

"Did you see him?" persisted Gilbert. "Out in the restaurant."

"I didn't go out in the restaurant," he said. "You have a job like mine, you don't go out in the restaurant. Busy, busy, busy. All the time, busy. Work, work, work."

"You didn't go out in the restaurant," said Lombardo, "but you went outside to have a smoke. It says right here: 'Witness went to back stoop for a cigarette.' "

"One cigarette," said Wen, holding up his chicken-claw of a finger. "I smoke one cigarette. I see a man. A big man. He sees me and he runs away."

"And this was around ten o'clock?" asked Gilbert.

"Ten o'clock," confirmed Wen.

"Did you get a good look at him?"

Wen nodded. "He had brown hair down to his shoulders. And a beard all over his face. And glasses. Tiny, round glasses. He ran away when I came out. Run, run, run. Like he was scared. He wasn't Chinese. I saw no Chinese man out there. Just a big white man."

CHAPTER
FIVE

ONCE THE DETECTIVES WERE THROUGH with Wen, they separated. Gilbert left by the front door. Lombardo went out the rear door, planned to drive by One Park Lane again to see if Pearl Wu had returned.

Gilbert ran through the rain to his Lumina, got in, and sat in the driver's seat for several minutes, thinking. He wasn't convinced by Dock Wen's story. Underneath the cook's veneer of cooperation, Gilbert sensed a snow job. In addition, he thought Wen was scared, that he had been forced to change his story. Officer Kennedy's report unequivocally described a Chinese. Now Wen was telling them a white man. Was that a lie? He glanced at the curb where he saw a dozen warped pool cues tied in a bundle beside a garbage can painted with crude flowers. When Gilbert thought of the details, he found he couldn't be sure: the long brown hair, the beard, the tiny round glasses. And maybe wearing beige Isotoner gloves, he thought ruefully? Details like that mitigated the possibility of a lie. Edgar's killer might, after all, be white, male, and large. Which nonetheless still left the discrepancy in Officer Kennedy's report about the Chinese man.

He looked at the door leading to the upstairs apartments, one of the few improvements on the otherwise late-Victorian facade. A steel door, no windows, double locks, now with a big police sticker on it telling any and all that the place was a crime scene. He looked up at the second-floor window. May Lau's apartment. He felt sorry for her, to lose a son like that. He thought of his own children, Jennifer and Nina, realized how much he missed Jennifer, now that she'd gone away to university. He wanted to wrap his arms around Jennifer and give her the biggest hug in the world. To get a better idea of how Mrs. Lau might feel, he imagined Jennifer dead, pictured Jennifer lying on the floor in a spreading pool of blood, with her own streak of blue dye through her hair, turning colder, motionless in the unnerving stillness of death, not sleeping, not resting, but eternally dead, never able to respond, talk, or breathe again. Echoes of grief filled his mind. He magnified those echoes. He felt suddenly heavy. Grief was crushing, as much in a physical way as an emotional one. He wondered whether May Lau was still staying with friends or if she had come back that morning.

Just as Joe had taken a look at the back alley in broad daylight, so Gilbert now thought he should take a look at Edgar Lau's apartment in the bleak light of this December afternoon.

He got out of his car, walked to the steel door, and, using the extra keys, let himself in. Cheap indoor-outdoor carpeting, smelling faintly of cat urine, covered the steps. He stopped at the foot of the stairs and listened. Over the sound of the rain he heard music. Chinese music. Someone played an instrument upstairs. A Chinese instrument. An instrument that sounded like a violin, only thinner, reedier, softer. Five notes to the scale, like the black notes on a piano—a pentatonic scale—mournful, ghostly, a parade of phrases and cadences that drifted down the steep stairwell like a lament, creeping into his skin the same way the damp did. So. She was home. And she was upstairs. Playing a Chinese instrument. Playing a song to her dead son, an accompaniment to the rain, a melody meant to ease her own suffering.

He climbed the stairs quietly. The steps slanted to the left, a sagging old staircase going more out of true every year. He didn't want to disturb her. He tried to shut the music out because it made him feel sorry for Edgar Lau. He didn't want to feel sorry for Edgar Lau. He had to remember what Edgar Lau had done to Pearl Wu—the stroke of a blade across her face, robbing her of the most precious thing she possessed. Feeling sorry for Edgar Lau would make him lose his impartiality. But the melody was like morning mist in a field, music he had to walk through, a song he couldn't avoid. He stopped on May Lau's landing and looked at her door. Steel, beige paint chipped away in spots, the dry remains of a dead fly flattened in the upper left-hand corner. A thick steel door. No wonder she hadn't heard the shot. At least not through this door. But what about through the floor? Her not hearing the shot bothered him. She still had at least one good ear. And the floors were thin. He had heard her wailing for her son through the floor. He continued upstairs. Why hadn't she heard the shot?

He stuck the brass key in the lock and opened Edgar Lau's apartment door. The sound of the rain immediately got louder, like rounding a bend on a quiet river and hearing rapids up ahead. He stepped into Edgar Lau's apartment and listened to it drum off the roof. Then he heard water dripping into a pail in the kitchen. He took a few steps into the apartment and saw rain leaking through the ceiling, the plaster ripped away, drops plummeting from one of the exposed joists into a half-filled plastic basket. Gilbert couldn't understand it. The man had a huge dose of China White worth millions of dollars in his attic and he had to live in a place like this? With pigeons and rats, and rain leaking through? With cheap carpeting on the outside stairs? And the smell of chop suey drifting up from below?

He looked at the blood. Flies, even in December, grazed on the thicker purple spots. He moved into the living room and took a look at some of the books on the shelf. *No More Vietnams,* by Richard M. Nixon. *West to Cambodia,* by S. L. A. Marshall. *The Fall of Saigon,* by Peter S. Bradley. *A History of China Since the Revolution,* by John C. Lai. *Hong Kong: Dream and Paradox,* by Roland Percival. Weighty, analytical volumes. He couldn't help thinking that Edgar had been seeking an answer in these books but had never succeeded in finding one.

Gilbert moved to the table, lifted the photograph album, and found the snapshots taken on the boat. Here was one that showed a view looking downward, directly over the side of the boat. Water snakes and flying tunny schooled alongside. He turned the page. And stopped. Stopped and stared at the photograph on the right-hand leaf. Stared at Foster Sung. A much younger Foster Sung. Sung had a kerchief tied around his head to protect it from the sun. He had a nickel-plated semiautomatic stuck in the waistband of his tattered salt-stained shorts, the bright nickel plate shining with starlike intensity in the unrelenting sun, a show piece as much as a weapon, the gun of a man who liked to kill in style. In the background Gilbert saw people passing buckets, basins, even pots and pans from the hold up to the deck and over the side in a human chain, bailing the ship.

He turned another page. And stopped again. This time because he saw a picture of that other man. From the photograph in Edgar's bedroom. The man who drove the yellow Honda. In this picture the man had his shirt off. His muscles were as sharply defined as Edgar's. Gilbert looked at the man's face. A handsome face. Like Edgar's. The resemblance was now readily apparent. The man held up a large fish by the gills, one that looked like a giant seagoing catfish, with whiskers around its nose, its pale eyes glistening in the sun. The man smiled at the camera with those big white teeth of his. A woman stood beside the man. May Lau. Much younger. But undoubtedly Edgar's mother. Wearing a light summer dress with girlish puff sleeves and a lace collar, a dress with as many wrinkles as an old lady's face, and as stained and dirty as a vagrant's only pants.

Then he realized that someone was looking at him. His peripheral vision sketched in a figure to the left. He turned.

May Lau stood there, having entered the apartment silently. They stared at each other. Neither said a word. The silence lengthened between them. May Lau finally spoke. She looked at the photograph.

"That's my husband," she said. "Ying. Edgar's father." The smile that came to her face was both fragile and melancholy. "The last picture we have of him."

She was a diminutive Chinese woman, in her late fifties, still handsome enough, but not beautiful the way she was in this picture on the boat. She wore a man's shirt. Over the shirt she wore a crocheted vest of olive-green cotton yarn. She wore black slacks and Mao slippers, had her long gray hair pinned up behind her head in a cheap plastic comb. She wore large square glasses.

"Mrs. Lau . . ." he said. "Mrs. Lau . . . I'm sorry about Edgar."

She nodded, accepting his condolences.

"I don't want you to think badly of Edgar," she said.

"Why would I think badly of him?" he asked.

Her eyes now glistened. "Because he's been in trouble with the police before," she said. "Because he's done some things he's regretted."

Gilbert raised his eyebrows, squeezed his lips together. He wondered how extensive Mrs. Lau's knowledge of her son's activities might be. He thought of Pearl Wu's slashed face again. He wanted to comfort May Lau. Children might grow up, become adults, but they never stopped being their parents' children. He was a father. He understood that.

"He's had some rough spots in his life," he offered, glancing down at the photograph album.

She nodded, acknowledging the photographs, and took a few more steps into the room. "That wasn't easy for us," she said. "We were desperate. We never wanted to leave but we had no choice." She glanced at some of the other photographs. "Ying had a business. Not a particularly thriving one, but he was proud of it. He was a mechanic. The Communist government took that away from us. We had no choice. We had to go."

Joe was right. The woman spoke English well. Her voice was soft, reminded Gilbert of the pure tones of a crystal glass being struck by a spoon. He flipped back.

"I see a picture of Foster Sung here," he said.

He watched her face. It changed. A darkness filled it, an intimation of a by no means placid emotion.

"Foster is a family friend," she said, her voice now devoid of inflection. "He's been much too generous to us. We owe Foster our lives. The boat in these pictures belonged to Foster. Foster lent my husband money whenever we needed it. Foster's always been much too generous to us."

Gilbert didn't know what to make of this. Her voice wasn't pure-sounding anymore. The crystal glass in her voice didn't ring.

"How did your husband die?" he asked.

She took a weak breath, faltering in the face of his question, her lips slackening, her eyes seeming to recede into some deep hidden spot inside herself. "The boat sprang a leak," she said, her voice straining, as if she had only the most tenuous hold on this fact. "He had to spend long hours bailing." She looked down at the floor, at the flies grazing on her son's blood. "He worked himself to death so everybody else could live."

"I'm sorry," he said. Inadequate words, but could words ever be adequate in a situation like that?

She looked around the apartment disconsolately. "I want to clean this up," she said. "When do you think I can clean it up?"

"We'll try to finish as soon as we can," he assured her.

The two of them just stood there. Gilbert had dozens of questions to ask Mrs. Lau but he found he couldn't bring himself to utter the necessary words when he saw so much grief in her eyes, hadn't meant to ask questions today anyway. But he was a homicide detective and it was his job to ask questions, to push forward even at the most hurtful times—more than just his job, a matter of his own integrity, a commitment to fight this bad thing that had never had any right to happen in the first place.

"Are you going to stay here?" he inquired. "Or are you going to move?"

She looked at him. "I don't know," she said. "I don't have much money and the rent's cheap here. Foster owns this building."

"You were playing an instrument," he said.

She nodded distractedly. "The *erhu*," she said. "I used to play that same melody to Edgar when he was a baby. It helped him sleep. He was a restless child."

Gilbert looked at his hands. "Is there anything you want to add to the statement you gave Detective Lombardo on Friday night?" he said. He felt like he was stepping over broken glass.

She shrugged weakly. "I told him everything," she said. "I wish I could be more use." She said this in a nearly guilty way.

"We can't find Pearl Wu."

Again, the shrug. "She comes and goes. She and Edgar have their episodes."

"Did Edgar know her well?"

"They've known each other for years. Ever since Hong Kong." She looked as if she might elaborate, but she turned away, as if she had decided against further comment.

"Does Edgar have any other friends we might talk to?"

She continued to stare out the French doors, her expression wistful and apathetic, a woman too grief-stricken to care about anything. "Edgar had his own life," she said. "He had his own friends. I would hear them come up and down the stairs, but he never bothered to introduce any of them to me." Acknowledging her own marginalization in her son's life, she grew sadder still.

Gilbert hesitated. If she had heard Edgar's friends coming up and down the stairs, why hadn't she heard the gunshot? The point stuck, something he couldn't find a way to explain, an inconsistency that made him think she might be filtering everything she told him.

"You have no idea where Pearl Wu might be right now?" asked Gilbert. "We really have to talk to her." Pearl had become the frustratingly absent center around which his investigation now revolved.

"Pearl's a busy woman," said Mrs. Lau. "She has three offices in Toronto. She looks after her husband's concerns here. She has meetings. She has appointments. She could be anywhere." May Lau looked at him with apprehension. "I take it you know what my son did to Pearl."

Gilbert again hesitated. He knew and understood this aspect of grief. The need to expatiate the sins of the departed. "We have it on file," he confirmed.

She turned away, looked at the coffee table. She appeared mystified, baffled. "I don't know why he did that," she said. Her voice was softer still. She adjusted her plastic comb. "He's never talked about it." She shook her head. "He confessed to the crime, he pled guilty, he went to jail, but he won't tell anybody why he did it, not even his lawyer. He's stubborn that way. Not even Pearl knows why he did it. It's against his nature to raise his hand against a woman. Or a man, for that matter. Edgar is . . . was . . . highly principled in his way."

Wind blew rain against the panes of the French doors. "We're a little concerned about Pearl," said Gilbert.

May Lau's face hardened. "I don't think she would kill my son," she said. But her conviction was forced.

"Under the circumstances, we're going to have to talk to her," said Gilbert. "She was up here around the time of your son's murder." Gilbert glanced at the French doors, wondering about them. "Did you see her leave at all?"

"No."

"You still have Detective Lombardo's card?" he asked.

"Yes."

"Please call us if you hear from Pearl. We've got to talk to her."

May Lau nodded tentatively. "I will," she said, but she said it as if she didn't mean it, and as if she didn't have the strength to do anything but grieve for her son.

When Gilbert got home from work that night, late as usual, his wife, Regina, waited for him in the front hall. She looked upset, had her head tilted to one side, a hand on her hip, and her blue eyes were solemn.

"What's wrong?" he asked.

"Jennifer's home," she said, glancing at the stairs.

"I thought she wasn't coming back for another three days," said Gilbert.

"I'm as surprised as you are," said Regina. "She came on the afternoon train. She broke up with Karl. She didn't even phone ahead, that's how upset she was."

Gilbert's first reaction was one of vast relief. Karl Randall, to his mind, was a supremely negative influence on his daughter's life, a young man who followed his dangerous impulses much too quickly, and who had a way of goading Jennifer into bad decisions.

"Is she all right?" he asked.

"She's in her room. Crying."

Nina, his younger daughter, fifteen years old, came out of the living room with pine cones and wire, raw materials for a Christmas wreath.

"I don't blame her," said Nina, with sincere sisterly commiseration. "Karl is such a hunk."

Gilbert stared at Nina. Men were hunks now. He had to make the adjustment. "She'll get over it," he said.

"No," said Nina, "she won't. How many chances do you think

she's going to get, dad? Look how tall she is. And look at the way she wears her hair. She was lucky to get Karl in the first place." Nina shook her head in a world-weary way. "I don't know why she had to go and blow it. I was hoping to see Karl this Christmas."

Coming from a fifteen-year-old, these words irked Gilbert. "If you want my honest opinion," he said, "I think the guy's bad news. He stole his friend's car, and he almost overdosed on heart medication. What kind of idiot would do that?"

"Let's not characterize Karl as an idiot just now," said Regina. "I think that's the last thing Jennifer wants to hear."

"Who dumped who?" asked Gilbert.

"He dumped her," said Regina.

"Then he's an idiot," said Gilbert, failing, despite considerable effort, to keep his hard line under control. "He won't find another girl like Jennifer."

"He's not going to want to find another girl like Jennifer," said Nina. "Have you seen the makeup she's wearing lately? No one goes Gothic anymore."

"Nina, sweetheart, please," said Gilbert. "I know you're a bright kid. I just wish you'd show it more often."

He wondered when Nina had become so opinionated; then he remembered that she had Regina as a mother.

"Could you go up and talk to her?" said Regina. He looked at his wife. Nineteen years of raising girls and they still hadn't figured it out. "I tried to talk to her but she won't listen to me. I think she needs her father."

Those words always scared Gilbert. "What do you want me to say to her?" he asked.

"You'll think of something."

"I liked Ben a lot better," said Gilbert.

"Dad, Ben was three years ago," said Nina. "And they weren't even intimate."

Intimate. He had to make the adjustment on that one too. "Do we have to go into the details?" he asked.

"At least Karl and Jennifer were intimate," said Nina.

"But that doesn't necessarily mean they were good for each other," said Gilbert. "And now look what he's done to her. She's all upset. God knows what it's done to her grades. I wish she would have stayed away from him."

"Dad, the world doesn't revolve around grades," said Nina.

"Yes, my darling, it does," he said, in a tone of anything but endearment. He took off his coat and dumped it over the banister. "He'd have to do this right now, around Christmas, wouldn't he? It's just what we need."

"Christmas is the most depressing time of year for over sixty percent of the population, dad," said Nina. "We'll be no different from anybody else."

"Tell her to come down and eat something," said Regina. "I have those ribs simmering in the Crock-Pot. I picked up a Caesar salad at Marvelous Edibles."

"This single household must keep that place afloat," he complained, slipping off his rubber overshoes.

"And by the way, a Jeremy Austin called from 52 Division," said Regina.

Constable Jeremy Austin, the constable Benny Eng said they should talk to if they wanted more information on the illegal Chinese gaming houses downtown, and which ones Edgar Lau might have worked at. But why would he call Gilbert at home?

"Did he leave a message?" he asked.

"No."

"I bet it's about a murder," said Nina. "You see what I mean about Christmas, dad? Joy to the world, goodwill toward men."

"Why don't you go watch *Old Yeller*?" said Gilbert. "It might cheer you up."

"Dad, don't make fun of my favorite movie," said Nina. "You're just going to make me resent you more than I already do."

Still, it was odd, thought Gilbert, as he climbed the stairs to Jennifer's room. Why would Austin call him here and not at headquarters? It made Gilbert think that Austin might know more about things in Chinatown than was reasonably healthy for a rank-and-file officer to know, as if the things he knew were things he'd sooner not tell anybody at headquarters. Maybe the man was in trouble of some kind.

He knocked gently on Jennifer's door. "Jennifer?" he said. "Jenn, hon, it's me. Can I come in?"

No answer. He knew she was at the age where he had to respect her privacy, but he yearned for her, needed her, hadn't seen her since Thanksgiving, and was aching to give his eldest a hug. He turned the knob and pushed the door open.

She sat at her desk slouched in her chair staring out at the rain. Gilbert couldn't help thinking that Nina might be right. Even though he himself thought Jennifer the most beautiful creature on earth, she might not get many chances after all. She was tall, man-like, didn't have such obvious pretty features as Nina, was a quiet and brooding young woman, characteristics that didn't lend themselves well to the social rituals of university life. Not only that, she was smart, with marks in the eighties and nineties, and that could scare away as many men as it might attract. She didn't turn. She continued to stare out the window. Her limp blond hair—with a turquoise streak—hung from a center part and looked as if it hadn't been washed in a few days. She wore bell-bottom jeans, seams split and filled in with faded paisley cloth. *Everything old is new again,* he thought.

"Mom told me you've had a rough time," he said. He looked around the room. Her suitcase sat unpacked on the end of her bed. A Limp Bizkit *Significant Other* poster hung on the wall. "Am I going to get a hug?" he asked.

She swung slowly round in her swivel chair and stared at him with her oversized blue eyes. He had to admit, Nina was right about the eyeliner too. Gothic. Too much eyeliner. The cult of the young urban vampire, after its initial craze, now seemed dated. His tall, gangly, socially graceless beautiful eldest daughter. He spread his arms. He felt like crying to see her so sad. She rose, came near, her lower lip quivering.

"He left me, dad," she said.

He left me. It sounded like such a grown-up thing for Jennifer to say. Okay. He had to make another adjustment. He put his arms around her, and was surprised, even startled, when she clung to him, arms around his back in a desperate squeeze, her body jerking with an agonized sob, as if what she had had with Karl were more than just puppy love after all. The prick, he thought. The absolute prick. To do this to his daughter. She had never held on to him like this. Squeezing him harder and harder. Shaking. Trembling. Crying. She couldn't control herself. He pictured her coming home on the train alone that afternoon, not bothering to phone, just running to the train station, traveling through the gray winter landscape, past the fallow cornfields and dull brown barns of southern Ontario, with the rain constantly coming down.

"I didn't do anything," she finally said. "I didn't do anything at all, dad."

He had never heard her cry like this before, as if her agony reached right to the marrow of her bones. She was a woman now. He could hardly believe it. It was as if the gyroscopic center of her soul, that which gave her all her emotional balance and poise, had been jostled, and jostled seismically, enough to rip her apart.

"I know you didn't, sweetheart," he said. "I know you didn't. And if it's any consolation, he's not exactly the best thing that ever happened to you. Sometimes bad things like this—"

But he instantly recognized his blunder. He felt her shoulders stiffen. She pushed him away. "What did you say?" she said, looking at him with accusatory eyes. "He's the *best* thing that's ever happened to me. I love him, daddy. I *love* him. And I know you've always hated him."

As if she had to blame anybody but herself or Karl for the breakup, choosing her father as the most convenient lightning rod around.

"I don't hate him," he said, wincing at her words.

"You don't know anything," she said. "You don't know anything at all. I slept with him, daddy." As if she were throwing down the gauntlet. "I slept with him a hundred times. And I loved every bit of it."

He didn't know what to say. He felt that any words, no matter what they were, would just backfire. "Mom wants you to come down and have something to eat," he said. That seemed safe enough.

"Just go, okay?" she said. "You have no idea what you're talking about, and I don't think you even care."

She fell on her bed in a heap. He wished he could do something. But she had to simmer down. So he left her there.

He went out into the hall. And found Regina standing there. Regina was crying too. Joy to the world. Goodwill toward men. This was going to be a great Christmas.

"You blew it, didn't you?" she said.

He nodded. "But good," he agreed.

IN THE HOMICIDE OFFICE THE next day, complimentary danishes, donuts, and coffee sat on trays near the front. Acting Staff Inspector Tim Nowak, after eight months of steering the squad through the pitfalls of employee reductions and budget restraints, had finally been appointed the official head of Homicide. Detective Support Command had sent the complimentary eats to the squad room to mark the occasion. Now the party was breaking up. Tim Nowak, a tall, thin, gray-haired man in his early fifties, stood at the office door shaking hands with well-wishers.

"He's more an administrator than Bill Marsh was," said Gilbert to Lombardo. "Marsh should have stayed in uniform. He was a street cop through and through." Gilbert sometimes longed nostalgically for the street. "The worst thing they ever did to Marsh was make him staff inspector of Homicide."

Lombardo looked at the new staff inspector doubtfully. "I hear Tim's in good with Command."

Gilbert raised his eyebrows. "Is that a bad thing?"

Lombardo took a sip of his coffee. "It can be," he said.

"I worked with him in Fraud twenty years ago," said Gilbert. He pondered his half-finished danish, the yellow lemon goop in the center a little too hard, a little too old. "He knows how to write a report."

"I can deal with that," said Lombardo, his tone brightening. "I write a good report."

They gazed at the new staff inspector. Nowak spoke as smoothly as satin to his well-wishers, handling the public relations aspect of his new appointment with a grace, diplomacy, and patience Marsh had lacked. Marsh had certain buttons. You had to be careful which ones you pushed. The problem with Nowak, he had no buttons. He was unflappable. The crowd dwindled to a half dozen. Two latecomers, looking as groomed and practiced as Nowak, men Gilbert had never seen before, entered the office. They said a few words to Nowak and shook hands with the staff inspector. Then all three glanced toward Gilbert and Lombardo. They exchanged a few more words and retreated to Nowak's office.

"Did you see the way they looked at us?" asked Lombardo.

"I saw," said Gilbert.

"What's that about?" asked Lombardo.

"I don't know."

The two detectives sat for a few moments. Every month, week, and year Gilbert worked with Lombardo, he felt a stronger-growing solidarity with the man. There might be sixteen years between them; Joe might be the last great playboy of the Western world while he himself was a happily married man; Joe might be a second-generation Italian and he a plain-as-white-bread WASP; but they both thought the same way about the job, *the* job, and so, under this new circumstance, with strange latecomers staking them out in their own squad room, they instinctively followed each other's lead and hunkered down together, waiting for whatever fecal matter was inevitably going to hit the fan.

Gordon Telford, one of the detectives in their squad, approached with a handful of magazines. Telford was a tall man with red hair, a mustache, freckles. He wore a double-knit suit, polished Bostonians, and a tie with conservative stripes. Today he had what looked like a ketchup stain on his shirt. His Bostonians were mud-splattered. The knot in his tie was askew. He looked, in fact, like a homicide detective.

"I thought you might want to take a look at these," he said, putting the magazines on Gilbert's desk. Chinese magazines, with dazzling Chinese writing all over them. Telford flipped to a spot halfway through the first one and pointed. "That's her," he said. "That's Pearl Wu. Before Edgar Lau performed his unscheduled surgery on her."

The woman in the fashion layout posed in a series of alluring evening gowns against the glittering nighttime skyline of Hong Kong. She couldn't have been more than twenty-five in these shots. Was she beautiful, wondered Gilbert? Within the definitions of her trade she indeed possessed those qualities that constituted the modern-day conception of beauty. But nothing particularly distinguished her. She looked as if she were made of plastic, doll-like and immutable, there simply for the purpose of being looked at.

"Oh, and by the way," said Telford. "The lab techs finally swabbed your glove."

"And?" said Gilbert.

"Positive for barium and antimony," said Telford.

"I don't believe it," said Lombardo, as if a lame nag had just trotted into the winner's circle.

Gilbert turned to Lombardo, feeling as if this might be the high point of his day. "I find a glove in a tree, it's dry on the inside, someone's just recently thrown it there, and you don't believe it?" One of the great pleasures of his partnership with Joe was making Joe eat his own words. "You must learn from me, my son."

Lombardo's handsome face twisted into a contrite but still incredulous frown. "Come on, it was a long shot," he said.

"Not so long when you think of the experienced criminals we're dealing with," said Gilbert. "They're going to know about barium and antimony. Shoot the victim wearing a glove, then throw the glove away. That way, when the police swab you, you come up dry. You're running from the crime scene, you have to get rid of the glove, so you fling it into someone's backyard. Only it lands in a tree." He turned to Telford. "Tell them to keep working on it. See if they can turn up fibers or hair, or dead skin inside the glove, something that might give us a chance at a DNA match. And I guess we should check how many men's beige Isotoners were sold city-wide, see if we can get names of purchasers from charge-card slips."

"Sure," said Telford.

Nowak's office door opened. "Barry?" called the new staff inspector. "Joe?" Nowak beckoned with a finger, his face sleek and composed. Gilbert and Lombardo glanced at each other. They would weather this together.

"Up, up, and away," said Gilbert.

The detectives went to Nowak's office. Nowak introduced Gilbert and Lombardo to the two men. "This is Sergeant Frank Hukowich of the

RCMP's Asian Organized Crime Squad," he said, "and this is Special Agent Ross Paulsen of the U.S. Drug Enforcement Administration."

Gilbert shook hands with the two men. He now recognized Hukowich, remembered him from an inter-agency baseball game three years back, how the man had been wearing a back brace at the time, nothing that interfered with his umping the game, just odd-looking, like the thorax of an insect. The brace was now gone. Hukowich was well over six feet, had his hair brushed back from his wide brow in a impressive wave. He had a bushy brown mustache and light green eyes that seemed unresponsive to their surroundings. Ross Paulsen, a far slighter man, had curly gray hair so short it reminded Gilbert of the nap on a tennis ball. He smelled strongly of cologne. The difference between the two men was like the difference between a wolf and a colobus monkey. Gilbert was anything but happy to see them. He knew these two men had come to run interference.

"Frank and Ross are here to help us with Edgar Lau," said Nowak, casually, easily, as if they were all good friends, all part of the same club. Nowak turned to Hukowich and Paulsen. "Barry and Joe are two of my best detectives," he said. "They've worked several gangland slayings over the years."

They talked about some of the gangland slayings Gilbert and Lombardo had solved, Gilbert offering short, to-the-point replies, sensing manipulation in everything Hukowich and Paulsen said, wondering when they were going to get to the point. Hukowich suggested that murder investigations, important though they were, might yield greater and potentially more vital results if they were handled with an eye to netting other suspects involved in related criminal activities.

"We've been investigating Foster Sung for a long time," said

Hukowich. "Benny Eng's case file is slim compared to ours." He paused, looked at Gilbert with something approaching pride, like an avid golfer about to show off his best set of clubs. Gilbert wasn't sure why Frank Hukowich eased toward Edgar's murder through Foster Sung's alleged criminal history. "We have intelligence photos of Foster Sung sitting with Bing Wu in a restaurant in Wiang Phran, in northern Thailand." Maybe Hukowich meant to discuss Pearl Wu, their strongest suspect, by the oblique route of Foster Sung's suspected association with Bing Wu, Pearl's husband. "Bing Wu is believed to head a major drug smuggling operation in Southeast Asia, centered in Hong Kong." Then again, maybe not. "And if you don't know anything about the city of Wiang Phran, it's heroin central, right in the middle of the Golden Triangle. I think you can guess why Foster Sung and Bing Wu were in Wiang Phran." Hukowich slid his hands into his pockets and jangled his keys with the savoir faire of a self-appointed expert. "So you see, Barry," he said, in the tones of an evangelist wearily converting a pagan, "this could turn into more than just an ordinary homicide investigation." He stopped jangling his keys, gave Gilbert a pointed look. Gilbert felt as if he had missed something, couldn't see how Foster Sung sitting in a restaurant in Wiang Phrao had anything to do with Edgar's murder. Hukowich's speech struck Gilbert as nothing but a long pointless non sequitur.

"I don't see how," he said.

Hukowich frowned, as if he thought Gilbert was obtuse. "Because Foster Sung is a suspect in this murder."

Gilbert looked at Tim Nowak, feeling as if he had just been forced to go the wrong way down a one-way street, then glanced at Joe. Lombardo's dark Mediterranean brow settled into a lethal line.

"He's one of our weaker suspects," Gilbert finally said, because even Gilbert had to acknowledge that Sung had been near Edgar Lau's apartment in and around the time of the slaying. "But we're really treating him like a witness. I'm afraid I don't see your logic. If you're at all familiar with the case file"—he gave Nowak a sour look—"you'll see that Pearl Wu is actually our strongest suspect."

Ross Paulsen spoke up. "Foster Sung's of great interest to us," he said, like an entomologist speaking of a rare bug. "He was at the scene in and around the time of the murder. He has suspected criminal connections to Bing Wu. We want to somehow put pressure on Foster Sung as a way of getting through to Bing Wu, and your murder investigation might give us the opportunity we need." Paulsen's faced was tanned, unnaturally so, with that freakish orange color that came from obsessive tanning appointments. "We know it's probably too early to write a warrant on Foster Sung, but we would certainly appreciate it if you concentrated your efforts in that direction."

Even to talk of warrants, especially one against Foster Sung, was so far removed from reality, Gilbert wondered how they could be talking about the same investigation. He glanced at Lombardo again, knew his young partner sensed the exact same thing, as if a trail had been blazed for them and they were now expected to follow it. But if Paulsen and Hukowich wanted to get through to Bing Wu, wouldn't Pearl be their obvious choice, especially since she was Gilbert's number-one suspect already? Foster Sung might know a lot about Bing Wu's organization, but wouldn't Pearl, as Wu's wife, know a lot more?

"About the most we can do right now is hope Foster Sung cooperates as a witness," said Gilbert.

All three men stared at Gilbert.

Tim Nowak shifted, and, with no appreciable change in his

demeanor, managed to lift the corners of his lips into a patient grin. "Frank and Ross would really like you to work the Sung angle," said Nowak, as rationally and calmly as a senior accountant reporting fourth-quarter earnings to company board members.

So. They were going to force him to be blunt. He loved being blunt. "I don't think Foster did it," he said.

"Why not?" asked Hukowich.

"For one thing, when Joe saw him at the crime scene, he didn't have rain on his clothes, and one of the theories we're working with is that our suspect came in the back through the rain. The other theory, and possibly the stronger theory, is Pearl." Gilbert shook his head in mystification. "I don't know why you're asking me to go after Foster Sung. Why not ask me to go after Pearl? Wouldn't she be just as useful to you as Foster? She's married to Bing Wu. I don't know why you've decided on Foster Sung."

Paulsen looked away, disgruntled. "Just take a close look at Foster, will you?" he said. The man obviously had his reasons. "Gather whatever evidence you can against him and we'll do the rest. You won't need much for a warrant. Not with the judge Frank has in mind."

Did the man have to be so obvious about the way he planned to bend jurisprudence for the sake of arresting Foster Sung? "Look, we'll talk to Sung," said Gilbert. "That's the most we can do for now."

Hukowich's face reddened. Gilbert didn't like the look he saw in Hukowich's eyes.

"Don't think Foster Sung's a saint, Barry," said Hukowich. "Benny told you about the immigration scam a few years back. But Ross has new sources who say he's smuggling human cargo into the country like cattle, at forty to fifty grand a head, refugees from China who work off their passages in illegal sweatshops south of the border. He's no Mother Teresa, Barry. Before he fled Vietnam he ran several prostitution rings as well as numerous illegal gaming houses. Extortion was his big thing—beating the crap out of laundry-shop owners for protection, threatening factory workers, paying bribes so the police would cooperate. You're not achieving anything by trying to protect him, Barry. He's no saint."

Gilbert stared at Hukowich expressionlessly. "I'm not trying to protect anybody, Frank," he said. "And believe me, in my line of work, saints are few and far between."

His meaning couldn't have been clearer.

DONCLIFFE TOWER STOOD ON UNIVERSITY Avenue south of Dundas Street in the heart of Toronto's Chinatown, a twenty-five-story office building of black stone and reflective glass owned by New Asian Holdings Incorporated, a Foster Sung assets management company. Sung's office was on the top floor, an expanse of teak and mirror, rosewood furniture, handwoven throw rugs, jade and brass statuary, a fully stocked bar, and a private sauna. A hundred-gallon aquarium, recessed into the wall, glittered with tiger barbs, neon tetras, and a half dozen other exotic breeds.

Sung greeted Gilbert cordially—a crisp handshake, a practiced smile—then asked the detective to sit down. Sung was in his late fifties. Impeccably groomed, he wore an expensive and elegantly tailored blue pinstripe suit, a fashionable silk tie, and a dress shirt from Harry Rosen's. His watch, tie clip, and cuff links were gold, each studded with a profusion of tiny diamonds. He looked robust, energetic, and forceful, the kind of man with an indefatigable capacity for work. The view from Sung's office would no doubt be spectacular on a clear day, but all Gilbert saw today was an uninterrupted layer of gray mist obscuring the large downtown bank buildings, hotels, and insurance towers, the cloud cover swallowing them at around floor thirty.

"There's not much I can add to the statement I gave Detective Lombardo on Friday night," said Sung. His English was good. The man had been in Canada since 1981. "I was sitting in the restaurant with some associates around ten o'clock when May came downstairs and told me her son had been shot. I asked her whether Edgar was still alive and she said she thought he was. I knew the situation might be dangerous, but I also knew I had to act. I climbed the stairs to give Edgar immediate assistance, even though I knew his attacker might still be in the apartment."

Sung's account was complete and succinct, a set piece, like a memo he might dictate to his secretary, with all the commas and periods in place, polished, yes, but also rehearsed, too perfect not to stir some doubt in Gilbert's mind.

"And Edgar was still alive when you got there?" asked Gilbert.

"Still alive but unconscious," said Sung. A man with all the answers. But then a faint tremor of concern played over his face. "I told May to stay downstairs." His polish evaporated and Gilbert saw a flicker of sorrow pass through his eyes. "Edgar was lying on the dining room floor. He was bleeding badly." Sung looked at Gilbert. "I've seen men bleed this badly before, back in Vietnam. I worked in a field hospital during the war. I knew Edgar was in bad shape." Sung shook his head, his concern and sorrow now capitulating to his genuine bereavement. "He had a ball of crumpled tissue paper clutched near his stomach, but as he was unconscious by the time I got there, he wasn't pressing it tightly to his wound anymore. I knew I had to stop that bleeding before I did anything else. So I took a dish towel from the rack under the sink, folded it several times, and pressed the dressing against Edgar's wound. Then I called nine-one-one."

The detail of the dish towel snagged Gilbert's attention.

"You say you stopped his bleeding with a dish towel?" said Gilbert.

Sung nodded. "Edgar was in bad, bad shape."

"We didn't find any dish towel when we got there." The fact of the dish towel blurred the emerging picture of the crime scene into sudden distortion. "Did you take it away?"

Sung raised his eyebrows, as if he were surprised by this news. "No," he said.

"A dish towel?"

"A yellow dish towel," said Sung. "Fresh. From the towel rack under the kitchen sink."

Gilbert thought about this. He was certain Officer Donald Kennedy had made no mention of this dish towel in his crime scene report. "You stayed with Edgar until the police arrived?" he asked Sung.

"I left the apartment only to get May," he said. "I was afraid that Edgar might die while we were waiting for help to arrive. I thought his mother should be there."

"And the dish towel was still there when you got back?"

"Yes."

"And when Officer Kennedy got there he asked you to leave the apartment?" said Gilbert.

"Yes," said Sung. "He wished to maintain the integrity of the crime scene. He was afraid we might inadvertently destroy evidence."

Normal police procedure. Any first officer at the scene would have done the same. Only now there was no yellow dish towel. Nor was there any mention of the dish towel in Officer Kennedy's report.

"And Officer Kennedy's partner stayed downstairs?" asked Gilbert.

Sung nodded. "Constable Szoldra took statements from diners in the restaurant," he said.

Gilbert thought of the other discrepancy in Kennedy's report, that there had been a Chinese man behind the restaurant, not a white one such as the cook Dock Wen had told them. One discrepancy was an anomaly. Two were suspicious.

"I understand you own the Laus's building," said Gilbert.

"I do."

"And that you're a longtime friend of the Laus."

"I am."

"And that you helped them escape from Vietnam twenty-four years ago."

"I did."

Gilbert glanced out the window at the gray sky. A few blocks to the south on Queen Street, he saw a streetcar rumble west across University Avenue. "Do you have any idea who might have murdered Edgar?"

"No."

"Do you know Pearl Wu?"

"I do."

"A waiter says he saw her leave Edgar's apartment around the time of the shooting."

"Yes, I saw her."

"You saw her?"

"Yes."

"You saw her leave?"

"Yes," said Sung. "I saw her arrive as well. As a matter of fact, she came to our table to say hello."

"But when she left, she left by the front door?"

"Yes."

"Because we think our perpetrator might have fled through the back," said Gilbert.

"Pearl left by the front door," said Sung.

Which didn't necessarily eliminate Pearl as a suspect. "Did Edgar use the back way often?" asked Gilbert.

"I have no idea," said Sung. "But he shouldn't. It's old. It's rusting through in spots. I've had the fire marshal look at it and he says I'll have to replace it next year. I don't like the Laus living in that old place. I plan to tear it down. I have much better buildings, but they won't move."

"Why not?"

"Because May will never take anything from me unless she absolutely has to," said Sung, with some irritation. "I tell her she can live wherever she wants. In any building I own. And pay me whatever she wants. But she refuses. She won't even let me pay for her son's funeral."

Gilbert stared at the suspected triad member. Did Sung feel a particular fondness for May Lau? He certainly seemed like a good friend to the Laus, a protector, there to support them, to lend assistance; but Gilbert now sensed something more, a tie between Foster and May, not a passion, exactly, but something that linked each to the other, a bond that balanced between Foster's persistent kindness and May's proud refusals.

"I understand Mr. Lau lost his life on your boat escaping from Vietnam," he said. He wanted more background, something that in the long run might help him in his search for Edgar's killer.

Sung nodded sadly, easing back into his chair, as if preparing to deliver another set piece. "Seven men, five children, and two women lost their lives on that boat." Sung rubbed his forehead, took off his glasses, and looked at the small mauve cockleshell inside his glass paperweight. "We all have our stories, detective, we who come to Canada as refugees. We all have good luck, we all have bad luck. We all take risks, we all gamble, and sometimes we win and sometimes we lose. Ying Lau was unlucky. He was a strong man, but even strong men, when they push themselves too hard, wear themselves out. Some men make their own luck. He never knew how to do that. He had a penchant for making wrong choices. About the luckiest thing he ever did was marry May. He never understood just how lucky that was. Our boat sprang a leak and he bailed night and day. He wouldn't take a rest no matter how hard May and I tried to make him. He pushed himself too hard and he died." He paused, reflecting on this tragic outcome, then turned to Gilbert with a little more brightness, as if he had learned to deal with the tragedies of the past. "We Chinese value family above all else. I suppose it's the same for everyone. For Edgar to lose his father like that . . . I tried to do what I could for the Laus once we reached Hong Kong. But as far as May was concerned I was a rough man, and she didn't want any help from a rough man."

A rough man? Was that how Sung romanticized himself?

"The boat must have been old," said Gilbert. "Edgar had some photographs of it."

Sung nodded. "She was a coastal freighter," he said. "Built in the 1940s. A lot of rust. She spent half her time in dry dock undergoing repairs. I used her to ferry goods up and down the Mekong River. I sometimes took her up the coast as far north as Da Nang, but never had her far out to sea until we had to leave. I knew it was a risk, but I couldn't afford a new boat. As an ethnic Chinese living in Vietnam I had to work hard for what little money I made, and there was little left over for that kind of capital venture. We were really treated like second-class citizens. My boat was never meant for the high seas. We hit rough weather our fourth day out. One of the seams split in the forward hold. Not a big leak, but one that would sink us if we didn't keep bailing."

"So Ying Lau worked himself to death bailing."

Sung lifted his chin, looked out the window where only the lower half of the CN Tower could be seen, the top half being shrouded by thick clouds. "Ying Lau was as stubborn as his wife," said Sung. Sung sounded as if he resented Ying Lau.

"And once you reached Hong Kong you tried to help the Laus," said Gilbert, now probing for the sake of Hukowich and Paulsen. "You obviously had connections in Hong Kong."

But Sung was too practiced to take such bait. "I told officials that May spoke four languages. Many of the civil positions were held by British nationals back in those days. With the refugee camps full of Vietnamese, she could translate from Vietnamese into English for the English-speaking officials, and from Vietnamese into Cantonese for the Cantonese-speaking officials."

Gilbert wasn't going to be put off so easily. "If you know Pearl Wu, you must know Bing Wu."

"Bing Wu is a business associate," said Sung. There was that word again. Associate.

"And he helped you when you reached Hong Kong?"

"We help each other. It's always been that way with Mr. Wu and I."

"And the Laus met Pearl Wu for the first time in Hong Kong?" asked Gilbert. "I understand Pearl and Edgar are . . ." He cast around for the appropriate euphemism.

Sung looked away, his brow creasing with displeasure. "Mrs. Wu has brought dishonor to her husband on many different occasions with many different men."

Gilbert saw his opening clearly enough. "Was Edgar one of those men?" he asked.

"The first and perhaps the most perennial." Sung occasionally spoke with a colonial turn of phrase, the influence of his years in Hong Kong, back in the days when the Jewel of Asia had been governed by British masters.

Connections. Pearl Wu and Edgar Lau. Was Edgar Lau's murder no more than a lover's quarrel then? Why did he get the sense that Sung was purposely trying to implicate Pearl? He had to be careful with Sung. Sung sat like a king in this opulent downtown tower, but he was a man who smuggled human cargo into Canada; he was a man who had been photographed with Bing Wu in Wiang Phran; a man who had been indicted on that immigration scam a few years back with Kung Lok Triad members.

"Who else was sitting at your restaurant table the night Edgar was murdered?" asked Gilbert.

"I was with Tak-Ng Lai, a concert pianist from Shanghai. I own an agency. I bring Chinese talent into the country. Lai is on a six-city tour right now."

Gilbert made a note of the name in his book, getting Sung to spell it for him. "Who else?" he asked.

"Xu Jiatun." Sung spelled that too.

"And what does *he* do?" asked Gilbert.

Sung leaned back in his chair and folded his hands over his

stomach complacently. "He's my bodyguard," he said, the admission calm and assured, yet with implicit challenge. Gilbert let it go.

"Anybody else?" he asked.

"Charles Peng. He's an agent and overseer for one of Bing Wu's export companies. If you wish to find him, he's staying at one of the many condominium suites Bing Wu owns at One Park Lane."

The next day, Wednesday, Gilbert took Jennifer and Nina Christmas shopping at Eglinton Square, a suburban mall a mile from where they lived. Toddlers crawled over the dollar-operated rides—a dinosaur, a helicopter, and a spaceship—while nervous parents weighted with bags and coats hovered around them, making sure they didn't fall. Storefronts glittered with tinsel and lights, green and red balls dangled from the indoor Japanese elms, and a chubby young Tamil woman, a Santa cap on her head, rang a bell collecting donations for the Salvation Army.

Gilbert kept glancing at Jennifer, who walked through the crowd as if in a trance, showing no interest in the festive shop fronts, her blue eyes dull, looking neither to the left or right, her lanky body leaning slightly forward as if into a wind as she trudged past other shoppers like an extra from a zombie movie. She still hadn't washed. Her face was pale. Her straw-colored hair hung in limp unattractive strands. The season was invisible to her.

"Let me get some money from the bank machine," he said. "We'll go to the food court and have something to eat." He put his hand on Jennifer's shoulder but she shook it away. "Can't we at least try to be friends?" he asked.

"He's made a few mistakes, dad," she said. "So what? You don't have to seem so happy he's gone."

"Who says I'm happy?" He felt as if he were walking through a minefield.

"This is turning into a real bummer," said Nina.

"Nina, why don't you and Jennifer go see if you can find something for Mom at Braemar's," he said. "Remember that blue dress she was talking about? See if you can hunt it down."

"Dad, that dress was three hundred dollars," said Nina.

"So?" said Gilbert. He thought of the Edgar Lau murder case. "I think I'm in for some overtime."

"I don't feel like buying a dress," said Jennifer.

He saw there was nothing he could do to raise Jennifer's spirits.

Nina hurried to Braemar's, always eager to shop for anything. Jennifer drifted over to Santa's Castle where little kids lined up to get their pictures taken with Santa, and young women in short red dresses, long black boots, and too much makeup acted as Santa's helpers. Gilbert stood in line at the bank machine. He felt unfairly picked on by Jennifer. He fought hard to conceal how he really felt about Karl Randall, but somehow it got through. If Karl had ever exhibited even a shred of responsibility, Gilbert might have felt differently, but Karl walked through the world like a mercenary on the loose, taking or wrecking anything he wanted while hurting a lot of people along the way. Rain beat against the skylights. He didn't mean to be an ogre about Karl. Easy-listening Christmas music— *Silent Night* with a backbeat—filtered through concealed speakers. But he simply couldn't help it.

He was three from the front of the line when he felt his pager buzz against his belt. He drew back his coat and had a look: 8081. Joe's extension at work. His partner was already working some overtime on the Edgar Lau murder case.

He felt for his cellular but discovered he'd left it in the car. He walked over to the nearest telephone booth.

As he dialed headquarters he kept his eye on Jennifer. She sat on the edge of the fountain next to Santa's Castle. She listlessly raked her fingers through the water, staring at the nickels and dimes on the tile below, seeing nothing, preoccupied with her own pain, oblivious to the happy sparkle of the coins in the water. Lombardo answered on the second ring.

"Bad news," he told Gilbert. "Pearl Wu is gone. She left the country. She's back in Hong Kong."

"Shit."

"She took a Canadian Airlines flight to Vancouver on Thursday, then a connecting Cathay Pacific flight yesterday morning."

"Is she running?" asked Gilbert.

"I'm not sure," said Joe. "Canadian Airlines says she's booked on a return flight a week tomorrow."

Gilbert glanced at a salesclerk handing out sample rum balls and marzipan at the Laura Secord candy store across the way, thinking this information through, then looked at Jennifer again.

"So she just went home for Christmas?" said Gilbert.

"That's a long flight," said Lombardo, sounding unconvinced. "Who knows if she's coming back? I'd hate to have to try and find her in Hong Kong."

Jennifer watched a young couple in love walk by. She had that look in her eyes, like she was completely alone in the world, and had been cheated out of the only thing that had ever mattered to her.

The uncertain nature of Pearl Wu's plans left them nothing to do but wait. Right now he was more concerned about his daughter.

"Look, Joe, I was wondering if you could do me a favor."

"Sure."

"Jennifer's a little down."

"The Karl thing," said Lombardo.

"It's turning Christmas into a disaster." Jennifer got up and wandered toward Braemar's, looking like a phantom, the soles of her black Doc Martins barely leaving the ground. "I thought you might take her to a show or something. I'll pay. What's on at the Royal Alex? Is *Les Mis* still playing?"

"Sure, I can get tickets to that," said Lombardo. Lombardo paused. "But why don't you take her yourself?"

"Because I rate a little below zero with Jennifer right now," he said. "And unless I give Karl the Citizen-of-the-Year Award, that's the way it's going to stay."

"The guy stole his friend's car," said Lombardo.

"I know," said Gilbert. "But maybe we think too much like cops."

"And he overdosed on some weird drug."

"Heart medication," said Gilbert. From down the mall he saw Nina come out of Braemar's, her face pinched with purpose. "I would really appreciate it, Joe." Nina met up with Jennifer. The two girls headed in his direction, Jennifer lagging behind. "Look, I've got to go. They're coming. When you phone her up, make it sound like it was your idea, okay?"

"Sure."

"Anything I do for her right now is going to be like poison."

"You have that effect on people," agreed Lombardo.

"Shut up, you schmuck," said Gilbert, and rang off.

When his two daughters reached him, Nina was solemn, looked as if she were about to announce the outbreak of World War III.

"Dad, they don't have the dress anymore," she said. "It's gone."

Gilbert didn't like shopping for just that reason; it always became problematic. "So what do we do?"

"I had the girl phone the Braemar's at Fairview, Scarborough, and Yorkdale." Gilbert stared at his youngest daughter with a flicker of renewed hope. "They don't have the dress in Fairview, only beige ones at Scarborough, and the blue ones at Yorkdale are a size too big." For a fifteen-year-old, she had uncanny investigative skills. "They're going to check their warehouse, but if the girl puts an order in today, it won't get here until after Christmas."

Gilbert felt his heart rate quicken. In some ways, this was more stressful than smashing open a door in a takedown. "So what do we do?" he asked again.

"You don't have to worry, dad. I found another dress, just the kind of dress I know mom will like," said Nina, her cheeks flushing. "I know she'll love it. And it's blue. Her favorite color."

Gilbert's shoulders sank. "Okay," he said, sacrificing his judgment to his daughter's shopping acumen. "Lead the way."

He was much too worried about Jennifer to venture into what to him were the uncharted waters of women's fashions, and would stick to offering up his credit card like a sacrificial lamb when the time came.

CHAPTER
EIGHT

ON THURSDAY AFTERNOON, FOUR DAYS before Christmas, Gilbert sat in the back booth of the Great Canadian Bagel Factory on University Avenue and Edward Street. Across the street he saw a Federal Express man double-park his vehicle in front of Kinko's Copy and run inside to make a pickup. At the next table, three lawyers from down the street—Osgoode Hall was no more than a few blocks away—argued over an arcane interpretation regarding capital gains tax law on heavy equipment, all of it in English, none of it comprehensible to Gilbert. Gilbert nibbled on his cinnamon-and-raisin bagel, no butter, waiting for Constable Jeremy Austin. Why they couldn't meet in 52 Division, a block away in Chinatown, Gilbert didn't know. He could only guess that Austin was, after all, in trouble of some kind. He looked out at the rain. He never knew rain could take so many forms. He remembered Austin's voice on the phone: tentative, nervous, reluctant. Today the rain came down like tendrils of silk, coiling in helixes, a fine particulate, not heavy rain, but penetrating. He was curious about what Austin had to say.

At the front he saw a tall, heavyset black policeman with a mustache and sideburns push his way through the glass doors. This was Austin. Austin glanced first to his left, into the Second Cup coffee-bar part of the eatery, then to his left, into the Great Canadian Bagel Factory. Gilbert raised his hand, catching the man's attention. Austin nodded, then glanced through the big windows out at the street, as if he suspected someone might be following him. The linebacker-of-a-man walked around the counter and moved past the soft-drinks cooler, reminding Gilbert of a big ship easing through a harbor. Austin wore a standard-issue blue parka with the crest of the force on both shoulders, and the usual police hat. He had a wide pleasant face, with a medium-dark complexion, congenial dark eyes, and a broad forehead. He slid into the booth. The man was anxious, tense, ready to talk. He launched right in, without preamble, perhaps incautiously, didn't even ask to see Gilbert's badge and ID.

"I've been hearing things," he said. He looked at Gilbert speculatively. "How long ago did you say you worked at 52 Division?"

"It was my first assignment," said Gilbert. "I was in patrol. I was there for my first two years before I moved up to the old headquarters on Jarvis. In '72 and '73. A long time ago."

Austin nodded, a man who'd heard it all, knew it all, an eminent historian of his own turf. "A lot has changed since then," he said. "I came on in '78 and I've been working there ever since. I've never wanted anything more than straight community policing in my career. I've always made a point of trying to know the people in my patrol community. The Chinese in and around here trust me. When they have a problem they come to me. Ask Benny Eng. I like to think I have an understanding with the immigrant Chinese. I'm an immigrant myself, came up from Tobago in 1969, so I think I have that experience, that understanding, and that's why these people come to me whenever they have a problem. They trust me. I try to do right by them."

From outside Gilbert heard the thump-thump of a helicopter air ambulance coming in for a landing on top of the Hospital for Sick Children up the street. He saw Austin was going to ease his way toward whatever information he might have, so Gilbert just sat back and played it like a conversation between friends.

"We had mostly Toishan Chinese back then," said Gilbert. "All from mainland China."

"That's right," agreed Austin, with a soft West Indian inflection. "But then you had a lot of Chinese moving in from everywhere else. Hong Kong, mainly. Some from Vietnam. Some from Cambodia. Now we're seeing a new wave of them, mostly from Fujian Province, most of them without legitimate papers. Ninety-nine percent of these people are decent, law-abiding folks."

Gilbert heard the man's reservations. "But we have to worry about the ones who aren't, don't we?"

Austin looked out the window, his eyes as dark as black coffee. "We've got some feuding, detective," he said. "You understand what I'm saying?"

"Between the Vietnamese and Chinese," said Gilbert. "All those shootings a few years back. I worked some of those."

"The Toishan Chinese and the new Hong Kong Chinese are the ones who are feuding these days," said Austin. "Each is trying to take over the other's operations. You get your shootings, but you also get the Toishans infiltrating the Hong Kong Chinese, and the Hong Kong Chinese infiltrating the Toishans. And that can create opportunities for a police officer like myself. That's why I'm here. To tell you about my latest opportunity. To tell you about the Toishan informant I've developed over the last three years. He thinks he knows who killed Edgar Lau."

Gilbert stared at Austin, noting for the first time the odd birthmark the constable had near his left temple, a dull brown patch that looked like a squid. "I'm not sure why we had to meet secretly in order for you to tell me this," he said.

Austin leaned forward. "Because there's more to this than just the Toishan and Hong Kong Chinese," he said, "and I'm in it up to my ears. Like I say, a feud like this creates opportunities for police officers." Austin's implication couldn't have been plainer. Opportunities for police bribes. Opportunities for police corruption. Gilbert was beginning to see the reason for the officer's initial nervousness. "You found a remote gunshot wound at autopsy?" said Austin.

Gilbert raised his eyebrows, surprised that Jeremy Austin should know this. "Yes, we did," he said.

"No one was ever arrested in that shooting," said Austin. "It happened in Vancouver. I don't know whether you've had that confirmed yet."

"No," said Gilbert, "we haven't."

"My Toishan informer tells me it was a contract shooting, tendered by the highest levels of the 14K Triad in Hong Kong, and that Tony Mok was the shooter."

"Tony Mok?" said Gilbert, taking a moment with the unfamiliar new name. He quickly scribbled it down in his notebook. "Who's Tony Mok?"

Austin glanced around again. "He's a member of the Kung Lok here in Toronto," said Austin. "Or at least he was. His status is unclear at the moment. He's young, a relative newcomer. He can't be more than twenty-five. But he's got a sheet six pages long, mostly assault charges from both here and Vancouver, a wildcat, my informer tells me, a dangerous man. My informant believes he's the one who killed Edgar Lau last Friday night, and that the killing was 14K instigated."

Gilbert sensed connections again, but the connections were vague, obscure, as intangible as the rain outside. A couple of dental students from the Faculty of Dentistry descended the faculty steps next to Kinko's and huddled under a big Fuji Film umbrella as they made their way toward Bay Street. The highest levels of the 14K Triad in Hong Kong. Bing Wu. Pearl Wu. Edgar Lau. And now Tony Mok.

"If this Tony Mok's a member of the Kung Lok, why's he taking tenders from the 14K?"

"Infighting between the 14K and the Kung Lok," said Austin, as if it were obvious. "This is dangerous territory, Detective. There's a lot happening right now. A lot of bad feeling. A lot of bad blood. You have the Toishans fighting the Kung Lok, you have the Kung Lok fighting the Toishans, and then you have the infighting between the Kung Lok and the 14K. All the triads are using everything in their power to come out on top, and the amount of money involved is enormous. Benny's been looking into it, but so far no charges." Austin leaned forward and glanced around the Great Canadian Bagel Factory. "That's what I want you to know. This environment . . . to have to solve a murder in it." Austin looked at Gilbert with true concern. "Be careful, man. It's not only Tony Mok you have to worry about. You have to worry about everybody. You have to be cautious. You have to watch your back. All this money they have floating around, available to anyone who wants to help . . . bad cops grow like maggots on a garbage heap with that kind of money floating around." Austin's eyes moistened and his look of concern turned to one of intense worry, as if his worry were an old wound that wouldn't heal. "I'm in some kind of shit right now, detective, I don't mind telling you. Things are bad at 52 Division, and they're getting worse."

Austin shook his head, looking defeated by the whole thing. Now all his nervousness made sense.

"Do you have any names?" asked Gilbert.

"I can't name names yet," he said, sounding angry with Gilbert. "I'm not in a position to name names yet."

"You've been threatened?"

"I've been threatened."

"By fellow officers?"

Austin nodded. "By fellow officers."

Gilbert leaned forward, shaking his head. "Jeremy . . . damn . . . Jeremy, you've got to come forward."

"I can't come forward," he said. "I've got a family."

"They threatened your family?" said Gilbert, growing more alarmed.

Austin nodded. "I have two grown sons and a little girl."

"Well . . . how . . . how bad is it?"

"It's bad. It's not like the old days, when just the Toishan Chinese were here. Back then, we turned a blind eye to the gaming houses, quietly collected our fines, you know. It's part of Chinese culture, all this gambling, so . . . they would show their appreciation by sending a gift or throwing a lavish dinner for us. We didn't even think of it as bribery. Hell, my wife got a jade necklace once, and I didn't think nothing of it because we were still giving out fines. Not closing the places down, you understand, but at least following some form of due process. These days it's a lot different. Cash payments totaling thousands of dollars. Bad cops collecting protection money. Bad cops involved in assault in their off hours. Bad cops protecting prostitution and drug rings."

"Jeremy . . . Jeremy, you've got to name names," he said.

"I can't."

"Have you told anybody else besides me?" asked Gilbert.

"That's just it," said Austin. "I have to be careful who I tell. At least until I get some proof. And I've been working on that. But I've had to go to people outside the force to help me."

"And who have you gone to?"

"There's only one person I *can* go to," said Austin. "And that person is Rosalyn Surrey." Connections. Strands hooking up with other strands in unexpected and startling ways. "She's looking into things for me." A pretty blond woman in a cheongsam, and Gilbert was at first startled by the connection, that he should find the councillor's name issuing from the lips of this poor scared constable who knew too much for his own good. "She's putting pressure on the Police Services Board to do something about it." But now that Austin mentioned the Police Services Board, she seemed an obvious contact for Constable Austin.

"You should let me help," said Gilbert. Nothing got to Gilbert like a scared cop; he wanted to do something about it.

"No, sir," said Austin. "The only reason I tell you all this in the first place is because I want you to be careful. You're in a jungle now, detective. You stick to Edgar Lau. You stay away from all the rest of this and you should be fine. You just try and track this Tony Mok down. That's what they pay you for. All this other stuff—just watch out for it, that's all. Stay clear of it. If I didn't feel you had to watch your back, I wouldn't have told you nothing about any of it in the first place."

Kitchener-Waterloo lies about sixty miles southwest of Toronto in the middle of southwestern Ontario, a small city with a large Germanic population, a city primarily known for its extensive Oktober-fest celebration each fall, but also for its university in the Waterloo part of town, and the numerous Mennonites who clip-clop to the suburban malls for supplies in their horse-drawn buggies and carts. Though not a particularly large municipality, the city supports a thriving arts community, including the Kitchener-Waterloo Symphony Orchestra.

On the evening of December twenty-first the orchestra featured guest concert pianist Tak-Ng Lai, from Shanghai, in a performance of composer Shau-Kee Kwan's masterpiece of social realism, *Evening Snow,* a concerto in one movement for piano and orchestra.

Gilbert sat in the green room as he waited for Lai to take his second bow. After another minute Lai appeared at the door.

He was a giant, nearly seven feet tall, disconcerting in a race of usually diminutive people, had big black-framed glasses, wore a tailored gray suit in a Mao cut, and had huge hands, gigantic appendages that looked as if they could uproot trees and lift cars. In contrast, his translator, a slender young woman in a pink dress, was a mere wisp, no more than a hundred pounds, and under five feet. Her name was Shen, and it was through her that Gilbert tried to verify Foster Sung's version of events on the night of the murder.

"Yes," said Shen, "the woman Mr. Lai later learned was May Lau came to his table at the Champion Gardens Restaurant shortly after ten o'clock." Shen translated stiffly and timidly, with a deference and respect for the concert pianist that was painful to behold. Tak-Ng Lai watched her intently. "Mr. Lai says this woman was distraught. He says she told Foster Sung that her son had been shot. Mr. Lai had just arrived from his performance at Roy Thompson Hall."

"Was Mr. Lai introduced to everybody sitting at Foster Sung's table?" asked Gilbert.

Shen translated the question for Tak-Ng Lai. Lai, as a means of verification, was, of all the men sitting at Sung's table, the most likely to tell the truth.

"Yes, he was," said Shen, translating for Lai.

"Can he recall the names of the men he was introduced to?" asked Gilbert.

Shen again translated Gilbert's question. Tak-Ng Lai's face stiffened. For some reason he seemed insulted by the question. Gilbert couldn't help thinking he looked like a Chinese version of Victor Frankenstein's monster.

Shen turned to Gilbert with apprehensive eyes. "He wishes you to know that he has perfect and total recall," said Shen. "This is his gift. He has had this gift all his life."

Tak-Ng Lai then recited, without the need of translation, the names of the people sitting at Foster Sung's table. "Foster Sung, Xu Jiatun, Charlie Peng, and Peter Hope."

Peter Hope. Gilbert checked his notes. No mention of Peter Hope from Foster Sung. He wrote the name down.

"Who's Peter Hope?" he asked Shen, who in turn asked Lai.

Lai grunted an answer, displaying a temperamental impatience that was beginning to grate on Gilbert. Shen translated. "He says he doesn't know," she said. "He says he was Foster Sung's guest, and that he and Peter Hope were introduced for the first time that evening."

Gilbert nodded, but made a mental note to himself to check Peter Hope out later on. "And when May Lau came to the table, Foster Sung went up to Edgar Lau's apartment with her?"

Shen again translated. "Yes," she said. "He was up there for at least fifteen minutes. Mr. Lai waited because he was of course concerned. When Foster Sung came down, he assured Mr. Lai that there was nothing he could do, that the police would look after it, and that there was no point in tiring himself by waiting around when he had such a busy concert schedule. At that point, Charlie Peng took Mr. Lai back to his hotel, and that's the last we've heard of this matter."

The next morning Lombardo dropped a canvas bag on Gilbert's desk.

"What's in there?" asked Gilbert.

"Take a look."

Gilbert loosened the drawstring and peered inside. He then looked up at Lombardo. "Keys?" he said.

"I had Rafferty down in Support make them," said Gilbert.

"Am I missing something here?" asked Gilbert.

"They're duplicates," said Lombardo, sounding amazed. "Of the key we found in Edgar's intestine."

Gilbert gazed at the big pile. "That's a lot of keys," he said. "What have you been up to?"

Lombardo grinned, proud of himself. "I talked to June Sayers in Community Services," he said. "She says she can promise a hundred auxiliary and volunteer support staff to help look for the locker. Then I talked to Ricky Munroe in Training and Education. They have a new cadet intake of sixty-six, and he's going to give every one of them a key. The auxiliary, volunteers, and cadets live all over the city. Ricky and June are going to ask them to check their neighborhoods for any public lockers. Everybody knows they're looking for locker 43."

It sounded like a good plan, but Gilbert still had some reservations. "Joe, how do we know what's going to be in locker 43 when and if we find it? What if it's a bomb? What if it's drugs? Or money?"

As a police officer of twenty-eight years, he always anticipated every eventuality.

"Everyone has instructions to call us immediately." Lombardo leaned against the desk. "How else are we going to cover all that ground? Missing Persons has pulled the same trick before. Why can't we do the same to find our locker? The man stuffs a key in a balloon and swallows it. You have to have a good reason for doing that. Who knows? We might find something that will let us write a decent warrant on Pearl Wu. We can nab her at the airport when she comes back and take her right downtown."

Gilbert nodded distractedly. "Just tell everybody to be careful, okay? I would hate anybody to get hurt. Or to get suddenly rich with money they don't own."

"Don't worry."

Gilbert shuffled through some papers on his desk. "I got the printout on Tony Mok." He found it under the Police Services Annual Report. Slipping on his reading glasses, he scanned the sheet. "Assault, break-and-enter, resisting arrest, reckless endangerment, three arson charges, vandalism . . . the guy's a punk, what can I say? I talked to Benny Eng. He knows Mok. He believes Mok is affiliated with the Kung Lok Triad. Not as a full member, never a blood initiation or tattoo, just a foot soldier who occasionally hires on when they need extra help."

"Do we know where he comes from?"

"Hong Kong. I checked with Immigration. He came here as a child. An orphan. Sponsored by a couple, Rose and Henry Kwon. We'll have to try and find the Kwons. Immigration tells me they're not sure where Tony was placed after the Kwons, only that he stayed with the Kwons for less than a year. They suggested UNESCO might have some information. UNESCO arranged his original placement with the Kwons. I haven't been able to get in touch with them. Christmas. As for his sheet, Mok became active seven years ago, when he was sixteen. He beat a Vietnamese gang member with a chain. He was charged but given a suspended sentence because the victim refused to testify, didn't even show up in court." Gilbert glanced over some of the background information. "Went to school at Eastdale Collegiate but dropped out when he was sixteen. By that time he was living on his own."

"Have you been able to find him?" asked Lombardo.

"No," said Gilbert. "The last address we have for him is Cecil Street. When I drove by there this morning the place was gutted. One of those old Edwardian brownstones. I'm sure it's slated for demolition. I saw a dog sniffing around inside."

"Maybe Mok's in Vancouver," said Lombardo. "If what Jeremy Austin says is true, about the shooting . . ."

"Maybe," said Gilbert. "But right now we have nothing that connects him to the scene of our particular crime, even though Austin has a source who tells him Mok might have been responsible for the Toronto shooting."

"What about Ballistics?" asked Lombardo. "Have they got the bullet from Vancouver yet?"

"Not yet. And there's no one down in Ballistics this week anyway," said Gilbert. "It's Christmas. Murphy says if the bullet arrives he'll come in for an afternoon and have a look at it."

"What about Peter Hope?" asked Lombardo. "Anything on him yet?"

Gilbert shrugged, sat back in his chair, and took off his reading glasses. "Not much," he said. "He's new. He's a Hong Kong resident but comes here regularly on two- or three-month visas. Benny hasn't been able to gain access over the holidays to any international file on Hope, but as far as our own file is concerned, we know Hope has a part interest in Kowloon Textiles, out in Agincourt. We also know that Bing Wu has part interest in Kowloon Textiles and that Wu has just reinvested significantly in the company. So Hope's obviously connected somehow, though whether there's any criminal connection is too early to say. He's down in Queens visiting relatives right now, due back on the twenty-eighth. I've e-mailed Hukowich in Ottawa to see if he has anything, but he hasn't gotten back to me."

"Damn this Christmas," said Lombardo. "I wish it would just go away."

"That's what I like about you, Joe," said Gilbert. "Your Christmas spirit."

"You know what?" he said. "I don't even have a date for Christmas Mass this year. My mother's going to wonder if I'm gay."

"Speaking of dates . . . have you . . ." Gilbert looked away. "You know . . . my daughter . . ."

Lombardo raised his chin. "Oh . . . sure . . . you have nothing to worry about, Barry. I'm taking her to *The Nutcracker* tonight. I couldn't get tickets for *Les Mis* after all."

"So you talked to her?" asked Gilbert.

"I listened," clarified Lombardo.

"And how did she sound?"

Lombardo stared at Gilbert, his eyes tactful, concerned. "She's heartbroken, Barry," he said. "You've got a heartbroken little girl on your hands."

"Goddammit."

"Actually, we talked for nearly twenty minutes."

Gilbert raised his eyebrows. "You did?" he said. He rubbed his brow with his fingers and shook his head. "I'm lucky if she says good morning to me these days."

"She really loved this guy."

Gilbert squinted irritably. "Don't say that."

"You got to think of something nice to say about him," said Lombardo.

Gilbert couldn't control his impatience. "Like what?" he said. "When he was here at Thanksgiving he had her out in my Windstar until two in the morning, even though I told him to be back by twelve. Not only that, he was drunk. Drunk, and driving my twenty-five-thousand-dollar Windstar, like the fact I'm a cop doesn't mean anything to him. What can I say nice about a jerk like that?"

"She's under the impression she's unattractive," said Lombardo. "She thinks she's undesirable. She cried a lot while she was talking to me."

Gilbert raised his hands in rigid claws, looking ready to strangle someone. "If I could get my hands on Randall," he said, "we'd have another homicide up on the board right now."

Lombardo put his hand on Gilbert's shoulder and gave it a comradely shake. "Don't worry," he said. "I'll see if I can cheer her up tonight." Then he gave Gilbert an arch look. "Maybe you should let me use your Windstar to take her out in. I'm sure I could have it back before midnight. That is if I don't get too drunk."

Dr. Blackstein, the coroner, dropped by the Homicide office later that afternoon with a gift box of deluxe nuts—cashews, pistachios, almonds, and a half dozen others, all in their separate pie-shaped segments of a red tinsel box, his standard Christmas gift to the squad. He gave the box to Carol Reid, the squad secretary, then moved through the office to Gilbert's desk at the back.

"I've been rereading my report on Edgar Lau," he said, "comparing it to the crime scene photographs you sent me."

Blackstein sat on the edge of Gilbert's desk, a knit in his brow, and folded his hands over his knee.

"And?" said Gilbert.

"I'm just thinking about the way he had all that Kleenex balled up in his hand," he said.

"What about it?"

"And then I read your addendum. About the dish towel?"

"We found no dish towel," said Gilbert. "We can't verify that."

"One way or the other," said Blackstein, "I don't think this man should have bled to death as quickly as he did. Not with the kind of pressure dressings we've got here. Not with the kind of wound he received."

Gilbert leaned forward, his eyes narrowing. "What are you saying?"

"Officer Kennedy says he found no dish towel at the scene, right?"

"Yeah."

"But Sung insists he tried to stanch the flow of blood with a dish towel?"

"That's what he said."

Blackstein shook his head. "Edgar should have made it, then," said the doctor. "He's young, he's strong, he was able to press a ball of Kleenex to his own abdomen." Blackstein glanced at the twelve-inch Christmas tree sitting on top of Gilbert's shelf next to some thick legal binders, a macabre little evergreen hung with the brass shell casings of .45-caliber bullets. "How long before the paramedics got there?"

"Seven minutes after Officer Kennedy did."

Blackstein shook his head. "I don't know, Barry," he said. "He survived that first gunshot wound out in Vancouver, and from what I can tell, it was a lot worse than this one, more point-blank. The bullet in our gunshot wound entered his abdomen on the left, grazed his stomach as it penetrated the diaphragm, and came to a stop against his rib cage on the right, really no more than a subsurface scratch, staying well clear of his vital organs and arteries. For him to bleed to death the way he did, someone would have to pull the dressing away and disrupt coagulation. And the only one who could have done that, according to all the time lines you've got in your various reports, is Officer Kennedy."

IT RAINED ON CHRISTMAS DAY. By four o'clock a major storm moved in. The clouds hovered low to the ground like a blanket of charcoal dust, dark and menacing. On the radio the weatherman cautioned people to stay home. Hail fell with menacing persistence for about five minutes, then changed into a heavy downpour.

Gilbert walked into the kitchen to see how Regina was making out. She wore her new dress, the blue one Nina had picked out for her. She cut celery sticks. He looked her up and down.

"What?" she said, turning to him.

"I haven't seen you in a dress like that for a long time," he said.

She smiled. "Do I look good?"

He stared at the dress. Finally he said, "It seems a little young for you."

She stopped cutting celery sticks. "Careful, buster," she said. "I've got a knife in my hand."

"I wouldn't wear it to school. Your students . . . I don't think they would . . . I don't know."

"I wouldn't wear it with my Reeboks," she said. "You need proper shoes for a dress like this."

"Maybe that's it," he said. "The shoes. With that kind of dress you need three-inch pumps."

"What do you expect?" she said good-humoredly. "You let your fifteen-year-old daughter pick it out. She forgets I'm fifty."

Gilbert's eyes narrowed. "Are you really that old?" he said. "You don't look a day over forty-nine."

She smiled. "Do I have to remind you about this knife again?"

"At least Joe's looking at you," he said.

"Joe looks at anybody."

He went up and slipped his arm around her waist. "Let's not make remarks about my partner," he said. "He saved Christmas."

Regina nodded with relief. "I'm glad she's come out of it," she said.

"It's the Lombardo charm," he said. "Teenage angst doesn't stand a chance against it."

But as Gilbert went back to the living room he still felt unsettled about Jennifer. The fire crackled, the Christmas tree glittered, and Nina had some forgettable *a cappella* pop group crooning love songs on the CD player. Joe sat on one sofa, Jennifer on the other. Joe stared at the fire. Jennifer stared at Joe. She had her hair washed. She had her hair up. The turquoise streak was gone. She wore her new dress, a Christmas present from her mother. She'd taken a tip from Nina about makeup. She didn't look like an extra from *Night of the Living Dead* anymore. She looked pretty, with wispy strands of blond hair shining like gold around her slender neck, her skin looking freshly scrubbed and healthy, her nails lacquered with a shade of rose-colored nail polish. She wore earrings. Her earrings made her look like a woman. If only she would stop staring at Lombardo with those love-sick eyes. Gilbert didn't like it at all. She was drinking rum and eggnog. That was something else he had to get used to. She could drink legally now.

He sat down and sipped his own rum and eggnog. Nina was off in the corner reading her new Danielle Steel. Good. Now he had to get rid of Jennifer. He had to talk to Lombardo, at least for a few minutes, in private about this.

"Jennifer, your mother said she needed help in the kitchen with the vegetable tray," he told her. "Before the other guests get here."

Jennifer continued to stare at Joe, a soft grin on her face, her eyes misty with romance, then turned to her father. "Sure, dad," she said, as if everything were perfectly normal between them.

She got up with what he saw was affected poise and moved toward the kitchen. Gilbert felt as if he had somehow gotten himself into a pit of quicksand he couldn't get out of. She was trying to make an impression on Joe.

Once she was gone he leaned forward. "So how'd it go on Friday night?" he asked. "She seems a lot better today."

"I think she had fun," said Lombardo, with a dismal attempt to downplay the damage.

"Did you go anywhere afterward?" asked Gilbert, annoyed at himself for prying. "I was expecting you home a little earlier."

"We went to Pat and Mario's for a drink," said Lombardo. "Do you know the place? A perfect place to take a nineteen-year-old girl. A lot of young people there."

Gilbert probed a little further. "I wasn't expecting such a quick result." He picked up a walnut from the wooden bowl and turned it in his fingers. "She usually keeps her moods a little longer." He looked at Lombardo. "What did you do?"

Lombardo nodded, as if anticipating Gilbert's question. "Little attentions, that's all," he said. "Helping her on with her coat. Pulling out her chair for her. Opening the car door. Making her feel like she matters."

The two detectives sat silently for a few seconds. In the fireplace the logs popped and sparked, then settled into a long slow hiss. The rain lashed against the windows, dull and persistent, the unending theme song of the day, of the whole month.

"Did you see the way she looked at you just now?" asked Gilbert.

Lombardo stared steadily into his rum and eggnog. "I saw," he said.

More silence. Gilbert shook his head. "What are we going to do about that, Joe?" he said.

The question had to be asked.

"I don't know."

"Maybe it wasn't such a good idea," said Gilbert.

Lombardo roused himself from his steady contemplation of his rum and eggnog and frowned. "What can I do now?" he asked, perplexed. "I don't want to hurt her feelings. She's your daughter."

Gilbert shook his head, as bewildered as Lombardo. "I don't know what we can do."

"She talked a lot about you last night," said Lombardo.

"She did?"

"You don't want to hear."

"That bad?"

"You don't want to hear."

"Is she ever going to like me again?" asked Gilbert.

Lombardo looked at him doubtfully. "She might," he said, sitting up straight. "But it's a crapshoot."

Before Gilbert could ask anything else, Jennifer appeared in the front hall with a tray of vegetables and dip. "Joe, do you think you can help me with some of this?" she said. "I've got three dips here."

Lombardo put his rum and eggnog down and got up quickly, as if she needed help crossing thin ice. "Sure," he said. He treated her like a vial of nitroglycerin. "You got a big load there." He went out to the hall to help her.

"Oh, look," she said, once he reached her, "we're under the mistletoe. That means you have to kiss me."

Gilbert saw she had contrived this circumstance.

Lombardo glanced nervously at the mistletoe, then back at Gilbert. He then turned to Jennifer and kissed her. On the lips. For longer than he had to. Trying to make Jennifer feel that she mattered.

Gilbert felt as if he had just stepped into an alternate universe.

Gilbert went back to work on the twenty-seventh of December. He sat with Officer Donald Kennedy near the duty desk of 52 Division on Dundas Street. A large mural of helpful-looking police officers stared down at them from above, and the food-drive box, decorated with red shiny paper and silver tinsel, overflowed with boxes of macaroni and tinned fruit and vegetables. Gilbert shared with the constable the latest developments in the Edgar Lau murder case. Kennedy's blue eyes peered with faint incredulity, as if everything Gilbert told him struck him as immaterial, an intrusion into his day. Gilbert smelled singed hair. Kennedy had just singed some of his hair while lighting a cigarette outside. Two square inches had gone all kinky and burned at the front. Gilbert told him about Pearl.

"We plan to pick her up at the airport tonight," he said, trying to ignore the singed hair. "Joe's going out there to get her. We thought you'd like to know what's going on."

Kennedy made a face, pressing his lips together in distaste. "But that's not the real reason you came down here, is it?" he said.

"What makes you say that?"

"Because you look like you have a paddle up your ass."

If the man wanted it straight, he would give it to him straight. "I want to talk about a few of the things in your report," he said.

"Like what?" he asked, as if Gilbert were nothing but a nag, nags being the lowest form of life.

"Like the statement you took from Dock Wen."

Kennedy's rust-colored eyebrows pinched toward the bridge of his nose. He wasn't faking. He looked puzzled. "I write a good police report," he said. "I took down every word. If your case is going to fall apart, don't go blaming it on my crime scene report. I'm no Shakespeare, but I write a decent report. Ask my captain. Ask anybody."

"I'm not saying you don't," said Gilbert. "But Wen says the man he saw out back was white, not Chinese. And you got the man down as Chinese. We're just trying to clear up the discrepancy."

Kennedy's face settled. "Wen told me the man was Chinese," he said. "If he decides to change his story, there's nothing I can do about that."

"And Edgar was still alive when you got there?" asked Gilbert.

"Yes," said Kennedy. "But he was going fast."

"Foster Sung says he tried to stop the bleeding with a dish towel. We didn't find any dish towel."

"Neither did I." He flung the words at Gilbert.

"Okay," he said. "Calm down."

"Why don't you ask Sung again?" suggested Kennedy.

"Did you leave the crime scene at any time?" asked Gilbert.

"I went out to the landing as the paramedics were coming up the stairs."

"And you found no dish towel?"

"I found no dish towel."

"But you saw the Kleenex?" said Gilbert.

"I saw the Kleenex. I got it in my report, don't I? I wrote down everything. I don't miss a thing. I never have. If someone tells me something wrong, or fucks with the scene afterward, don't go blaming me. I write my report, and what I write in my report is what I saw at the scene, nothing more, nothing less."

Lombardo was waiting for Gilbert back at headquarters with the ballistics comparison report. The bullet from the Vancouver shooting, the one that had wounded Edgar Lau back in August, had finally arrived. The young detective held up the printout.

"The Vancouver bullet was badly mashed," he said. "Murphy said the comparison was difficult, but he says he can be at least seventy percent sure that the gun used on Edgar in Vancouver back in August might have been the same gun used in his murder a week ago Friday."

"That's great," said Gilbert.

"I know, but seventy percent still leaves a jury considerable room for doubt."

"At least it's a start," said Gilbert. "Did he say anything else?"

"He says he didn't get a perfect set of lands and grooves on the Vancouver bullet, but the ones he did get matched. Not only that, the killer used the same unusual wadcutter slug in both cases, so as supporting evidence it's fairly strong. If what Jeremy Austin told you about the Vancouver shooting is true, that Tony Mok was the shooter, then he might indeed be the perp in the Toronto shooting as well. I think we have the beginnings of a case against Mok."

Gilbert stared at his paperweight made of bullets, his hands clasped before him in an inadvertent gesture of supplication. "Only we don't have Mok," he said.

"Not right yet," said Lombardo. "But I've been busy."

"You've found Rose and Henry Kwon?" said Gilbert.

"I have," said Lombardo. "Like Immigration told you, Mok came over as an orphan. When he was eight. UNESCO arranged it through a program for orphaned children. I got in touch with someone at UNESCO today, and they filled in the picture. They said they had a case file on Mok, which they sent to the Children's Aid Society here in town back in 1985, when Tony came over. I phoned the Children's Aid Society and they're going to send us his file. For Mok to come over here legally, he had to have a sponsoring guardian or relative in Hong Kong."

"In Hong Kong?" said Gilbert.

"Foster Sung was his sponsoring guardian in Hong Kong," said Lombardo. "Sung got him placed with the Kwons. Don't look so surprised. Sung sponsored all sorts of orphaned refugee kids in Hong Kong. Tony's just another. When I run across a connection like this, maybe I'm surprised at first, but you finally realize that it's all got to join up somehow. Tony Mok connecting through a tangent like this, what else could we expect? You dig deep enough, you always find something like this. I bet half the orphans Sung sponsored turned into gang members. For sponsored orphan read recruit."

Connections, Gilbert again thought. Foster Sung connecting to Tony Mok. Like the bonding element of an increasingly complex molecule, a structure of intent and motive, of crime and loss, of blood and community.

"We'll have to talk to Foster Sung about Mok," he said.

"I've tried contacting Sung but he's not returning any of my calls," said Lombardo.

"Christmas," said Gilbert.

"Christmas," agreed Lombardo. "But I had better luck with Rose and Henry Kwon. I found them. They're on Beverley, north of the Art Gallery."

"And you spoke to them?"

"I spoke to them."

"And they know where we can find Tony?" asked Gilbert.

The smile disappeared from Lombardo's face and he shook his head. "No," he said, "they don't know where we can find him."

From the front of the office, Carol Reid's telephone rang.

"Okay, I'm listening," said Gilbert.

"Shouldn't we get Carol's phone?"

"She's in the Xerox room. She'll get it."

"And then you'll give her the extra lump of coal?" said Lombardo.

"I ask you, why do I have this reputation? I'm one of the kindest homicide detectives I know."

The two detectives watched Carol walk from the Xerox room to answer her phone. Gilbert felt secretly rankled by the comment but he buried it for now. He knew he sometimes took Carol for granted and made a quick mental note to change his ways. Lombardo continued.

"The Kwons had Tony for only three months," he said. "Under

a year, like you said. But then Tony broke their own child's arm by pushing her off some monkey bars. Not only that, he was constantly stealing from them. Rose said she finally had to hide her purse."

"And Tony was only eight?"

"Yep."

"Some kid."

"So you know who looked after Tony when he left the Kwons?" asked Lombardo.

"Who?"

"Are you ready for this?" said Lombardo.

"It's not like you're going to tell me the earth is really flat, Joe," he said. "Get on with it."

"May Lau did."

Gilbert paused, long enough to become a devout flat-earther. He made the next bond, like adding a renegade isotope to a heretofore stable and understandable structure.

"In fact," continued Lombardo, "May Lau looked after Mok for the next eight years."

Adding family to blood and community, a connection now archetypical of murder; Gilbert should have guessed, should have looked at the lethal molecule from a different angle to discern its predisposing outlines. The discovery was simple and satisfying, like stumbling on a rudimentary mathematical equation to finally explain the exact nature of the universe.

"We really have to check this guy out," he said. "We've got to find him and we've got to find him fast, before he takes off somewhere."

*   *   *

May Lau looked away, her face creasing with unmistakable woe when Gilbert told her they were looking for Tony Mok. Her eyes misted over and she took off her big square glasses. She wore an odd brooch today, a Siamese cat holding a lily in its mouth, and was dressed in black. Though it was only four in the afternoon, the sky was already getting dark and the rain came down like water from a broken dike.

"I haven't seen Tony in nearly six months," she said. Her voice sounded faint.

"Had your son seen or talked to him?" asked Gilbert.

"Tony and Edgar weren't on the best terms," she said. She looked up at Gilbert, as if challenging Gilbert to understand. "Edgar never really liked Tony when they were growing up. I don't know when they saw each other last."

She seemed too spiritually bruised to talk about Tony.

"We have an address for him on Cecil Street, but the place is abandoned, ruined," said Gilbert.

She nodded, as if she knew about Cecil Street. "I don't know where he went after Cecil Street," she said.

Gilbert stared at the torn suit jacket on the coffee table she was mending, a mix of gray and charcoal tweed with the left arm torn off; maybe Edgar's jacket, maybe something she planned to sell to make a little extra money for herself.

"You didn't mention Tony when I talked to you last week," he said.

She turned to him. A calico cat with orange, white, and black fur jumped up on her lap and she gave its head a careless stroke. The cat moved on, up onto a high side table, where it stepped over a broken Chinese fan.

"Tony left us when he was sixteen," she said. "That was seven years ago. The only reason he ever comes around these days is to ask for money. I took care of him for eight years, but he's never really thanked me for it. If it hadn't been for the money Foster Sung gave me to look after Tony, I think I might have tried to place him elsewhere. But when he first came to Canada he spoke no English at all, and to place him with another Chinese family, especially after what had happened with the Kwons, would have been difficult. Also, I needed the money."

"He's been in a lot of trouble since he was sixteen," said Gilbert.

"I know." She smiled, but it was a melancholy smile. "And he was in a lot of trouble before he was sixteen." Her smile disappeared and she picked up the broken fan, pink roses on black silk, the weave of the silk shredding near the edge, two of the bamboo supports cracked. "I tried to love him." Her face hardened, as if loving Tony Mok had been nothing but bitter effort. "I thought the reason he acted so badly was because maybe he thought no one loved him. I tried my best. But I naturally loved my own son more. Tony would compete fiercely for my attention. He would break things to get my attention. He thought he could make me love him as much as I loved Edgar. But I was often angry with him." Her voice took on a resentful tone. "And he was so ungrateful. He never did what he was told. I thought the refugee camp in Hong Kong might have made him that way." Under her big square glasses, her eyes narrowed in speculation. Then she looked at Gilbert, a serene smoothness coming to her brow. "I can't say I was sorry to see Tony go." She pressed her lips together. "I couldn't find any natural feeling for him."

"We think he might have been involved in Edgar's murder," said Gilbert. He felt he had to nudge her.

"I wouldn't know," she said. She stared at him. She moved the fan up and down a few times. "He was a difficult boy." On the mantelpiece she had a stick of incense burning around a small shrine to Edgar, with some of Edgar's things up there, and an old school photograph with Edgar in a school blazer and tie. "He was more trouble than he was worth."

He continued to nudge. "And if he was always competing with Edgar for your affections—"

She held up her hand, stopping him. "Tony would never kill unless he had something materially to gain from it," she said. "He might have competed for my attention when he was a boy, but he stole from me as well. He stole from Edgar. I used to lock my jewelry in a closet. Edgar had a hand-carved ivory mah-jongg set. Tony stole that from Edgar. Tony denied it, but we both knew he did it. His denials were always so obvious."

Gilbert wondered what could have made Tony that way. "Any idea who his real parents were?"

Outside, rain blew against the window, blurring the pane, obscuring the decrepit Victorian brownstones across the broad truck-congested street.

"His mother's name was Fang," she said. "She was on our boat." May Lau put the fan down, looking distressed by these memories. "I don't know if Fang had a husband." She shook her head. "She came alone. She was terribly pregnant. All the ladies on the boat fussed over her constantly."

"And she gave birth on the boat?"

"No," said Mrs. Lau. "She gave birth three or four days after we reached Hong Kong. In the refugee camp. And then she died. We had an outbreak of diphtheria in our camp. Fang contracted it and she died from it." May folded her hands on her lap. "Foster took responsibility for the child. We didn't even know if Fang's family name was Mok. We just picked a name out of a hat for the boy. Foster helped the child as much as he could. Foster did well in Hong Kong. He already knew people there. He helped dozens of children who were orphaned during that outbreak of diphtheria. We didn't have enough medicine. There were just too many of us."

"When was the last time you spoke to Tony?" asked Gilbert.

Her eyes narrowed. She shook her head. "I can't remember," she said. "I try to forget Tony." She looked at him, pleading. "I don't like to think about him." She glanced at a flimsy dress pattern draped over the end of the couch, a rat's nest of lines and instructions. "Whenever I think of Tony, it always reminds me of all the bad things that happened to us. And I'd just as soon forget all those things."

Gilbert got back to headquarters on College Street around six. Lombardo had just returned from the airport. Without Pearl Wu.

"She had Peter Hope waiting there to pick her up," said Lombardo.

"Peter Hope?" said Gilbert.

"It turns out he's her personal assistant. Wouldn't you know it? He wouldn't let me talk to her."

Peter Hope, Foster Sung's unmentioned tablemate from the night of the murder. "Were you able to talk to her at all?" he asked. He wished Hukowich would get back to him about Hope.

Lombardo arched his brow. "What was I going to do?" he said. "Twist her arm? Hope didn't let her say a thing. He was pushy. I tried to talk to Pearl as she came out of Customs but he took her by the arm and pulled her away. He said she was much too tired to talk to me, that she had just spent the last twenty-two hours on an airplane, and if I thought it was really necessary I could phone him in the morning and make an appointment to see her."

"So you saw her walk through the airport?"

"I saw her."

"And?"

Lombardo glanced at the overhead fluorescent lights, pondering, then looked at Gilbert. "Try to imagine the most beautiful Chinese woman you've ever seen," he said, as if he were setting the scene for a dream come true, "then multiply it by a hundred times."

Lombardo so often got dreamy over women. And it was beginning to bug Gilbert, especially because of Jennifer. His eyes narrowed with skepticism. "You know, I don't mind you dating witnesses, Joe, but try to stay away from suspects, okay? It's like sleeping with the enemy."

"Who said I was sleeping with her?"

"Should we start taking bets around the squad room?"

"I don't even know her," said Lombardo.

"When has that ever stopped you?"

"And besides, she's married."

"When has that ever stopped you?"

"Hey!"

"Did you see her scar?"

Lombardo looked down at his Italian leather shoes, then picked a piece of lint from his expensive pleated pants. "I saw her scar," he said.

"Is it bad?"

Lombardo put his hands on his hips, thought about it, then nodded tentatively. "It's bad," he said. "But it's bad in a good kind of way."

"You speak in riddles, my son," said Gilbert.

"It . . . I don't know . . . it elevates her beauty." Here he went with his dreamy stuff again. "It gives her . . . character. It goes right down here, diagonally along her left cheek, the color of cream, and it's . . . it's like a tribal scar, like some of the tribesmen in Africa have, nearly looks as if it were put there on purpose."

Gilbert stared at Lombardo, his jaw sinking. "You're hooked," he said.

Lombardo shook his head. "I would never get near her," he said. "Not the way Hope hovers around her. He might be her personal assistant, but I think there's a lot more to it than that. Think chaperon, and that's the impression I got. He gave me his card. He was like a pesky old nanny around her, yanked her this way and that, talked to her sternly, like he was scolding her, treated her like a child. She didn't look too happy about it. You think she would be the one giving the orders to Hope."

"But he gave you his card," said Gilbert.

Lombardo pulled out Peter Hope's card and showed it to Gilbert. "It's got a little fake emerald up in the corner," said Lombardo. "Have you ever seen a card like that before?" He handed it to Gilbert. "It has his name in both Chinese and English, plus telephone numbers for here and in Hong Kong."

Gilbert gazed at the card. He raised his eyebrows. "Isn't that something?" Gilbert gave the card back to Joe. "So do you think the pesky old nanny will let us talk to her?"

"He told me to phone tomorrow," said Lombardo.

"Does he know we want to talk to him as well? Because if he was sitting at Foster Sung's table on the night of the murder, we definitely want to talk to him."

Lombardo nodded. "He knows," he said. "He's going to try and set some time aside."

Gilbert shook his head. "This is the end of Western civilization as we know it, Joe," he said.

"Why's that?" asked Lombardo.

"Interrogation by appointment only. Have you ever heard of such crap?"

Lombardo went home but Gilbert stayed an extra hour to write reports on everything they had done that day on the Edgar Lau case. He was just shutting down his computer when Roger Pemberton, from Missing Persons, walked in. Gilbert was surprised to see Pemberton. Pemberton was a tall meek-looking man with stooped shoulders.

"I thought you were off all week," said Gilbert.

Pemberton, wearing a loosened tie around his neck, his shirt-sleeves rolled up, shook his head despondently and shambled forward, his long arms hanging ape-like at his sides.

"Merry Christmas," he said, his voice barely audible.

"What's up?" asked Gilbert.

"I just did a search through your case files," he said.

"How's that working out?" asked Gilbert, remembering the initiative taken by Security and Information to link the Missing Persons database to Homicide's database.

"It's okay," said Pemberton, as if he were talking about a healing canker sore. "The search time is a little slow, but Dave says we're getting upgrades in February. Our hard drives, they have only one hamster apiece inside them."

"And did you get a hit?" asked Gilbert.

Pemberton nodded disconsolately. "We're looking for a Garth Surrey," he said. "I got a hit in your Edgar Lau file. I thought I'd better tell you. I know you've got other agencies involved. The more the merrier, huh?"

"Garth Surrey?" said Gilbert.

Pemberton flinched. "Rosalyn Surrey's husband," he said, as if he wondered why Gilbert had to talk so loudly.

Gilbert leaned forward, felt the blood rush past his temples. "He's missing?" he said. He couldn't help thinking of Playmate-of-the-Month Rosalyn Surrey, how the cameraman had been none other than Edgar Lau, and how that might mean a jealous husband somewhere in the picture. Now the jealous husband was missing. Maybe the jealous husband was running. Maybe the jealous husband was Edgar's killer.

"She filed the report with us on the twentieth," said Pemberton, oblivious to Gilbert's excitement. "He's been missing since the day of your murder."

Outside, the rain and the wind played a chaotic tattoo against the windowpane. "So you followed up on all the leads?" asked Gilbert.

"Until the leads ran out," said Pemberton. As if he believed the whole universe was running out of leads, slowly, surely, dying toward a state of coma-like leadlessness.

"And you checked our case file?"

"To see if he'd been murdered." He shrugged, an embarrassed twitch of his shoulders. "As a last resort. I wasn't going to. I was hoping to put it off for as long as I could. And when I finally went ahead, I was hoping for a dead end so I could go home and spend the rest of the week with my family. But now I guess I've got to talk to Rosalyn Surrey. A woman like that makes me nervous. I don't know how they ever let her on the Police Services Board. She might start blaming me for something. Even if I didn't do anything wrong."

Gilbert glanced at Roger Pemberton's shoes, about as big as shoes could get, then looked up at his small gray eyes. "Look, Rog, just bring your missing persons file on Garth Surrey down here," said Gilbert. He got up, patted Pemberton on the shoulder. "I think we better handle it from here."

Pemberton raised his blond eyebrows. "Really?" he said, the decibel level of his voice for the first time reaching the normal range.

"We're working some angles, and your case file might help us."

Pemberton managed to hoist the corners of his lips into a weary smile. "Thanks," he said. "I was hoping you'd say that. I've got the case file right here." He handed Gilbert a manila folder with his long arm.

Gilbert took the file and glanced through it. His eyes immediately stopped at Garth Surrey's description: tall, six feet four, 280 pounds, long brown hair, a beard and mustache, small round glasses. Exactly the same description Dock Wen had given them. Gilbert looked at Pemberton.

"Thanks, Rog," he said. "Thanks a lot. You have a Happy New Year."

"Is there anything in there you can use?" asked Pemberton.

"Everything," said Gilbert.

CHAPTER
TEN

GILBERT WENT BACK TO NEW City Hall the next day. The large concrete arches spanning the skating rink had iced over and a frigid north wind blasted Nathan Phillips Square, snaking through the half-arches of the two towers and seeming to concentrate its full bitter force on Gilbert's face. The wind moaned through all the towers of the financial district south of City Hall and the piped-in Top 40 skating music at the rink could hardly compete. Three large articulated streetcars were backed up behind a traffic accident at Queen and Bay, stuck in their tracks, unable to move around the mishap, while bumper-to-bumper cars and trucks fought contentiously to squeeze through the one open lane. He wondered why people still brought their cars downtown; there was no place to park, and hardly any place to drive. The few people he saw walking across the square had to bend into the wind, collars or scarves up, hanging on to their hats. Toronto was bracing for its first blast of winter.

Despite a possible match on bullets in the Toronto and Van-

couver shootings—physical evidence that at least partially implicated Tony Mok as the killer—Gilbert couldn't rule out this new possibility of Garth Surrey, especially now that he had Roger Pemberton's
missing persons report. He hurried to the podium office block, passing a sullen blond woman in a yellow rain slicker working a hot-dog
stand. With the Vancouver bullet badly mashed, affording only a
limited comparison, he couldn't eliminate anybody yet. Gilbert
opened the big pine door and entered the welcome warmth of New
City Hall. Tony Mok and Pearl Wu might be their strongest suspects.
Gilbert climbed the broad stairs to the second level. But Garth Surrey, because his physical description matched the description given
by Dock Wen of the white man seen behind the restaurant at the
time of the murder, came a close second.

Rosalyn Surrey was with one of her constituency volunteers
when Gilbert arrived. She came out and told Gilbert to wait.

"No Cindy today?" he said.

"She's on holiday," said Rosalyn. Rosalyn looked exhausted.
"She'll be back after the New Year." She waved to the waiting area.
"Take a seat. I won't be long."

He sat down as Rosalyn went back to her office. He glanced
out into the hall. No one here today. He again looked at the photographs on the wall.

He had to admire Edgar's handiwork; he had been a gifted
photographer. Up in the corner Gilbert saw a photograph of Metro
Councillor Rosalyn Surrey shaking hands with Chief of Police Michael K.
Moore, a stone-faced man who had once been Gilbert's captain in
patrol. In another photograph, she cut the ceremonial ribbon at the
opening of the Bedford Heights Community Center with a girls'
broomball team gathered round her. In another, she celebrated the
Chinese New Year, stood on a platform in front of the Art Gallery

with some dignitaries, clapping her hands as she watched a dragon parade go by. He grew suddenly still. He stared harder at the parade picture. He got up and had a closer look. She wore gloves. Beige Isotoners, much like the one he had taken from the tree, like the one that had tested positive for barium and antimony. They looked a little big on her. Men's gloves? Compositionally, the photograph focused on Rosalyn's hands, the way she applauded, as if to stress her appreciation of Chinese culture; a hallmark of Edgar's photography seemed to be the conscious use of symbolism. Gilbert examined the photograph carefully, detected a stain on the right glove similar to but more apparent than the one on the glove he had in the evidence locker back at headquarters. He heard the meeting break up. He couldn't be certain of the glove. But now it looked as if even Rosalyn Surrey might be a suspect. He returned to his chair.

Rosalyn came to the door, wished her volunteer, a pudgy young Chinese woman in a faded Rodeo Drive sweatshirt, a Happy New Year, sent her on her way, and turned to Gilbert. Her expression was at once hard and fretful, her lips pressing together, her eyes narrowing, her brow pulling toward her nose. Again, it was a game of silence between them. The emptiness out in the corridor seemed to echo, caught stray sounds from the lobby, magnified the scant traffic noise from outside. Whether she thought he was here about Garth, or Edgar, or both, he couldn't be sure.

"Your husband is missing," he said.

More silence. A look of quick calculation crossed her face, the politician regrouping. But then her burden crushed the politician right out of her. She turned away, took a few distracted steps to the functional-looking sofa against the wall, and sat down, her green skirt riding up over her knees, her knees demure and girlish in her nylons.

"Is he dead?" she asked.

For her to ask such a question about her husband raised several startling possibilities. Was Garth Surrey suicidal? Was he in trouble with the wrong kind of people? Was he the kind of man who might find himself in a situation where he might wind up murdered? Or did she just think that because he was a homicide detective there could be no other explanation?

"We don't know," he said. "But I wish you'd tell me what's going on."

She collected herself, raised her chin. A vague defiance settled into her cat-green eyes. "Detective Pemberton was handling this case," she said. "I don't know why you're here."

"Take a guess," he said. If she wanted to skirmish, he would skirmish.

"I haven't a clue," she said.

"We have evidence that links your husband to the murder of Edgar Lau," he said. "There's your clue."

Her eyes widened and she stared at him. Her mouth opened, but the shock he saw on her face looked more like an act. He knew she was the kind of woman who was going to play the game for as long as she could, who would be tenacious in protecting herself and her husband, and who wouldn't give anything away unless she saw she had something to gain from it.

"I have no idea why my husband would ever want to murder Edgar," she said. "They don't even know each other."

"Are you close to your husband?"

"What kind of question is that?"

"Do you know where he was on the night of Edgar's murder?"

She looked away. She might have been a product of big-city

politics, a great dissimulator, but she was so obviously thinking on her feet Gilbert wondered why she even tried. "No . . ." she finally said. "No, I don't." As if she had decided that at least a little truth might appease him.

"So he doesn't tell you where he goes?"

He could see she was annoyed by this unwarranted and inappropriate assumption. He was glad. Anything to get her off balance.

"I don't know why you think he had anything to do with Edgar's murder." Back to the party line.

"We're just trying to find him," said Gilbert, softening his stance, going back to his own party line. "That's why I'm here. We're trying to find your husband for you, Mrs. Surrey." Gilbert paused, glanced at the glass sculpture on the shelf, a modernist piece, abstract, hard and reflective on the outside, but fluid and soft-looking with a number of different dyes on the inside. "And if we're going to do that, we have to know something about him." Gilbert took a few steps and sank into one one of the waiting-area chairs. "I note from Detective Pemberton's report that he's presently unemployed."

Rosalyn looked away. "Yes," she said. She offered the truth, as long as the truth remained innocuous.

"Has he been unemployed long?" asked Gilbert. "There's no mention of any previous employers we might contact to help us find him. Does he have any old work friends he might go to?"

She looked at him. "Have you checked Florida yet?"

"Detective Pemberton's sent a description to the Florida State Police."

"What about Tampa?"

"He's sent a description to them as well," he said. "Have you phoned all your friends down there?"

She nodded. "I've phoned the lot," she said.

"You have no children?" he asked.

She frowned. "What's that got to do with anything?"

"Sometimes couples who don't have any children drift apart."

"Sometimes they do," she conceded, with a trace of contempt.

"He disappeared on the night of the fifteenth, the night Edgar was murdered." He looked at her inquisitively. "Did you have a big fight that night?"

"No."

"I came here the next day. Before I even had a chance to tell you why I was here, you asked me about Garth. You were concerned about him? Why?"

This stopped her. This was like a brick wall to Metro Councillor Rosalyn Surrey. She looked at her knees. Her cheeks flushed. She was scrambling. The silence lengthened. Outside, the north wind howled. He felt sorry for her. He felt he had to give her a chance.

"Rosalyn . . ." he said. "Rosalyn . . . it's only going to get worse. You might think you can play a decent game against me, but I know what I'm doing, and what I'm doing is trying to help you. So don't try and fight me. Your position might intimidate some people, but it doesn't intimidate me. You're a woman who has a lot of up-front confidence, but your confidence means nothing to me. Your constituents think you deserve to be where you are, and believe me, I'll be the last to take that away from you. But if you don't cooperate with me, what am I supposed to do? Why don't we work together on this and figure it out? I'm sure we can minimize the fallout. I know you feel you have to be perfect in front of your constituents, that your political viability depends on it, but I look at you, a young woman, thirty-two or -three, and I see you're scared, and that you're not telling me everything you know. Maybe I should get Detective Bannatyne down here to yell at you, to shake some sense into you. Or maybe you can learn to trust me. Because like I say, if you don't trust me, it's going to get worse. Do you know Bob Bannatyne?"

She nodded grudgingly. "I met him at a community fund-raiser once."

"Bob doesn't know how to be diplomatic. He likes to shake out witnesses, and he likes to shake them out fast, regardless of the damage he does. If I were to let Bob Bannatyne take over, he would call Ronald Roffey at the *Star* and tell him we're looking for Rosalyn Surrey's husband. In connection with Edgar Lau's murder."

He saw she was like that glass statue up on the shelf—hard on the outside, soft and fluid on the inside. Her shoulders sank, her head bent forward, her blond hair hung around the sides of her face, and she raised her thumb and forefinger to her nose. Then she looked at him. He had to admire the resilience he saw in her eyes.

"I'm not the political animal you think I am," she said. Her tone was different now, broad, incisive, without the usual obfuscation of most politicians, but still as tough as leather.

"Rosalyn, I want to help you."

"I see what you're doing. Barry."

"Good, good," he said, sitting up straight, putting his hands on his knees. "You're cynical."

"And so are you."

"I never said I wasn't."

"Don't think you can manipulate me," she warned.

"Why do you fight me when I'm trying to help you?"

"And don't think you can use my political ambition as leverage. Call Bob Bannatyne. I don't give a shit."

"Is that what you tell your constituents?" he asked.

"My constituents mean a lot to me," she said, regaining some of her poise. "But I'm beginning to dislike municipal politics. Especially since the amalgamation. Megacity. A definition for nothing that works. Barry, you're so transparent you're practically invisible."

"I'm forty-nine years old," said Gilbert. "I've been a homicide detective for seventeen years. You want me to speculate? You want me to tell you why I think your husband killed Edgar Lau?"

She shook her head, grinned bitterly. "You don't have to tell me," she said. "I can guess."

"I think you loved Edgar Lau," he said. "And I think he loved you. I don't know you, and you don't know me, but I know by looking at those photographs, with you in that cheongsam, that they're the work of a man who felt nothing but tenderness for you. And I can tell by the way you smile in them that you felt nothing but tenderness for him too."

"You're forty-nine and you watch too many old movies," she said. She tilted her head to one side. Her green eyes glowed in the overcast light coming in through the window. "Edgar was my photographer," she said. "That's all. A volunteer. Whatever you saw in those photographs was meant solely for my husband. I'm sorry Edgar's dead. I have no idea what he got himself mixed up in. You can call Bob Bannatyne. You can do anything you like. It's a free country and everybody's allowed to make a fool of themselves any way they please. But facts make a case, Barry. Not speculation. When you have some facts, you can make an appointment to see me again. Until then, I wish you wouldn't bother me anymore. If you bother me too much, I might have to raise the matter with the Police Services Board. And you wouldn't want that, would you?" She looked at him sweetly. "Not when there's still more cutbacks on the way. Not when so many of your colleagues have already been down-sized out of their jobs."

That afternoon, when Gilbert got back to headquarters, he found Frank Hukowich of the RCMP waiting for him in the squad room. Pearl Wu was coming for an interview and Hukowich wanted to observe. Lombardo walked Hukowich through the case file on the computer.

"And Peter Hope's a player," said Hukowich, shaking his head with a gleeful look in his eyes. "This is great. I knew we were going to get a nibble on this thing."

Gilbert wondered if Hukowich's obvious familiarity with Peter Hope meant a deeper degree of unwanted interference in the investigation.

"Where's Paulsen today?" asked Gilbert.

But Hukowich was too caught up in this newest development to pay any attention to Gilbert. "I wonder why we never got a flag from Customs and Immigration on him," said Hukowich. He shook his head, bewildered by this breakdown in the system, perplexed by how Hope could have entered the country without someone person-ally notifying him about it. "Something went wrong somewhere."

"Who *is* Peter Hope?" asked Lombardo. "He says he's Pearl Wu's personal assistant, but Barry and I think it goes further than that."

Hukowich turned to the young detective. Something about Hukowich, thought Gilbert, some sleight of hand about his person-ality, something Gilbert didn't trust.

"Benny hasn't filled you in?" asked Hukowich.

"Benny has a local file," said Lombardo. "Nothing interna-tional."

Hukowich nodded. His hair, sculpted to perfection, was a cheesy masterpiece, a pompadour sweeping back in a mathematically precise curve to the crown of his head. "We think Peter Hope is a highly placed member of Hong Kong's 14K Triad," he said. "Our sources suggest he's the triad's Red Pole, the Hung Kwan, the number 486. That means he's the triad's enforcer, its top fighter and battle tactician. In his day he was a much feared master of the martial arts, but he must be well over seventy by now. Hope hasn't been active for a number of years, so that's why I'm surprised to see him turn up in your file like this. He has close connections to Bing Wu. Bing Wu is seventy-four. We have a whole album of surveillance photographs of the two of them together. He was Bing Wu's best man when he married Pearl seven years ago."

From down the aisle of desks, Carol Reid's telephone rang.

"He didn't seem particularly fearsome to me when I saw him out at the airport," said Lombardo. "Just annoying."

"Don't underestimate him just because he's old," said Hukowich. "The Hong Kong Police have never been able to touch him but they believe he's ordered ninety-six murders in the last decade alone, eleven of which have been in Canada. He's a ruthless man, Joe, and as cold-blooded as any killer you have in any of your case files," said Hukowich, waving to the computer screen. "And if he's here in Canada, it can mean only one thing. There's trouble somewhere. Bing Wu's called him out of retirement to deal with it. And that's just the kind of mud we like to see stirred."

"Barry?" called Carol from her desk, holding the phone against her shoulder. "Your appointment's here. Do you want me to go downstairs and card her in?" she asked.

Gilbert remembered Lombardo's comment about the lump of

coal. "No, it's all right," he said. "I'll go down." He turned to Lombardo and Hukowich. "Do you guys want to get a look at our beauty queen of the East from the atrium gallery?"

Hukowich shrugged. "Sure," he said. "Why not? Let's see the old man's trophy."

Gilbert, Lombardo, and Hukowich left the Homicide office.

Like so many of the newer buildings in Toronto, the first few floors of police headquarters on College Street were arranged around an open-air atrium, with galleries overlooking a broad and spacious lobby downstairs. They followed the gallery to the right, past Sexual Assault, and paused to look over the stone barrier to the ground floor. Gilbert looked for a beautiful Chinese woman. But there were no beautiful Chinese women down there.

"Holy shit," said Hukowich.

"What?" said Gilbert.

"It's him," said Hukowich. "Hope. Sitting on the bench by the elevators." Hukowich looked like a kid in a candy store. "This is starting to turn into something we can really use." Gilbert didn't at all like the sound of that. "I'm going to have to call our guy in Hong Kong and see what he can dig up about this. Something's going on and it might be big."

"Where's Pearl?" asked Lombardo. "I don't see her."

Gilbert scanned the lobby again. "I don't know," he said. "Maybe she's in the washroom."

All three men stared at Hope. He was a small aging Chinese man with gray hair combed to one side, longish hair for someone so old, unruly hair, as if the man had just stepped in from a windstorm, rakish and theatrical hair. He wore a simple gray overcoat. A silk scarf hung loosely around his neck. He sat forward on the bench, feet firmly planted on the marble floor, hands braced against his knees, looking as if he were ready to spring.

"I better go down," said Gilbert.

Hukowich nodded. "I'm going back. I can't let him see me. I'll watch through the glass."

Gilbert turned to Lombardo. "Joe, better check the video camera," he said. "It was acting up a few days ago."

"Sure," said Lombardo.

Lombardo and Hukowich went back to the Homicide office. Gilbert continued toward the elevators. Using his security access card, he took the elevator to the ground floor. The doors slid open and he approached Peter Hope. Gilbert searched his memory, trying to recall if he had seen Peter Hope in and around the Champion Gardens Restaurant on the night of the murder. Now he thought he might have. The man sprang from his spot on the bench and hurried forward, spry for one so old, smoothing out his long gray hair with his hand as he approached Gilbert.

"Are you Detective Gilbert?" he asked. His English was moderately accented but nonetheless easily understandable.

Gilbert looked at the small man, his face like stone. "And you are?" he said, playing along with the charade.

"Allow me to introduce myself," he said, with elaborate formality. "My name is Peter Hope. I'm Pearl Wu's personal assistant. I'm here to answer your questions."

Gilbert looked past the elevators toward the public washrooms. "And where's Mrs. Wu?" he asked. "I was expecting her to come alone. I asked her to come alone. Can she not follow simple instructions?"

Hope bowed. "Mrs. Wu cannot come today," he said. "I tried

to work a spot into her appointment book, but at the last minute she had to meet with some potential buyers for a restaurant we own in Markham, and she couldn't make it. She sends her sincere apologies."

This didn't in the least please Gilbert. He was sick of interrogation by appointment only. "You know what I'm going to do?" he said, unable to hide his annoyance. "I'm going to phone York Regional Police and have them go get her. Where is she? I want the exact address."

Hope lifted his hands, trying to placate Gilbert. "There's no need for that," he said. "Really, there isn't." The man smiled, but he smiled the way a shark might smile. "I've come in her place. I can answer all your questions."

"This isn't a dinner date," he said. "She can't decide not to show up. I'm not her hair stylist, I'm a homicide detective. And she doesn't cancel on a homicide detective."

Hope now looked like an excitable old man, a retiree who was easily discombobulated by small things, if only it weren't for the shark-like smile.

"But I was there in the restaurant on the night of the murder," said Hope. "I saw everything there was to see. I can help you. Trust me. I can really help you."

Like an old man pleading with muggers not to take his Social Security check.

Gilbert stared at Hope. He knew Hope was trying to protect Pearl Wu, even suspected he had been ordered to protect Pearl from any untoward attention by Bing Wu. Whether Pearl Wu had canceled her appointment was now beside the point. What mattered was Hope's assurance that he could help Gilbert, weighted as it was with unmistakable innuendo, that he could perhaps provide inside information about the murder. They could still talk to Pearl. They could pick her up any time they liked. She didn't seem to be running.

For now, though, he had this man in front of him, this Red Pole, this Hung Kwan, this number 486 who in his capacity as 14K enforcer had ordered the murders of ninety-six people. And maybe that was an opportunity a homicide detective shouldn't be so quick to pass up.

IN THE INTERVIEW ROOM UPSTAIRS, Hope calmly surveyed his surroundings. He picked out the small camcorder mounted on the tripod in the corner, the overhead microphone, the window of one-way glass, then took off his coat and slung it over a chair. He sat down, but instead of perching on the edge of his chair, hands on his knees, as he had done downstairs, he lifted one knee over the other, leaned back, and folded his hands across his lap in a pose of studied ease, as if he were used to such rooms. He regarded Gilbert with a blank expression, his dark brown eyes unwavering behind the inscrutable folds of his Chinese eyelids. Liver spots covered the backs of his hands.

Hope glanced at the one-way glass. "They watch us?" he asked.

Lombardo and Hukowich were out there.

"Mr. Hope," he said, "I'm a homicide detective. I'm interested in one thing. Finding Edgar Lau's killer. Some people want to broaden this investigation." He glanced at the one-way glass. "I don't." He could fairly sense Hukowich bristling in the squad room. "As the primary investigator on this murder, I've looked into the history of my victim, and I know that criminally he's not untainted. I know the people he deals with aren't untainted." Gilbert paused. He saw that Hope, an astute old man, understood the meaning of his pause—that not only had Gilbert looked into the history of Edgar Lau, but into the histories of everybody connected to Lau. Gilbert acknowledged Hope's own criminal past with this pause. Hope realized this. They both moved on. "None of that means anything to me unless it has a direct bearing on who killed Edgar Lau."

"I admire your pragmatism, Detective Gilbert."

"You were sitting at Foster Sung's table in the Champion Gardens Restaurant on the night Edgar Lau was murdered?"

Hope nodded. "I was."

"And which way were you facing?"

"I was facing the street."

"And could you see out the windows?" asked Gilbert.

"I could."

"And did you see Pearl Wu?" He was double-checking Foster. Sung's story about Pearl.

"I saw her arrive, yes."

"You saw her arrive?"

"She came to our table."

"She did?" He was getting confirmation again.

"Yes."

"For what reason?" asked Gilbert.

"To say hello. Plus I had a word with her about her flight arrangements to Hong Kong the next day."

"Did you see her leave?"

"Yes, I saw her leave," said Hope.

"And she left by the front door?"

"She left by the front door."

Gilbert shook his head, as if he were perplexed by the whole thing. "And the next day she went to Hong Kong," he said.

Hope's lips parted in a smile. His teeth looked like sharpened pieces of ivory in his leathery face. He lifted a bent index finger, shifted in his chair, looked as if he were about to make a major and heretofore undiscovered point about the celestial arrangement of the universe.

"You see?" said Hope. "That's why I'm here. To clarify. Yes, I saw Mrs. Wu. Yes, she did indeed visit Edgar Lau shortly before he was murdered. And then the next day she left for Hong Kong. No doubt you've had witnesses tell you the same thing. So even one such as I, one so woefully ignorant of police matters, understand why you made such erroneous assumptions about Mrs. Wu's culpability when she flew to Hong Kong. But I assure you, her flying to Hong Kong had nothing to do with Edgar Lau's murder. She wasn't running away. Quite simply, she went home for the holidays. She has a large and loving family in Hong Kong. She wanted to spend Christmas with her husband. That she should freely return to Canada thirteen days later should allay at least some of your suspicions. She flies back and forth to Hong Kong all the time. She'll be flying there again for the Chinese New Year."

Gilbert shrugged. "Maybe so," he said. "But six years ago Edgar Lau slashed her face, destroying her career as a model, and excuse me, that's a motive. Not only that, we know about the gun charge, the Derringer she had in her purse. These are facts that do nothing to allay my suspicions."

"Perhaps it's appropriate for me to now point out that Mrs. Wu wasn't the only one to visit Edgar Lau in and around the time he was murdered," said Hope. Hope's smile disappeared and a reflective expression came to his face. "Foster Sung went up ten minutes after she did."

Gilbert nodded. "When Mrs. Lau came and got him."

"No, no," corrected Hope. "This was before."

"Before?"

"Yes," said Hope. "A full half hour before Mrs. Lau came down and got him. A full half hour before we learned Edgar Lau had been shot."

Gilbert leaned forward, his eyes widening. "You mean Foster Sung went up twice?" He couldn't believe it. Maybe going after Foster Sung might be the right route after all.

"Yes. He was up there while Pearl was up there. The two of them were up there together."

Gilbert glanced at the one-way glass. Hukowich had to be dancing a jig. "The two of them were up there together?" he said, wanting to get it right.

"Yes."

"And the two of them came down together?"

"No. Pearl came down first. Foster came down five minutes later."

Gilbert felt his lips stiffening. He was galled. "And Pearl went home?" he asked.

"I assume so. She had an early flight."

"And Sung came into the restaurant when he left Edgar's apartment that first time?"

"Yes."

"Did you notice any outward change in him?"

"No," said Hope. "Or at least . . . he seemed preoccupied. I understand he's experiencing some business difficulties just now."

"Do you have any idea why he went upstairs that first time?" asked Gilbert.

"He was going to ask Edgar and Pearl if they wanted to join us," said Hope. "At least that's what he said."

"And when did Mrs. Lau come into the restaurant to get Sung?"

"About a half hour later."

"Who was sitting at your table?" asked Gilbert.

"Foster Sung, myself, Xu Jiatun, Tak-Ng Lai and Charles Peng. I should mention that Pearl came with a friend."

"She did?"

"Yes."

"Who was her friend?"

"A man I scarcely know. Tony Mok."

Gilbert studied the Red Pole; either he was the best of liars or he was telling the truth. Tony Mok was there? In the restaurant? In and around the time of Edgar's murder?

"Could you describe Tony Mok?" He had to be certain that Hope had the right man.

Hope nodded. "Chinese, twenty-four or -five, short but muscular, broad across the shoulders, long hair, wearing a leather jacket with a Harley-Davidson logo on the back, unkempt blue jeans, and sneakers. I sometimes wonder where Pearl finds her friends."

Hope's description was detailed and perfect, as one might expect from a battle tactician.

"I gather you don't approve," said Gilbert.

"Mrs. Wu isn't particularly prudent in her choice of friends," he said.

"And is that why you're here?" asked Gilbert. "To make sure she doesn't choose the wrong friends?"

"My duties are various and many, Detective Gilbert. If I must guard Mrs. Wu against her more naive proclivities, then that's what I'll do. This Tony Mok . . ." Hope shook his head. "I've had the man investigated. He's nothing but an extortionist and rip-off artist."

"And you hardly know the man?"

"I know what I must do to protect Mrs. Wu."

Was this a break in the case, wondered Gilbert. They had the possible match on the bullets. They had Constable Austin's story that Mok shot Edgar in Vancouver, and possibly in Toronto. Now Peter Hope placed Mok at the scene.

"Did Tony Mok go upstairs to visit Edgar Lau with Pearl?" he asked.

"No," said Hope. "He waited at the front of the restaurant while Mrs. Wu came to our table to say hello."

"Did she tell you why she had come to visit Edgar Lau?"

"She said she had a Christmas present for him." Hope's eyes brightened. "You see? Despite her horrible injury, she's forgiven Edgar."

"And Tony waited at the front of the restaurant while Pearl said hello?"

"Yes."

"And when Pearl went upstairs, where did Tony go?"

"He went outside," said Hope. "I saw him walk south on Spadina, toward Baldwin Street. Frankly, I was relieved."

Gilbert thought of Baldwin Street, how it was just south of the Champion Gardens Restaurant, how it connected to the alley behind the restaurant. Rainwater on Edgar's floor suggested the killer might have come through the French doors. And if Mok had been heading toward Baldwin Street . . .

"When you saw Tony Mok, was he behaving strangely in any way?" asked Gilbert.

Hope raised his eyebrows. "He was behaving the way you would expect someone of his background to behave," he said. "Hands in his pockets, looking all over the place, waiting for the next opportunity to steal anything that wasn't nailed down."

After Hope had gone, Gilbert, Lombardo, and Hukowich went to the fourth-floor cafeteria for coffee. A water pipe had burst above the drop-down ceiling. Building Services had removed seven of the large acoustical tiles and had secured the area with police tape—POLICE LINE DO NOT CROSS. Gilbert, Lombardo, and Hukowich watched the men work for a while. Water damage looked extensive. Even now, two days after the discovery, the smell of damp acoustical tile lingered in the air, mixing with the smell of Tuesday's Special, sauerkraut and sausage.

"Hope puts Sung in Edgar's apartment at the time of the murder," said Hukowich. "I think you should write a warrant."

"Frank, you're not looking at the other circumstances," said Gilbert. "What about the glove? I find a glove in a tree, it's dry on the inside, it hasn't been up there long, and then the lab tells us it tests positive for barium and antimony. Sung was in the restaurant. Ask Joe. Did he have gloves on? No. He had his coat hanging on a coat-tree. His face wasn't red from the cold and his hair wasn't wet. He hadn't been outside."

"I don't like your glove, Barry," said Hukowich. "And neither does Ross. You found it too far away from the crime scene to make it fit plausibly into your investigation."

"That's not true," said Gilbert. "I found it in a tree, discarded in a hurry along the most likely escape route." Gilbert shook his head, frustrated with Hukowich. "Then you have the two bullets, both thirty-eight-caliber, both soft-nose wadcutters, a kind of ammunition you don't see often, both fired from the same gun."

"I talked to Murphy," said Hukowich. "He's only seventy percent sure. I don't buy it."

"The only reason you don't buy it," said Lombardo, getting fed up, "is because you want to arrest Sung any way you can."

"So?" said Hukowich. "If we arrest Sung, we have a way of getting to Wu. You guys have no idea what's tied up in all this. Millions of dollars have been spent on this investigation."

"I still don't know why you're not going after Pearl," said Gilbert. "She's a far stronger suspect, and she's married to Bing Wu."

"Because our intelligence suggests she knows next to nothing about Bing Wu's operations," said Hukowich. "Maybe a bit about the laundering, maybe a bit about the shipping procedures, but Wu's kept her largely in the dark. He adores her. He worships her. He wants to protect her any way he can. So he keeps her out of it. At least as much as he can. Foster, on the other hand, worked with Wu extensively through the 1980s and most of the 1990s. He knows Wu's organization inside and out. He's in a position to name names. He has evidence. If we can turn him into an informer we can build prosecutable cases against dozens of Wu's people, maybe even against Wu himself. But we need leverage if we're going to do that, and that's where you guys come in."

Gilbert couldn't help thinking how Hukowich seemed to be losing sight of Edgar Lau, how Edgar's death didn't matter to him at all, how it had become a side issue. He had to make Hukowich and Paulsen understand that there were other possibilities, that their single-minded witch-hunt was out of place when measured against the evidence in hand.

"But can't you see we have to look into these other suspects?" said Gilbert. "What about Garth Surrey? He's missing. He went missing on the night of the murder. The cook sees a man matching his description behind the Champion Gardens Restaurant on the night of the murder. This man is seen running away from the crime scene. Was he wearing beige Isotoners? I don't know. But he could have been. Was he Garth Surrey? I don't know. But he could have been. Before we can go after Sung, we've got some winnowing to do."

"How can Surrey be a suspect?" asked Hukowich. "Why are you guys needlessly complicating this thing with those photographs of Rosalyn Surrey? Why don't you just cut through all that crap and do your job? Write a warrant on Sung."

"We can't do that," said Gilbert.

"You're forgetting the central aspect of this case," said Hukowich.

"And what's that?" asked Gilbert.

"Twenty-four hundred grams of China White in Edgar Lau's attic."

All expression left Gilbert's face. "As far as I'm concerned, Frank," he said, not bothering to hide his disgust anymore, "the central aspect of this case is Edgar Lau lying dead on his dining room floor."

Gilbert had to go for a walk after that. Lombardo came with him. They walked east along College Street toward Yonge, Gilbert stamping a few pigeons away with more force than necessary. Lombardo glanced at him. Gilbert shrugged helplessly.

"The guy bugs me," he said, exasperated.

"So you take it out on the birds?"

"They were in my way," he said.

"You want a hot dog or something?" said Lombardo, pointing to a vendor up the way. "You hardly ate a bite in the cafeteria. Maybe you're hungry. Look, he has onions. You love onions. Pile them on thick. Go for broke."

"You're the one who usually gets mad," said Gilbert. "Why don't you punch that mailbox? Just seeing you punch that mailbox would make me feel better."

"That's government property," said Lombardo. "You'd arrest me."

"He doesn't seem to understand why we became homicide cops," said Gilbert.

Lombardo shrugged innocently. "I just drifted into it," he said. "All I ever wanted to do was sell shoes."

"You know what? You're not government property. Let me punch you. That'll make me feel better."

"Everyone has their own agenda, Barry," said Lombardo. "Hukowich is no different."

"But he doesn't even care about Edgar. I'd like him to take one good look at May Lau. If he could see her eyes, and hear the way she plays that Chinese violin, the way it sounds so sad . . . that's why we do it, Joe. That's why we put up with all this crap. So we might make a difference to someone like May Lau."

They walked in silence for a bit, past an old Fran's Restaurant, a landmark from the 1950s, one of those places that never close down. They finally came to Yonge Street, the city's main drag.

"You want to walk down Yonge?" asked Lombardo.

"I hate Yonge Street. The prostitutes and pushers keep getting younger every year. Plus I hate that guy who plays the drums. There should be a law against drum solos in public places."

"You don't like drum solos?" said Lombardo. "Drum solos are cool."

"Even when I went to rock concerts, I hated drum solos."

"You went to rock concerts? How can that be true? I heard you whistling *King of the Road* the other day. I thought Burl Ives was more your style."

Gilbert grinned, feeling a bit better. "You might make a good mailbox yet," he said.

They crossed Yonge Street. College turned into Carleton. They came to Maple Leaf Gardens. Gilbert glanced up at the impressive gray building, no longer home of the Toronto Maple Leafs, just an old discarded arena where they held monster-truck rallies and other culturally edifying events. He kept thinking of Hukowich. He didn't mind taking advice from outsiders, but when the advice was dead wrong, he had to put his foot down.

"What's with that guy?" he asked Joe. "Does he think we can write warrants any time we feel like it?"

"Like I say, he's got his own agenda," said Lombardo.

"But what doesn't he understand about it?" said Gilbert, as they continued east along Carleton toward Jarvis Street. "We've got someone who matches Garth Surrey's description behind the restaurant at the time of the murder. We've got Pearl upstairs. We've got Tony Mok in the restaurant—along with two matching bullets and Constable Austin's claim that Tony Mok killed Edgar. And okay, I admit, we've got Foster Sung going up to Edgar's apartment twice. But if we arrest Foster Sung now, that's it, the investigation's over.

What doesn't Hukowich get about that? If Foster Sung didn't do it, Edgar's real killer goes free. And what good does that do May Lau? The only comfort she'll have is playing sad songs on her Chinese violin."

Rain started again late in the afternoon, a persistent gray precipitation that seemed to permeate every bit of concrete, glass, and asphalt in the city, running in the gutters in half-hearted trickles, blighting the sky with its damp pall.

Having received an unexpected call from Rosalyn Surrey, Gilbert drove his unmarked Lumina to the Annex, a trendy residential neighborhood just west of the University of Toronto's St. George Campus. She lived on Palmerston Avenue, a street lined with globe lamps on black metal posts, in a detached renovated Edwardian house with granite pillars and pilasters supporting an impressive portico, the kind of house Gilbert, as a former student of architecture, dreamed of owning some day. He climbed the steps and knocked.

She opened the door. He was surprised by the difference. She no longer looked so hard. She wore a pink Roots sweatshirt, faded blue jeans, moccasin slippers, and had her blond hair tied in a ponytail with a piece of turquoise yarn. She was thirty-two, but she now looked twenty-two.

"I'm sorry," she said. "I didn't want to keep you working late. You probably want to go home."

"I'm used to working late," he said.

She looked down at the welcome mat, as if she were unsure of how to proceed.

"I'm sorry about this morning," she said. She looked up at him and grinned, and he could see that her grin was genuinely contrite. "I shouldn't have threatened you."

She was demure. She was amenable. She was ready to talk. He smelled the faint scent of *eau de lavande* coming from behind her ears.

"It's all right," he said.

"And I'm sorry about the phone. I don't feel safe talking on the phone."

He still had no idea why she didn't want to talk on the phone, why she had to talk to him in person.

"If you don't feel safe . . ." He shrugged, accepting her conditions.

"Let's go inside," she said.

"Sure."

He followed her inside. The hardwood floor glowed like gold in the soft lamplight. Group of Seven reproductions—melancholy depictions of northern Ontario's pine, rock, and lakes—hung on the walls. A variety of ornamental dried grasses, some yellow, some blue, stood in large cut-glass receptacles on the floor. She had a fire going. She had a Christmas tree, but the Christmas tree looked sad to Gilbert, an artificial one, entirely silver with small red lights, and three unopened gifts wrapped in gold paper under the glimmer of its lowest boughs. A bone-white baby grand piano, scuffed and battered, with a Montreal Jazz Festival sticker stuck on the underside of its opened lid, stood in the corner.

"Do you play?" he asked.

"It's my husband's," she said.

"He's a musician?"

"Well . . . was . . . had a brief recording career in the early nineties, but then ran into tax problems and . . . he's not that active anymore. He's had that piano for a long time. It's got a cracked soundboard and it's really not worth fixing, but he insists we keep it."

"I'm sorry about your husband."

She looked away. "Would you like a drink?" she asked. "I was about to pour a sherry."

"You go ahead," he said.

He watched her move to the liquor cabinet, her walk fluid and easy, a bright example of feminine poise. The cabinet looked like an antique, walnut or oak, with ten beveled glass panes in the framework of each door. The fire cracked and embers leaped up the flue, and the rain suddenly seemed far away to Gilbert. The furniture was soft, comfortable, upholstered in off-white fabric. The walls were white and the trim was wood, varnished in muted tones. She came back. She smiled in a girlish way. She kicked off her moccasins, revealing white socks with a pink frill around the top, and folded her right foot under her left thigh with yoga-like flexibility.

"I have information that might help you solve Edgar Lau's murder," she said.

He took the statement calmly, and, considering how uncooperative she'd been thus far, expected nothing from it.

"And that information might be?" he asked.

Her eyes focused and her smile dropped away, and he saw the iron-hard city councillor coming back. "Ever since I was elected," she said, "I've received complaints about illegal gaming houses in and around the Chinatown area of Ward One. If you read the minutes of any of the Police Services Board meetings, you'll see that I've raised the issue again and again, and that again and again the chairman says she'll contact officers at 52 Division to deal with the problem. I respect Julie Winslow, I think she's an excellent

board chairman, and I think she's established clear lines of commu-
nication with the various command sectors in the police force. But
somehow this particular problem doesn't go away." Gilbert kept
quiet. He saw no reason just yet to tell Rosalyn that he knew about
the connection between herself and Constable Jeremy Austin. "So
I've had a closer look at the problem on my own time. I grew up in
Ward One, Detective Gilbert. I went to Orde Street Public School,
and I went to Jarvis Collegiate. I know the Chinese community. Most
of my friends in high school were Chinese. I know I have to expect
at least a modest amount of gambling in Chinatown, despite the
complaints. It's part of the culture and I don't want to disrupt
things too much. I can accept the gambling."

He nodded. "We all have to get along," he agreed.

"I've identified at least eighteen such gaming houses in my
electoral district and that's all right, that's okay. But I've determined that at least seven of these are acting as fronts for drug-
smuggling and prostitution rings. I've developed sources within the
Chinese community, and one of my primary sources happened to be
Edgar Lau." She paused, took a sip of her sherry. She looked at the
wine magazine on the coffee table, an issue devoted to the wines of
South America, with a bottle of Isla Negra, from Chile, on the front
cover. "Before he was murdered Edgar told me he had conclusive
evidence that linked certain officers at 52 Division to these drug-
smuggling and prostitution rings. You have to understand. I don't
mind the gambling. But drug-smuggling and prostitution rings? No
way. The reason these places haven't been closed down is because
of corrupt police involvement at 52. Edgar was up to his neck in it,
trying to find things out for me, and I believe Edgar may have been
discovered." A shadow of grief darkened her face. "I believe one of
these bad officers might have murdered Edgar."

He stared at her. Here was an alternate canvas, a different pic-ture, yanking suspicion not only away from Garth Surrey, such as she obviously intended, but also away from Tony Mok and Pearl Wu.

"Why didn't you tell me this before?" he asked.

"Because I was afraid if you began investigating along these lines you might possibly jeopardize some of my other sources. And I didn't want to jeopardize anything, particularly at that point, because Edgar was so close to handing over documented proof to me."

Gilbert looked through the gauze curtains. The chimney next door looked distorted and faint through the curtains. "Why come to me now?" he said.

"Because you said you wanted to help me," she said. "And because I've had a chance to think about it." She looked down at her knees, and, in a softer voice, said, "And because I'm scared."

He stared at her. "You've had threats?" he asked. He thought he was going to get a replay of Jeremy Austin.

"I really want to trust you," she said.

"Why would Edgar help you?" asked Gilbert. "Why would he risk it?"

She looked up at him. "I don't know why," she said, and she looked truly perplexed. "He started as a volunteer. I saw his pho-tography skills as an asset and I tried to get him on board. Then we became friends. I began to trust him. He understood the Chinese in Toronto as only a Chinese can. And he helped me with that. He advised me on that. He was a paid member of my staff for a while. When I told him what I was doing, how I was sick of these drug and prostitution rings, he told me to be careful, that there was a lot of infighting just now, that a lot of the older Toishan establishments were being taken over by the Hong Kong Chinese, and that the Hong

Kong Chinese could be dangerous. That's as far as it went. For six months, whenever I talked about it, he would just keep quiet, never say anything about it. Then, one day near the end of November, he told me he would help me."

Gilbert took a deep breath. "Any idea what prompted the change?" he asked.

Rosalyn's eyes narrowed. "I don't know . . . but a change . . . yes, a definite change . . . a change in his character." She turned to Gilbert. "One thing I always admired about Edgar was the control he had over his emotions. But when he came to me and told me he wanted to help me, I saw this black, this dark . . . something in his eyes. His face was like stone, not a muscle twitched, but in his eyes I saw the most ominous and frightening . . . determination. He looked . . ." She shook her head, bewildered by the memory. "I couldn't believe the change. I asked him about it but he never talked about it."

Gilbert paused to consider. He still couldn't understand why she would wait two weeks to tell him this. He was suspicious. If her story was true, certain 52 Division officers, as yet to be identified, would now become suspects in Edgar Lau's murder too. And that meant that he would have to take a closer look at Donald Kennedy, what with the dish towel and Chinese-man discrepancies in his report. He would verify what he could with Jeremy Austin. As for now, he couldn't rule out the possibility that she was attempting to deflect suspicion from her husband. This soft interior, the fire in the grate, the offer of a drink, her casual clothes—these all seemed part of a carefully orchestrated plan to steer Gilbert away from Garth Surrey.

"How close was Edgar to having concrete documented proof?" he asked.

"He said he had it," she replied.

"And when did he tell you this?"

"Two days before he was murdered."

"Because we checked every square inch of his apartment. We examined every single file on his computer, once we had our technicians hack through his password. There's nothing there that indicates corrupt police involvement in his murder."

"He said he had the proof hidden away in a locker somewhere," she said. "That's the thing about Edgar. Everything is planned. He was going to fly to San Francisco. Some friends down there were going to hide him for a while. He was going to mail the locker key with instructions to the Solicitor General's Office. Then he was just going to watch the whole house of cards collapse from a safe distance."

CHAPTER
TWELVE

THE FOLLOWING MORNING, AFTER WORKING a domestic stabbing in Riverdale—
a dunker complete with a repentant husband in blood-spattered jeans
and a dead wife lying on the kitchen floor—Gilbert and Lombardo,
both on rotation for Saturday, drove to Toronto's exclusive Bridle
Path, a posh community of thirty-room houses, three-car garages,
and private tennis courts a world away from the government-
subsidized high-rises of Riverdale. On the way up Leslie Street,
Gilbert, having done some homework on the subject, told Lombardo what Edgar Lau had done with himself over the last few
months. He kept remembering Rosalyn Surrey's words, that Edgar
had changed at the end of November, and he was trying to find out
why.

"Canadian Airlines has him flying to Vancouver on the twenty-
eighth of November," said Gilbert, "but they don't have him flying
back. I've checked all the other airlines. I've checked Via Rail, Canadian Pacific Rail, and all the bus lines, but there's no indication he

took any kind of public transportation back to Toronto after flying out there."

"What about a rental car?"

"I've checked," said Gilbert. "No rental car. So how did he get back to Toronto? I thought about that for a while. I think he drove a private vehicle back to Toronto. He flew out there so he could drive something back—*deliver* something back to Toronto. In a private vehicle. Maybe the product we found in his attic."

Lombardo nodded. "I think you might be right," he said.

Gilbert passed a bus. "He had to get the smack from somewhere," he said. "I figure he got it in Vancouver and drove it back here. I phoned the Vancouver Police and talked to a Detective Pam Nichols of the Asian Crime Squad. I asked her to retrieve the twenty-four-hour report on the shooting of Edgar back in August. No suspects, but it referenced Edgar's name to another report, one that ties into a major investigation the Vancouver Police are conducting on a Ling Han Lam, a suspected major narcotics trafficker with connections to the 14K Triad. They've been watching Lam for a long time. One of their undercover agents spotted Lam talking to Edgar in a *pai-gow* parlor on East Pender in November. Edgar's just a footnote in this much bigger investigation, but I think it's safe to assume he was in Vancouver for business, not pleasure." Gilbert glanced at Lombardo. "How'd the neighborhood canvas go?" he asked. "Did Benny Eng give you any leads about who you might talk to, people who might actually know Edgar, or who might have some guesses about how he got himself killed?"

"He did."

"So you made progress?"

"I did," said Lombardo. "I covered the downtown Chinatown as well as the one by the Don Jail," he said. "I talked to one of the older Chinese out there, a Danny Leung, a guy from Canton who runs a tearoom, but the place is really a gaming house. Leung told me Edgar worked for him as a bouncer a few years back. He also mentioned Tony Mok. He has the same information Jeremy Austin does—that Tony Mok was responsible for the Vancouver shooting. As for Edgar's murder, he doesn't know anything about it. But he's heard rumors about a split between the 14K and Kung Lok triads, and he's convinced that Edgar was somehow caught in the cross fire."

"It wouldn't surprise me." Gilbert shook his head. "This is really starting to smell," he said.

"This is starting to *reek,*" said Lombardo.

Foster Sung's mansion came into view a few minutes later. It was new, made of flesh-colored brick, ungainly and huge, too modern and functional-looking to be attractive in any but a conventional, suburban way. The driveway passed a shrubbery garden of a few blue spruces in a bed of white quartz stones. Two garish Chinese lions stood on either side of the front door. The thermal pre-fab windows looked plugged into their spots, displaying an architectural disregard, as far as Gilbert was concerned, for the more enchanting possibilities of fenestration.

Gilbert and Lombardo got out of the Lumina and walked up to the door. Gilbert rang the doorbell. Two cocker spaniels leaped at the window beside the door and yelped. Gilbert saw someone yank the spaniels away. The barking grew fainter as the dogs were shoved into a nearby room. The door opened and a middle-aged black woman in a white apron confronted them with inquiring eyes.

"Yes?" she said.

Gilbert showed his badge and ID to the woman. "We're here to see Mr. Sung," he said. "He's expecting us."

The woman looked him over suspiciously, then nodded. Her dark face remained immobile. "Come with me," she said. "He's waiting for you in his study."

They followed the woman down the hall to a room at the back. She gave the door a few discreet taps and pushed it open. Foster Sung was on the phone talking in Cantonese.

"Detective Gilbert is here to see you, Mr. Sung," said the woman.

Sung beckoned to the woman and the detectives while he continued to speak on the phone. The woman ushered them halfway into the room. "He should be done in a minute," she said. She retreated.

Gilbert and Lombardo took the opportunity to glance around the room, looking for anything that might be of evidentiary value, conducting a plain-view search while Sung continued to talk in Cantonese on the phone. Gilbert didn't see anything in the least incriminating. Sung sat behind a vast walnut desk. Intricately carved rosewood panels covered the walls. Taking a closer look at the wall, Gilbert saw antique sheets of music framed under glass, the brass plaque under the frame identifying them as Chopin's *Nocturne et Berceuse,* the original handwritten manuscript, penned with a quill in brown ink by the composer himself. He turned to Sung. So, he was a collector. He continued to glance around the room. The expensive furniture was upholstered in liver-colored leather. This was as much of an office as it was a den. Sliding glass doors opened onto a rain-drenched deck, and beyond, backing against a small wooded area, Gilbert saw a kidney-shaped swimming pool covered with a blue pool cover. Sung waved them toward some chairs in front of his desk. The two detectives sat down. Sung, after a few more words, hung up. He swung his swivel chair in their direction and gave them a neutral smile.

"Gentlemen," he said. The man looked impervious.

Gilbert started first by comparing Sung's version of events on the night of the murder to Peter Hope's version.

"He has Pearl going up the stairs first, then he has you following ten minutes later."

"Yes, this is correct," said Sung. Today, the suspected triad member wore a blue blazer with a nautical crest above the left breast pocket, gray flannels, and a silk scarf tucked down the front of a pale yellow shirt. Gilbert couldn't help thinking how young he looked for his fifty-seven years.

"I think you can guess why this has us so concerned," said Gilbert.

"I'm afraid I can't," said Sung, still smiling.

"Because it puts you at the scene of the crime right around the time of the shooting. You went up twice. Once ten minutes after Pearl went up, and once later, when May Lau came and got you. Why didn't you tell us you went up twice?"

Sung raised his eyebrows. "Because it didn't pertain," he said.

Gilbert and Lombardo glanced at each other. Lombardo spoke up. "Of course it pertained," he said, feeling his way around the odd word, a word a Chinese man learning English in a British colony might use. "Everything you did that night—" Before Joe could finish, his pager went. He pulled his sporty blazer aside and looked down at the number. Then he looked at Sung. "I've got to use your phone."

Sung gestured at the telephone on the desk. "Be my guest," he said.

"Is there somewhere private?" asked Lombardo.

Sung swept his palm toward the door. "There's one out in the hall," he said.

"Thanks."

Lombardo got up and left the room. The page was really a ruse designed to widen the plain-view search. Telford had beeped Lombardo for that specific purpose.

With Lombardo gone, Gilbert went over things in more detail with Sung. He started with Tony Mok, telling Sung what they knew about him. "We know Mok was born to an unmarried refugee woman by the name of Fang who escaped Vietnam on your boat, that he was interred in a refugee camp in Hong Kong for the early part of his life, and that he then came to Canada. From what we understand, you more or less acted as the boy's guardian. You took a personal interest in Tony."

Sung's smile disappeared and he leaned forward, folding his hands on the red blotter. "I took a personal interest in a lot of orphans," he said.

"We understand Mok was in the Champion Gardens Restaurant on the night Edgar was murdered."

"Yes, he was there," said Sung, but apparently didn't think that pertained either.

"And you didn't mention him?"

"Why would I mention him?" he said. "He stood there for a minute or two, waiting for Pearl. When Pearl went upstairs, he left. I can't see what he has to do with any of it."

"We'd like to find Tony Mok," said Gilbert, "but we have no idea where he might be."

Sung smiled in an honest and unconcerned way. "Neither do I."

"We have strong evidence that ties him to Edgar Lau's murder."

"You shouldn't waste your time on that," said Sung quickly. "I saw him leave the building. He was nowhere near the building when Edgar Lau was murdered."

"Does he have any friends?"

"He has a few."

"Can you give me names?"

"I'm afraid I can't," said Sung.

"Because you won't, or because you can't?"

"Because I don't remember their names. Have you talked to Pearl Wu yet?" asked Sung.

"Not yet."

"She's the one you should be talking to."

"Why?" asked Gilbert.

"Because she's Edgar's old flame, for one thing." Sung turned his head, looked at a giant carving of a turtle on his desk. "And because she was . . ." He unfolded his hands and tapped the blotter a few times. "I went up there the first time to invite them both to my table in the restaurant. I believe in the traditional forms of hospitality. I didn't want either of them to feel slighted. I thought they might enjoy talking to Tak-Ng Lai, our guest from China, an exceptional musician, one who's done much to promote Chinese music throughout the world." Sung shook his head. "They were having an argument. I don't know what they were arguing about. I didn't ask."

Was Sung now trying to implicate Pearl? Many arguments turned into homicides. Gilbert shook his head. "Why didn't you tell me this when I came downtown to see you at your office?" he said.

Sung looked out the sliding glass doors at the swimming pool. The pool was a depressing sight in these first days of winter, with rainwater collecting in the dips of the cover. The man no longer looked so impervious. In fact he looked downright worried. He couldn't possibly say that Edgar and Pearl having an argument didn't pertain. It *did* pertain. Why the evasion?

"To understand that, you must first understand who Pearl is, and who she is married to," said Sung. "Mr. Wu prizes his wife more than anything. He's an extremely powerful man, and he wields that power calmly, wisely, and deliberately." Within the context of the Asian crime world, Gilbert had to wonder how wisely anyone could wield power. "The only thing I've ever seen him get angry about is his wife. When he's angry, he becomes persistent. When he's persistent, he becomes dangerous. It's not my place to make trouble for Mr. Wu or his wife. It's not my place to implicate Pearl in this business. I hope this may give you at least some understanding of my various omissions."

Why the evasion? Gilbert now saw it plainly. Fear. Concealed behind Foster Sung's careful expression. Sung didn't want to implicate Pearl Wu in the murder of Edgar Lau because he was afraid of Bing Wu. Yet in the end he had done just that, perhaps to save himself from further police inquiry.

"So you heard them arguing and what did you do?" asked Gilbert.

"I knocked on the door and asked them if they would like to meet Tak-Ng Lai. They of course stopped their argument the moment I knocked."

"Who answered the door?"

"Edgar answered the door."

"And what was his emotional state?"

"He was angry."

"What was Pearl's?"

"She was crying. She wouldn't look at me."

"Where was she standing?" asked Gilbert.

"In the hall."

"Did she have her coat off?"

"No."

"Was she carrying a bag of any sort?"

"Detective Gilbert," said Sung, "before we go any further, I must stress to you that what I tell you in this room should never be in any way connected or attributed to me. There are certain loyalties and bonds you are forcing me to jeopardize, and certain risks you are asking me to take. I would never be able to appear in court should this ever come to litigation. In the world of our . . . our so-called little societies . . . we must always guard against the possibility of . . . of a stubborn grudge now and again."

He had to admit, Sung was a master of euphemism. "I understand that."

And with his understanding, Sung seemed willing to make a concession. "She had a bag," he said. And a bag could mean a concealed weapon.

"And the two of them were alone in the apartment?" asked Gilbert.

"As far as I could tell, yes."

"Could you tell if the French doors were open?"

"The French doors were closed."

"Did you see any rainwater on the floor?"

Foster Sung frowned. "I wasn't looking at the floor," he said.

"And you saw Tony Mok leave the restaurant?"

Sung looked exasperated by the question. "I saw him leave the restaurant," he said. "I saw him get into a taxi. I saw the taxi drive away."

Warning bells went off in Gilbert's mind. Sung's story diverged from Hope's. Hope had Mok walking down Spadina Avenue toward Baldwin, not getting into a taxi and driving away. He tucked the discrepancy away for future use.

"So you asked Edgar and Pearl whether they wanted to meet Tak-Ng Lai, and what did they say?"

"They said another time."

"And then what did you do?"

"I rejoined my party in the restaurant," said Sung.

The warning bells went again. Peter Hope had Pearl leaving Edgar's apartment first. Foster Sung had himself leaving first.

"Did you see Pearl leave?" He had to pick at this.

"You ask me dangerous questions, detective."

"You have my solemn promise," said Gilbert.

"I saw her leave," said Sung.

So. Sung had himself leaving first. Hope had Pearl leaving first. Who was lying? Gilbert played along with Sung for the time being.

"Did she come into the restaurant to say good-bye to you?"

"No. She left in a hurry. She had her sports car parked outside."

Gilbert wondered if there was much point to this. Might as well try to establish a few more facts rather than try to figure out who was lying.

"Was she wearing gloves?" asked Gilbert.

Sung's brow knitted; he was puzzled by the question. "Gloves?" he said. "I don't know . . . I suppose she was . . . it's December, and she still had her coat on, so I—"

"Beige driving gloves," said Gilbert, trying to jog something. "Isotoners?"

Sung thought about this, tried to remember, but finally shook his head. "I don't recall," he said. "It was . . . rather a quick encounter."

Gilbert heard a ruckus out in the hall, Lombardo cursing someone, and, a moment later, saw the door open. A gigantic Chinese man in a fern-green business suit had Lombardo by the scruff of the neck.

"I was trying to find the bathroom," Lombardo protested. "Let me go."

The gigantic Chinese man uttered an explosive phrase of Cantonese to Foster Sung. Sung gazed at Lombardo like a judge passing sentence.

"Let him go, Xu," he said. A cool smile came to Sung's face. The bodyguard let Lombardo go. The difference in size between the two men was marked. Sung turned to Gilbert with an expression of dismissal. "Gentlemen," he said, "if you have no further questions, I have a busy day ahead of me."

Gilbert saw that Foster Sung knew exactly what Lombardo had been trying to do, and under those circumstances thought it best not to press any further. If subsequent questions developed, he would simply make an appointment to see Sung again.

On the way back to headquarters, Gilbert told Lombardo about his conversation with Sung.

"He was reluctant," said Gilbert. "He didn't want to implicate anybody. He gave me the minimum." Up ahead, where Leslie Street dipped to the Taylor Creek ravine, water flooded part of the road. Gilbert covered his brake as they coasted through. The car sent a Maui-like curl of water onto the curb. "But in the end, he more or less implicated Pearl. He has Pearl and himself up in Edgar's apartment at the same time, like Peter Hope says, but in his version he's the one who leaves first, not Pearl. Ergo, Pearl's guilty." His eyes narrowed as he went over the conversation in his mind. "Then he has . . ." He pictured the snake plants at the front of the Champion Gardens Restaurant, tried to imagine Mok standing there by the glass counter and cash register waiting for Pearl Wu. "He has Tony Mok leaving in a taxi instead of walking down the street."

"And Hope has Mok walking down the street, not getting in a taxi," said Lombardo.

"Exactly."

"Tony Mok is starting to bug me," said Lombardo.

"Me too."

"I think Sung's trying to protect Mok," said Lombardo.

"Why do you say that?"

"He puts Mok in a taxi so he can get Mok as far away from the crime scene as possible. He's obviously got some interest in protecting the guy. Especially if he's willing to risk the consequences of implicating the China bride of the 14K."

"The man was Mok's legal guardian in Hong Kong," said Gilbert. "That's got to count for something."

"Plus I found photographs upstairs," said Lombardo.

"You went upstairs?"

"I decided why not take a risk?"

"The plan was for a plain-view, Joe."

"I didn't touch a thing. Everything I saw was in plain view." Lombardo looked away, defensive.

"All right," said Gilbert, giving Lombardo the benefit of the doubt. "But what do these photographs have to do with Sung wanting to protect Mok?"

Lombardo squinted as he thought about it. "Because they're photographs of Tony," he said. "Some of May Lau too. Weird photographs. Like surveillance photographs. They had that telephoto quality to them. All in gold frames on top of Sung's dresser. Some of Tony, some of May Lau. I recognized Tony from the mug shot we have of him. Quite a few of May Lau by herself in Saigon. She doesn't even know she's being photographed. One of her leaving a Chinese temple. Another of her in a park with Edgar. One of her in an outdoor café with a friend. And then these ones of Tony. There's one of him standing by himself. I guess when he's about sixteen or seventeen. In front of the President Restaurant downtown. The big Chinese place they tore down a few years ago. He's wearing a suit. Like it's a special occasion. Why would Sung have a photograph of Tony in a suit if he didn't have some feeling for the guy?"

Gilbert flicked the left-hand signal on as they passed the Inn-on-the-Park. He thought about the whole thing. He realized that Lombardo had a point. But while he was interested in the Tony Mok photographs, he was also interested in the ones of May Lau. "Those photographs of May Lau," he said. "I think Sung's got a thing for her. I've been thinking that right from the start."

"Me too," said Lombardo. His eyes narrowed as he glanced up at the landmark Inn-on-the-Park sitting on its grassy hill. "Only it's a one-way street, isn't it? May doesn't give a shit."

"May doesn't give a shit," agreed Gilbert.

"I wish we could find Tony," said Lombardo.

"Maybe we should broaden our posted lookout," said Gilbert. "Send it further afield. Go nationwide on it."

"Do you think Nowak will let us?"

Gilbert turned left on Eglinton, sighed, raised his eyebrows. "We can only try," he said.

*   *   *

When they got back to headquarters, Gilbert had a Post-It note stuck to his phone with Carol Reid's handwriting on it. From Dock Wen, the cook at the Champion Gardens Restaurant. Please call. So Gilbert called.

"How are you, sir?" asked the cook when Gilbert got through.

"Just fine," he asked. "What's up?"

"I think about what I say to you, and now I remember something I didn't tell you."

"And what might that be?" Gilbert couldn't believe it, a civic-minded citizen, someone who was actually willing to inconvenience himself for the sake of a police investigation.

"I see a car," said Wen.

"You saw a car?" said Gilbert, grabbing some notepaper and a pen. "When did you see a car?"

"When the big man ran away," said the cook.

"You saw a car out in the alley?"

"It go very, very fast."

"Which way?"

"Baldwin Street."

"So it came from the west end of the alley, came around the corner, and went down to Baldwin Street," said Gilbert, writing it down.

"That is correct," said Wen. "Very fast."

"Did you happen to get the make and model?" asked Gilbert.

"Volkswagen," said Wen. In the background Gilbert heard the banging of pots. "Could be Golf. Could be Jetta. It had gold hubcaps."

"What color was the car?"

"White."

When Gilbert was done with the cook, he immediately went

to his computer and called up the case file. He wasn't sure about cars. Lombardo had done all the Ministry of Transport networking on the case.

He was gratified by what he found. Tony Mok drove a late-model white Volkswagen Golf. No taxi for Tony Mok, he thought. The getaway car had been around the corner all the time.

FIFTY-TWO DIVISION MADE A BIG stink about it but they finally handed over Constable Kennedy's run-sheet for the evening of December fifteenth. At nine o'clock on the night of the murder, Kennedy answered a shoplifting call. The store owner decided not to press charges and the perp got off with a warning. At nine forty-five, down at the corner of King and Jarvis, he ejected an unruly drunk from the Shamrock Restaurant and Tavern. Gilbert leaned back in his chair, frowning at the next entry. The shooting call. What Gilbert didn't get was how Kennedy could report himself as the closest officer to the scene. The Shamrock was down at King and Jarvis, miles from the scene. Officer Janvier, answering a domestic call at nine thirty, had in fact been the closest officer to the scene, right around the corner from the Champion Gardens Chinese Restaurant, on Phoebe and Beverley.

Gilbert pressed the button on the Marantz four-track tape deck, an old piece of equipment that had been kicking around

Homicide for twenty years, never replaced because of Homicide's tight budget, and listened to the radio tapes of the dispatch calls one more time.

"This is seven-four-three," said Kennedy, announcing his unit number to Officer Janvier. "Repeat, this is seven-four-three; cancel that ten-seventy-one, I'm eastbound on Harbord, west of St. George, en route to that ten-seventy-one; do you copy, six-oh-two-nine? Do you copy, six-oh-two-nine?"

"Roger that, seven-four-three," said Officer Janvier. "Will assist when able." In other words, when his domestic-dispute call was over. "Ten-four, seven-four-three."

"Ten-four. Dispatch, this is seven-four-three. Dispatch, this is seven-four-three; do you copy?"

A nasal female voice came onto the band. "Copy that, seven-four-three."

"Code four that ten-seventy-one at 504 Spadina Avenue," said Kennedy. "Am en route, east of Salem, westbound on Harbord, ETA in three minutes."

"Copy that, seven-four-three. Code four. Ten-four."

Time of transmission was three minutes past ten. The run-sheet had it down as nine fifty-five. A minute or two was fine. But eight minutes? That was too suspicious to believe.

On New Year's Eve, Gilbert heard the doorbell ring and went to answer it. He found Joe Lombardo standing there with some flowers in his hand and a pair of ice skates slung over his shoulder. Lombardo wore his black leather jacket, a pair of stone-washed blue jeans, and fur-lined mukluks, about as casual as Lombardo ever got.

"Hi," he said. "Happy New Year." Lombardo peered past Gilbert's shoulder. "Is Jennifer ready?"

Gilbert again had the sense that he had stepped into an alternate universe. "Is this real?" he said. "Tell me this isn't real."

"I'm taking her skating at Nathan Phillips Square for First Night," said Lombardo. "She didn't tell you?"

"And you bought her flowers?"

"No," said Lombardo. "The flowers are for Regina."

"First you charm my daughter, now you charm my wife?"

"It's in the blood," said Lombardo.

Gilbert felt exasperated. "Joe, I thought we agreed that you were going to ease out of this."

Lombardo looked at him doubtfully. "Jennifer didn't tell you, did she?"

"No," he said. "She didn't."

"I told her to tell you." Lombardo looked away. "Carumba," he said.

"Joe, c'mon."

"I know, I know," said Lombardo. "But it was her idea. What was I supposed to do? Tell her I didn't want to go to First Night with her after we had such a nice time at *The Nutcracker*?"

"She's having rebound, Joe," said Gilbert. "You're going to end up hurting her all over again, and that's the last thing we want."

"I know," Lombardo said, raising his hands. "And that's why I wanted to have this one last evening with her. I plan to let her down easy tonight. I plan to boost her confidence. When she goes back to school I want her thinking she's somebody special, that she can have any man she wants."

"I'm never going to get used to this," said Gilbert.

"Used to what?" asked Lombardo.

Gilbert put his hands on his hips and stared past Lombardo at the light rain. "Her having any man she wants," he said. "Just be careful." He looked at Lombardo. "And for God's sake, try not to kiss her again."

Gilbert woke up at two o'clock in the morning on the first day of the New Year. Having spent the evening watching First Night on City TV and working his way through a half bottle of President's champagne with Regina, he hadn't even made it to midnight, the combination of champagne and big enteric-coated aspirins making him so drowsy he conked out at eleven-thirty. He turned to Regina. She slept soundly. He pulled the bed covers aside and sat up. He hated champagne. He didn't know why he drank it. He always felt so dried out afterward. He got out of bed and walked to the window. The rain had turned to snow, but a wet snow, ugly and pelting, the flakes whipping past the streetlight like tiny kamikazes. He bent his knees carefully, one after the other, felt the usual nighttime stiffness, as if his knee joints needed oil. He slipped his feet into his slippers and shuffled quietly to the hall.

He hoped, even prayed, that Jennifer would be in bed, but when he saw her door open he knew she hadn't come home yet. He moved into the middle of her room and stared at her bed. Her room smelled of the potpourri she kept on her windowsill. He walked to her bedside table and turned on the lamp. She had *The Lippincott Manual of Nursing Practice,* a heavy blue tome the size of a telephone book, on the floor beside her bed, as well as Gray's *Anatomy* and a paperback medical dictionary. She was in the nursing program at Queen's University in Kingston. He was proud of her. An old candy tin commemorating the coronation of Queen Elizabeth II in 1952, something that had once belonged to his mother, sat on the windowsill, full of loose change. He looked up, checked some of the other books in her bookcase. What was this? She had three of his own books on top of her bookcase: *Toronto Observed—Its Architecture, Patrons, and History; Architecture in North America Since 1950;* as well as his big book on Frank Lloyd Wright and the Prairie School of Architecture. This was their common interest. Architecture. He remembered the family trip to Europe three years ago, how Jennifer had been content to wander for hours through old Norman churches, French châteaus, and German castles, talking architecture with her father while Regina and Nina strayed to the nearest shop or boutique to alleviate their boredom. A common interest. Yet now they seemed to have nothing in common. Now they seemed to come from different planets.

Outside, he heard a car drive up. He walked to the window and saw Joe and Jennifer in Joe's flashy Fiat, a sports car with a black removable top and a school-bus-yellow body. He took a deep breath, happy to see them. Lombardo got out of his car, opened his big golfing umbrella, walked around to the other side, and opened the door for Jennifer. He helped her out of the low-slung sports car and they walked arm in arm to the house. Gilbert grew apprehensive. He was afraid Jennifer might be devastated by Joe's gentle letdown. He heard the front door open. Despite his New Year's resolution not to interfere, he left her room, hurried along the hall and looked over the railing, was just about to go downstairs but stopped when he heard Jennifer giggling. This was letting her down easy? He leaned over the railing, his knees seeming to pop from their sockets, and peered through the banister posts where, to his great consternation, he saw them kissing, their faces partially illuminated by the porch light. He didn't know what to do. He felt paralyzed by the sight of his partner kissing Jennifer. Before he could stop himself he spoke out.

"Do you think that's a good idea?"

The two broke apart, startled by his intrusion.

"Barry?" said Lombardo. Jennifer reached for the light, turned it on, and gazed at her father with contempt. Lombardo frowned at him. "Happy New Year, Barry," he said, his voice flat, sounding as if Gilbert had just ruined his plan for a gentle letdown. Lombardo shut the door.

Gilbert walked around the end of the railing and descended the stairs, not sure what to do. "Did you have fun?" he asked, forcing an innocent tone to his voice.

"Were you waiting for us?" demanded Jennifer.

"No, I . . . I just woke up." Now it was his turn to frown. "And please don't speak to me like that," he said.

"Jennifer, look, I'll call you, okay?" said Lombardo.

She turned to Lombardo, scrutinized him, trying to sniff a turncoat. "Okay," she said. "But don't let him ruin things." She glanced at her father as if he were the most despicable man on earth. "He always likes to ruin things."

She dropped her skates on the floor, took off her coat, flung it on the chair beside the telephone table, and marched up the stairs. Gilbert felt disoriented, out of step with reality, trapped by his own behavior. He heard her tramp down the upstairs hall into her room. She slammed the door. Gilbert cringed at the sound.

"Shit," he said.

"Barry, I'm sorry," said Lombardo.

Gilbert felt more confused than ever. "You were supposed to

let her down easy, Joe," he said. "Do you call kissing her letting her down easy?"

Lombardo glanced up the stairs uneasily. "Maybe we should go to the kitchen," he said. He took his gloves off and stuck them in his pockets. "Before we wake everybody up."

Gilbert shook his head. "I think we already have," he said.

They went through the dining room into the kitchen and sat down at the kitchen table. Gilbert stared at Lombardo, fighting to keep himself under control, to understand all this, comprehend how his good intentions could have gotten so out of control. Lombardo looked at him sheepishly.

"I could use a coffee," he said.

Gilbert had to remind himself that this was Joe, and that Joe would never do anything to intentionally hurt his daughter. He got up distractedly. "Yeah," he said. "Sure." He walked over to the stove and put the kettle on. "I'm sorry, Joe. I'm sorry I'm acting this way. I'm sure you have it all figured out."

Lombardo stared at the brass napkin holder on the table, looking unsure of the situation. "The last thing I want to do is hurt Jennifer," he said. "You know that."

This new dynamic bewildered Gilbert. "Sure I know it."

Lombardo picked up the brass napkin holder and turned it end on end. "She's a wonderful girl, Barry," he said. "You've got a wonderful daughter."

Gilbert stared at Lombardo as the kettle began to hiss. "Is this where you ask me for her hand in marriage?" he said.

Lombardo's face remained set. "I'm serious, Barry," he said. "She's a wonderful girl. Karl was an idiot dumping her like that."

Gilbert was touched by how fervently Lombardo seemed to feel about his daughter. "I think he was too, Joe." Gilbert wondered how he was ever going to find his way out of this alternate universe. "Though I can't say I'm sorry. All I want . . . I just want Jennifer to be happy."

"Then you'll understand why I had to kiss her."

Gilbert tried to make the stretch but he couldn't. "I'm not sure I do," he said.

Lombardo put the brass napkin ring aside and looked up at Gilbert. "Because she was expecting it." He paused. "Because we had a great time. Because we danced, skated, had a drink over at the Sheraton Center, then went back to the bandstand and danced some more. Because it was a romantic evening and all romantic evenings have to end with a kiss. She's a wonderful girl, Barry, but she's also bright. She's not expecting much out of me besides a few pleasant evenings."

"I'm not sure that's true, Joe. She's vulnerable right now."

Lombardo's brow creased in frustration. "What else was I supposed to do?" he asked. The kettle whistled on top of the stove. "She expected it. I didn't want to hurt her feelings. Don't worry, she knows it can't last."

"Yeah, but if you kiss her too much she's going to get other ideas."

"No, she won't."

"Yes, she will."

"She's going back to school in a couple weeks," said Lombardo. "She's got more sense than to make a thing about me. By February I bet she has a new boyfriend."

"Spoken like a true heartbreaker."

"I would never break your daughter's heart."

"I know you wouldn't," said Gilbert. "But it might just end up getting broken anyway."

Gilbert got up and made coffee. While he was stirring the Coffee-Mate into the mugs, Regina came into the kitchen.

"What happened?" she asked. "She's up there crying."

He continued to stir the coffee. He felt as if he were sinking into his alternate universe even deeper. "I caught them kissing at the front door," he said.

She looked at him as if he were speaking a foreign language. "What did you say to her?" she asked.

He shrugged. "I just asked her if kissing Joe was such a good idea," he said.

Regina glanced at Joe, who looked like a fox caught robbing the henhouse. "What's so bad about that?" she asked. As if kissing Lombardo seemed like a good idea, even a desirable one. Gilbert felt his face settling. Joe immediately brightened.

"Tell her I'll call her tomorrow," he said. "Tell her I've got everything under control."

Regina stared at the steaming cups of coffee, then finally nodded. "Okay," she said. "I'll do that." She glanced at Gilbert. "And try not to stay up too late, Barry. You're always cranky in the morning when you stay up too late."

Gilbert watched his wife leave the kitchen. Why was he the culprit here? He brought the coffee over to the table and sat down. He slouched. He felt defeated. He wasn't going to fight anymore.

"Look, Barry, you've got to trust me on this," said Lombardo. "I'll make sure she's all right. She's going to be fine by the time she goes back to school."

"Whatever you say, Joe."

"Don't worry."

"Can't I worry?" he said, looking up. "I'm her father. Just let me worry, okay?"

"She'll go back to school, she'll get caught up in her classes, she'll make new friends, she'll forget about me, and by March break she'll be fine."

Gilbert nodded sullenly. "Whatever you say, Joe."

"Trust me," said Lombardo. "That's how it's going to happen."

"Are you going to see her again?" he asked.

Lombardo looked away. The man looked as guilty as a skunk. "We've got a date a week this Friday," he said. "It was her idea. I swear, it will be the last."

"Why didn't you just tell her no?" said Gilbert. "It's not that hard, you know."

Lombardo looked as if he were growing impatient with Gilbert, his dark Mediterranean eyes simmering. "Because I just didn't, okay?"

"This is bad, Joe."

"I know it's bad, but what do you want me to do?"

Gilbert took a sip of his coffee. He hardly tasted it. He finally said, "Could you please cancel?" He looked at his hands. "I'm asking you as a friend . . . and I'm asking you as Jennifer's father . . . please . . . think up some excuse. Maybe wait until the day, then tell her you've got to work late on the case. Anything. But please . . . let's just end it. It's time for cold turkey, okay?"

Lombardo nodded weakly. "Okay," he said. "I'm sorry, Barry. I'm sorry it turned out this way."

"Me too, Joe."

* * *

Roger Pemberton from Missing Persons came to Gilbert on the morn-ing of January second, shuffling around the desks and down the aisle carrying a slip of paper in his hand, his huge feet barely leav-ing the floor, his ape-like hands hanging straight down at his sides.

"I got a call from a Detective Doug Pilch earlier today," he murmured. "He's with the City of Tampa Police Department."

Gilbert looked up from his report writing. Outside, sleet fell from the sky. He'd fishtailed twice driving to work today. "They found Garth Surrey?" he asked.

Pemberton shrugged equivocally. "Uh . . . no," he said. "They found a friend of Garth Surrey's."

"A friend?" said Gilbert, pushing back from his desk.

"Steve Zidner." Pemberton paused. Paused for ten seconds, looking around the squad room as if he couldn't remember how he got there. His eyes finally settled on the Christmas tree hung with brass cartridge shells. "Someone he's known for years. Pilch says Zidner came in and told him about Surrey. Zidner and Surrey shared some drinks at a bar in Tampa just before Christmas. Zidner's a drummer." Pemberton lifted his big hand and scratched behind his ear, checked his fingernails, then looked at Gilbert. "Got a little bit of eczema," he informed Gilbert. "The halog cream doesn't seem to be working."

"What about Zidner?" said Gilbert.

"He was playing a job at this place. A place called the Con-cord, one of the local jazz clubs." Pemberton raised his eyebrows, about as animated as his expression ever got. "After the two of them got drinking for a while, Surrey boasted he'd killed his wife's boyfriend, shot him to death. He told Zidner the boyfriend was a Chinese gang member." Pemberton shrugged lethargically. "Thought you might like to know."

"How long before Christmas?" asked Gilbert, sitting forward.

"Well, let's see . . . December the twenty-first."

"And it took Zidner that long to tell Detective Pilch about it?" said Gilbert.

"Don't blame me," said Pemberton.

"Surrey could be anywhere by now."

Pemberton tried to hoist the corners of his lips in a helpful smile, but the effort was too much for him, and he abandoned the attempt. "I got Pilch's number, if that'll do any good," he said, and handed the slip of paper to Gilbert.

Gilbert phoned Tampa and got in touch with Detective Doug Pilch. Pilch sounded like an older man, with the rough voice of a chronic smoker.

"Zidner came to me on the afternoon of the twenty-ninth," said Pilch, "just as I was getting ready to go home. I've been read-ing your lookout posting every day at roll call, especially because we know the Surreys have a place down here, so I immediately knew who Zidner was talking about. I've had Zidner in a few times on drunk and disorderly conduct. I'm not about to believe every damn thing he says. But then he started talking about this Chinese gang member, like you got in your posting, and I knew he had to be telling me something close to the truth."

"Why did he wait so long to come forward?" asked Gilbert. "Eight whole days."

Pilch paused. "Well, he . . . he says he first thought nothing of Surrey's claim. Just a hollow boast. Anybody can start bragging about anything they like, especially when they're drunk, even killing a Chinese gang member. But then Zidner kept thinking about the details. How Surrey climbed a fire escape, how he broke into the Chinaman's third-floor apartment, how the sky had been pissing rain. Zidner figured Surrey wouldn't go to the trouble of all those details if there weren't some truth to it. That's when he came to see me. He gave it to me like he was swearin' on a stack of Bibles, and he was able to confirm at least one of the details in your posting."

"Which one?"

"Zidner says Surrey knew about the fatal gunshot wound to the stomach. So I expect Surrey's your boy."

Gilbert felt his blood quickening. Pilch was right. Garth Surrey could know about the gunshot wound to the stomach only if he had been there. So maybe this had nothing to do with tongs and triads after all. Maybe this was just a jealous husband.

"And Surrey and Zidner saw each other on the twenty-first?" said Gilbert, now thinking about the logistics of tracking the man.

"That's what Zidner says."

"And does Zidner have any idea where Surrey might be?" asked Gilbert.

"No," said Pilch. "Not a one."

FOURTEEN

ROSALYN SURREY, WHEN TOLD OF her husband's boast to Steve Zidner, turned from Gilbert, her hands reaching forward to clutch her knees as she sat in the passenger seat of Gilbert's Lumina. He had the car parked on the sidewalk near the ferry docks, not far from the turnstiles and the boarding area, right next to the Harbor Castle Hilton. He wanted her out of her office, in a place where she could react freely. On the other side of the harbor he saw Ward's Island, low and gray, with a small collection of tiny clapboard houses bearing the brunt of Lake Ontario's worst. The trees out on Hanlan's Point, leafless and gray, huddled like stubble close to the cold wet grounds of the park. The sleet had again turned to rain and lashed against the windshield with an angry persistence. He saw a commuter airplane come in for a wobbly landing at the Island Airport. He was surprised that the control tower hadn't shut the place down, what with all this wind.

"So you know Steve Zidner," he said.

She looked up, gave him a distracted nod. "He's one of Garth's oldest friends," she said. "They played in a band a long time ago." She wore a dark woolen coat and a black beret. Her gloves, he noted, were new, black leather lined with rabbit fur.

"Would you mind telling me what's going on, Rosalyn?" asked Gilbert. "Could we have another go?"

She hesitated, struggled, lifted her hands from her knees, looked at them as if she weren't sure what to do with them, then swung her head quickly away, sniffling, fighting to control herself. She was a strong woman. She was willing to stand up to a lot. But under these circumstances he wondered how far she would go, whether she would tell the truth once and for all. She didn't fall back or regroup as she had done on previous occasions. She simply allowed the news to wash over her, to confuse her, and, at last, to overwhelm her. She showed her grief. She mourned for the loss of Edgar, he knew that. He could tell it in her grief-blasted eyes. She finally allowed Gilbert to see her grief. She reached into her purse and pulled out a small package of Kleenex. She withdrew one from the cellophane wrapping and dabbed her eyes.

"I was going to leave Garth," she said. Rosalyn got her tears under control. "When I was younger, I admired Garth. I adored him. Ten years ago I was a much different woman." Her lips squeezed together, and she seemed to be swallowing against a hard knot in her throat. "I didn't want then what I want now." She shook her head. "All I wanted was Garth. I worshiped him. Not only was he a consummate musician, but he had mastered the art of . . . well, the art of living." She turned to him with a deprecating grin. "Foolish, isn't it, the way that sounds? But everything he said or did seemed to have meaning." She looked at the dashboard with unseeing eyes.

"He had this energy, this power . . . and he hypnotized me with it. I gladly let myself be hypnotized. I was so young then. I didn't know any better. I didn't know how things could be so easily ruined by . . . by marriage. When I married him, I began to expect things from him. And that was a mistake. Garth's not that sort of man. You can't expect anything from him. You have to take whatever he wants to give you."

Gilbert saw this was hard for Rosalyn. Though he had specific questions he wanted to ask her, he let her go, allowed her to continue as she might. "Marriage is a funny thing," he said, offering this neutral comment to let her know he understood.

"I don't know whether he lost interest in me," she said, "or whether he felt he could just take me for granted, that I was safe and secure, and would stick with him no matter what he did. He had his music. He had his friends. And there wasn't much time left over for our marriage." She looked at Gilbert, her eyes wide. "How would you feel?" she asked. "You spend all this time in the sun, and the minute you marry him you suddenly have to spend all your time in the shade. We have a spot on the front lawn under our maple tree. Every year I try to plant new grass there. I plant it early, before the leaves come out, and at first it grows well, green and lush, but as soon as the leaves get big, and the shade grows thick, the grass pales, and finally dies. That's what I mean. I married him, and suddenly I didn't have any sunlight. He never spent any time with me. I had nothing to do. He was never around."

"It must have been hard," said Gilbert.

"I thought I would go mad with boredom." She nodded to herself. "So I decided I had to do something with all my extra time." She sniffled again, looked out the window. "I thought, to hell with

Garth. I started seeing some of my old friends. Patricia Wong was one of them. She's Arnold Wong's daughter. This was around election time eight years ago. I went to her parents' house for dinner one night, and I saw all these political pamphlets, and I started talking to Arnold, and I found him interesting, and believed in what he was trying to do for the city. I volunteered to work as a member of his campaign staff. I threw myself into it, and it really helped me, really made me forget about how bad my marriage was. I was thankful to Patricia. I was thankful to Arnold. Arnold got me interested in politics. That's made a big difference in my life."

"Life's a lot better when you believe in something," he said.

She nodded. "Working for Arnold made me feel useful. It made me feel as if I were doing something worthwhile. It gave me a sense of accomplishment, a feeling that I really mattered, like I was in the sun again." She looked away, stared out at the rain. "Then when Arnold had his heart attack and had to step down, and it looked like Sam Petronis was going to become councillor, I made the decision to step in, especially because I knew Petronis would wreck half of Arnold's work if I didn't do something to stop him. I got the mayor to support me, fought one of the dirtiest campaigns this town has ever seen, and won. I was twenty-eight, the second-youngest councillor ever."

He waited. "And how did Garth feel about that?"

She nodded, facing the question bravely, yet now with unmistakable woe in her eyes. "I wanted his support," she said. "Not his political support, just his . . . his support. I longed for his support. His emotional support. I asked for his support." She shook her head. "But he didn't seem to care. He couldn't take it seriously. He couldn't see how municipal politics could matter to anyone but the

politicians involved in them." She turned to Gilbert, her eyes focus-
ing with silent entreaty. "So I switched off. We somehow got
through the next few years, but it was like I was dead to him. I still
love him, but I . . . when you don't feel there's anything connecting
you . . . he always thought I'd be there for him, no matter what he
did, and I guess he was surprised when I . . . I'm afraid he feels he
has a lot to be bitter about these days, Barry. But he brought it on
himself. He keeps griping about an emotional shortfall on my part."
Her expression softened. "And that's what we're here to talk about,
isn't it?" she said. "This emotional shortfall? How he and I don't
connect anymore?"

"I'm sorry?" he said.

She looked at him with deepening grief. "Edgar," she said,
simply, her voice clear, riding over the sound of the rain. "Can you
blame me? Edgar gave me all the things Garth wasn't able to give
me anymore."

So, thought Gilbert. Here it was. After a brief history of her
sunless life with Garth, Rosalyn Surrey had finally brought herself to
the brink. "No," he said. "I can't blame you."

She smiled at the concession. "Thank you," she said.

"I'm sorry about Edgar," he said.

She looked away. She shivered and he turned up the heat.
"Edgar was like . . . like a promise to me, a promise that life could
turn out to be something more than it was turning out to be," she
said. She chuckled despondently at her tangle of words. Then she
grew still. Her grief took hold again. "Those photographs," she said.
"Edgar insisted we take those. He said I had to be recorded for pos-
terity." She smiled at the memory, but the smile was weak, fleeting.
"He knew how to flatter me. But most of all . . . most of all, he knew

how to make me feel lucky. He made me understand what it was to live again. I didn't even care when Garth found out. I felt so lucky to be with Edgar that I didn't care about anything."

"And when Garth found out, was he jealous?" he asked. "Because that's what we're here to talk about too."

"Oh, yes, Garth was jealous," she confirmed. "But Garth had his chance. And he blew it. I wasn't going to wait forever."

Gilbert's shoulders tightened. Time to jump in. "Do you think Garth killed Edgar?" he asked. "Out of jealousy?"

Rosalyn shook her head. "No," she said. "He exaggerates a lot of the time. I can see how he might tell Steve he killed Edgar. But I don't think he would ever actually do it. One thing about Garth, he talks a lot. Speaks first and thinks later."

Gilbert sighed. He had to sketch a broader picture for her. "The details he gave Zidner are details only the killer could know," he said.

She turned to him. "Really?" she said.

"Yes," he said.

She turned, stared at the glove compartment, her lips pursed in worry. "I still don't think he would do it. He hasn't got the nerve. He used to have a lot of nerve. But he drank his nerve away. He's just a sad drunk now. The details . . . I wouldn't know about that. A lucky guess? I think it would be awfully sad if Garth turned out to be the one who killed Edgar. I'd never forgive myself."

"And you have no idea where he was on the night of the fifteenth?"

She turned to him. Her face looked pale now. "No," she said. "He never tells me where he goes. He never did. He insists we're not that kind of couple."

*   *   *

A short while later, Lombardo paged Gilbert. Gilbert answered the page just as he got back to College Street. Lombardo was in Oakville, a well-to-do community thirty-five kilometers west of Toronto. Communicating by cell phone, Lombardo told him Halton Regional Police had discovered Tony Mok's Volkswagen Golf parked on a side street near the lake.

"I've called a tow truck from work but I thought we better make a thorough check before anyone touches it," he said. "How soon can you get here?"

Gilbert glanced outside at the freezing rain. "Have you seen the crap that's falling from the sky?" he asked.

"So an hour?" said Lombardo.

"At least."

On the way to Oakville, Gilbert thought about Garth Surrey, went through the items of evidence against him one by one. He knew the details of the crime scene. Then there was Dock Wen's description. And what about the beige Isotoner? Might Garth have been wearing those gloves? He passed low modern factories, sleek, bright, many made out of reflective glass. The case against Garth Surrey seemed to be getting stronger. Despite all the evidence they had against Tony Mok. Gilbert took the turnoff to Trafalgar Road and headed for the lakeshore.

He found Joe Lombardo on Windermere Street, a street lined with gracious stucco homes. The street ran straight to the lake. The wind was up, blowing from the south, feeding the province yet more rain-saturated air from the Gulf of Mexico. The waves, eight-foot breakers, stormed onto the beach in a gray flood of curl and foam, and the air had a faint underwater smell, of old algae and dead fish. Mok's white Golf with gold hubcaps stood at the curb, three limp parking tickets under its windshield wiper. The car looked abandoned. Lombardo sat in one of the older unmarked Luminas. A police tow truck had nudged up to the sidewalk across the street and Gilbert saw the tow-truck operator looking at them, his face blurred by the rain against the glass.

Gilbert got out of his car. Joe did the same.

"Christ, this rain," said Lombardo. He had to raise his voice to make himself heard over the sound of the waves at the end of the street.

"You look cold," said Gilbert.

Lombardo nodded at the old Lumina. "There's something wrong with the heater," he said. "I had barely enough heat to keep the steam off my windshield."

"You should have climbed in with the tow-truck driver."

"He just got here," said Lombardo.

The tow-truck driver rolled down his window. "You want me to hook it up?" he called.

The rain came down in squalls around them. "No," called Gilbert. "We'll tell you when. But do you have a slim-jim? We need to get inside."

"Sure," called the tow-truck operator. He yanked the hood of his anorak over his head, got out of the truck, went to the back tool compartment, and pulled out a slim-jim. Walking over to the Golf, he slid the slim-jim between the window and door, hooked the lock, and had the car door open in seconds. He looked at the two detectives. "Call me if you need me." He hurried back to his truck.

Gilbert pondered Mok's white Golf. "Let's take a look," he said.

The first thing Gilbert noticed when he opened the door was the brown stain on the shoulder harness.

"What's that?" asked Lombardo.

"Looks like blood," said Gilbert. "Here's some more on the headrest."

"Want me to get the leuco?" asked Lombardo.

Gilbert stared at the stains. "I think you better," he said.

While Lombardo got the leuco malachite applicator out of his car, Gilbert edged his way into the Golf looking for more blood. Other than these few smears on the shoulder harness and the headrest, the car looked clean. The interior reeked of stale cigarettes—the ashtray overflowed with half-smoked butts, as if Mok didn't have the patience to smoke cigarettes more than halfway down. Lombardo came back with the applicator.

"Here," he said.

"Thanks," said Gilbert.

Gilbert daubed the cotton-tipped applicator to the smear on the shoulder harness. The applicator turned blue.

"Bingo," said Gilbert, forgetting the cold and the rain.

"Really?" said Lombardo.

"Really," said Gilbert.

But whose blood, wondered Gilbert. He would have to press the lab on this.

They continued to search the car. While they searched, Gilbert asked Lombardo about his date with Jennifer.

"Have you canceled yet?"

"No," said Lombardo. "But I'm going to. I think if I cancel on the day, like you said, it will look more legit."

"As long as you cancel," said Gilbert.

"Don't worry," said Lombardo. "I will."

Fifteen minutes later Lombardo said, "Hey, look at this." Lombardo stood at the rear of the car, at the hatchback, holding up a bullet. "I found it in the tire well."

Gilbert halted his inspection of the glove compartment and came round to have a look. "Is that what I think it is?" asked Gilbert.

Lombardo nodded. "A thirty-eight-caliber soft-nose wadcutter." He shook his head. "Why do they have to be so dumb, Barry?" he asked. "It takes all the fun out of it."

Gilbert shook his head in mock commiseration. "I don't know, Joe," he said. "I don't know."

Yet he still couldn't help thinking of Garth Surrey. And of Pearl Wu. And of Foster Sung. All were still red-flagged as suspects as far as he was concerned, despite this blood in the car and the bullet in the tire well.

They finished their search, bagged their evidence, and sat in Gilbert's Lumina. He had the heat on. "Get yourself good and warmed up," he said. "You have a long drive back."

"Thanks," said Lombardo.

They sat there talking for another few minutes, and were just speculating how long it would take the lab to test the blood, when Gilbert's pager went. He checked the number and looked up at Lombardo. "It's Carol," he said.

Gilbert lifted his cell phone, dialed the Homicide office, and got Carol Reid on the phone.

The squad secretary had news for him. Unexpected news. Bad news.

"Your wife is in the Emergency Department of Toronto East General Hospital," Carol said. "I don't have any details. They wouldn't give me any details because of their confidentiality policy, only that Regina had sustained some nonthreatening injuries, and that she was asking for you, wanted you to come to the hospital to get her."

The darkness of the afternoon took on a whole new cast, as if the contrast on a television set had been changed.

"Thanks, Carol," he said, and rang off.

Gilbert deadened his panic, accepting how the whole mood of a day could alter with a single unexpected phone call. The afternoon really seemed quite dark, as if he were looking at the world through a smoky lens. He realized he should have asked Carol for the hospital number. Maybe it didn't matter. If he put the light on top of the Lumina's roof he would get there quickly anyway. He ignored his adrenaline, and, in what he thought was a slow and deliberate way, turned to Lombardo. Joe looked flat and distant.

"You all right?" asked Joe.

Like shifting gears without a clutch, as if somewhere inside him metal scraped against metal. "Regina's in the Emergency Department at Toronto East General," he said. The noise of the rain seemed to fade around them.

"What happened?" asked Lombardo. Lombardo's words sounded far away. Blood drummed past Gilbert's ears.

"Look, Joe, I've got to go," he said. Even his own voice sounded muted. "I wish I could let you warm up longer." He smiled but his face felt stiff, awkward. "I'm going to talk to the garage about that damn heater."

"Sure," said Lombardo.

"Make sure no one fucks with Mok's car."

"Keep an eye on your speed," said Joe, opening the door. "Keep looking at the little red needle."

Gilbert nodded, a tense grin on his face. He already felt a world away from Lombardo. "I'll see you at headquarters," he said.

Once he got to the highway Gilbert grabbed his police light from under his dashboard, stuck it on the roof, and turned on his siren. He sped down the inside lane at 140 kilometers per hour. After he hit one-forty, he didn't bother keeping his eye on the little red needle. Few cars traveled the expressway inbound to Toronto at this time of the day, but just over the rail, coming the other way, the traffic inched bumper-to-bumper, stop-and-go all the way, with people coming home from work. The few cars on his side of the highway eased away from him, giving him plenty of room. His mind churned with speculation. A car accident? A fall? Or something more ominous?

In twenty-five minutes, Toronto's skyline came into view, the CN Tower rising like a futuristic needle high above all the financial towers, the Skydome nestling like a giant dinosaur egg at its base, with the Convention Center just beyond. In this weather, with the sky dark, and the clouds low, and the rain turning to ice, the city was anything but a welcoming vision, more like a gray and hellish Babylon glittering with the hurtful glare of its million lights under the pall of an overcast sky. Off to the right, invisible from view, but with the palpable presence of a bad nightmare, surged Lake Ontario, black, cold, and polluted. He raced onto the elevated Gardner Expressway, his car like a fury, red light flashing wildly, his siren screaming as he passed the canyon-like streets.

He arrived at the hospital twenty minutes later. The triage nurse smiled at him reassuringly and told him to follow the blue line along the wall. He followed it left, then right, knew the way by heart, had been here many times, had seen many assault casualties turn into homicides here. He passed an old woman lying on a gurney with tubes up her nose; a drunk in a wheelchair, the front of his pants covered with blood from a gash on his forehead; and two young doctors viewing X rays of a fractured hand on panel lights. He passed cubicle after cubicle until he finally saw Jennifer, then Nina peeking out from behind a curtain at the end. Nina hurried toward him with that innate self-control that was the hallmark of her personality.

"She was mugged, dad," she said. "Can you believe it? She was mugged in the school parking lot right after her meeting. You should see her. She's got bruises all over her face. And she's got a gash on her head."

Gilbert sped ahead of his youngest daughter and went into his wife's cubicle.

Regina sat cross-legged on the bed, the sheets nested around her hips and thighs. On the right side of her head, blood matted her hair, and she was busy cleaning it out with an alcohol swab. Her left eye was swollen, her lip was split, and she had an angry bruise on her cheek.

"Shit," said Gilbert. He sensed Jennifer staring at him sullenly. "You were mugged."

"No."

"Nina said you were mugged."

"They didn't take anything. They could have taken my purse."

"Did you call the police?"

"You're here, aren't you?" she said, grinning through her split lip.

"I'm going to get the badge number from the triage nurse."

"Barry, calm down."

"I want to get a copy of his report."

"Her report."

"Her report."

"Look, just sit down, okay?" said Regina. "You look like you're in worse shape than I am."

"What happened?"

"I was attacked."

"I know, but . . . did you get a good look at him?"

"They were wearing ski masks."

"They?" he said, growing even more alarmed.

"There were two of them," said Regina.

"Tell him what the guy told you, mom," said Jennifer.

"Jennifer, please," said Regina.

Barry looked first at Jennifer, then at Regina. "What are you talking about?" he asked, annoyed with Jennifer. "What did the guy tell you?"

Regina looked away, a picture of calm. "He gave me a warning," she said.

"A warning?"

"Or at least something to pass along to you."

"To me?" he said. "What did he say?"

She looked at him, her face growing serious. "You're to stay away from Chinatown."

He lifted his hand to his temple and rubbed. "Shit," he said, breathlessly, the expletive issuing from his mouth like a hatchet chop. "And the guy was for real?"

"Barry, calm down."

"I'm going to get a twenty-four-hour security detail for you and the girls," he said. "And I'm off the case as of right now."

"Don't be ridiculous."

"Look at your lip," he complained.

"I didn't even want to come here," said Regina. "Jennifer made me come. All I needed was a little ice and a Band-Aid."

"My first responsibility is to my family," said Gilbert.

"Then why don't you spend more time with us for a change?" said Jennifer, now past the point where she could contain her sullenness. "No wonder we all turned into losers."

"Was that really called for?" asked Regina.

"You might be a loser," said Nina, "but I'm not."

"Barry, I don't want you to quit the case," said Regina. "That would just be giving in to them. I don't mind a couple of plain-clothes officers around for a while, but I'll be really mad if you quit the case for my sake. They didn't really hurt me all that badly."

"Mom, how can you say that?" asked Jennifer. "Look at your head."

"What happened to your head?" asked Gilbert, peering through her thick blond hair.

"Oh, it's nothing," she said, looking even more annoyed with Jennifer. "I slipped on the ice when they pushed me and I hit my head against the Windstar's side-view mirror, that's all."

"She's got nine stitches, dad," said Jennifer, now sounding as if she were gloating. *"Nine,"* she repeated. Her face turned red, blotchy, as if beneath her sullenness she were seething. He knew this wasn't about Regina's nine stitches; he knew this was still about Karl Randall. "And it's all your fault, dad," she said. "Every last bit of it."

He looked at his daughter, but he didn't know who she was anymore. He heard her voice, but it didn't sound like Jennifer's voice at all. He looked into her eyes, but he couldn't find her there.

And the afternoon seemed darker still . . .

*   *   *

The next morning, Gilbert and Lombardo were called to investigate a suicide at Forest Hill General Hospital. From one hospital to another, he thought. They had to wait several minutes to get an elevator up to the twelfth floor—the Otis Elevator guys had three of the five out of service for repairs. Gilbert shifted impatiently from foot to foot. He felt he should have taken the day off work, that he should have stayed home with Regina—but she insisted he go. So here he was, with Joe.

"It had to be either the Kung Lok or the 14K," he said. "I get physically weak just thinking about it. Nowak's going to send some guys up today to park outside the house. He's not such a bad guy, you know."

"I've been thinking about that," said Lombardo.

"What? About Nowak?"

"No. About your wife. It doesn't make sense."

"What doesn't make sense?"

"That the Kung Lok or 14K should send someone to beat her up."

"They want us off the case," said Gilbert. "That's obvious."

"Yes, but they're not stupid," said Lombardo. "Take a look at Foster Sung. And at Peter Hope. They wouldn't do something like that. I know you're a little freaked out, Barry, but this may not be as bad as you think. I don't think the Kung Lok and the 14K are after Regina."

"You don't?"

"Foster Sung's too smart to send someone after your wife. And so's Peter Hope. They're both sharp. Neither of them would need-lessly make extra trouble for themselves by sending some guys after your wife as a way of giving you a warning. They'll try to sidestep Edgar's murder as quietly as they can. These guys are pros."

"But if not the 14K or the Kung Lok, then who?" asked Gilbert.

"Donald Kennedy," said Lombardo, "that's who."

Their elevator came, and they squeezed on with fifteen doctors, nurses, and other hospital staff. This was what he admired about Lombardo. The elevator began its slow climb, stopping at floor after floor. The man could take a problem and look at it from all sides. Gilbert felt Lombardo was becoming the partner he had always wanted, a savvy, street-smart guy he could count on, a man who was willing to do the work, put in extra hours, and not just punch a clock until he retired.

The elevator doors opened on the twelfth floor and they got out.

"So why Donald Kennedy?" asked Gilbert.

"The guy smells," said Lombardo. "First we have the discrepancy in his report about the Chinese man behind the restaurant at the time of the murder." They began walking toward the nursing station. "Then we have the discrepancy between his run-sheet and the dispatch tapes. Eight minutes. *Eight* minutes. That's unreal. Eight minutes in court can make or break a case. Then there's that bit about the towel. Foster Sung says he used a yellow dish towel to stanch the flow of Edgar's blood. Dr. Blackstein says Edgar might have lived had he had that towel. Kennedy says he saw no towel. Did someone take that towel away? We don't know. Was it Kennedy? We don't know. But Kennedy was there by himself, and he could have easily taken the towel away." Lombardo shrugged. "For what purpose? To ensure that Edgar bled to death? That's what I think. The guy knew Edgar had information, like Rosalyn Surrey was telling you. He saw his opportunity to keep Edgar quiet, and he took it.

Kennedy hears the ten-seventy-one and he goes for it, even though he's on the other side of town."

On the overhead, Gilbert heard switchboard calling out a code blue—a heart attack—in the MRI suite.

"And after he does all that," said Gilbert, "he sees I'm sniffing too close, so he beats the crap out of Regina as a warning." He shook his head. "You know, Joe, I think you might be right. I think Kennedy might be stupid enough to try something like this."

Gilbert saw Detective Gordon Telford come out of a patient room down the hall.

"I certainly don't think it's a triad thing, Barry," said Lombardo.

Telford, the primary on the suicide, came up to them. "It's open-and-shut, guys," he said. "But if you want to have a look . . ."

Gilbert nodded. "Sure."

They went inside and discovered that the patient had hanged himself from the shower rail in the bathroom with a sheet. The bathtub was splattered with urine and fecal matter and the man's face was blue.

Gilbert shrugged. "If you're determined, you're determined," he said. He turned to Telford. "Did you speak to the nurse on duty?"

Telford nodded. "I got her statement," he said. "She's still here if you want a few words with her."

Gilbert contemplated the suicide. Poor guy. But his mind was elsewhere. He was thinking of Kennedy. "No," he said. "Tell her she can go home. Get the body out of here. I imagine they're going to need the bed."

Still thinking of Kennedy. And of how he had beat the crap out of Regina.

CHAPTER
FIFTEEN

GILBERT MET CONSTABLE JEREMY AUSTIN the next day. They parked on Victoria Street next to Massey Hall, and after getting a couple of cappuccinos from a nearby coffee place, Gilbert once again asked Austin to name names. Austin's wide black face settled with reluctance as he looked away. Gilbert glanced up at Massey Hall and waited. Thirty years ago, with hair down to his shoulders and his ragged denim bell-bottoms sweeping the dusty gallery floor, he had seen Jefferson Airplane perform in this venerated concert hall. Now he was a homicide detective with two teenaged daughters, daughters who had never even heard of Jefferson Airplane. The years marched by so quickly; 1971 seemed like such a long time ago. He could hardly remember his life before Regina.

"I can't name names yet," said Austin, with a harried stubbornness that exasperated Gilbert. "I told you that."

"Donald Kennedy," said Gilbert. "There's a name."

Austin didn't react. He neither denied nor confirmed. He just sat there looking uncomfortable.

"Paul Szoldra," said Gilbert. "There's another name."

Now Austin looked even more uncomfortable. He looked ashamed of himself. "I've got to protect my family," he said. "Until these guys are off the street, I stay neutral in all this."

When Gilbert tried to reschedule his appointment to see Pearl Wu, Peter Hope again gave him the runaround. Gilbert was tired of it. So was Lombardo. Interrogation by appointment only wasn't going to work. If they didn't necessarily have enough probable cause to arrest Pearl as a suspect in the murder of Edgar Lau, they certainly had enough for a limited search of her dwelling. Not that Gilbert particularly wanted to search her condominium at One Park Lane. He just wanted access. Access to Pearl. By herself. Without interference from the Red Pole.

He walked around her condominium, waiting for her, having obtained entrance from the building manager. Lombardo was following up on the blood found in Tony Mok's car. Gilbert expected more opulence. He expected her condominium to face south, toward the lake. But it faced east, where, across the street, he saw the National Life Building, a generic office tower too drab for words. Her furniture looked like department-store stuff. He expected at least a Maytag dishwasher in the kitchen, but there was no dishwasher at all. Pearl's Toronto residence was more like a cheap hotel suite, a place to crash when she flew in from Hong Kong, with all the furniture scuffed and used, the way furniture in a cheap hotel looked. She had a few Chinese prints on the wall, one of a temple, another of a junk on the water, and another of a Chinese fan dancer in a traditional costume, but these did little to personalize the place, were of such poor quality Gilbert guessed they had to be items from the boatloads of Chinatown tourist-trade garbage Bing Wu sent over from Hong Kong.

He walked to the bedroom. The bedroom looked the same: secondhand furniture, track lighting with one of the fixtures missing, beige walls, wall-to-wall carpeting with a few coffee stains here and there. Her clothes lay all over the floor. He stared at her clothes. She was a former fashion model and she just threw her clothes on the floor? Not only that, they looked junky: jeans, sweatshirts, sweatpants, not exactly high-fashion threads.

He went back to the living room and sat down in one of the chairs, feeling the unevenness of old foam underneath the beige corduroy upholstery. He had to slouch. He had no choice; it was that kind of chair. The chair smelled sickly sweet, as if something had died inside it. He waited. Fifteen minutes later he heard a key in the door. He struggled out of the chair—like getting out of a hammock—and reached the front part of the living room just as Pearl entered the condominium. She turned on the vestibule light.

When she saw him, she immediately drew her gun. He looked at the gun. A two-shot Derringer. With elaborate silver scrollwork all over the barrel. Despite all her junky clothes, she still felt she had to make a fashion statement, at least when it came to firearms. The gun looked so small in her hands. She had strong-looking hands, big hands, hands that looked purposely strengthened through exercise.

"Hello," she said, not alarmed, just ready. "Please to identify yourself."

She was indeed stunning, even with the scar across her face, an almond-shaped mark an inch across, the color of bamboo.

"I'm Detective-Sergeant Barry Gilbert of Metro Homicide," he said. "I have a warrant to search your residence in regard to the murder of Edgar Cheng Lau. The warrant's over there on the dining room table."

Keeping an eye on Gilbert, she moved to the dining room table, lifted the document, and scanned it quickly. When she was finished, she put the warrant down and looked at Gilbert. He contemplated Pearl Wu. Her coat was what Nina might call retro-funk—artificial brown leather with poodle-like rims of artificial black fur trimming the collars and sleeves, so tacky, so 1970s Motown, he knew it had to be stylish, even in vogue. Her pants were made of white polyester, slightly flared, widening discreetly over her black platform shoes. She wore peach-colored eye shadow and had hoop earrings. And a diamond wedding ring with a rock the size of a peanut on her finger.

"You are armed?" she asked.

He pulled his jacket aside and showed her the grip of his Glock 9-mm semiautomatic handgun.

"Please to put the pistol on the table," she said.

"No."

She raised her Derringer higher, steadied it with both hands, and narrowed her eyes. How easily she handled that gun. Women rarely murdered, and when they did, they rarely used guns, were fonder of knives. But Pearl Wu, living in the crucible of the Chinese gang underworld, was undoubtedly an exception. Pearl Wu, he decided, would use a gun, had maybe even used one on Edgar Lau.

"Put the gun away," he said, "or I'm going to arrest you. Not only that, when you pull a gun on a police officer, you take your own life into your hands."

She stared at him, remained perfectly still. Then put the gun down. She smiled. "I didn't kill him, you know," she said, almost cheerfully. "I would never kill Edgar. I always nice to him. I rub his shoulders when they get sore. I buy him presents. I buy him candy. I always buy him candy. I would never kill him. Whenever I come from Hong Kong I give him presents. So much to buy in Hong Kong," she said. "Everywhere you look. Lots of clothes. Lots of candy. He likes candy. So do I. He addicted to candy. I keep lots here for him." She looked at him slyly. "You want some?"

As if suddenly the subject of Edgar's murder were of secondary importance to candy.

"No thanks."

"I buy gourmet candy," she said. "You like it."

Her obsession struck him as odd and inappropriate. "I'm not really fond of sweets," he said.

"You like these," she said. "Edgar eat them all the time."

"Mrs. Wu, I'm here to ask you some questions," he said.

"I got plenty," she coaxed.

"No, it's all right."

Before he could stop her she hurried to the kitchen, overcome by this weird enthusiasm for candy. She came back with a big bowl of it, expensive stuff from a specialty shop: peanut brittle, saltwater toffee, French nougat, Turkish delight, designer jelly beans, marzipan balls, and Scotch kisses. All of it wrapped in small individual packets of decorated cellophane.

"Try these," she said, pointing to the marzipan balls. "They're really good."

He looked at her, caught off guard by her insouciance, her seeming lack of grief over the passing of Edgar Lau. She was gorgeous, sweet, frivolous, unpredictable, impulsive, even wacky, reminded him of a silver ball in a pinball machine bouncing all over the place. She lifted one of the marzipan balls, unwrapped it, shoved it in her mouth, then looked at him with wide-eyed curiosity. He found he couldn't stop looking at her hair. Her hair shone like black satin.

"So, Barry, you find what you looking for?" she said, her Cantonese accent sharp but piquant as she nodded toward the warrant.

She now didn't seem at all concerned that he should be here in her condominium waiting for her. That she should so familiarly use his first name suggested some sly nose-thumbing, as if she had indeed lived and breathed in the triad underworld a long time. What unusual survival skills she must have. What a bizarre journey her life must be.

"You know as well as I that I'll never find those things on the list there," he said. "The gun and so forth. I'm here to talk to you. Peter Hope was making that difficult. So I used the warrant as an excuse."

She raised her eyebrows. "He always like that," she said. "He like a tennis player. Always bounce the ball back at you."

Gilbert took another moment. This was a woman who had three offices in Toronto? A woman who handled millions of dollars in real estate transactions each day? He was going to have to discard his preconceptions about Pearl Wu. She was singular. No wonder Hope wanted Gilbert to stay away from her. She showed not the slightest trace of nervousness, maintained her zany cheerfulness despite the seriousness of the situation.

"As far as we've been able to determine," he said, "you were the last one to see Edgar Lau alive before he was killed."

For the purpose of this interview, he was going to go with Foster Sung's version of events. Not Hope's.

"This is correct," she said.

He stared at her. Did this mean that Foster Sung had been

telling the truth, and that Hope had been lying? Did Pearl not realize how badly she incriminated herself by confirming Foster Sung's
version of events: that Sung came up to ask them to his table in the
restaurant to meet Tak-Ng Lai, then left them alone, to finish their
argument, while he went back downstairs?

"And you had an argument," he said, wanting to get the
details straight.

Her brow arched, an acknowledgment to Gilbert; she smiled
with some noticeable admiration, as if she believed he might have
more skill than she had at first assumed. "Who tell you that?" she
asked.

He suddenly felt as if he were in a game of parry and thrust.
How much to reveal? How much to hide? He liked to use his facts
carefully, and only if they might shake loose yet other facts. In this
case, he had a name, and he thought he might use that name as a
wedge.

"Foster Sung," he said. He waited, gauged her reaction, but
her face was as still as a painting, poised in a half-smile, as if she
were prepared to be gracious under any and all circumstances. "He
said he went up to ask you and Edgar to join him and his guests at
his table in the restaurant, and that he heard the two of you arguing before he knocked on the door."

She nodded, the same half-smile still on her face, yet he now
sensed a glimmer of concealed hysteria in her eyes, as if maybe Foster Sung's name had acted as a wedge after all. "Why you care if we
argue?" she asked. He heard an echo of strain in her voice, a nuance
that suggested the grief he was looking for. "We argue. All the time,
argue. That night not any different."

"I'm trying to establish a clearer picture of what went on that
night," he said. "Would you mind going over it with me? Foster Sung

came up to Edgar's apartment and asked the two of you to come to his table in the restaurant, you both declined, then Foster Sung went back downstairs?"

She had to think about this. "That is correct," she finally said.

He stared again. Foster Sung had just become a much weaker suspect. Too bad for Hukowich and Paulsen. And Peter Hope had lied. Lied to protect Pearl? To cast suspicion on Foster for the purposes of taking it away from Pearl? If so, why didn't Pearl seem to care? She was alone with Edgar in the apartment, sketching in for Gilbert her window of opportunity. Why would she admit to it so freely? Particularly if she was guilty? Was she innocent after all? He began to think she might be, particularly because their harder evidence pointed toward Tony Mok. Tony Mok coming through the French doors. After Foster had gone. After Pearl had gone. There to steal again. There to take away Edgar's China White. That was the most plausible scenario.

"And you came to the restaurant with Tony Mok?" he asked.

This was also a name he could use, a way to make her understand he knew about the murder, to imply that his knowledge was far-ranging and potentially damaging, to further unbalance her in her grief and strain. But she recovered. The momentary hysteria left her eyes. And she looked as fun-loving and gamesome as ever.

"Tony Mok, he a nice guy," she said.

He smiled, tried to play the game right along with her. "I'm sure he is," he said.

"He not so serious," she said. "Everybody so serious all the time. You too serious, Barry."

He smiled mildly, pretending to be taken with her. She didn't seem to realize she was trying too hard to be cute.

"Was Edgar Lau always serious?" he asked.

He hated to be cruel, but sometimes he knew he had no choice. He knew that lovers argued. He felt sorry for her in her sudden transparency. Her strain and grief came back, and now, at least to his eye, she looked faintly ridiculous, even pathetic, in her poodle-like coat, a poor kid whose mother had dressed her in funny-looking clothes, a woman who in striving for this kinetic retro-funk look had sacrificed some of her own dignity.

"Why you do this?" she asked. The piquancy was gone from her voice, her tone was leaden, and her emotional barometer had plunged. The plunge was so precipitous, so unexpected, he quickly wrenched her back to what he was really after.

"Do you have any idea where Tony went when the two of you parted?" he asked. Regardless of who was alone in the apartment with Edgar, Tony, because of the tangible evidence, still had to be found, and found as quickly as possible.

Pearl looked up, like coming up for air, her Chinese eyes hooded and sweet under their epicanthic lids, her lips pursed to a rosebud, and gazed at him as if from the balcony of a tall building.

"I meet him later in video arcade," she said, her voice soft.

"You did?" said Gilbert.

She stared at him, as if she were still trying to understand him. Gilbert felt there existed a gulf between them, a cultural demarcation that made any meaningful answers and questions difficult and approximate.

"We play Samurai Shodown over and over again," she said. She seemed to brighten a little. "You know that game?"

"No," he said. One of the challenges with Pearl, he decided, was to keep her from getting distracted by her own conversation. "Which arcade?"

"Downtown," she said. "I always forget name."

That didn't surprise him, considering she was from Hong Kong. "And you had fun?" he asked.

"Lots and lots of fun," she said, brightening even more. "Him a riot. All day long I talk, talk, talk, sell, sell, sell. Tony just what a girl need. Him play Samurai Shodown like a pro."

"You wouldn't know where he is now, would you?" asked Gilbert.

Her brow arched, as if she were giving his question serious thought. Finally she said, "He go this way, he go that way, he moving all the time."

Gilbert stopped. She wasn't going to give him anything. So he tried again to unbalance her. "Edgar loved you," he said.

She idly picked some saltwater taffy out of the cut-crystal bowl and put it back. It was as if a veil had been lowered over her face.

"Edgar so serious all the time," she said.

"Was he?"

"He like to argue."

"And do you?" he asked.

"No," she said. "That why I leave early that night. Who know who kill him that night, but it not me. I left. Lot of people see me go."

As an alibi, this was ridiculous. He knew it, and she knew it, but she didn't seem to care.

"And you met Tony Mok later on? Down at the arcade?"

"I already tell you that."

"Okay," he said. "I need to talk to Tony."

"I tell him."

"Will you?"

She suddenly looked impatient with him. "You go now," she said. She no longer seemed willing to be gracious under any and all circumstances. "I a tired girl." She was dismissing him, and he recognized something familiar about the dismissal, an edge to her voice that suggested he shouldn't argue with money and power, that she was through with humoring him. "I need sleep." But there was something more to it than just dismissal. She seemed broken in some way, crushed not only by the death of Edgar, but oppressed by the way she had to live, by her role as a trophy wife to an Asian crime lord. "I have many meetings I go to tomorrow." Beneath her gamesome veneer he now sensed a young woman who had made a mess of her life, who felt trapped by her life. "So you go now." She gave him a brief acquiescent nod, then looked up at him with pleading eyes. "I call you if I see Tony. I tired."

Yes, she was tired. She was exhausted. Exhausted by everything. He felt sorry for her. He didn't come here meaning to feel sorry for her, but he did. And he decided he wasn't going to press her. At least not yet. Not until he had another fact or two that might shed some light on why she looked so trapped. So he left, taking his warrant with him, left her to her sad exhaustion and oppressed soul. She could dismiss, she could evade, she could refuse, but she couldn't hide what he saw in her eyes. And what he saw in her eyes was a thread, a piece of the puzzle, something that connected her to everything, something that, when the time came, she wouldn't be able to deny.

Lab techs retrieved usable blood samples from the shoulder harness and headrest of Tony Mok's Volkswagen Golf, and were quick to match the blood type to Edgar's blood type. But half the world's population had Edgar's blood type. To further individualize the blood required DNA testing, and that meant sending samples to the

Center for Forensic Science, near the university, where the backlog was well over a month long.

"We can't wait forever," said Ross Paulsen, not pleased that Tony Mok should become their prime suspect, wishing simply to eliminate Mok by getting DNA results on the blood samples as quickly as possible. "I'm flying to Washington tonight. I have a meeting there tomorrow. I'll take the samples to our lab, have them work on it around the clock, and fax the results to you Friday morning."

Which he did. On Friday morning, as Gilbert read over the results, he thought Paulsen had to be climbing the walls. The blood did indeed belong to Edgar Lau, and gave Gilbert just the evidence he needed to write a viable warrant on Mok, derailing Paulsen's hope for an indictment against Foster Sung.

Just before noon that same day, the UNESCO case file on Mok from the Children's Aid Society arrived. Much of it confirmed what they already knew: that Mok had been born to a single Vietnamese female by the name of Fang, last name unknown; that Fang subsequently died of diphtheria in the refugee camp; and that Foster Sung had then become Mok's guardian. The case worker's entries charted Mok's emigration from Hong Kong to Canada, his placement with the Kwons, and finally his placement with May Lau. An inclination toward delinquency was noted.

Then came copies of various medical reports—the required documentation immigration officials needed to confirm Mok's state of health prior to granting the boy landed immigrant status. Among these various reports Gilbert found the results of an unusual blood test, not the standard blood test used to determine hemoglobin, platelet, and white cell counts, but something called a blood phenotype. Blood seemed to be the theme of the day. This particular blood phenotype test had been requisitioned by the Prince of Wales Hospital, a hospital not actually in Metropolitan Hong Kong but in the New Territories. The New Territories were a suburban and rural area north of Hong Kong, far from the refugee camp where Mok had been born. The hospital had farmed out the test to a private lab nearby. The blood phenotype, conducted on the date of Mok's birth, puzzled Gilbert. Its origin and date suggested Mok might have actually been born in the Prince of Wales Hospital, not in the refugee camp, as May Lau had originally told them. He checked for a hospital birth record but couldn't find one.

He phoned Dr. Blackstein at the Coroner's Building, asked the doctor about Mok's blood phenotype, and why the test would be performed on a newborn infant.

"For paternity testing," said Blackstein.

"Paternity testing?" asked Gilbert, surprised.

"That's right."

Gilbert thought about this.

"Would the parents need blood phenotypes done as well?" asked Gilbert. "In order to get a match?"

"Yes."

Gilbert took a deep breath. This was indeed odd. Why would anybody want to find out who Mok's real father was when Mok's mother had fled Vietnam in Foster Sung's boat all by herself? What possible interest could anybody have? Gilbert once again flipped through the medical reports but found neither a mother's nor a father's blood phenotype report.

"Is there any other reason why a blood phenotype might be performed on a newborn infant?"

Blackstein paused. "Possibly if the infant had hemolytic disease of the new-born," he said. "But that's rare. Trust me, Barry. Your blood phenotype was done for paternity testing, plain and simple."

That afternoon, while Lombardo took Detectives Telford, Halycz, and Groves to the suburban Chinatowns in Mississauga and Agincourt, Gilbert went to visit May Lau one more time. He hoped Tony Mok might have contacted her since the night of the murder.

The rain, having abated for the last few days, now came down as if making up for lost time. She had tea ready for him, scalding and green, in a teapot adorned with red-and-gold dragons. Shopping coupons were spread out on the table, clipped from flyers and sorted into neat piles, a shopping list in ballpoint Cantonese characters beside them. When he told her Tony Mok was their prime suspect she turned away, looking deeply saddened but not particularly surprised. She finally faced Gilbert with a look of resignation in her eyes. She seemed particularly fragile this morning.

"I wasted a lot of effort on Tony," she said, "and it was all for nothing."

"You're sure you don't know any of his friends?" asked Gilbert. "Friends he might stay with?"

She shook her head. "He had a lot of friends when we lived on First Avenue. But he never kept them for long. He always ended up fighting with them."

"Can you remember any of their names?" he asked.

She stared at her cat. The cat slept on the chair in the corner. But then the cat jerked awake, roused by the sound of banging upstairs. May Lau looked toward the ceiling. Gilbert looked up too. He heard men calling to each other in Cantonese. Then more banging.

"What's going on?" he asked.

"Foster's fixing the ceiling up there," she said. She frowned. "I wish they wouldn't shout like that. It carries right through the floor." She turned to him, doing her best to ignore the banging and shouting. "We used to live in Chinatown East," she said. "Out by the Don Jail. Tony hung around with a gang of street kids there, just before we moved over here. Rough kids. If he's in touch with anybody, he'd be in touch with them. But if you're asking me to remember names . . ." She shook her head, looking much older than her fifty-four years. "It was such a long time ago."

"So Chinatown East," he said. "And you say you lived on First Avenue?"

"Over by Logan," she said. "Right near the railroad tracks."

Gilbert thought this over. "Please get in touch with us if you hear from Tony," he said. He gave her another card in case she'd lost the one Lombardo had given to her.

"I will," she said.

As he went down the stairs into the rain he once again thought about the sound the gunshot had made on the night of the murder. If May Lau could hear the banging and shouting upstairs so easily, why hadn't she been able to hear the gunshot that had killed her son? And if she had heard the gunshot, why was she now trying to hide it?

He came back much later, well past ten in the evening, when the windows in May Lau's apartment were dark. He climbed the stairs to Edgar's apartment and let himself in with the extra set of keys. He turned on the light.

With the scene relinquished a number of days ago, any useful evidence from Edgar's apartment had all but disappeared. But he wasn't here for evidence. The ceiling was patched with drywall compound, and a fine coating of plaster dust covered the kitchen counter. He was here for confirmation. The blood was gone, as were the slashed futons. The books had been put back on the shelves. He was here for comparisons, compelled by that same instinct which had forced him to take the glove down from the tree. He was here to look at the photograph album again.

The photograph album had been put away in a box full of others on the bedroom floor. He lifted it out of the box, placed it on the desk, turned on the desk lamp, and found the picture he was looking for, the one of Foster Sung standing on the boat, the nickel-plated semiautomatic stuck down the front of his pants. Gilbert took out his mug shot of Tony Mok. He looked at Mok's face, then at Sung's face, then back at Mok's face. He thought of the blood phenotype performed by the Prince of Wales Hospital, wondered if there might be other records of Tony to be found there. Why hide it, he wondered? If indeed there was anything to hide. He studied the contours of Mok's cheekbones, then the contours of Sung's cheekbones. Why go to such elaborate lengths to blur the facts? Or was Gilbert just being a desperate detective? He looked at the picture of Ying and Edgar on the yellow Honda in Saigon pinned askew on the bulletin board. He looked at Ying's eyes, then at Mok's eyes, then at Ying's eyes again. Was there anything there, he wondered?

He shook his head.

Nothing was sadder than a desperate detective.

CHAPTER
SIXTEEN

LOMBARDO, GROVES, TELFORD, AND HALYCZ recanvassed not only the suburban Chinatowns but the inner-city ones as well. Lombardo got lucky with Danny Leung again, the *pai-gow* operator out by the Don Jail, who now knew where Tony Mok might be hiding—a converted factory just off First Avenue in the heart of Chinatown East. Gilbert got Judge Dave Lembeck to sign an arrest warrant based on the blood and bullet evidence found in Mok's car. With the warrant on Mok signed, Gilbert and Lombardo moved in on Chinatown East. Neither of them were surprised that Mok should choose this particular community to hide in. Having been raised here as a boy, Mok no doubt felt safest here.

Chinatown East nestled on the slopes of the Don Valley. Chief landmarks in the area included the Don Jail, the Riverdale Palliative Care Hospital, and the Riverdale Public Library. Here in the center of Chinatown East, the King and Gerrard streetcars creaked and moaned through the constantly busy intersection at Broadview. The night sky pelted rain. The shops were dirty, plastered with Chinese posters, and packed closely together. As Gilbert and Lombardo turned left onto Gerrard, Gilbert read some of the shop names: Hoi Toi Salon, Sun Hao Food Market, Best of China Herbs Market. He saw a Chinese man in denims riding an old Monarch bicycle through the rain, a big basket of dried salt cod tied to the handlebars. Nearly all the pedestrians were Chinese. This was more of a real Chinatown than the Chinatown downtown was. The downtown Chinatown was a tourist attraction, a place for white people to buy trinkets from the East, find cheap produce, and eat dim sum. Chinatown East could have been a neighborhood in Shanghai—there were hardly any white people anywhere.

"Up here on the right," said Lombardo. "Boulton."

Gilbert turned right on Boulton.

They came to a small red brick factory; it looked as if it had been built in the 1920s. To the right stood the Que Ling Seafood Restaurant, a dilapidated white clapboard structure with a green shingle roof and a faded bristol-board sign in the window advertising fresh lobster and shrimp. To the left, an alley ran west along the side of the old factory. Across the street stood Eastdale Collegiate Institute, Mok's old high school.

"How do you want to work this?" asked Lombardo. "There's a buzzer at the front door and an automatic lock."

Gilbert looked at the door, a big glass one leading into a small foyer. "Let's wait awhile, see if he comes out," he said.

"A regular stakeout then?" said Lombardo.

"I think so. We'll duck into the school parking lot here. We'll have a perfect line of sight."

Gilbert drove into the parking lot, did a three-point turn, and eased under a leafless chestnut tree. He turned off the headlights but left the windshield wipers going so they could see better.

"Should we call our backup yet?" asked Lombardo.

"No point until we actually see him," said Gilbert.

He stared at the front of the factory. An odd facade, with a big aluminum garage door right in the middle of the front wall, painted with flaking brown paint, bent in spots. Windows lined the second floor. The structure had a flat roof. Gilbert wondered if there was any way to get up onto the roof from the inside, a way that Mok might escape. With the buildings so close together in Chinatown East, he wasn't looking forward to a roof chase, even if the uniforms did most of the chasing.

"See those two doors down there at the side of the building next to each other?" said Gilbert.

"Yeah?"

"He'll use one of those if he makes a break for it," said Gilbert.

"Strange, the way they put those doors right together like that," said Lombardo.

"One's the fire exit for the first floor, the other's the fire exit for the second floor," said Gilbert. "Quaint old building."

"You call that quaint?" asked Lombardo. "With all those garbage bags out front? And those two old sofas? I don't call it quaint. I call it a dump."

They waited for an hour, then waited some more. Gilbert wondered how his knees would behave tonight. As he listened to the sound of the rain against the car roof he felt oddly detached from the prospective takedowns, was so familiar with the process, had done so many takedowns, not only as a detective but as a patrolman, he couldn't get worked up about it, simply viewed it as a normal part of everyday life, part of his job.

At ten-thirty, Joe went to get a couple of coffees. Gilbert was left alone in the car. Alone with his thoughts. He stared at the old building. Converted into a boardinghouse now. He wondered if the arrest of Tony Mok would make a difference to anybody whatsoever. Lombardo came back with the coffee fifteen minutes later. Gilbert was about halfway through his coffee when someone turned the corner.

"Is that him?" he asked. He put his coffee in the dashboard cup holder. "Joe, I think that's him."

A short Chinese man walked down Boulton Street, hands in the pockets of his Harley-Davidson bomber jacket, shoulders huge, legs slight and wiry. He wore black denims and running shoes. Lombardo took the identification photograph, a mug shot from a previous arrest, off the dashboard and had a look.

"That's him," he said.

As Mok passed the Que Ling Seafood Restaurant, he glanced in their direction, then looked away.

"We've been made," said Gilbert. Gilbert lifted the radio and immediately called backup. "He's not going to wait for the uniforms to get here. He's going to go upstairs. He's going to get whatever he can and then he's going to bolt. We're going to have to do this now, Joe, and hope the uniforms get here fast." They watched Tony Mok enter the building. "Looks like I'll have to break that glass," he said. "Let's go. You guard the back entrance. I'll go in and take him down."

Lombardo glanced skeptically at Gilbert. "You know what?" he said. "I think we should do it the other way around."

"Why?" said Gilbert. "We've both got flak jackets."

"I know," said Lombardo. "But he's twenty-three, and you're

forty-nine, and I think I might have the lungs and the moves to handle him better." Lombardo smiled uncomfortably. "No offense."

Joe had a point. Forty-nine. Like an old jet with metal fatigue. "Okay," he said. Still young enough to fool himself into thinking he could beat someone like Tony Mok. "I'll give it a minute or two at the side entrance, then I'll come in after you." But wise enough to realize he couldn't trust his body to perform like it once had. "Let's go."

Both men got out of the car and drew their guns. They hurried across the rain-soaked street. Gilbert walked down the alley and stationed himself by the rear fire doors. Would have to shoot the lock off, if it came to that. Wise enough to understand that though he might feel well at the moment, his cardiovascular ice was getting thinner every year and he had to watch himself. He had to tread carefully, had to open the door a little wider for the unwelcome guest of his own mortality. He had to remind himself that his father had died of a heart attack one cold morning at the age of sixty-four while starting his bus in the transit barns on Coxwell Avenue five months before his retirement. Spray-painted graffiti covered this side of the building. Five discarded tires sat stacked across the way. Rear-echelon now, in these kind of takedowns, despite all the swimming. He heard the tinkle of glass out front—Joe smashing the glass in the door to get inside. Gilbert pointed his gun skyward, elbow bent, and pressed his back against the wall, hiding himself in the shadows. The smell of fish drifted up the alley. The swimming could only retard his slow decline. Far in the distance he heard the sound of police sirens approaching. If they could only restrain Mok until the uniforms got here.

He heard thumping on the stairs from inside, footsteps, somebody racing down the steps, and he knew that Mok, right on cue, was making a break for it, behaving the way all Gilbert's other fugitive suspects had behaved, true to type, running, fleeing, in a mad panic to get away. The fire-exit door burst open and Tony Mok came out with the energy of a runaway train.

Gilbert grabbed him by the shoulders and immediately felt the man's bristling strength. "Stop! Police!" he commanded.

Mok clutched his hands together, brought both arms up in between Gilbert's, and, in a martial arts move, broke Gilbert's grip by pulling his own arms apart. Then he darted away with such speed, Gilbert knew he had little chance of catching him. But he tried anyway, struggled to convince his body one more time that he was really a young man, told himself that swimming three nights a week really did make a difference.

He chased Mok down the alley past all the garbage, his black wing tips slipping on the slick pavement. He forced his lungs into a rhythm. To his right rose the backs of shops; to his left, over fences and garages, dark backyards lay soaking in the rain. Tony Mok ran like a black streak ahead of him, the Harley-Davidson logo with the catch phrase *More Than A Machine* jumping into relief on his jacket as he passed a streetlight. The sirens got closer. Gilbert saw headlights swing into the other end of the alley, his backup, cutting off Mok's retreat. Gilbert kept running, despite his weakening knees. Tony Mok searched for a way to escape, spotted a small warehouse to his left, and ran for it.

"Stop!" Gilbert shouted again. "Police!"

Security bars crisscrossed the warehouse windows. With the agility of an acrobat, Mok leaped to the nearest security bar, climbed the succeeding ones like the rungs of a ladder, pulled himself up onto a junction box, and struggled from the junction box to the roof. Gilbert stopped, awed by the display, immediately knew he was dealing with a different caliber of fugitive, that their takedown might not succeed after all. Mok darted over the roof and disappeared into the dark.

Gilbert ran the rest of the way to the warehouse, pulled himself onto the security bars, climbed them to the top, grabbed the junction box, but simply didn't have the strength in his arms or upper body to pull himself up, couldn't make the awkward maneuver to the roof. He eased himself back to the pavement. The radio car skidded to a halt in front of him and the uniforms got out.

"He went over the roof," he called. "Can one of you climb that?"

"I'll go," said the younger of the two. Gilbert glanced at the older patrolman, a man of about fifty. Something passed between them, an acknowledgement that they were both losing the fight, that they now had to step aside to let the younger men do their work.

The young patrolman scaled the security bars on the windows to the junction box and pulled himself up onto the roof. Whereas Mok had made it look easy, even this young patrolman had difficulty, possessed none of the simian strength Mok possessed. Mok was a force, a phenomenon, and Gilbert regretted not having gathered more intelligence on the man's ability before attempting to arrest him.

Gilbert turned to the older constable. "Let's get in the car and go around to First Avenue," he said.

They got into the radio car and sped down the alley. They turned south on Boulton, then right on First Avenue, heading against one-way traffic. The officer punched on the siren so oncoming traffic would get out of their way. They sped past the Toronto Alliance Chinese Church, the tires making a ripping sound as they rolled over the wet pavement. Gilbert wondered if Lombardo had been hurt. It took less than a minute to get to the other end of the street, but even so, Mok had vanished. Gilbert scanned the front yards, guessed the one Mok might have escaped through, squinted, and saw the young officer lying on the ground up ahead, down but not dead. Gilbert lifted his arm and pointed.

"There," he said. "On the front lawn. Your man is down."

The older officer bounced the car up onto the curb and came to a quick stop. He snatched up the radio. "Ten-three-five to Dispatch. We have an officer down, repeat, an officer down at First Avenue and Broadview. Dispatch, do you copy?"

Gilbert left the older officer to the radio work and got out to help the young one. He found the whole thing galling, especially because Mok knew they were after him now. The young officer groaned, shifted. As Gilbert got closer to him, he saw blood all over the poor guy's face. Gilbert knelt beside him. Galling, yes, but there was also a bright side. If nothing else, the whole frustrating episode helped confirm Mok's guilt in the murder of Edgar Lau. Why else would he run?

"He took my gun," said the officer, who looked as galled as Gilbert felt. "I don't know how he did it, but he took my gun. He came out from that bush at me, all hands and feet." He waved groggily toward a huge cedar bush. "A real kung-fu guy. I was down before I could draw my weapon." He pushed himself into a sitting position and touched the big gash at the corner of his eyebrow, then pulled his fingers away and looked at the blood. "He kicked my feet right out from under me. I went down hard. Can you imagine? A small guy like that doing that to a big guy like me." The officer tried to catch his breath. The rain made the blood run in diluted rivulets down his cheek. "I should have had him pinned. I should have had him cuffed by now."

"You did your best," said Gilbert. He looked down the street, his eyes roving quickly from pedestrian to pedestrian, hoping to see Mok. "Did you see where he went?"

The young constable bent his elbow carefully a few times. "He went that way, toward Broadview. Maybe some of those guys at the Salvation Army saw him."

Gilbert got to his feet and looked up and down the street. Mok had to be an extremely able street fighter to subdue such a large and youthful constable. Garbage cans and blue boxes lined the curb. Discarded Christmas trees, sparkling feebly with bits of tinsel, sat on the sidewalk ready to be collected. He sniffed the air. Cat piss. He saw a couple of toms squaring off under the bumper of an Oldsmobile across the street. His shoulders eased, his knees started to ache, and he knew he had to let this one go. He saw a small Chinese boy staring out a window at him. He had to admit, reluctantly, that Tony Mok, at least in this first encounter, had eluded him.

"Barry!" a voice called.

He turned. Lombardo limped toward him from the direction of the Toronto Alliance Chinese Church. In the flashing of the police-car light, Lombardo squinted, as if there were something wrong with his eyes. Gilbert hurried toward his partner.

"What happened?" he called.

The two men met up. "He threw something in my face, vinegar or something," said Lombardo, "then whacked me over the head with a chair. This guy's fast, Barry. I was out cold for a minute or two. I've never seen anybody move so fast."

"But you're okay?" asked Gilbert.

"I got his gun," said Lombardo.

Gilbert felt his pulse quicken. "You did?"

"I found it in a dresser drawer," said Lombardo. Lombardo pulled a revolver from his pocket. "I guess I spooked him before he could get it. A Colt Diamondback thirty-eight."

"A thirty-eight?" said Gilbert. "That's great, Joe."

"And not only that, look at this." Lombardo pulled a plastic Ziploc freezer bag from his coat pocket. "There's got to be at least six hundred caps of horse in here. The guy must be a major heroin dealer around here."

Gilbert and Lombardo got back to College Street Headquarters around ten o'clock that night. Policy dictated that Lombardo go to Occupational Health immediately to have his injuries assessed.

While Joe was downstairs having the nurse practitioner look him over, Rosalyn Surrey telephoned Gilbert. He was surprised to get a call from her so late.

"Garth's here," she whispered, her voice tense and scared. "He's come back. He's here right now. He's on the couch, drunk and asleep. Can you come over? He's insisting he killed Edgar. I don't want to be alone with him."

So Gilbert went over to Rosalyn Surrey's house on Palmerston Avenue. But before he went, he phoned Occupational Health and talked to Lombardo.

"Can you come with me?" he asked.

"No," said Lombardo. "They want to keep me here for at least an hour. I shouldn't have told them I was out cold. They've got to observe me now." Lombardo said this as if he thought it was a big waste of time.

"Okay," said Gilbert. "I'll call you in the morning."

"Barry?"

"What?"

"Be careful," said Lombardo. "We don't want two of us down here."

Rosalyn opened the door quietly for him when he finally got to Palmerston Avenue, and put her index finger to her lips, urging him to be quiet. The rain had stopped, at least for now, and a distinct chill had settled into the air. Rosalyn wore a double-knit skirt and blazer, looked as if she had just come home from work despite the late hour. Gilbert took off his coat and rubber overshoes and followed her into the living room.

A large man lay on the couch. His jeans and denim shirt were filthy. He lay facing away from Gilbert, snoring quietly. Despite a profusion of long, ringleted brown hair, Surrey had a bald spot on the top of his head. Gilbert smelled alcohol fumes rising from the man.

"I guess you better wake him," said Gilbert. "He won't try anything, will he? We've already had a bit of a fight tonight."

"I've never seen him hurt anybody," she said.

"Okay," he said. "Go ahead. Wake him up."

She walked to the couch and shook Surrey's shoulder. "Garth?" she called. "Garth, wake up. There's someone here to see you."

Surrey groaned, turned, opened his eyes, and looked at Gilbert through tiny round glasses. Glasses just like the ones Dock Wen had described. "Who are you?" he asked, in a rough dry voice.

Gilbert pulled out his shield and ID. "I'm Detective-Sergeant Barry Gilbert of Metro Homicide, and I'm here to ask you some questions about the murder of Edgar Lau."

Surrey turned to his wife. "You called a cop on me?" he asked.

Rosalyn looked at her husband with distant distress, the corners of her lips turning downward, her eyes dull with helpless pity, her hands unconsciously coming together in a gesture of nervous tension.

"I had to, Garth," she said. "I'm sorry, but I had to. The minute you came in the door, you told me you killed Edgar. What was I supposed to do?"

Surrey, an affable-looking man with intelligent eyes, gazed at his wife in dim wonder. A man who knew how to live, as Rosalyn had described him. A man with a special energy. But Gilbert now saw the energy was gone. Surrey looked like a hitchhiker who, having been dropped at the side of the road in the middle of nowhere, was now lost.

"I only told you that to scare you," he said. As if this were a logical and appropriate course of action, something anyone would have done. "I wanted to make you understand how much I loved you." His voice sounded windless, defeated.

Gilbert glanced at Rosalyn. He saw she was at a loss. She gazed at her husband as if she suspected he might be a figment of her imagination. Here was a man who had entombed himself in alcohol and self-pity, who had lost his judgment, and who couldn't figure out that scaring someone and loving someone were two entirely different things.

"Mr. Surrey, we have an eyewitness who puts you at the scene of the crime on the night Edgar Lau was murdered," said Gilbert. "And that doesn't look good." He tried to be kind. To serve and protect. Surrey looked so . . . so shell-shocked. "I wish you could explain that to me."

Surrey struggled to rally himself. Maybe he realized he had reached a crucial watershed in his life. But his reply was nearly flippant.

"And if I tell you I was there, you'll lock me up and throw away the key?" he said, as if he found the whole situation darkly humorous; he'd lost his wife, his livelihood, his dignity; wouldn't it now be hilarious if Gilbert locked him up?

"I just want to know what happened," said Gilbert.

Surrey raised his eyebrows. He looked like a stranger in this immaculate living room. Dirty, his black jeans covered with mud, the alcohol fumes rising from his pores like methane from a swamp, Surrey looked as if he didn't belong here. As if he were an outcast here, in this clean room. This was Rosalyn's living room, not his.

"I hardly know what happened," he said. "I can barely remember it." He lifted his hand to his head and rubbed his right temple. "But somehow I found myself sitting in a restaurant with Edgar on the night he was murdered."

Gilbert and Rosalyn looked at each other. A stillness came to Rosalyn. Gilbert wondered what Rosalyn and Surrey must have been like in the sunshine years of their courtship, before Surrey had forced her to live in the shade all the time. He couldn't make the stretch. Rosalyn and Surrey were in the same room but they might as well be galaxies apart.

"Do you remember which restaurant?" asked Gilbert.

Surrey squinted, his large sensitive brown eyes narrowing as he tried to dredge up from his alcohol-addled memory any remnants of his evening with Edgar. "Down around College and Dovercourt," he finally offered. "A Portuguese place. Had Portuguese plates on the walls, and a lot of rooster pictures. I remember being really mad that day. And . . . and upset. I was sitting here . . ." He motioned toward the bone-white baby grand. "Playing the piano . . . playing some old songs I wrote years ago, working my way through a bottle of wine, and I just . . . I just wanted to fix things . . ." He shook his head. "I don't actually remember getting up from the piano or making the phone call to Edgar, but I guess I must have. The next thing I knew I was walking down the street to meet him." He pressed two fingers to a leather coaster on the table, long dexterous fingers, piano-player fingers, and moved the coaster a few inches along the beechwood finish. "I got soaked. I was drenched by the time I got to the restaurant. It was raining so hard that night."

"So you phoned Edgar because you wanted to talk to him about Rosalyn?" asked Gilbert, wanting to get it right.

Surrey looked at his wife, ignoring Gilbert's question for the moment. Rosalyn's eyes were like green ice. *Ouch,* thought Gilbert. To see such coldness in the eyes of the woman you loved. Surrey turned glumly his way.

"I phoned Edgar because . . . because I wanted to make him understand . . . that he was wrecking our lives . . ."

Gilbert was disappointed. Here was a crucial watershed, a moment Surrey might have used to regain some of his dignity, to shake off all the booze and show some courage, but . . . he let it go, as if he didn't recognize it as an opportunity. He blamed everything on Edgar.

"I talked to him," continued Surrey. "And I . . . I said that I . . . that I still loved my wife. I remember ordering a couple of drinks, something to warm me up after walking all that way in the rain. Edgar stuck to tea." He turned to Rosalyn. "I talked for a long time. I tried to get him to tell me that he wouldn't go near you anymore."

"You didn't kill him, did you?" she said, her eyes now fretful.

"You think I'm a killer?"

"I don't know what you are anymore, Garth."

"I'm your husband," he said weakly.

She had nothing to say to this. She looked at Gilbert. He negotiated his way carefully through the wreckage of their marriage. *Husband*. Rosalyn was dead to the word. He could see she just wanted to get on with it.

"Did you leave the restaurant together?" asked Gilbert.

"No," said Surrey, rousing himself as if from a dream. "He left first. I stayed behind. I ordered another drink. I don't know how long I sat there. But eventually I decided I had to go after him. I had to try again. So I paid up, went outside, and started walking east along College. The rain was really cold. I thought it might turn to snow. It woke me up a bit. I took a couple deep breaths to clear my head."

"And you finally caught up to him?" asked Gilbert.

"No," he said, his voice softer. He glanced at Rosalyn. It was painful to see how deep the fracture was. "I walked all the way over to his place on Spadina. I thought I might catch him before he actually went inside. But I didn't. I had to knock. I tried the front door next to the restaurant first. I knocked and knocked but no one came to answer. So I went round back." Surrey gripped the right lens of his round-rimmed glasses, centering them on his nose. "That's when I saw the little guy run like crazy down the stairs."

Gilbert waited. Outside, he heard the furtive rhythm of yet more rain. *The little guy*. The atmosphere of the room felt different, thicker, resonating with incipient revelation.

"What little guy?" asked Gilbert.

Rosalyn seemed to recede; if the living room had been a stage set, the lighting technician would have been steadily dimming her spotlight by hopeless and heartbreaking increments as a way to further isolate her from Surrey.

"I don't know," said Surrey, glancing at Rosalyn, as if he

sensed her receding. "At first I thought it was Edgar." His eyes narrowed and he rubbed his beard with the back of his hand. "But then I saw that he was actually smaller than Edgar. He froze me to the spot because he had a gun in his hand."

Gilbert felt the atmosphere change again. He felt as if he had turned a corner in the case. Every so often a suspect turned into a witness. Every once in a while the pieces fell into place in the most unexpected ways.

"He had a gun?" said Gilbert. "How old did he look?"

"Young," said Surrey. "In his twenties."

"Was he carrying anything else?" asked Gilbert.

"Looked like a pair of gloves. Holding them in his other hand. He ran right past me and I thought for sure he was going to shoot me. But he ran right past me and went down the alley. I've never seen a little guy run so fast."

"Did you see what color the gloves were?"

"No, it was too dark."

"Can you remember what he was wearing?" asked Gilbert.

Surrey shrugged. "Black, I guess," he said.

Gilbert pulled out his mug shot of Mok and showed it to Surrey. "Is this the man you saw?"

Surrey looked. "That's him."

"And which way did he run?"

"Out behind Gwartzman's, toward Kensington Market."

"And once he was gone what did you do?"

"I looked up the fire escape," said Surrey, shrugging again, looking more helpless than ever. "I saw that the French doors were open. I thought I'd better go up. You know, make sure Edgar was all right. And I still wanted to . . . to talk to him. I thought if I could just find the right words . . ." He swallowed, shifted. "So I climbed the fire escape." He looked at the big metal radiator on the far wall under the window, scared, unsure, as if he were a D-Day recruit about to step ashore in Normandy. "And that's when I saw him lying there. On the dining room floor. Clutching this dish towel to his stomach. I got scared. He was shaking like crazy. He was having a convulsion of some kind. I know I should have gone in and helped him. But I just got scared, and I . . ." His eyes misted up. "The dish towel was soaked right through. It didn't look like it was doing any good. I just . . . I just got out of there as fast as I could." He turned to his wife. "I'm sorry, Rosie. But I . . . I let him die. I'm sorry I did that. I wished I could have saved him for you."

Rosalyn's hand went to her mouth, and her eyes moistened. God, this was awful. Gilbert felt he was in the middle of her grief, that he was drowning in her grief, and that he was swimming around in the shipwrecked pieces of their broken marriage. He hardened himself to it, pushed on.

"Was there anybody else in the room with him when you saw him?" he asked.

Surrey looked distractedly at his wife, extra solicitous, now that she was crying. "No," he said.

"How long did you stand in the back lot before you climbed the fire escape?"

"Couldn't have been more than thirty seconds after I saw the little guy run out."

"What was the condition of the apartment when you looked inside?" asked Gilbert.

Surrey yanked his attention away from Rosalyn and peered at Gilbert, puzzled. "What do you mean?"

"Did anything looked disturbed, books taken down from the shelves and so forth?"

Surrey shook his head. "No," he said. A knit came to his brow. "He had a stepladder in the middle of the floor. Other than that, the place was neat."

"And you left?" asked Gilbert. "You left right away?"

"When I saw him lying on the floor like that . . . sure . . . I got scared. I wanted no part of it. The cook saw me coming down the stairs. That scared me even more. I thought I'd better disappear for a while. I thought the cook might think I was the one who shot Edgar. So I went down to our place in Florida. I thought if the police came asking, I could just say I was down there the night Edgar was murdered."

Gilbert tried to piece it all together. Edgar gets home from the Portuguese restaurant around nine. Pearl visits at nine-thirty. Ten minutes later Foster Sung goes up and invites them to his table. They decline. Foster Sung goes back downstairs. Witnesses see Pearl leave at ten to ten. Shortly after, Surrey sees Mok race down the fire escape. Thirty seconds later, Surrey goes up, looks through the French doors, sees Edgar lying there with the dish towel already there, already pressed to his stomach, long before Foster Sung came up the second time to put it there. What was going on? Why would Foster Sung lie about the timing of the dish towel? They *had* Mok— the blood, the bullets, and now the eyewitness account. These were enough to convict. But with so many discrepancies like the dish towel remaining, Gilbert felt that maybe he hadn't turned a corner in the case after all.

He left the Surreys in the rubble of their demolished marriage, feeling as if he were stranding them; neither of them was in any shape to be alone, and especially in no shape to be with the other. But what else could he do? He had to go home. So he ventured out into the rain. The rain was cold. He thought it might turn to snow.

The sky was dark. Lives were wrecked. A victim was murdered. And a suspect was still on the loose. Jennifer despised him. His wife was bruised and beaten. Joe was under medical observation. Their murder remained unsolved. And he had no idea what he was going to do next. Another day, he thought. Seventeen years as a homicide detective, twenty-seven as a cop. He shook his head. Was he ever going to get used to it?

CHAPTER
SEVENTEEN

ON MONDAY, THE BALLISTICS TEST on the recovered Colt Diamondback .38-caliber revolver came back positive—the gun recovered from Mok's room on Boulton Street was indeed the gun that had killed Edgar Lau. And Murphy was at least seventy percent sure the gun had been used in the Vancouver shooting as well.

The evidence against Mok was now overwhelming. Bullets used in both attacks were soft-nose wadcutters. The blood evidence found in Mok's car was irrefutable. And now they had Garth Surrey and his eyewitness account. Any jury would convict with such evidence. He had to go after Mok.

Yet Gilbert remained equivocal. As he sat at his desk waiting for Frank Hukowich and Ross Paulsen to get there, he couldn't help thinking about the dish towel again. And what about May Lau? How could she hear the workmen upstairs, but not the gunshot? Then there were the gloves—not worn, but carried by Mok. Running from the crime scene with gloves in his hand? No. There was something wrong with that picture. What bothered Gilbert most was the condition of the apartment, how the apartment had at first been neat, according to Garth Surrey, with no sign of slashed futons or unshelved books, but ransacked later, in and around the time the first officer had arrived. Was Donald Kennedy really part of the corrupt police ring at 52 Division? Had Donald Kennedy been responsible for the ransacking, looking for Edgar's evidence against the police ring? Had Kennedy ripped the dish towel from Edgar's wound, speeding his death as a way to keep him quiet? Maybe. Maybe not. He had no way of knowing. Which meant he could only operate on the established certainties. The blood, the bullets, and the eyewitness. Despite all the discrepancies—and Donald Kennedy's possible involvement—the hard evidence demanded he arrest Mok.

When Hukowich and Paulsen finally came, Gilbert told them what they had on Mok. He stressed Mok's connection to Foster Sung, as well as how Mok had been hired by the 14k to shoot Edgar in Vancouver last summer in the hope they would lend him some support. He wanted to tell them about Mok's interesting blood phenotype test, and recount to them how he had gone up to Edgar's apartment late at night to make comparisons between Mok's mug shot and the photographs of Foster Sung and Ying Lau. But he knew both men would instantly discount this particular investigative hypothesis as groundless—the conniving speculation of a desperate detective who wanted to get their help any way he could.

"We have no idea where Mok might be, and it's going to take a lot of manpower to find him," he said. "We thought you could supplement our squad with some of your own resources. If we're going to mount a dragnet for this kind of skilled and experienced criminal, we'll need more officers."

Both men stared at Gilbert for several seconds. Then Paulsen leaned forward. "From our standpoint, we believe our resources would be wasted mounting a dragnet for Tony Mok." Paulsen shrugged apologetically. "Sorry, Barry, but we can round up any number of petty thugs any time we want. Mok simply doesn't fit the profile we're after."

"What about the six hundred caps of heroin we found in his room?" said Gilbert. "That's got to mean something."

Paulsen nodded. "I'm glad you got them off the street."

Gilbert turned to Hukowich. "Frank?"

Hukowich looked straight ahead. "I'm sorry, Barry. I'm afraid it's a no-go from our end as well. Mok's just too small-time, with no real connections to anything worthwhile."

"What about his connection to Foster Sung?" asked Gilbert, knowing if he didn't get more manpower he would never find Tony Mok. "Foster Sung was Mok's guardian way back when."

"Barry," said Tim Nowak, "I've had Benny Eng review Mok's file. There's no current evidence that links Mok to Sung in any criminal way. You and Joe are going to have to work this one yourself. We can send an updated lookout notice to patrol, but other than that, you're on your own. We've got more pressing cases now."

Lombardo returned after lunch and took the bad news solemnly. His dark Mediterranean eyes smoldered.

"You know what?" he finally said, looking ready to hit something. "We don't need their help. We can do it ourselves. Paulsen bugs me. And I can hardly keep a straight face when I look at Hukowich's hair."

"Nowak came to me later," said Gilbert. "After Hukowich and Paulsen had gone. He said we could work overtime on Edgar for another week. After that . . ." Gilbert raised his palms.

"So we work like hell for the next week," said Lombardo.

"I'm going to talk to Peter Hope," said Gilbert. "Let's ask the Red Pole if he knows where we can find Tony Mok. If I tell him we're going to ease up on Pearl, he might go for it."

Lombardo's eyes narrowed. "But I thought he lied to us about Pearl coming down the apartment stairs first on the night of the murder. Are we going to trust him?"

"One way or the other, we've got to talk to Tony," he said. "If I tell Hope we're going to eliminate Pearl as a suspect, he might help us."

Lombardo nodded. "Okay," he said. "But she's still a suspect, no matter what."

"Agreed. Hell, Foster Sung's still a suspect. So's Garth Surrey. So are Rosalyn and May. So's Donald Kennedy. But when you look at everything we have, Tony Mok is our strongest suspect by far. It was his gun. It was his bullet. And it was Edgar's blood in his car. We've got to go after him any way we can."

Lombardo gave him a wry grin. "Even if we sleep with the enemy?"

Gilbert conceded the point. "Even if we sleep with the enemy," he said.

Gilbert asked Lombardo about May Lau's medical record. Lombardo had spent the morning tracking it down. "Did you get her doctor's name?" asked Gilbert.

"A Dr. William Tse, on King Street."

Gilbert raised his eyebrows. "So you got her chart?"

Lombardo frowned, looked away. "Tse has it in storage," he

said. "He keeps all his inactive charts in a warehouse behind the medical building. She hasn't been to see him in a while." Lombardo's frown deepened. "May Lau's was on a high shelf." Lombardo looked away. "I couldn't reach it."

Gilbert stared at his partner.

"You couldn't reach it?" he said, enjoying this. "Well . . . how high was it? Five feet?"

"Not funny."

"Four?"

Lombardo again looked ready to hit something. "It had to be at least nine feet up."

"And you couldn't reach it?"

"They didn't have anything to stand on."

"No shoe boxes lying around?"

"Watch it."

"Or a step stool?"

"What I lack in height I make up for in looks," said Lombardo.

"So your mother tells you."

"And Dr. Tse is six-one. He wasn't there. He's going to get it for us later. His secretary's going to fax it to us. She couldn't reach it either. She's short too. So you see, I'm not alone. The short shall inherit the earth."

As if on cue, the fax machine bleated, and, watching the number on the display, they saw that it was coming from Dr. Tse's office. Both detectives watched as the machine began to hum.

"Was it a big chart?" asked Gilbert.

"Twenty pages."

The fax machine finished a few minutes later and the two detectives went over to have a look.

They found a report of a general physical on May Lau dated

July 24, 1993, years after the Vietcong artillery shell had supposedly damaged her hearing. Item number 4 was about hearing. Both ears were normal, with no deficit in either. The two detectives looked at each other. Gilbert knew they were both thinking the same thing. Why would May Lau lie about the circumstances surrounding her own son's murder? Many incongruities complicated this case, but that was one of the most perplexing ones.

Gilbert sat in the Golden Bamboo Restaurant on Spadina and Cecil at a table near the back sipping a Diet Coke. He found himself in the ambiguous position of having to treat Peter Hope, the 14K enforcer, not only as an adversary but as an ally. Chinese lanterns hung from bamboo poles overhead. He looked out the window where he saw the traffic going by on Spadina Avenue. Lots of it. A lot of garment places around here, so there were dozens of garment trucks going back and forth. His goal was simple. Find Tony Mok. He looked behind the counter where he saw the short-order cook serving up Chinese noodles, scooping quickly into the pot as if he were catching a fish, twirling the noodles with three quick turns of his wrist and sliding them in a neat knot into a bowl, a deft and skilled maneuver that took all of three seconds. Gilbert believed Tony Mok had disappeared into the impenetrable world of triads and tongs. If he was going to find him, he needed someone who knew the way. Who better than Peter Hope? What choice did he have? He wasn't going to have the investigation stalled here, when they were so close to clearing it. He had to walk through the snake pit, careful of his ankles, and hope for the best.

A black Mercedes with tinted windows pulled up in front of the Golden Bamboo. Gilbert expected the aging and diminutive Red Pole to emerge from the rear door. But a much younger Chinese man dressed in a plain brown suit, wearing a black chauffeur's hat, a black tie, and black leather driving gloves, got out of the driver's side. He walked around the front of the car and entered the restaurant, where he stood at the WAIT-TO-BE-SEATED sign and scanned the tables. When he finally saw Gilbert, he moved through the restaurant, ignoring the solicitations of the maître d', and came to Gilbert's table.

"Mr. Hope is waiting in his car," he said.

Gilbert stared at the young man, then placed a few dollars on the table and followed him out to the car.

The chauffeur opened the back door of the Mercedes for Gilbert. Gilbert got in and found the Red Pole waiting for him. Hope wore a navy-blue overcoat, gray flannels, a white shirt, and a red silk scarf. He looked fragile today, his skin nearly transparent, his rakish hair looking more like an old woman's than an old warrior's. The two men stared at each other. The Red Pole finally gave Gilbert a small bow.

"What do you want?" he asked, his tone flat, direct.

The driver got in and they drove north on Spadina Avenue. The road sloped gently upward. Three-story brownstones from 1910 lined the broad avenue, and there was an inordinate number of Chinese restaurants, taverns, trading companies, boutiques, money-exchange places, and immigration agencies. They drove next to Spadina's streetcar-only lanes. The rails were collared by concrete meridians to keep automobiles and trucks out; the intersections had duplicate traffic lights—one set for the streetcars and another for regular traffic, timed so regular traffic could still make left turns over the tracks while the streetcars waited.

"I want your help," said Gilbert.

He gave Hope a brief sketch of his situation, how he had enough evidence to convict Tony Mok—the blood, the bullets, their witness—recounted their attempt to apprehend Mok, and his own subsequent appeal for greater resources. He told Hope how the other agencies were now backing out of the investigation.

"And Detective Support Command is easing away from the investigation as well," he said. "They won't allow me the necessary resources to mount an effective manhunt. I thought you might be able to help me find Tony Mok."

He studied Peter Hope. The man's eyes narrowed. The Mercedes turned left on College and headed for Little Lisbon.

"And why do you think I can help you find Tony Mok?" asked Hope. "Why do you think I should?"

Gilbert knew that Hope was fishing, that the deal-making had begun. "I'm sure it would be a great comfort to Mr. Wu if we were able to close the file on Pearl as a suspect in this case," he said. Gilbert paused, looked out the window, where a short rotund Portuguese widow dressed in the usual black pulled a bundle buggy west along College Street, the buggy stuffed with a dozen board-like loaves of Portuguese bread. "We can't do that unless we arrest Tony Mok. Mrs. Wu will continue to be investigated, as will our other suspects, until we can bring the case to a satisfactory conclusion. As much as we might wish to spare Mr. Wu and his various business enterprises any embarrassment, and as much as we're sure Tony is our man, I'm afraid we would still have to continually inconvenience Mrs. Wu with persistent inquiries. As you're her personal assistant, I'm sure you're eager to prevent that."

Was he being too hasty, he wondered?

Hope, of course, instantly saw what he was being offered. As he'd told Gilbert before, it was his job to protect Pearl; and if he had been purposely brought out of retirement by Bing Wu to extricate her from the difficulties surrounding Edgar's murder, here was a chance he seriously had to consider. But like a good man of business he wanted the specifics of the deal.

"And you have enough evidence to convict Tony Mok?" he asked.

"We have the ballistics. We have the blood. We have a witness. What more do we need?"

Hope sighed, skeptical. "I suppose that's . . . that's good news," he said.

"Then you'll help?" he asked.

Gilbert let Hope consider the deal as they continued west along College Street. Gilbert glanced out the window, saw a street sweeper sweeping up cigarette butts outside a pool hall. Toronto the clean, he thought. He wasn't going to tell Hope about his reservations in the case. The driver braked at a streetcar island and they waited while the exiting passengers walked to the curb. He wasn't going to tell Hope how Pearl would remain a suspect no matter what. They moved on, passed a Portuguese gift shop full of silver, baby clothes, and ornamental ceramics. He was just going to play it with the facts against Tony: the blood, the bullets, and Garth Surrey's eyewitness account.

"And will Mrs. Wu be free from further inquiries if I decide to help you?" asked Hope, seemingly not the least bit interested in what Gilbert was offering him. "She's much too busy for anything but her work just now. And she also finds the whole business distressing."

"Once we convict Tony, the case will be closed," he said.

Peter Hope nodded doubtfully. "Let me think about it," he said. Hope's face revealed nothing. "Let me think about it, and I'll get back to you." And that was that. Nothing more. No questions. No wrangling. Just a dismissing *I'll get back to you*. The Red Pole leaned forward, his red silk scarf falling free of his navy-blue overcoat, and spoke to his driver. "Jian, you can let Detective Gilbert off at the corner."

Gilbert was disappointed, unnerved by the Red Pole's lukewarm response, and feared that the investigation might be all but over if Hope didn't help him. The 486 leaned back in his seat with a tight civil grin on his face, and Gilbert had the fleeting fear that he might have insulted the man in some way. He thought Hope would have gone for it, no questions asked, as a way to protect Pearl from her . . . her more naive proclivities. But he hadn't. He didn't even seem to care. Jian eased up to the curb. Gilbert opened the door.

"You know where I am," said Gilbert.

Hope nodded. "I have your card," he said.

Gilbert got the feeling he was never going to hear from the man again. Or maybe Hope was just playing poker with him. He got out of the car and shut the door. He watched the car drive off, then looked around. He was over near Clinton Street. In front of a gelateria. Maybe this was a bad idea. Behind the shop fronts across the street he saw the steeple of a large Catholic church rise into the gray air, smog-darkened red brick, slate shingles, and a crucifix right at the peak. Was it not said that the cobra sometimes danced and swayed to hypnotize its prey? He started walking east along College. Damn. Was the Red Pole doing the exact same thing to him? Gilbert had opened negotiations with the Hung Kwan, the feared enforcer of the 14K, and now he thought that maybe he shouldn't have. But what else could he do? Hukowich and Paulsen weren't going to help. Nowak wasn't going to help. And any overtime on the case was going to be gone by the end of the week. He had to make his moves. Only his moves didn't seem to be working. Pigeons again got in his way and he stamped at them. At least the man had promised to think about his offer. Or was that just so much cobra dance too? One way or the other, he could only hope he would hear from the Red Pole soon.

Gilbert walked over to Mount Joseph Hospital. He descended the stairs to the basement and followed a long corridor past the House-keeping Office, the Materials Management Office, the Morgue, and the Linen and Lab-coat Exchange Unit, until he finally came to the Medical Records Department. He took a court order out of his brief-case and presented it to the department's release-of-information secretary, a pretty young mulatto woman with a faint wash of henna in her hair. She put on glasses and read the court order.

"It's for a Foster Ling Sung," he told her. "He was brought to your Emergency Department seven years ago for a stab wound. We understand he needed a transfusion, but that there was a problem with the transfusion. He had a delayed transfusion reaction. Your blood bank had to run some tests on him and we believe that one of those tests might have been a blood phenotype."

The secretary looked up from the court order. "Could I see your badge and identification?" she asked.

Gilbert produced both items for the secretary. He glanced toward the main file. "What's going on?" he asked, curious. "The last time I was here you didn't have near as many staff. Where did all those young people come from?"

The secretary glanced at the main file. "We're having all our charts scanned into electronic form. Those kids are from the company who's been hired to do it. They're packing up the charts and taking them off-site to be scanned. We're working toward an electronic chart." She held up the court order. "Do you mind if I show this to my department head?" she asked.

"No, not at all."

"Have a seat," she said. "I'll be back in a minute."

"Thanks."

Gilbert sat down.

A few minutes later, the secretary came back with the department head, a tall black woman wearing a corporate-style business outfit and discreet studs in her ears.

Once she and Gilbert had introduced themselves to each other, the department head said, "I'm afraid Mr. Sung's chart has been sent off-site to be scanned. I'm not sure we can lay our hands on it right away. All we have on this patient right now is a computer list of visits, four over the last ten years, one of them for the stab wound you're interested in."

"Does the stab wound visit-entry list any tests that might have been performed?" he asked.

"Yes," she said. "But the test results won't be listed."

"Would it say if a blood phenotype was performed?"

The department head went to the nearest terminal and checked. She looked up from the workstation. "Yes," she said. "A blood phenotype was performed. But like I say, we don't have the result, just a record that the test was performed."

"How soon would you be able to get the actual report?"

he asked. "I realize you've got a big changeover going on here, but I—"

"We'll try to get it to you as soon as possible, Detective Gilbert," she said. "But I can't promise sooner than a week."

WHEN GILBERT GOT HOME A little after eight that night, Regina was waiting for him in the kitchen. The bruises on her face had faded and she looked a lot better. She was marking papers at the kitchen table, with a dictionary and a copy of Shakespeare's *Macbeth* at her side for reference, a red pen poised in her hand.

"Joe canceled on Jennifer," she said. She stared at him, her eyes wide with inquiry.

He paused, trying to figure out how he could put a positive spin on this. But he found he couldn't. "I had him cancel," he admitted.

A wrinkle came to Regina's brow and she put her pen down. "Why?" she asked.

He moved to the back of the chair. "I thought it would be for the best," he said. She continued to stare, her blue eyes searching. He felt he had to explain. "I didn't want her to think Joe . . ." The rain beat against the window, and the clock above the doorway chimed the quarter hour. He looked at the table, where she had a pot of tea and a half-finished raisin scone. "I didn't want her to get hurt again."

"She's nineteen, Barry," she said. Regina sat back in the chair, put her hands on top of her grade-twelve English papers, and contemplated him like a sentencing judge. "You can't be protecting her for the rest of her life."

"I know I can't," he said, wincing. "But I just . . ." He looked out to the hall where he saw their old Barcelona chair, something they'd owned since the place on Merrit, a relic from his bachelor days, now reupholstered in a pale green material with paler green birds stitched into the fabric. "Is she upstairs?"

"She and Nina are having dinner at Marvelous Edibles tonight." Regina's lips stiffened. "With some of Nina's friends." As if that were a punishment she wouldn't wish on anyone.

That Jennifer should have to spend her time with Nina's giggling fifteen-year-old girlfriends made Gilbert feel even worse. "You know what?" he said, annoyed with himself, annoyed with the rain, with work. "I'm through with interference." He put his briefcase on the table. "She can make her own mistakes from now on."

Regina frowned, lifted her pen, and went back to marking papers. "At least that's better than you making them for her," she said.

Two days later, Gilbert stood at the east end of the Bloor-Danforth viaduct, the girder-and-concrete bridge spanning the Don Valley. He peered through the rain at the oncoming traffic, looking for a green Oldsmobile Cutlass Supreme, holding his umbrella close to his head, pointing it into the wind to stop it from blowing inside-out.

After fifteen minutes, Gilbert saw the car ease up to the curb and come to a stop just before the exit ramp to the Don Valley Park-way. The driver blinked his high beams. Gilbert walked toward the car, noted the dented fender, the rust by the front bumper, the faded STP decal on the tinted windshield. He opened the passenger door and got in.

The driver, a Chinese man in his early forties, with sloping cheeks, sloping eyes, and a pronounced brow that gave him the appearance of a Mongolian horseman, looked him over. He wore faded blue jeans, white socks, slip-on deck shoes, a brown leather jacket, a Calvin Klein T-shirt, and had thick, collar-length hair. A cig-arette was clutched between the first and middle fingers of his right hand. He gazed at Gilbert, his expression showing nothing. A blue-and-green tattoo of a dragon ornamented the back of his right hand.

"You have a gun?" asked the man.

"Yes," said Gilbert.

The driver put his cigarette in his mouth and proffered his palm. "Hand it over."

Gilbert pulled his gun from his shoulder holster. The driver took the gun, snapped the clip from the grip, and put both compo-nents on the floor behind his seat.

"You can have it back when you leave," he said, looking more at ease now that they had passed this first hurdle.

The man shifted gear, squeezed out into traffic, flicked on his right-hand signal, and took the steep twisting down-ramp to the Don Valley Parkway.

As they drove north on the parkway, the driver took huge drags on his cigarette. Invariably, he blew the smoke out his nose. The car had white leather upholstery and a V-8 engine. A getaway car. A string of ivory beads hung around the rearview mirror, and a com-pass sat on the dashboard, fixed there by a suction cup. Gray, leafless trees clung to the slopes of the Don Valley, and below, Gilbert saw the Don River, swollen and muddy with all this rain, overflowing its banks onto the grassy and willow-lined floodplain next to the six-lane highway. Take a pretty river valley and put a freeway through it—he supposed Toronto wasn't much different from any other North American city that way.

They exited the parkway onto the 401 and drove east, all the way to Agincourt, weaving their way in and out of traffic.

When they got to Agincourt they drove through a suburban commercial area of strip malls, drive-through fast-food joints, brake-and-muffler places, parking lots, furniture discount joints— the usual suburban car-oriented purgatory—to the warehouse of Kowloon Textiles, in the new Chinatown. The new Chinatown had strip malls, fast-food joints, and all the rest of it—only all the signs were in Chinese. The driver parked outside the warehouse and they both got out. They walked past stacks of empty skids to the ware- house door, where the driver pressed an intercom button and spoke in Cantonese, presumably telling whoever was inside that they'd arrived.

A minute later another Chinese man, older, stouter, reminding Gilbert of Buddha, opened the door.

The driver and the older man exchanged rapid-fire Cantonese. Then the older man patted Gilbert down.

"Are you wearing a wire?" he asked.

"No," he said.

The older man made him unbutton his shirt. When he was satisfied that Gilbert was clean, he nodded. "Okay, I'll take you in," he said.

As the old man led Gilbert into the warehouse, Gilbert felt as if he were crossing a border—as if in asking the Red Pole for help, he had ventured into uncharted territory, had gone outside regular procedure, and perhaps was risking not only the whole investigation but even his own job. Crates and giant ship containers, some stacked three high, formed a network of aisles in the warehouse. Despite the risks, he knew he had to do this. He had to do it because he now felt a compelling sympathy for Edgar, this man who had escaped Vietnam in a boat all those years ago, who had been fighting to expose a corrupt police ring at 52 Division, who had evidence in a locker somewhere, who, despite all the incriminating circumstances surrounding his murder, was now turning into a dark-horse hero of sorts. In the corner, he saw a few men working on a car; they stopped working and watched him suspiciously.

"In here," said the older Chinese man, leading him to an office at the back.

They entered the office.

And there he was. The Red Pole. The Hung Kwan. The 14K enforcer, as mysterious as an unknown river, as unreadable as a book without words.

Peter Hope sat behind a battered metal desk on a cheap foam swivel chair, legs crossed, hands clasped over his bent knee. He greeted Gilbert with a dip of his head, then turned to the older man and said something in Cantonese. The older man retreated. The Red Pole had his shirtsleeves rolled up, revealing not only his thin mottled forearms but also a tattoo, a blue-and-green dragon, one similar to the one the driver had worn.

Hope gestured at a chair. "Sit down, Detective Gilbert," he said. The corners of his lips rose in a bright but hard smile. With that particular smile, Hope reminded Gilbert, for some reason, of a creature—a mongoose or a snake—who ate raw eggs, eggshell and all, his teeth small and sharp, ideal for chiseling through hard substances. "I have news for you."

Gilbert sat down. "I'm listening," he said.

"Tony Mok is in Hong Kong."

Hope's hard smile remained in place. Gilbert glanced at the calendar on the wall behind Hope's shoulder, a cheap promotional one with a lot of Chinese writing on it, and a picture of a Chinese model in a traditional red silk cheongsam serving tea next to a fountain. So. The Red Pole was going to help him after all. The Red Pole had actually found Tony Mok. In Hong Kong. Half a world away. To some detectives the great distance might have been disheartening, an obstacle all but impossible to overcome, but to Gilbert it was simply a matter of degree. This man from the other side had moved quickly and efficiently. Hope might be old, but the Red Pole was still a force. Gilbert gave Hope a small bow.

"Thank you," he said.

The hard edges eased from Peter Hope's smile and a genuine friendliness came to his face. Gilbert felt as if he had passed a test. Hope's smile no longer looked so predatorial.

"Have you ever been to Hong Kong, Detective Gilbert?"

"No."

"Because you'll have to go. I've had some of my associates detain Tony Mok for you. I should point out that I was personally opposed to any cooperation with you. As far as I'm concerned, and as far as Mr. Wu is concerned, Mrs. Wu is innocent. Certainly I would like to spare her any further questioning, but Mr. Wu and I both think that any inconvenience she might suffer isn't worth the time and trouble—and the considerable risk—we took in finding and apprehending Tony Mok for you. The police can ask her as many questions as they like, as far as we're concerned. Mr. Wu and I feel we have nothing to gain in detaining Tony Mok for you."

Gilbert's brow arched in puzzlement. "Then why did you help me?" he asked.

"Because Mrs. Wu wanted us to. Mr. Wu knows how Mrs. Wu feels about Edgar. And while this angers him a great deal at times, he knows that sometimes it's difficult for Mrs. Wu. He can see Mrs. Wu's grief. Mrs. Wu insists we help you. She grieves for Edgar and she wants to see his killer brought to justice. Mr. Wu dotes on her, and is willing to do anything for her. Pearl wants us to help you. So that's why we're here, Detective Gilbert, you and I. And that's why you'll have to go to Hong Kong."

Gilbert let the challenge settle. He thought through his various questions quickly. First and foremost, why would he personally have to go to Hong Kong when it made better sense for police counterparts in the former British colony to apprehend Tony Mok? And if he in fact had to go to Hong Kong, would Detective Support Command be able to find the necessary money in the expediency fund for hotel and airfare to Asia? And what kind of cooperation would Gilbert get from Hong Kong's new Communist masters?

"Can't we have Hong Kong Police apprehend Tony Mok?" he asked.

Hope nodded, as if he fully expected Gilbert's question. A quietness came to Hope, as if he, too, felt that the border between them was no longer so guarded, that they had met each other halfway, and were now engaged in a most unusual and perhaps notable undertaking.

"There have been many changes in Hong Kong since the People's Republic of China took over a few years ago," said the Red Pole. "Hong Kong is still one of the best places in the world to do business—everyone will tell you that—but there have been many reforms." Hope's eyes narrowed. "As you might expect, many of these reforms have been in law enforcement."

Gilbert waited. He sensed conditions on the way—the Red Pole setting up the situation to suit whatever safety net he might need.

"Police are more vigilant in the new Hong Kong," said Hope. He lifted his chin and stared at Gilbert with eyes that seemed charged with electricity. "What can you expect? They have five thousand new officers, and look where they come from. Look what their traditions are. Look how punitive their justice system is."

Gilbert studied the Red Pole, realized that Hope was truly concerned, and that the impact of Hong Kong's handover to Communist China was both real and highly feared by those who had connections to the triad underworld in Hong Kong. The Red Pole sat back in his chair, seeming to measure the effect of his words on Gilbert.

"Because of the unusual nature of our cooperation, Detective Gilbert, I must ask you to make the arrest personally." Hope raised his hands, as if to qualify. "I know that as a man in your senior position a simple arrest is usually left to uniformed officers, but let us admit, this arrest won't be so simple. There are certain risks on both sides."

Gilbert again waited. The Red Pole's conditions loomed on the horizon ever closer, like a thunderstorm. He watched Hope. Hope took a deep breath and shifted in his chair, looking as if he were now ready to go into greater detail.

"Like I told you, Detective Gilbert, I've had associates in Hong Kong apprehend your suspect." The Red Pole grinned, and Gilbert saw that the irony of the situation wasn't lost on Hope. "He's being held as we speak. He is part of . . . part of *our* world. The Hong Kong Police would . . . would never have found him . . . in *our* world. So we found him for you." Hope's oblique admission—about his shadowy connection to the tongs and triads of Hong Kong—unsettled Gilbert. "We found him because Mrs. Wu *wanted* us to find him. And we incurred a great deal of risk. Holding Mok, a Canadian citizen, against his will, has opened my associates to all sorts of legal danger. I have to do what I can to protect them. To involve the Hong Kong Police in any but the most superficial way, to get them physically anywhere near my associates, would in the end only jeopardize the freedom of my associates who, after all, are only trying to help you. The only way I can give them protection is by keeping the Hong Kong Police Force at arm's length. I'm in no position to trust the new Hong Kong Police Force. You might make special arrangements with them to collect Tony Mok from us, but given the slightest opportunity, they would most certainly move in on my associates and indict them on kidnapping charges."

Hope rubbed his chin with his fingers and looked out the window, where a forklift operator moved a large crate from the back of a flatbed truck and put it next to the receiving dock.

"I've thought through all the possibilities," he continued. "Drug Tony, put him in a car trunk somewhere, have the Hong Kong Police pick him up and save you the trip of going all the way over there. But I can't let the Hong Kong Police question him in any great detail. He must remain in your custody until he returns to Canada. Given the opportunity, Mok would most certainly divulge to the Hong Kong Police the names of those who . . . who have so graciously detained him for you. That's why I must insist on my arrangements. That's why I must insist you make the arrest yourself."

Gilbert thought about this.

"What if the Hong Kong Police don't go for it?" he asked. "What if they're unwilling to let us go ahead with your plan?"

"Then there can be no arrest," said Hope. "It will be up to you to smooth things over with them."

Gilbert nodded. "I'm willing to make the arrest myself," he said, "and to smooth things over with the Hong Kong Police, but I'm concerned about making an effective arrest. I'm a forty-nine-year-old homicide detective with bad knees, a family history of cardiovascular disease, and not the best eyesight. I'm brave but not stupid. I know Tony's fast. I know he's a good street fighter. I'd like to bring my partner Joe Lombardo with me if I could. He's not Hong Kong Police. He's young. And he's a great boxer. He works out. I'd feel a lot safer having him along. I think we'd have a better chance of making a successful arrest."

The Red Pole thought this through and finally nodded. "Very well," he said. "You can take your partner. But no one else. You'll be watched, I'm sorry to say, but what choice do I have?"

"I understand."

"The main thing is to keep the Hong Kong Police physically away from my associates at all times," he said. "They're like wolves. They'll go in for the kill at the smallest opportunity." Hope opened the desk drawer and pulled out a Chinese money envelope, bright crimson with gold Chinese writing all over it. "We start with this."

Gilbert gazed at the envelope tentatively. "With that?" he said, not sure he understood.

"It's a Chinese money envelope." He offered the envelope to Gilbert. "Don't look so perplexed. I assure you, it's all very practical. I want you to take this money envelope to the Yellow Moon Tea Room in Tung Loi Lane once you reach Hong Kong. It's really very simple. You'll find the address inside the envelope. This envelope will establish your credentials with your first contact. Like a letter of introduction, if you will. Give the envelope to the manager at the

Yellow Moon Tea Room and sit down. In an hour or so you will receive a similar-looking envelope from the manager. In this next envelope you'll find some instructions. These will guide you to another destination. At this second destination, if we see you're not alone, the arrest will be called off. As I say, you'll be watched, so please make sure any police escorts are nowhere in sight at this point."

"Okay," said Gilbert.

"Once we're certain you and your partner are alone, your next contact will come forward and take you to Tony Mok." Hope took a deep breath and leaned back in his chair. "These arrangements might seem troublesome to you, Detective Gilbert, but believe me, they're the only way I can protect the people who work for me. If you're prepared to accept them, then all you need do is book your transportation, your accommodation, and we'll be set to proceed."

STAFF INSPECTOR TIM NOWAK REACTED with dismay to Gilbert's latest initiative in the Edgar Lau murder case. As he sat behind his desk staring at his half-finished cup of coffee, with the rain coming down outside harder than ever, he shook his head wearily at Gilbert's written request for expediency money.

"Barry," he said, "I have to think of my budget. We're near the end of the fiscal year and there's not much left. If it were Vancouver, I wouldn't hesitate. Even if it were San Francisco, I would say okay. But Hong Kong? For the two of you, that's five thousand dollars in airfare. Then there's accommodation. I had Carol check the hotel prices there. Three hundred a night for double occupancy, up to five hundred if you want to stay in any of the upscale places, and that doesn't include the ten-percent service charge or the three-percent tax. I don't have ten grand in my budget to throw away on this. And the possibility of getting that much money from the expediency fund is nearly nil."

So Gilbert reluctantly outlined his second proposal. "Why don't we contact Frank Hukowich and Ross Paulsen and tell them I've worked my way into the confidence of the Red Pole?" he said. "Maybe they'll offer us some funding. Who knows what I might be able to unearth? That's got to mean something to them."

Paulsen took a flight from Virginia that same day. Hukowich drove down from Ottawa. Paulsen had a hard polyester case with him. He opened the case to reveal what looked like an ordinary package of Camel filter cigarettes. Gilbert stared at the package of cigarettes, knowing exactly what it was, sensing, just as he had sensed with the Red Pole, conditions looming on the horizon. He felt as if he were venturing even farther into a no-man's-land, that he was being pulled in two different directions by two different camps, that he was not so much a detective wishing only to make a simple arrest for murder, but a pawn in a much bigger game.

"This is one of our latest body bugs," said the American. "It's better than most of the wires we use, operates on fifteen-hundred milliwatts of power, and can transmit up to fifty miles if the conditions are right. It has a crystal-controlled frequency, so if anybody tries to intercept they'll have to match the band exactly. It has a microchip to scramble transmissions, so even if somebody manages to intercept they won't understand any of it anyway, not unless they find a way to decode."

Paulsen, on a techno-high, spoke more quickly than he usually did, and with a lot more enthusiasm. Gilbert stared at the device. Having spent a number of years in Narcotics, he was familiar with such devices, though this was by far the most sophisticated one he had ever seen. The ones they had downstairs in Technical Support had to be strapped around your waist or worn like a back brace, bulky and cumbersome devices that could easily be discovered. This bug, in its simple disguise, was beyond the reach of the MTPF's fiscal resources. Only an agency like the Drug Enforcement Adminstration could afford something like this. He didn't want to wear it. He was willing to be Ross Paulsen's ears, to pick up whatever he could when he went to Hong Kong, and then report it back to Paulsen by word of mouth, but he thought wearing this bug would be a major risk.

"Look, all I meant to offer was some background information on some of the things the Red Pole was telling me, and whatever I might hear from his associates in Hong Kong. I'm a cop. Whatever I hear will be good. I'm a watertight witness. Isn't that enough?"

"For someone like Wu, we need it on tape," said Paulsen.

"I know . . . but a wire. Won't that be risky?" He thought of how he was patted down at Peter Hope's warehouse. "All I want to do is arrest Mok."

"They won't find the wire," said Paulsen.

"Hong Kong is the gadget capital of the world," he said. "They'll find it. At the very least they're going to have a boomerang detector."

Paulsen grinned, as if he were glad Gilbert had raised this point. "We've got it shielded with lead." He was like a car salesman selling a fully loaded sports car. "A boomerang detector's not going to touch it." Paulsen's shoulders sank and he made an attempt at being personable. "Look, Barry, you've gained the cooperation of one of the most highly placed triad members in the world. Any of his associates—*any* of them—particularly the ones you'll talk to in Hong Kong, are going know things and say things that we can add to our library of evidence against Bing Wu. This is a rare opportunity. We've got to take it."

He had to expect this—that in dealing with Paulsen his investigation would in some way be co-opted.

"If they find this thing, I'll never get Tony Mok. And I'll wind up dead."

"They won't find it, Barry," said Paulsen. "Look at it. It's top-of-the-line. We never send our agents into the field wearing junk. We've learned the hard way."

Paulsen lifted the pack of Camels out of the polystyrene mold and handed it to Gilbert. It had the exact same weight and feel of a package of cigarettes. Gilbert opened it and took out one of the cigarettes. It indeed was an actual cigarette. He took out the next cigarette. That too was a cigarette.

"Where's the battery?" he asked.

"We've got a mercury battery concealed in the last cigarette at the end here. You'd have to break the cigarette apart to find it because it's packed right inside the tobacco," said Paulsen. "The electronics and the microphone are hidden in the foil."

Gilbert contemplated the device with growing astonishment. The budget Paulsen must have to work with!

"And if I refuse to wear it?" said Gilbert.

Paulsen shrugged. "Then you don't get your money," he said. "It's as simple as that."

A few hours later he received a telephone call from the department head of Mount Joseph Medical Records. She had disappointing news.

"I'm afraid we haven't been able to find the chart on Foster Ling Sung," she said. "We have it marked as going out to the scanning company, but they say they have no record of receiving it. We've done a computer search in our chart location system, as well as a physical search here in the hospital, but we haven't been able to find it. I'm sorry, Detective Gilbert, but I'm afraid we're going to have to put Mr. Sung's chart on our missing list for the time being."

Gilbert shook his head, disappointed. There was only one thing left to do. Check any Tony Mok records at the Prince of Wales Hospital once he got to Hong Kong in the hope he might find matching phenotypes on Foster Sung there.

His luggage was packed and standing by the front door in the hall downstairs. Lombardo sat in his Fiat in the driveway outside, afraid to come in because of the way he had cancelled on Jennifer a few days ago. Gilbert knocked quietly on his eldest daughter's bedroom door.

"Jenn?" he said. Thunder rumbled distantly to the west. In January. Bizarre. "Can I come in?"

No answer. As much as he wanted to respect her privacy, he had to try and patch things up before he left for Hong Kong. He opened her door and went in.

He found her sitting at her desk making a sketch of the lymphatic system from her Gray's *Anatomy*. He was glad to see she was taking an interest in her schoolwork again.

"You're sure you don't want to come down and say good-bye to Joe?" he asked.

She continued to shade her sketch lightly with a pencil crayon. "How do you think it makes me feel, dad?" she asked.

"How what makes you feel?"

"You really don't like me, do you?"

He frowned, looked away. "Jennifer, don't say things like that."

"Do you have any idea how infuriating you can be at times?" she asked. "Mom's right. You're too wrapped up in yourself."

"She said that?"

"She said that. You don't know how lucky you are to have someone like mom. Someone who tolerates you."

"I know I'm lucky."

"I don't know how she puts up with you."

"Jennifer, please don't be like this, not before I go."

"You have to earn the right to be a husband and a father," she said, putting her pencil crayon down. She turned around and faced him with hard accusatory eyes. "Or didn't you know that?"

"Yes, I knew that."

"Why do you think you have the right to interfere in my life?"

"Jennifer, I'm sorry about Joe."

"No, you're not," she said. "You're glad about it. Just like you're glad about Karl."

"The whole thing with Joe was a mistake from beginning to end."

She looked at him more closely. "What do you mean by that?" she asked.

He knew he had blundered again, but he didn't want to lie to her. He slid his hands into the pockets of his gray flannels and sighed.

"I put Joe up to asking you out to *The Nutcracker* in the first place," he said. He wasn't sure he should be telling her this, but he felt she deserved the truth. "I felt sorry for you. I thought if Joe took you out you might snap out of it. But then it started going too far. You know . . . the way you were looking at him, the way you kissed him. I thought you were going to end up getting hurt all over again."

She looked at her father in astonishment. "Shit, I don't believe this." Her voice sounded raspy, breathless, and he knew she was precariously close to tears. "I don't believe this."

"I thought I was doing the right thing."

"I don't need your help, dad," she said. "I don't *want* your help."

"Jennifer, all I want is what's best for you."

She exploded. "How can you know what's best for me? You don't even know me. You can't even stop your own fucking wife from getting beaten up."

She turned around and made a pretense of shading her sketch again. Gilbert saw a tear fall onto the sketch paper. He felt perplexed. He could make no right move as far as Jennifer was concerned. Everything he said to her was like pouring gasoline onto flames. He was afraid that this new discord between them might be permanent. She went back to school on the eighteenth and he was afraid the emotional distance between them might become even greater if they didn't patch it up before then. He had no idea why this was happening to them.

"I just want you to know that no matter what happens," he said, "I love you."

She kept shading her drawing.

Twenty-two hours on an airplane. His knees started to hurt halfway to San Francisco. At first he tried to alleviate the ache by walking up and down the aisle, but by the time they landed in San Francisco to change planes, his knees hurt so badly he dosed himself with two of his enteric-coated aspirins and ordered a double Scotch and soda, hoping to concoct his own improvised goofball to send him to sleep.

At ten in the evening, the flight attendant dimmed the lights and handed out blankets and pillows. Gilbert put his seat back but the steady hum of the aircraft kept him awake. He kept thinking about his family. He stared at the little air nozzle on the ceiling while Joe snored quietly. He wondered what he could do to make Jennifer like him again. He glanced across the aisle where an overweight Chinese man no more than five feet tall, with a paunch the size of a basketball, slumped a good way over his armrest. His mouth was open, his eyes closed, and his tongue, moist and purple, was making unconscious forays over his lower lip. Gilbert felt alienated from his own family, as if he were an outsider, as if, because he was the father—the traditional authority figure—he could never quite belong to his own family, at least not the way the girls and Regina belonged to one another. That gave him a great big ache right in the middle of his chest.

By hour eighteen, he felt as if he were in a surreal dream. His knees were numb and the only thing he felt happy about was the prospect of apprehending Tony Mok. He felt as if the jet somehow traveled outside of time and space, that it was a jet that would never land, one that would fly forever through the dull gray void of the pre-dawn sky. A flight this long was a test of endurance. Because they were racing away from the rising sun, the night seemed to stretch on forever.

He thought of Jennifer and Nina swimming up at the cottage, how Jennifer liked to take the snorkel and goggles and swim along the sheer rock face of the south point, where the granite was pink, and minnows schooled in groups of twenty or thirty. As the sun finally caught up with them from behind, he smelled coffee brewing.

This revived his spirit. He thought of coffee up at the cottage, thought of Regina in her big soft white terry-towel bathrobe, of her fair skin, skin so fair it shone in the morning light. He lifted the recessed window shade and looked down at an unbroken layer of cloud below. It looked like a carpet of cotton, tinted purple, gold, and pink by the rising sun. The tilt of the jet was nose-down now. He was lucky to have his family. The lights came on and flight attendants emerged to take away pillows and blankets. Sometimes he forgot just how lucky he was. Passengers drifted to the washrooms. Gilbert got up and stretched his knees in the aisle. He went to the washroom, noting how over half the passengers on the jet were Chinese, and splashed some water on his face. He'd gone on several homicide-related overseas flights in the past—to India, Ireland, South Africa, one even to Hawaii—but this was by far the longest. He'd never brought back presents for Regina and the girls. This time he was going to. Desperate measures, he thought, something to get in his family's good books again, but that's what he was going to do.

Once he got back to his seat, the flight attendants wheeled breakfast down the aisles. Lombardo was up, rubbing the thick dark growth on his chin with his palm. He looked bleary-eyed and his hair was disheveled.

"How are the knees?" Lombardo asked him.

"They hurt like God's own judgment," said Gilbert.

Lombardo lifted his wrist and looked at his watch. "Christ, I guess we're almost there," he said. "That's a long haul."

"Another hour and we should be landing," said Gilbert. He looked at his hands. "I think I'm going to call Jennifer when I get there. Things were a little shaky when I left and I want to see if I can fix them up."

A doubtful expression came to Lombardo's face. "You know what?" he said. "I'd leave it alone for now if I were you. I'd give it some time."

Lombardo's advice bothered Gilbert; Joe seemed to know Jennifer better than he did. He stared at the cover of *Discovery,* Cathay Pacific's in flight magazine. "Maybe you're right," he said.

Lombardo glanced out the window and ran a hand through his hair. "Let her cool off."

Gilbert was grateful to Lombardo. Grateful for reminding him that no matter what he tried with Jennifer right now, nothing would work. The man was only thirty-three, but he had a lot of common sense. Even if he occasionally did spend up to seventy-five dollars on a haircut.

They got their breakfasts. The coffee made Gilbert feel better. One of the best airline coffees he had ever tasted, as a matter of fact. A short while later the seat-belt warning rang and the captain made his pre-landing announcement. He reported the weather in Hong Kong as balmy and overcast, with a temperature of 72 Fahrenheit, 24 Celsius, and rain expected by evening. The jet's nose dipped down and the rosy clouds came up fast. They went into the clouds.

After a few minutes, the clouds shredded, and Gilbert saw the South China Sea. The pilot said a few words about the new Chek Lap Kok Airport, opened in July 1998 to replace the old Kai Tak Airport in downtown Kowloon. Gilbert saw rocky islands now, and fishing junks. As they rounded a few final mountains they came upon Metropolitan Hong Kong. Tall financial towers clustered thickly on the north shore of Hong Kong Island, jammed against the peaks and hills of the interior, while across Victoria Harbor, on the south shore of Kowloon Peninsula, smaller buildings, no taller than twenty stories, congregated shoulder to shoulder in a toy-like collection of cubes and monoliths. Ships, freighters, ferries, sampans, and junks crowded the harbor. Gilbert glimpsed a double-decker bus driving on the left-hand side of the road.

They continued west toward Chek Lap Kok Airport, banking over Lantau Island, getting ready to come in for their final approach. Lower and lower they flew. Gilbert saw a profusion of tiny islands everywhere. The runway got closer and closer. Finally, the landing gear touched down and the jet engines squealed. The jet slowed; they came to a halt next to the terminal.

Their liaison officer, Inspector Ian Dunlop of the Hong Kong Island Region Administrative Wing of the Hong Kong Police Force, greeted them at the airport. He was about forty, had deep-set blue eyes, a narrow aristocratic nose, and blond hair cut in a Mersey-Beat style. He wore a gray pinstripe suit, a maroon shirt, and a black tie. Dunlop told the detectives a little about himself. Though of British ancestry, Dunlop was a longtime Hong Konger, born and raised here, and had been recruited at the age of twenty-one into the then Royal Hong Kong Police Force.

"My dad was a surgeon," he told Gilbert and Lombardo on the twenty-five-minute train ride via the Tsing Ma Bridge from Lantau Island to the city. "He worked out of Princess Margaret Hospital for thirty years, saved more lives than I can possibly count, but finally left in April of 1997, just before the handover. Went back home and bought a farm in the Cotswolds, where he plans to read the complete poems of Gerard Manley Hopkins and make stained-glass windows as a hobby. Me, I could never leave here. This is my home. I might have blond hair and blue eyes, but I feel like a bleeding Chinese most of the time." He glanced out the window, where workmen laid concrete for a new overpass. "I'm one of three white officers left in the force's HKI Administrative Wing. That doesn't make any difference to me. But some of the new PLA officers regard me with a certain degree of suspicion. Of course, they're born to suspicion, aren't they?"

"PLA?" said Gilbert.

"People's Liberation Army. We now have over five thousand PLA officers in the Hong Kong Police Force. And they've sent down about five hundred new vehicles from Shenzhen. That's good. We could use them."

"So there's been a lot of change," said Lombardo.

They passed through a corridor of densely populated government-subsidized high-rise housing. Gilbert had never seen streets so crowded, congested with trucks, cars, double-decker buses, pedestrians, and hundreds of bicycles.

"There has been and there hasn't been," said Dunlop. "We've had an overall reduction in crime, and certainly the way in which we police the place has been more stringent since the Communist takeover, but oddly enough our homicide rate is going up. So is our suicide rate. I can't help reading something into that. We still allow peaceful demonstrations, and people are still allowed to make huge piles of money, and to spend huge piles of money, and we still have all our so-called hostess clubs, and the seedier side of our nightlife, and we can partake freely of our nastier habits. Hong Kong's still very much an island of the Gucci Chinese, and everybody still wears designer clothes. But there's an overall sense that our civil liberties have been curtailed. You've got to watch what you say now, and that's truer for me than for most because of the position I hold in the Administrative Wing."

Despite Gilbert's excruciating jet lag, he was interested in what Dunlop had to say.

"Just before the handover," continued Dunlop, "the Chinese introduced some amendments to our various ordinances." He glanced out the window, where a man walked along the street with five dead roosters slung over his back. "For instance, if I were to say or do anything to advocate the independence or sovereignty of Taiwan, Tibet, or Hong Kong, I would lose my job instantly and probably be jailed for sedition." Dunlop raised his eyebrows. "And that's taken some getting used to. I like to say what I like without anybody telling me otherwise. My dad always taught me to speak my mind. But I can't do that anymore. Not if I still want my paycheck."

They stayed at the Ritz-Carlton on Connaught Road in the Central District, a narrow finger of a hotel squeezed next to the landmark Furama Hotel. The American Government had an expense account with the Hong Kong Ritz-Carlton, and because Gilbert and Lombardo were acting under the partial auspices of the Drug Enforcement Administration, both were given account cards. This allowed them free dining at the hotel's main restaurant, Toscana, as well as access to the Executive Business Center, with its Internet, e-mail, and fax machines. From an architectural standpoint, Gilbert liked the building because of the way its exterior recalled Art Deco New York. The interior was refined in an Old-European style—reproductions of Gainsborough, Constable, and Turner hung on the walls. From their window they had not only a view of Victoria Harbor but also one of the Peak. On the opposite corner rose the Bank of China, a colossus of glass and steel, with its two radio antennas pointing skyward, the most recognizable building in Hong Kong. The whole city seemed squeezed into the meandering corridor of land between the harbor and the various sparsely populated peaks of the interior.

They reached the hotel at ten o'clock in the morning local time—ten P.M. Toronto time—and made arrangements to meet Ian Dunlop later that afternoon, after they'd had a chance to rest and clean up. Before they went up, Gilbert asked Dunlop if he could send someone to the Prince of Wales Hospital in the New Territories to retrieve the original and any related blood phenotype records on Tony Mok or his parents.

"Be happy to," said Dunlop, "if you think it will help your case."

When Dunlop was gone, Lombardo turned to Gilbert. "What was that all about?" he asked.

Gilbert hadn't yet told Lombardo about his theory. He knew his theory was a long shot. Just as the glove had been a long shot. No point in getting ridiculed about it until he had to. Now was the time. Gilbert explained his theory to Lombardo.

When he was done, Gilbert said, "Blackstein assured me that this particular blood phenotype had to be done for paternity testing only. I'm hoping to find the corresponding parental phenotypes at the Prince of Wales Hospital."

Lombardo shrugged doubtfully. "I don't know, Barry," he said.

Gilbert pressed his point. "If Foster Sung turns out to be Tony's biological father," he said, "it might explain why he was trying to protect Tony when he told us Tony took off in a taxi on the night of the murder. And if we can bolster that particular angle with a phenotype record, proving their blood relation to each other, our case against Tony grows stronger."

Lombardo shook his head. "But what about Tony's case file

from the Children's Aid Society?" he asked. "They have Tony documented as an orphan. They have Foster Sung documented as his legal guardian, not his father. Why would Foster Sung go to all that trouble to hide his biological connection from Tony?"

Gilbert stared at the rainy harbor. "I have no idea, Joe," he said. "But I think it's an angle worth looking at."

At four o'clock, they went outside. The doorman gave them complimentary umbrellas as they left. The rain that fell was more like a summer rain, warm and silky, glossing everything with a satiny coating of wetness. The temperature was balmy—Hong Kong was about as far south as Cuba and enjoyed subtropical weather. Ian Dunlop waved to them from a parked police van across the street. The driver was a uniformed police constable. He opened the sliding side door and Gilbert and Lombardo got in. Sound equipment packed the back of the van: a Mitsubishi broadcast-quality tape recorder as well as a lot of receiving apparatus.

"Have a seat," said Dunlop. "It's going to take us a while to get through this traffic."

At this time of day, gridlock always slowed traffic in Hong Kong to a crawl. They inched west along Connaught Road, turned left up Jubilee Street, edging higher into the hills, then right on Queen's Road Central until they came to Bonham Strand East, the tall buildings flashing with hundreds of neon signs, the sidewalks crowded, dance clubs beckoning, stalls offering everything from Calvin Klein knockoffs to stuffed baby crocodiles, buskers playing strange Chinese instruments Gilbert had never seen before. At Bonham Strand East, they pulled up to the curb.

"This is the heart of the Western District," said Dunlop. "The Yellow Moon Tea Room is just up there on Tung Loi Lane." Gilbert glanced up the street where he saw several open-air fruit markets.

"The Western District is a veritable warren of alleys and lanes too narrow for this van, and not exactly safe for pedestrians either." Dunlop glanced at Gilbert and Lombardo questioningly. "You've got your guns?"

Both detectives nodded. Outside, the light faded quickly. The weatherman called for the rain to clear by midnight.

"Right," said Dunlop. "Here's a little map I've drawn." He gave the map to Gilbert. "Walk up here to Wing Lok Street, then turn left. That's Tai Street. Follow Tai Street until you reach Tung Loi Lane. Turn left again. The Yellow Moon Tea Room is about five doors past the Post Office. Can we check the microphone to make sure it's working?"

Gilbert spoke into his body bug. "Testing, one, two, three."

The needle on the sound meter jumped. "It's working," said Dunlop. "If you get into trouble, all you have to do is call. I'm sure your weapons will be taken away from you at some point, but you might as well take them along for now. Good luck."

CHAPTER
TWENTY

GILBERT AND LOMBARDO GOT OUT of the police van and ventured into the rainy night. They passed a temple from which Gilbert smelled the aroma of heavy incense. Looking inside the open door, he saw several devoted worshipers burning paper prayers in a giant urn, the flames leaping as high as a good-sized bonfire. The buildings in the Western District were old, shabby, and the streets so narrow and crowded, he and Lombardo at times had to squeeze their way through. Following Dunlop's map, Gilbert and Lombardo walked farther into the thicket of streets. Through front windows they saw fan-makers, jade carvers, and fortune-tellers. Gilbert saw shops selling snake wine, ginseng, funeral wreaths, and hundred-year-old eggs—dingy shops where the shelves were stocked with bags and chests of goods exuding the fusty smells of dried mushrooms, shark fins, and abalones. He saw as many shopkeepers using modern computerized cash registers as he did old abaci. As they turned left onto

Tung Loi Lane, a man tried to sell them a knockoff Rolex but instantly grew annoyed when he found they couldn't speak Cantonese. He moved off quickly.

The Yellow Moon Tea Room was on the fourth floor of a low mean structure five stories tall, had its own neon sign extending on a pole over the street. Mini-skirted Chinese women hung around outside waiting for customers. Gilbert and Lombardo climbed the few steps to the building and entered a dim lobby. The place smelled of cooking oil and, faintly, of marijuana. The cracked tile floor was strewn with rubbish. People had set up vending stalls in the lobby. One man sold live squid from an aquarium tank. Another sold stuffed birds. Through a glass door to the left, Gilbert saw several bamboo mats spread out on the floor—the place was a low-cost hostel of sorts and was packed with Chinese men. He looked at the stairs. A mush of impenetrable garbage covered the steps.

"I guess we take the elevator," he said.

"Do you think it's safe?" asked Lombardo, peering at the cage-lift doubtfully. "It doesn't look safe."

Gilbert pointed at the stairs. "Do you want to climb through that?"

"No," said Lombardo, scrutinizing the garbage in bewilderment. "I guess I don't."

They rode the lift to the fourth floor.

Once there, Gilbert looked down the hall and saw a neon sign at the end blinking off and on, big Chinese characters, smaller English letters underneath—the Yellow Moon Tea Room. The smell of mildew and fish hung thickly around them. The two detectives walked down the hall, Gilbert noting how the floorboards sagged beneath his feet. A mouse, dark and quick, bolted along the baseboard and disappeared into a hole under the quarter-round. Gilbert went into the tea room first, the Chinese money envelope ready in his hand.

He was surprised by how small the place was, no more than twenty feet long by twelve feet wide, roughly the size of his rec room at home. Old Chinese men played *pai-gow* and mah-jongg at folding card tables. Many had birds in bamboo cages on their tables.

"What's with all the birds?" asked Lombardo.

Gilbert shook his head. "I don't know."

Lombardo shrugged, looking ready to accept anything.

A middle-aged pockmarked man in a white short-sleeved shirt—a shirt decorated with what looked like little purple TV antennas—came up to them. *"Nay ho mah?"* he said. The man wore a hairpiece, not a good one, one that fit him like a hat, the hair so black it looked blue.

Gilbert handed the money envelope to the man, who inspected the gold writing on it carefully. His face grew still, cagey. He looked at the two detectives, first at Gilbert, then Lombardo, as if he was trying to ascertain something about them. Finally, he beckoned with an index finger.

"You come," he said.

He led them to a table at the back beside a window. On the wall next to the window Gilbert saw a faded, water-stained poster for the Miss Asia 1983 Beauty Pageant, nearly twenty years old, replete with lovely young Chinese women, all wearing the same identical one-piece pale orange bathing suit and pale orange high heels. Gilbert and Lombardo sat down. The manager brought them tea, a pungent green steaming liquid that both detectives looked at suspiciously.

"You going to drink it?" asked Lombardo.

Gilbert gave it a whiff. "I don't think so," he said. "I'll wait until I can find a coffee somewhere."

Lombardo pushed his own little Oriental cup away. "Me too," he said.

An hour later the manager brought them an identical Chinese money envelope. Gilbert opened it and found further instructions inside. He handed the computer-printed missive to Lombardo.

"They want us to cross the harbor to Kowloon," he said. "We're to wait on the corner of Shantung and Ferry Streets."

Out in the police van Ian Dunlop looked over the instructions. "Right," he said. "We've got a four-mile drive. Shantung and Ferry. That's right next to the water."

They drove east until they came to Causeway Bay, then took the Cross-Harbor Tunnel to Kowloon.

Kowloon huddled on the peninsula directly north of Hong Kong Island, a densely packed municipality of multi-story apartment blocks. They passed apartment block after apartment block. Security bars covered many windows, laundry hung everywhere, and Gilbert saw tired-looking plants and canary cages on several of the cramped concrete balconies. The traffic moved as slowly as molasses, even at this time of night. Gilbert saw dozens of shanties in narrow alleys— squatters finding refuge wherever they could. An old man living in a refrigerator crate sold oranges and smoked oysters to passersby. A few palm trees sprouted from a brown scrap of park in front of an apartment complex. Up ahead, a truckload of naked department store mannequins had fallen off a truck. Farther on, teenagers swarmed around a man who had a box of Britney Spears T-shirts. An old man with a Confucius beard and mustache stared drearily at the melee from behind the smoke of his thick hand-rolled cigarette, then shook an old noodle container at passersby, hoping for coins. Barbecued dog hung in windows. So did barbecued rat.

"I'll be dropping you at the Yau Ma Tei Typhoon Shelter," said Dunlop. "Ships and boats cast anchor there whenever we have a typhoon. People live there. On their boats. They run businesses there. A lot of floating brothels, some drug dens, dozens of water taxis. At any given time there's over a thousand boats out there."

Twenty minutes later Inspector Dunlop slid the van door open at Ferry and Shantung Streets.

"Now, look," he said, "I don't know where this crowd came from, maybe there's something on somewhere, but half the people here already look suspicious to me, and we know you're being watched. That man over there in that doorway, I'm sure he's triad. And so's that man over there. Something in the way they hang about. The constable and I will hide a few blocks back. We should still get good radio reception from that distance. Nathan Road should be far enough. If you happen to lose your transmitter, or if it's taken away from you, you can call me on any public pay phone afterward. Don't try anything dangerous. You're my responsibility. Your safety comes first. Those are my orders." Dunlop smiled thinly. "Let's not risk my pension playing hero, shall we?"

Gilbert and Lombardo got out and waited on the corner. Across Ferry Street, Gilbert saw the Yau Ma Tei Typhoon Shelter, a dim expanse of boats moored up and down channels in regular rows, with larger access channels intersecting smaller ones at measured intervals. An old man in a peaked bamboo hat steered a sampan through the shelter by standing at the stern, moving a pole back and forth, shaking his hips from side to side, looking as if he were performing a bizarre dance. The sampan, garlanded with old tires, protected from inclement weather by a tin awning, moved slowly over the green water. Gilbert turned around and gazed west along Shantung Street. Dozens of signs hung from overhead poles—a thicket of neon placards so abundant they blocked out much of the night sky, bold and bright, their Chinese characters glowing like embers. Cars packed the street. Pedestrians thronged the sidewalks. Vendors hawked their wares amid the noise and smoke of the Kowloon evening. Gilbert covered his Camels with his hand and turned to Lombardo.

"Dunlop bothers me," he said. "I smell fish, and the fish aren't kosher."

Lombardo looked at the covered listening device, then at Gilbert. "You think so?" he asked.

Gilbert couldn't define his distrust. But it was there, as unsavory as the smell coming from the harbor.

"He's trying too hard to convince us of his own legitimacy," he said.

Lombardo peered down the street, thinking about this, and finally nodded. "He's not the genuine goods, is he?"

Gilbert shook his head. "I don't think so," he said.

They waited an hour.

Ten minutes into their second hour, Gilbert saw two men in a large speedboat motor up to the dock across the street. The speedboat looked out of place, a rich man's plaything, glimmering with orange sparkle paint, hardly typical of the ragtag and idiosyncratic collection of vessels out in the typhoon shelter. The driver, a short man whose skin looked momentarily blue in the fluorescent lights along the pier, cut the engine and said a few words to the other man, who got out, glanced briefly up Shantung Street, then tied the boat to the dock. The speedboat driver got out also, and the two Chinese men climbed the steps to Ferry Street.

The rain had stopped and the clouds began to clear. The two men dodged traffic across Ferry Street. They picked Gilbert and Lombardo out quickly—the only two white men around—and walked along the sidewalk toward the detectives in long, purposeful strides. The driver, a man of about thirty, wore a nightclub singer's blazer—purple velour with black satin lapels—pointed black shoes, and had a cigarette wedged in the corner of his mouth. His epican-thic eyelids were so pronounced Gilbert could hardly see his eyes through the slits. When the driver reached Gilbert he looked him up and down, slid his hands into his back pockets, struck a tough-guy pose, glanced at Lombardo, then turned back to Gilbert. Despite his tough-guy pose, the man had ridiculously big ears, didn't look threatening at all. Gilbert glanced at Lombardo. Lombardo raised his eyebrows. The man's posturing was comical.

"You have the second envelope?" the man asked in English.

Gilbert pulled out the second envelope and handed it to him. The man apparently took this cloak-and-dagger aspect of the arrest extremely seriously; he looked over his shoulder like a spy and acted so suspiciously that Gilbert thought a beat cop might come along any moment and arrest him. He first examined one side of the enve-lope, then the other, as if he were looking for a code, then shoved it in his pocket.

"Come to the boat," he said. "We have Mok out there, in the shelter."

He spoke in low tones, obviously thinking he was impressing the hell out of the two detectives. Gilbert and Lombardo followed the two men across Ferry Street, down the steps to the pier, and onto the boat.

Once in the boat, the driver drew his gun on Gilbert and Lom-bardo in a lazy and routine way, trying to make it look as if drawing his gun on police officers were something he did a hundred times a day. Gilbert couldn't get over the blazer, purple velour with black satin lapels, something Hugh Hefner might have worn in 1962 at the Playboy Mansion, a barbarous garment, but a garment the driver no doubt thought was the height of style. The nightclub blazer looked diseased, with balding spots on the velour.

"Your weapons," he said.

Gilbert and Lombardo opened their jackets and relinquished their guns. The driver said something in Cantonese to the other man. This other man was older, had a crabby face, an extremely red face for a Chinese, and wore a brown polyester blazer that looked two sizes too small for him, pinching him at the armpits, the sleeves riding up his forearms every time he reached for something. He frisked both detectives, checking for concealed weapons. His body odor, at once salty and sour, assaulted Gilbert's nostrils. His hair looked waxy from lack of washing, and had chunks of dandruff in it. The man took out Gilbert's cigarettes. He knocked one out, stuck it in his mouth, and gave the rest to Gilbert. He looked at Gilbert, as if challenging Gilbert, but Gilbert simply ignored him, and put the cigarettes back in his shirt pocket without comment.

The driver started the boat.

They pulled away from the pier and angled out into the channel. They veered north until they came to the first access channel. They followed this channel west, passing sampans, two junks, and six houseboats coming the other way. Several narrow channels led directly south, each lined with hundreds of boats. Gilbert saw the Hong Kong skyline, towers of glittering light, Eastern-looking, ultra-modern, with the dark peaks of the island rising in a ragged and ungainly line behind. He felt on edge. Having to go out on the water like this struck him as an added risk, yet he had to admire Hope's tactical choice, using the barrier of the water as a way to give his associates double protection against arrest, from any kind of physical contact with the Hong Kong Police Force.

They traveled at five knots for ten minutes. The channel widened and the driver increased speed. Up ahead Gilbert saw open water. The driver puttered to the last channel and turned left. Dozens of boats—cabin cruisers, houseboats, junks, and sampans—lined the channel. The driver eased up to the side of one of the larger houseboats and turned off the engine. The outboard Johnson shuddered a few times, then grew silent, leaving a cloud of blue exhaust drifting above the stern.

The other man climbed onto the houseboat and tied the speedboat to the railing. The houseboat looked as if it had at least three decks, was as large as a bungalow, painted green and brown, and listing to port.

The clouds broke up overhead, but to the southwest another cloud bank moved in. To the east, Gilbert saw a full moon the color of copper magnified by Hong Kong's blanket of smog, its craters and seas showing up like dim blue bruises. The typhoon shelter stank of diesel exhaust and drifting seaweed.

The driver left the wheel. "Let's go up," he said, smiling, his white teeth protruding, angling out from his gums, reminding Gilbert of the white keys on a piano. "We've got him in the cabin." He treated Gilbert as if they were old friends now.

Gilbert and Lombardo followed the driver onto the houseboat. They negotiated a walkway around the back of the boat and entered the cabin. The other man followed behind, his body odor clinging to him in a dismal cloud of stinkiness.

Tony Mok sat on the cabin floor of the houseboat guarded by two old men, several small cuts and bruises on his face, his wrists tied behind his back, his ankles bound with packing tape. The two old men looked like grandfathers; they wore caps and were minding Mok the way they might mind grandchildren—with benign grins on their faces. The cabin reeked of whiskey, and if the shards of the broken J&B Scotch bottle in the tin pail were any indication, the old men had obviously knocked a fifth of the stuff to the floor in their geriatric drunkenness and were now working on a fresh one.

"He's all yours, Detective Gilbert," said the speedboat driver, looking as if he were about to salute, endearing despite his utter lack of style. "I'll give you a lift back to the pier with him."

The speedboat driver spoke in Cantonese to his other men. Instructions of some sort?

Gilbert and Mok looked at each other. In Mok's eyes Gilbert saw something he never expected to see, an unspoken plea, an attempt to make Gilbert see that there might be more to this than just a handover. A quick intelligence and awareness emanated from Mok's dark Chinese eyes. Mok looked tired but alert. His jeans were dirty, had a grass stain on the knee, and he didn't have any shoes on. His leather jacket had a tear in the sleeve. Mok was a fighter, wild and unpredictable, but looking into Mok's eyes now, Gilbert saw an awareness that went beyond the wild and unpredictable.

The driver finished talking to his men. He turned to Gilbert. "Are you ready?" he asked.

Gilbert nodded. "Can we get our weapons back?"

"I'll return your weapons when we reach the pier," he said.

Mok stared at his Chinese captors. His eyes changed. They went dead. They showed nothing. It was as if he had lowered a veil over his eyes. Mok was gagged. Gilbert removed the gag. Mok had deep welts on either side of his lips. He moved his jaw from side to side and looked at Gilbert. He said nothing, but again, something passed between them, an attempt, at least on Mok's part, to establish a common ground. One of the grandfathers cut the packing tape from around Mok's ankles. Gilbert leaned down and helped the suspect to his feet. Mok got up and followed them outside.

They escorted Mok into the speedboat without difficulty. He sat docilely in one of the backseats. Lombardo sat beside him, guarding the small, wiry, and amazingly fit young gang member. Gilbert sat next to the driver.

"Aren't we going to bring anyone else to guard him?" asked Gilbert.

The driver looked at him, dismissing the idea with a careless shrug, smiling with those big teeth of his. "He's not going to cause any trouble," he said. "He's had the trouble beaten right out of him." The driver glanced at Mok. "Isn't that right, Tony?"

Mok didn't answer, stared straight ahead.

"Shouldn't we at least have our guns?"

"I told you before," said the driver, "you'll get your guns at the pier. Don't worry. Everything's fine. Everything's okay."

The driver started the boat, eased away, puttered down the narrow channel, and veered east toward Ferry Street. Clouds floated like tattered sailing ships across the sky, drifting in front of the moon. A warm wind meandered up from the south. Gilbert grew apprehensive. He glanced over his shoulder at Mok. The prisoner continued to stare straight ahead. Gilbert remembered Mok's energy, strength, and agility from the night of the failed takedown. He glanced at Joe. Joe jogged a few miles a day and belonged to a boxing club.

But Mok was young, so vitally young, chiseled into shape, as quick as a bird, as decisive as a thunderclap, and ten years younger than Joe. Twenty-six years younger than Gilbert. Next to Mok, Gilbert's own flesh felt corrupt, withered by age into an undignified mass of wrinkles, flab, and graying hair. He felt energy coming off Mok, like sparks off a flywheel. In sensing that energy he grew even more apprehensive, knew then and there that Mok was going to try something—but was too late in formulating a response, even as he saw the precipitating twitch in Mok's shoulder, the widening of his eyes, and the spring in his knees. A microsecond later, Mok jumped for the speedboat driver. His hands, though ostensibly bound behind his wrists, came suddenly free, the cords slipping from them as if they were no stronger than yarn, his left thumb bloody, as if cut by glass. Gilbert remembered the broken J&B bottle. Had Mok been able to cut the cords with a piece of broken glass?

Mok reached under the driver's nightclub blazer and secured the driver's gun from the waistband of his pants. Both Gilbert and Lombardo lunged for Mok, but Mok was too fast. Mok fired the weapon, blasted the speedboat driver's head with three quick rounds. The driver slumped forward onto the throttle, pushing the throttle forward so that the boat gained speed. The wheel twisted right and the boat lurched. Mok swung round and, using both hands clasped around the weapon as a club, hit Lombardo in the head. Lombardo stumbled backward. The boat gained yet more speed. With no one steering, it careened sharply to the right, pitching Gilbert off balance. He clutched the windshield, steadied himself, tried to grab Mok's weapon, but the weapon disappeared like smoke, Mok pulling it away in a blur of speed. Lombardo regained his balance and landed a punch to the side of Mok's head, but the punch seemed to have no effect. The boat lifted on its side, bobbed nervously on the water, cut a reckless arc through the typhoon shelter, narrowly missing several old pier supports. Gilbert grabbed the wheel and tried to steady the vessel. In those two or three seconds, out of the corner of his eye, he saw Mok strike Lombardo in the face, once, twice, three times, hands clenched over the grip of the gun, stunning Lombardo, knocking him off balance. Gilbert thought for sure that Mok would shoot Lombardo, but for one reason or another he didn't. Mok pushed Lombardo. Lombardo stumbled backward and tripped over the twenty-gallon gas tank. Tripped just as Gilbert turned the wheel to avoid an oncoming boat.

That's all it took.

Lombardo tried to regain his balance but he couldn't. He tumbled over the side of the boat into the water.

"Joe!" cried Gilbert.

The boat gained yet more speed. Gilbert looked over the stern and saw his partner break the surface in a foam of white and green bubbles. Lombardo cleared the water from his eyes, gazed after the boat, and started treading water.

Mok swung round, pointed the gun at Gilbert's head, then flicked his eyes beyond the windshield.

"Turn," said Mok.

Gilbert whirled around. The typhoon shelter's concrete embankment loomed dead ahead. He wrenched the wheel to left. The boat shuddered, came within a few yards of the concrete embankment, knocked against an unoccupied sampan, then heaved 180 degrees, breaking free of its own wake, hopping over its own waves in a breathtaking leap, the propeller leaving the water for a second and howling in the air. Mok flung himself in the chair next to Gilbert's. Gilbert hunched over the dead man. He maneuvered the boat into the access channel, steering clear of obstacles.

"Head for open water," said Mok.

Mok spoke English without a trace of accent, a flat, generic, mid-continent North American English. They sliced through the water, Gilbert leaning against the dead man to keep control of the boat, the right leg of his pants absorbing blood like a surgical dressing. So many small boats out here. He weaved in and out, dodging them like a skier through a slalom.

"Can we move this guy?" he called. "It's hard to steer."

Mok remained silent, kept his gun pointed at Gilbert's head, scanned the horizon, then looked behind the boat. As they moved out into the harbor, the waves grew larger and the boat rocked. Spray flew over the bow. Mok turned around and looked at the horizon again. He finally nodded.

"Okay," he said. "Move him."

Keeping one hand on the wheel, Gilbert grabbed the dead man by his collar, dragged him from the chair, dumped him in the middle of the boat, and sat behind the wheel. He clutched the throttle and pulled it back, hoping to gain a measure of control by slowing the boat down.

"Keep going," called Mok, flicking the gun forward. "Push it back up."

Gilbert reluctantly pushed the throttle back to full. "Where are we going?" he asked.

"That way," said Mok.

They passed the western tip of Hong Kong Island and headed

well out into open water, leaving the city far behind. Gilbert saw a few low peaks rise out of the surf ahead of them.

"Take that channel over there," said Mok.

Gilbert steered to the right and negotiated a channel between two islands, afraid but controlled, not yet sure what Mok planned to do with him. Beyond the two islands, the sea once again opened up.

"Straight that way," said Mok.

They traveled west for another ten miles, covering the distance in twenty minutes.

"Okay," called Mok, "cut the throttle."

Gilbert eased back on the throttle until it clicked into the neutral position.

"Now come over here," said Mok.

Gilbert got up from behind the wheel. He stepped over the dead man. Mok kept his finger poised on the trigger.

"Sit over there," said Mok, waving the gun at one of the backseats.

Gilbert did as he was told.

"Put your hands behind your back."

Again, Gilbert did as he was told.

Mok tied his hands behind his back with the dock twine he had cut from his own, looping it around Gilbert's wrists, then around the chair, making sure Gilbert couldn't get up. Mok then stuffed the gun into the waistband of his jeans. With this done, he grabbed the dead man, and with surprising strength, hoisted him to the side of the boat and dumped him overboard. He turned to Gilbert.

"I didn't want to kill him," he said. "He was actually a friend of mine. But what choice did I have?"

Mok got into the driver's seat, pushed the throttle forward, and headed northwest, out into the open sea.

CHAPTER
TWENTY-ONE

THEY DROVE FOR A LONG time through the darkness. Sometimes Mok looked behind the boat, checking for pursuers. Sometimes he looked at the sky. Gilbert tried to keep track of direction but because the moon went behind the clouds again, and Mok made so many crazy turns, he eventually gave up. Northwest, northeast, due north, that's about all he could make out. Gilbert saw no land, no boats, no islands anywhere.

Mok finally slowed the boat and cut the engine. The outboard motor coughed a few times and shuddered to a stop. Cutting the engine way out here didn't seem particularly prudent to Gilbert—what if it didn't start again?—but there was nothing he could do about it. The silence was like a shock, sudden and disorienting. The shifting clouds, brightened by the moon, provided just enough light to see by. Mok went to the back of the boat and tossed a twenty-pound anchor overboard. He then sat in the seat next to Gilbert and peered at the detective.

Mok had a handsome face, his skin smooth, dark, molded over distinctive cheekbones. Gilbert couldn't help thinking of Foster Sung. Sung had similar cheekbones. Mok's long black hair had some curl, unusual for a Chinese. So did Foster Sung's. The moon struggled out from behind a roving pack of six or seven clouds.

"You know how to be quiet," Mok said. "I like that." He gazed at the bubbles in the water where the anchor sank. "I remember you. From that night on Boulton. And I know why you're here. You're here about Edgar, aren't you?" Mok grinned, as if he somehow found the thought of Edgar amusing. "You're here to arrest me, aren't you?" He shook his head, grinning even wider, as if behind this one isolated moment, this strange and increasingly protracted moment, there existed a vast construction of fact and circumstance he somehow couldn't help feeling happy about. "Let's talk about Edgar," he said. His eyes were congenial now. "He's the soup of the day, isn't he? He's the reason we're here. Funny how a dead man can have such power over our lives." For a man so young, Mok sounded self-assured, was at ease with the situation. "I understand what you have against me." He turned to Gilbert, his grin widening to a smile, as if he had nothing against Gilbert personally. "I know about the gun, the bullets, the blood, and your witness."

In the scant moonlight, Gilbert studied Mok's face, waiting, trying to find something predictable in this unpredictable man. Gilbert wasn't sure how Mok could know about the evidence—but he did, and that was that. He was a connected gang member; no doubt he had his sources; maybe even sources leading right back to 52 Division's corrupt police ring.

"You didn't have to kill the boat driver," said Gilbert.

Mok's face settled. He looked at Gilbert, an unwelcome challenge in his eyes; he stared at Gilbert for close to ten seconds, then turned and looked into the water, as if trying to find in its murky green depths an explanation for why his life had become so crazy. He seemed to lose track of time as he stared at the water, of where he was and whom he was with.

"I'm sorry I had to do that," he finally said. "But what choice did I have? Hoi would have killed me." Remorse flickered in Mok's eyes. His shoulders sank. His previous challenge was now replaced with regret. "Hoi has a wife. He has two small girls." Mok shook his head. "One of the first things I'm going to do when I get back to Hong Kong is give some money to his widow. She'll need it. So will her children. I have some money stashed away. I'll make sure her kids are okay. I'll make sure they're looked after."

Mok stood up, walked to the front of the boat, turned around, and jumped onto the seat, a natural acrobat. He scanned the sea, still looking for pursuers, then glanced at the sky. The boat heaved up and down in the swell.

"And as for Edgar?" asked Gilbert.

Mok turned his attention back to Gilbert. He rocked his hips in time to the waves. He was handsome. He was capable. But he was also unnerving. He carried the gun loosely in his hand. "As for Edgar," he said. He shook his head, at first slowly, then more quickly, and the smile came back to his face. He looked as if he were going to laugh about Edgar. "As for Edgar . . ." He paused, as if Edgar were an enigma he still hadn't figured out. Mok looked at Gilbert. "That scar on Pearl's face?" he said. "You've seen it?"

A few waves slapped the side of the boat. "I've seen it," said Gilbert.

"Edgar did that to Pearl."

"I know."

Mok's face settled, as if he were disappointed that Gilbert

should know about this already. "But do you know *why* Edgar did that to her?" he asked.

"No."

"Because Bing Wu made him do it."

Gilbert's eyes narrowed with puzzlement. "Bing Wu *made* him do it?"

Mok nodded. "Bing Wu won't be dishonored by anybody," he said. "Isn't that ridiculous? He thinks up punishments for people who dishonor him. Retired people like him have nothing better to do. He made Edgar slash her face. That's why the scar looks so neat and careful. He made him slash her face as a punishment and a warning to both of them. It was either that or be killed." Mok rested his hand on the windshield of the boat. "Isn't that the craziest thing you ever heard?" Mok smiled, as if he believed such cruelty otherworldly. "Bing Wu shows his love for Pearl by making her understand he owns her." Mok nodded. "He made Edgar slash her face because Edgar was her lover. And as far as Bing Wu's concerned, that's dishonor. Someone should put the old fool out of his misery."

Gilbert now wished he had questioned Hukowich and Paulsen more closely about Bing Wu. A cloud poured across the moon like a spilled glass of milk. He wondered if in their encyclopedic file on Bing Wu they had anything about the marriage between Bing Wu and Pearl. Several questions came to mind. Why would such a young beautiful woman marry such an old dangerous man? How did they meet? Where did they meet? And what was the original connection between Edgar and Pearl? Was Bing Wu so far removed from everyday society that the facial mutilation of his bride might seem like a reasonable punishment for her infidelity? The cloud passing in front of the moon, in its transparency, took on pink and purple hues; the moon was just visible as a murky disk underneath. And if facial mutilation was a just punishment for a wayward bride, was there then not something warped about Bing Wu, something that should have scared Pearl off in the first place? How could she have ever made such a disastrous mistake? How could she have ever found herself in a seemingly unbreakable bond to the Hong Kong crime baron?

Mok shook his head as the smile faded from his face. He continued. "She and Edgar had to be careful after that," he said. "They really had to take it as a warning. You'd think the old man would realize his mistake. That in doing something like that to Pearl it would only make Pearl want to get away from him. But he didn't. And Pearl wanted to get away from him. He knew she was trying to get away so he had her watched. He didn't seem to realize that he couldn't keep her as his wife by having his guys watch her all the time. But that's what he did. How would you feel, having to live like that? Like you're in prison. Guarded all the time. Having Peter Hope follow you around all the time. You would want to get away too. Pearl certainly did. So she and Edgar made up this plan. It couldn't be any plan, not with Bing Wu watching her all the time. It took some doing but they finally got all the pieces into place. They were going to run away to San Francisco together. They were going to scam some drugs, or money, or both, and they were going to use that to start a new life in San Francisco. Go underground there for a while."

Gilbert remembered the quotes for flights to San Francisco on Edgar's desk. "So you killed Edgar because Bing Wu knew he was going to take her away to San Francisco?"

"No," Mok said, surprised by this.

"One of our informants tells us you were hired by the 14K to kill Edgar."

Tony shook his head. "No," he said. "No, not at all. You're not following me. I didn't kill Edgar. It wasn't *me*. It wasn't me at all." A short incredulous guffaw escaped Tony's lips. "You miss the point, my friend. I thought you were a detective."

Gilbert was rankled by this. "Then what's the point?" he asked.

"*Pearl* killed Edgar," he said. "That's the point. That's the real soup of the day. That's the main course, too. That's the fuckin' bill with a tip, my friend."

Gilbert frowned. "Then why does all the hard evidence point to you?"

Mok jumped from the seat of the boat and came nearer. "Piss on the hard evidence," he said. "I'm telling you what happened, and I'm telling you for a reason. Pearl killed Edgar. I saw it with my own eyes. Who needs hard evidence when you've got a motive as big as hers?"

"And what motive is that?" asked Gilbert.

Mok calmed down. The light of the moon illuminated his face. "Edgar changed his mind," he said. "There's your motive. He told her he wasn't going to take her to San Francisco anymore. There's your motive. Three years in the planning, she's living in fear of Bing Wu all the time, and at the last minute Edgar changes his mind and burns her. That's her motive." Mok shook his head, as if he truly commiserated with Pearl. "I don't know whether there was another woman . . . but . . . Pearl thinks there was." He raised his eyes toward the sea. The sea undulated. The waves rocked the boat from the south. "November was a strange month for Edgar," he said. "Back in November, Edgar was always changing his mind. So I wasn't surprised when he changed his mind about Pearl. I don't know what happened to Edgar in November, but he wasn't the same old Edgar I knew. He wasn't the same man at all. He really had something on his mind."

Mok lifted a rusted juice can, lowered it over the side, filled it with water, and sluiced the blood from the driver's seat.

"Usually he'll play with the . . . the other players," said Mok. "But starting the end of November he played only for himself, didn't give a shit about anybody, not even Pearl." Mok lifted his hand to his face and rubbed his eyes with his fingers. "He hires on as a courier for Foster—that was part of his and Pearl's plan to scam some drugs and money. He goes to Vancouver to buy some drugs for Foster, but then he hijacks the deal on the way back, steals the product from Foster and stashes it somewhere. Foster won't kill him. He can't. Not when he feels the way he feels about Edgar's mother. Edgar and Pearl are going to split the product. But Edgar rips her off. Half that product is Pearl's. She helped broker the deal with Bing Wu in the first place. She gets burned. There's your motive, my friend. There's your full-course meal."

Mok paused. He folded his arms in front of his chest and shook his head. Gilbert thought about it. Edgar going to Vancouver. He had Detective Pam Nichols's report sitting in the case file at headquarters, verifying Mok's claim. Edgar squirreling away a multimillion dose of China White. He had that dose sitting in the evidence locker at work, verifying Mok's story yet again. He was beginning to believe Mok. He stayed quiet, let Mok continue.

"He's got all this product," says Mok. "He has everything he needs to start over in San Francisco with Pearl. But then he makes the big mistake of saying no to Pearl. Of turning around and burning her. And not only did he burn her, he broke her heart as well. And breaking her heart like that just pushed her over the edge."

Mok leaned against the side of the boat, got more water, and washed away yet more blood. The man looked exhausted, hungry. Gilbert remained silent. He had the wire. He was getting all this on tape. He would just let the man talk.

"Pearl asked me to talk to Edgar," said Mok. Mok put the juice can down and turned to Gilbert. "But I tell her it's probably better if she talks to him. Edgar and me don't get along, and for some reason, near the end of November, he detests me more than ever."

More corroboration, thought Gilbert; Rosalyn Surrey telling him how Edgar had changed near the end of November, how a darkness had come over him. The detail stuck, seemed to charge the damp sea air between Gilbert and Mok. Mok tapped the edge of the boat a few times. What in heaven's name could have changed Edgar?

"I tell her that I'll back her up, that I'll go with her, and that if things get too rough, I'll step in. She pays me. I do this. I earn money this way. I stand there looking tough. Like I'm a trained pit bull. Edgar doesn't scare me. I can take him any time." Mok shook his head, as if he were bewildered by everything. "He has the product somewhere, we don't know where, but we go over there thinking we'll be able to get it from him." He scratched his wrist; Gilbert saw rope burns from the dock twine. "Pearl still wants to get away from Bing, and she says she's going to need her half of the product to do that. So we go to Edgar's. I say to her, here, take my gun, that little two-shot isn't going to be worth much if things get out of hand."

"So you gave Pearl your gun?"

"I gave her my gun."

The gun explained, he thought. Mok's gun. Mok's bullets.

"She went up to Edgar's apartment first," said Mok. "Once she got inside she unlocked the French doors while Edgar was in the kitchen doing something. That's how I got in later on. The plan was, she would go in first. I would sneak up the back way and be ready on the fire escape if things got out of hand." Mok shook his head. "I spied on them from the back landing. Pearl kept moving around at first, talking and talking. She can talk a lot when she wants to. She was trying to convince Edgar. This went on for about ten minutes, her just talking, pacing around, moving her hands. Edgar just sat there, not saying a word. I could see Pearl getting madder and madder." Mok nodded at the memory. "She started yelling. Edgar got up and gave her a shove toward the door, like he was trying to get rid of her. I got nervous. Things were heating up. Edgar had his gun on the table. I didn't like that at all."

Gilbert remembered the clip of ammunition to the gun they had never found.

"And I thought to myself, only a man hiding a lot of horse in his apartment keeps a gun on his table," said Mok. "I decided I had to go in. Pearl was paying me to protect her, to help her get the product, so I figured I had to do my job."

"So you went in."

"I went in."

"And what did Edgar do?"

"He lifted his gun and pointed it right at me. I thought for sure he was going to shoot me. I was unarmed. I say to him, 'Edgar, calm down, Pearl wants me here, Pearl asked me to come. We just want to talk about this product.' Then, before you know it, Pearl pulls out *my* gun. Edgar turns to her. 'Put down the gun, Pearl,' he tells her, but she just stands there, like she's through with talking to him. 'Put the gun down,' he says again. 'And then leave,' he says. 'I never want to see you again,' he says. That's when her face goes blank. I've never seen it go blank like that before. A few seconds later she pulls the trigger. I couldn't believe it. Everything happened so fast. Bang. A single shot right in the gut. We just stand there. Edgar goes to the chair and sits down. He pulls some Kleenex from the box but he can't hang on to it and he drops it to the floor. He looks at his stomach and he's bleeding all over the place. He looks at Pearl. Like he's really disappointed in her. Pearl just keeps looking at Edgar with this blank look on her face, pointing the gun right at him, as if she's going to shoot him again. May comes racing up the stairs. You should have seen her move. I've never seen an old woman move so fast. She was practically flying." So May heard the shot after all, thought Gilbert. "She comes in, she sees Pearl with the gun in her hand, and Edgar sitting in the chair bleeding." Mok turned to Gilbert, his eyes widening. "May starts yelling at Pearl, 'Put the gun down, put the gun down, put the gun down,' and then she hurries to her son to see if she can help him. I just stood there doing nothing. I didn't think things could get out of hand so fast. But Pearl was mad. I'd never seen her so mad. She just went right over the edge. Bonkers. But in a cold quiet way. It was the most amazing thing to watch."

CHAPTER
TWENTY-TWO

AT THAT POINT, FAR TO the southeast, a boat appeared. All Gilbert could see were its lights. Mok's body stiffened and he stared at the boat with animal intensity, his concentration razor-sharp. The boat moved to the northwest. Mok hoisted the anchor, then went to the wheel of their own boat and started the engine. Keeping the running lights off, he drove slowly to the northeast, away from the other vessel.

They moved at no more than five knots, driving quietly through the dark for the next twenty minutes, leaving only a small wake behind them. *Pearl killed Edgar*. Gilbert could see it now. She was impulsive. She was prone to mood swings. Her emotional barometer, as he had witnessed firsthand, was fickle, prone to wild and sudden changes. The swell of the sea was even, with perfect aquamarine arches and dips, translucent and smelling of brine, making the boat bob. He couldn't help thinking of the gunshot wound. Ripping Edgar's flesh open on the left, tracing a superficially damaging path to the right, coming to a stop just above his duodenum.

If Mok had fired, the bullet would have followed an entirely different trajectory. The sideways trajectory meant Pearl had fired. From the hall.

Far to the rear, the lights of the passing boat grew intermittent, twinkling, and finally disappeared. Poor Pearl. Confused, trapped, desperate, making one last futile attempt to escape from the tyranny and brutality of her husband. Heartbroken and double-crossed. Burned, as Mok called it. Was pulling the trigger really such a hard thing to do under those circumstances?

"Why did Pearl marry Bing Wu in the first place?" he asked.

Mok increased his speed; their small wake began to bubble more insistently, frothy and silver, churning the water into whirlpools, leaving an ever-widening train of foam behind them. Mok glanced over his shoulder.

"Because her family was in debt to him," he said. "Her parents owed him money. They couldn't pay him. So Wu came up with this alternative. To marry Pearl. Pearl had no choice."

This made Gilbert pity Pearl all the more. He thought of her stunningly beautiful face, the childlike quality of her eyes, their veiled desperation, and remembered how on that night in One Park Lane she had seemed somehow ruined, lost, beyond redemption. The China bride, as Lombardo had called her. But she hadn't been a bride at all. She had been a sacrifice. Payment for a loan gone bad. She had been a victim. Now, in her desperation, pushed by her changeable and erratic personality, she had shot Edgar. It didn't seem fair that she should go to jail for that. At least not for the next twenty-five years.

"How did she and Edgar meet?" he asked.

Mok eased up on the throttle, turned on the lights, stood up and peered over the windshield, looking for something, or maybe afraid of running aground. Satisfied that the way was clear, Mok again glanced at Gilbert. He raised his voice over the noise of the engine.

"They met as kids in Hong Kong," he said. "When Edgar first got there from Vietnam. He was in a boarding school for a while. Victoria College. They met there. She went to the girls' school next door. St. Michael's. Foster knew Pearl's parents. I think that's how Pearl and Edgar got introduced. They became friends. They always kept in touch. Even after Edgar moved to Canada."

Gilbert remembered the China White knapsack from Edgar's attic, the one with the Victoria College emblem on it. Pearl was thirty-five now. She must have been extremely young when she'd met Edgar for the first time. Childhood sweethearts maybe? Two kids in love? Perhaps with plans to marry from way back? But then Pearl's parents borrowed money from Wu. A big mistake. And Pearl had had to sacrifice herself—and her love for Edgar—so that her parents might live. The whole thing oppressed him. He wanted to help Pearl. He didn't want to see her go to jail for any unreasonable length of time, not when events had so unreasonably conspired against her.

"We found Edgar's blood in your car," said Gilbert, believing he still might yet shift the guilt to Mok.

"I was standing right next to Edgar when she shot him," said Mok. "I got blood all over me."

Perfectly plausible. He knew Mok was telling the truth. But what he didn't get was why Mok was taking all this trouble to *tell* him the truth. What was his agenda? What did he hope to gain? Why not just take Gilbert out to the middle of the sea, shoot him, and dump him? What was Mok's motive? Gilbert knew he had to have one.

"Deal?" said Gilbert. "What deal?"

They were now anchored within sight of land, a dark low strip on the eastern horizon with a few lights showing here and there.

"We had a deal and Bing Wu broke it. Now he has to suffer. The only way he suffers is through Pearl. I want him to suffer badly. I want him to understand that he can't get away with what he's done to me. And Pearl's got to understand too. She played right along. She knows what's going on. As much as I like her, and as much as I feel sorry for her, she's got to be made to understand that she can't do this to me."

Gilbert raised his eyebrows. "And what have they done to you?" he asked.

"Bing hired me to take the fall," said Mok, as if it were obvious. He folded his arms in front of him. "He hired me as a defendant to take the fall for Pearl on Edgar's murder. If she was ever arrested for Edgar's murder, I was to step forward."

"As the perpetrator?"

"As a way to keep Pearl clear of trouble for shooting Edgar." Mok nodded. "When Wu found out how seriously you were investigating Edgar's murder . . . when he discovered that the police were taking a close look at Pearl . . . and at me . . . he offered me a million dollars to take the fall. He knew if I stepped forward, the police, because of all the circumstantial evidence against me, would likely arrest me and make me stand trial for Edgar's murder. That would remove Pearl from risk." Mok gestured toward the south, where the Jewel of Asia—Hong Kong—cast a misty glow into the scattered clouds from behind the dark ridge of coastline. "He invited me to Hong Kong to get my money. That's why I'm here. To get my million dollars."

Bing was obviously willing to go to a lot of trouble and expense to protect Pearl from what Peter Hope called her more naive proclivities. The scheme was original, and Gilbert, beginning to understand why Wu was so close to the pinnacle of the organized Asian crime underworld, had to concede at least that the man might have a true and dire weakness for Pearl. Wu wanted to protect her. Did that mean he loved her? Honestly and truly loved her? Was such a man—the dark vortex at the center of all this—capable of love? And if so, was his love unrequited, just as Foster Sung's love for May Lau was unrequited? Here was an interesting parallel, he thought. Two men driven by women who didn't love them.

"He said he would hire the best lawyers for me," continued Mok. "That was part of the deal. I talked to a couple of lawyers on my own. They said any good lawyer could argue the killing down to a manslaughter." Twenty thousand feet up, a jet hissed by. "So I said yes to Wu. I told him I would take the fall. I might catch eight years for manslaughter, but the lawyers said they could get me out in three. That's over three hundred grand a year for just sitting around. That's good money as far as I'm concerned." Mok took a deep breath. "So I came to Hong Kong," he said. "And I was treated like a king. At least for the first few days. I was Pearl's savior. I had dinner with the old man twice." Mok looked up at the jet. "Then Wu's guys came and got me in the middle of the night at my hotel." The frequency of the waves momentarily increased. "They beat me." Mok looked proud of his beating. "They tied me up. It took seven of them. They kept me on that houseboat." The waves lessened, and for several seconds the speedboat was still. "Bing Wu came to the houseboat and personally told me the police had watertight evidence against me. Bing likes to gloat whenever he can. He likes to parade in front of his enemies. When you're his age, there's not much else to do. He asked me why he should waste all that money on me when officers in Toronto were already convinced I was the one who had killed Edgar?" Mok shook his head and sighed in irritation. "He burned me. Burned me just the way Edgar burned Pearl. And now he has to pay. He has to learn that no one burns Tony Mok. The only way you can teach Bing Wu anything is by hurting Pearl. You've got my testimony. I knew you were coming. When you send Pearl to jail, Bing might finally learn his lesson. I hope you send her away for a long time."

So. Here was the reason Mok was telling him all this. For revenge. Three hundred grand a year. For just sitting around. Now it was gone. To a young man like Mok, it must have seemed like a fortune. And now he was, to use his own word, burned. Gilbert's knees started to ache as the adrenaline eased from his body. He saw now that he had been duped by the Red Pole. But that didn't bother him so much. What bothered him was how Pearl was going to suffer. Gilbert had everything on tape. Even a mediocre lawyer could argue that the tape was admissible evidence. And Pearl would take the fall, not Mok. Hukowich and Paulsen would have a field day. They would go in for the kill. They would hurt Bing Wu—just as Mok wanted to—by hurting Pearl. Because they couldn't get Foster Sung, they would take Pearl as a consolation prize. He *knew* they would. And he couldn't let that happen. Not when she was such a victim in the first place. He had to do something.

"So Edgar drew his gun on you," he said, "and then Pearl drew *your* gun on Edgar?" said Gilbert.

"Yes."

"I want to get this straight."

"That's the way it happened," said Mok.

"Do you think there's any possibility that Pearl might have shot Edgar to defend you?"

Hukowich and Paulsen would have yet more conniption fits. But he had to do this. His own moral sense forced him to forge ahead. A line came to Mok's brow. Mok sucked in his lower lip, chewed it, nodded.

"Maybe," he said. "Maybe."

There. That's all it needed. Even a mediocre lawyer could take that somewhere. Victimized into a marriage she detested, her beauty barbarously mutilated, her lover double-crossing her at the last minute—Pearl didn't deserve anything more than a few years as far as he was concerned. Pearl pulling the gun in defense of Mok might help. Crime, law, morality, compassion. Not many people suspected how often a homicide detective had to deal with these things, and how sometimes it ultimately came down to the homicide detective to decide the fate of a perpetrator like Pearl. What had him scared, what had him thinking his little effort for Pearl might not work, was the messed-up apartment. The messed-up apartment could easily be construed by any jury to be the aftermath of a robbery. Even if Kennedy had been the one to ransack the apartment, looking desperately for whatever incriminating evidence Edgar had against the corrupt police ring at 52 Division, Hukowich and Paulsen would inevitably try to prove first-degree murder by contending Pearl was responsible for the ransacked apartment. With the time lines so close, and the China White sitting there like a beacon, even a *mediocre* lawyer could argue away Kennedy's involvement. Pearl shooting Edgar during the commission of a felony robbery, even if it was in defense of Mok, was first-degree murder, plain and simple, according to the criminal code. The judge would sentence Pearl to twenty-five years under stiff parole stipulations. Bing would get his comeuppance. And they would send the poor woman away. She would be victimized yet again.

"So she shot Edgar, and then what happened?" he asked, thinking more details might help. "How does Foster Sung fit into all this?" he asked Mok. "When did he come up?"

"He came up a few minutes after May Lau did," said Mok. "I'm not sure why he came up . . . obviously he came up for something. By this time, May had Edgar lying on the floor. Pearl still had the gun in her hand. She looked white. I'd never seen her look so white before. I was standing there trying to get the blood off my coat with a piece of newspaper." Gilbert remembered the bloodied piece of newspaper from the apartment. "Foster came in and took control of the situation. He knelt beside Edgar and had a good look at his wound. May had this ball of Kleenex pressed against it. Foster took that away and lifted Edgar's shirt. The blood was coming out fast but he said he didn't think it was a fatal wound. He went to the kitchen and got a dish towel. He got May to press the dish towel tight against the wound. He said he thought we better make up a good story. We had to protect Pearl. The police and ambulance would have to be called and the last thing we wanted was Pearl to get in trouble. We all knew Bing Wu would make us pay if Pearl got into trouble. So we made up this story. Edgar is surprised by an unknown assailant coming through the balcony door. We all cooperated. Even May cooperated. That's how afraid we are of Bing Wu. My part was small. I got rid of the gun. I got rid of Pearl's gloves. We didn't want the police testing them for residue. I threw them in some back yard as I was running to my car. But then I thought I better not leave them there, so I went back to look for them. I only found one. I wanted to get out of there fast, so I didn't stick around to look for the other. Foster got rid of Edgar's gun. We all went our separate ways. Foster and May were going to pretend to discover Edgar ten minutes later, which I guess they did. I took off in my car. I met Pearl downtown later on. Just to make sure she was all right."

They put to shore in a small fishing village on a rocky beach well after midnight. Mok puttered into a protected cove and turned off the engine as they drifted to a rickety dock. He jumped onto the pier and tied the boat to a mooring ring. He then got back in and freed Gilbert's hands.

"I'm sorry I have to leave you like this," said Mok. Mok looked at the village. "But I have to make my getaway now," he added facetiously. "Wu will be after me. I guess I'm going to have to hide for a while. I hope you can use what I told you. If it hurts Bing Wu, then all this was worth it."

With a final few twists, the twine came loose from Gilbert's wrists. "Can I have my gun?" he asked. "It's under the front of the boat where those paddles are."

Mok smiled. "Sure," he said. "I'll toss it to you once I'm moving."

Gilbert nodded. He climbed out of the boat onto the dock. He felt sorry for Mok. He didn't hold out much hope for Mok. Mok was right. Wu would be after him.

"Tony, you should really come back with me," he said.

"Just go for Pearl," said Mok. "That's all I ask. I'll be fine."

"You should come back with me," he said. "We'll see what we can work out in the way of protection. And immunity. Other agencies are going to be interested in what you have to say about Wu.

And what you have to say about Pearl. You should really give your-self up. Wu's going to come after you."

"I'll be fine," he said. "Just go after Pearl."

Mok eased the throttle forward, moved away from the pier, and tossed Gilbert's gun to the dock. Mok waved, put the throttle to full, and sped away. Gilbert watched him go—watched him until he rounded the point. He sighed. He picked up his gun and put it in his holster. His shoulders eased, as much from relief as disappointment. He turned around and looked at the village.

He felt as if he had stepped into the fifteenth century, that's how old the village looked. He walked down the pier to the village. He counted the number of dwellings—twenty-three—plus an official-looking building in the village square. All the lights were out. As a foreigner, he wasn't about to go knocking on doors in the middle of the night. He was just going to lie low till morning.

He walked to a tree and sat down. He sat there thinking about Bing Wu. The invisible monster at the center of it all. Forcing Pearl into marriage. Making Edgar slash Pearl's face. Getting Tony to take the fall for Pearl's crime. A monster. He shifted, made himself more comfortable. He took a deep breath. Bing Wu. He could see why Hukowich and Paulsen were so eager to go after the guy.

At ten o'clock the next morning, having not slept at all, Gilbert sat in a barren but functional office in the village post office. He had a telephone pressed to his ear. A man in an olive-drab uniform with a red star on his cap stood before him staring at him suspiciously. He was in Kwangtung Province, nowhere near Hong Kong. A portrait of President Jiang Zemin hung on the wall. A few villagers peered through the window. Gilbert was covered in blood—Hoi's blood. His gun had been taken from him yet again. He looked a ruin. He was the only white man—the only *Westerner*—for miles around. The man in the uniform had every right to be suspicious.

"Ian?" said Gilbert into the telephone.

"Barry!" said Dunlop. "Blast it all, where are you, man?"

Gilbert glanced at the Chinese officer, exasperated by the whole long evening. "In the People's Republic of China," he said. "Without my friggin' passport." His lips stiffened. He wanted to see Regina. He wanted to see the girls. "Could you please come and get me? And bring me a decent cup of coffee while you're at it."

CHAPTER
TWENTY-THREE

UNIFORMED OFFICERS OF THE HONG Kong Police Force came to get Gilbert from the Chinese fishing village of Yencheng. They forgot to bring him coffee, but he didn't care, he was just glad to be getting out of there. They took him back to Hong Kong, following a coastal road through Kwangtung Province. Gilbert saw walled villages, temples with pagoda-style roofs, and bamboo-hatted peasants plowing rice paddies with ox-driven plows. He was anxious to get back to the hotel.

They crossed the defunct colonial border forty-five minutes later.

As he and the police officers made their way through the New Territories—the semi-rural and suburban area immediately north of Metropolitan Hong Kong—his suspicions about Dunlop were renewed. Something not right about the man, he thought again. Probably Wu's man. But then again maybe not. Just because there were corrupt police officers in 52 Division didn't mean there were corrupt police officers everywhere.

Still, being around the man irked Gilbert. The road veered close to the Kowloon-Canton Railway. Gilbert saw a train clanking north toward China. If Dunlop was indeed Wu's man, Gilbert wondered what role he was playing in this whole sad business.

He expected Dunlop to debrief him, but Dunlop mercifully allowed him to sleep first.

"We have everything on tape," said Dunlop. Gilbert didn't like the smile on Dunlop's face. Something told him he had to act fast if he was going to arrest Pearl successfully.

When he got back to the Ritz-Carlton, he phoned headquarters and had Gordon Telford write a warrant on Pearl for unlawful possession of a firearm. He was going to nab her on the Derringer, just as a way to hold her until he himself could write a more detailed warrant on the . . . yes, on the *manslaughter* charge.

"Phone me the minute you have her in custody," he said. "You're going to have to move fast."

He and Joe had lunch after that.

"Jesus, you really had me worried," said Lombardo. "I thought for sure he was going to kill you."

"No," said Gilbert, and took a sip of his second merciful cup of coffee. "No, he treated me fine. I was more worried about you. Man overboard, and all that."

Lombardo looked to one side, ignoring his eggplant with garlic sauce. "I'm going to have to work out more," he said. "It took me an hour to swim back to Ferry Street. It was a lot further than I thought. By the time me and Dunlop got in the helicopter and were heading out to sea, you were long gone. I'm sorry about that, Barry.

I'm a slow swimmer. I should come with you to Leaside Pool. I'm starting to lose my edge."

Gilbert shrugged. "I'm okay, aren't I?" he said. "Other than a bit of caffeine withdrawal, I'm perfectly fine." Gilbert grinned. "Eat your eggplant," he said. "The hotel's got a swimming pool. We can go for a swim later. I'll help you sharpen your stroke."

"You better phone your family first," said Lombardo. He shook his head. "I called them," he said. "I had to let them know that you were . . . you know . . . that you were out there with Tony. I felt it only fair that they should know the situation."

Gilbert nodded. "Okay," he said. "Thanks."

Because it was two o'clock in the morning in Canada, he put off phoning his family until six, Toronto time.

In the meantime, Dunlop called and asked Gilbert and Lombardo to come to HKPF headquarters. They took a taxi. Together with Dunlop and one of the DEA's Hong Kong agents—a proxy Paulsen—they sat around with coffee and croissants and listened to the Tony Mok conversation.

Once the tape was finished, Dunlop lifted his chin, curious. "What do you plan to do about Tony, now that he's on the run again?" he asked.

Gilbert gazed at Dunlop. His face settled. "I don't know," he said.

"Because he's murdered Hoi Hsien now, hasn't he?" said Dunlop. "And that's changed the complexion of the whole business." Dunlop raised his chin. "I think he's rather our bag of groceries now, don't you?"

Gilbert stared at his croissant. "I suppose he is," he said.

*   *   *

When Gilbert got back to the hotel, he had a message to call Gordon Telford. He called immediately.

"We got Pearl," said Telford. "We nabbed her at One Park Lane. We found the gun."

As Gilbert hung up, he grinned. Dunlop could sound the alarm to Wu's people any way he wanted now. They had Pearl, and nothing Dunlop could do was going to change that.

He phoned his family. Nina answered. Nina always answered. She was at that age where the phone was a necessary umbilical of life.

"You're okay," she said, sounding surprised but immensely relieved.

He smiled, overjoyed to hear her voice. "I'm okay," he said. "Is mom there?"

"Dad, you're really okay?" she said, her voice climbing into its higher range. This was his little girl, his little Nina. "Are you really all right? Did that guy hurt you?"

"I'm all right. I'm just tired. I want to see you guys badly."

He heard her pull the phone away. "Mom, it's dad. He's alive." Her voice now quavered with excitement. God, he loved that girl. The father-daughter connection between them vibrated all the way across the Pacific.

He heard the phone change hands.

"Barry?" said Regina.

"Hi," he said.

"Are you okay?" she asked.

Nothing made him feel better than hearing Regina's voice. A mellow soprano, supremely feminine, it made him think of her perfect white teeth and pink lips.

"I'm fine," he said. "Joe said he phoned you."

"What happened?" He heard the chronic worry in her voice. "I thought I was going to lose you." Her voice grew thin, as if the trials and tribulations of a homicide detective's wife were too great to bear.

He took a deep breath. "It didn't go quite according to plan," he said.

"But you're all right?" she said. "He didn't hurt you, did he?"

"I'm fine. I was thinking of you guys, though. Especially when I got to China. I spent a night under a tree there. And I thought about you guys constantly."

"Jennifer wants to talk to you."

"She does?"

"She's emotional, okay?"

Gilbert paused. "Okay," he said. He swallowed, prepared himself. "Put her on."

He heard the phone change hands again.

"Dad?" Jennifer sounded as fragile as a snowflake.

"Hi."

"Hi," she said.

"Are you okay?" he asked.

A long pause. "Dad, I'm sorry," she said at last. "I'm sorry I treated you the way I did. I thought I was never going to see you again."

"It's okay," he said. "I'm okay."

Another pause. Her voice got shakier. She started crying. "I'm really sorry I said all those things, dad. Mom said you looked so sad when you left. I really felt bad about that. I don't want you to be sad. That's not the way I want you to be. You're my father. You're my dad, dad."

Here was his firstborn. He remembered her as a child. Smart. Inquisitive. But dark. Prone to long periods of silent contemplation. Able to feel. And feel deeply. What he felt from her now was nothing but love. Nothing would ever change that, he realized. Her fiery passion for Randall, her passing infatuation with Joe . . . they were all ephemeral emotions compared to what he felt coming from her now.

"I'll be home in a day or two," he said.

"Good," she said. She paused again. He heard her sniffle. "That's good," she repeated. "I just want us to be normal again, okay? I don't know what happened to us. But it was like we were on different planets for a while. I don't want that to ever happen again."

"Neither do I."

A silence hung between them. The silence was more eloquent than all their words. "Love you, dad," she finally said.

"And I love you, too," he said.

"Here's mom."

He heard the phone change hands a third time. "Well?" said Regina.

"Well what?"

"Just a sec . . . she's going . . . she's leaving the kitchen." He waited. "Okay, she's gone. How'd it go?"

He took a deep breath and exhaled in relief. "It went a lot better this time," he said.

An hour later, Gilbert received another call from Ian Dunlop.

"I'm afraid Tony Mok's been murdered," said the HKPF officer. "Have a uniformed constable bring you to the Happy Valley Sports Ground apartment complex on Wong Nai Chung Road. I'm at the scene now. Apparently Tony was trying to give Hoi Hsien's widow some money. Two gunmen opened fire from the stairwell."

A driver came and got Gilbert and Lombardo at the Ritz-Carlton Hotel fifteen minutes later.

"Dunlop still bugs me," Gilbert told Lombardo. Lombardo's face was awash in the dim neon light coming from the street. "How could two gunmen be waiting for Tony? They would have to know Tony had plans to give Hoi Hsien's widow money. How could they know that without knowing about the tape? One of the first things Tony said to me was that he was going to give money to Hoi's widow. Dunlop heard the tape. He told those gunmen to go wait there in the stairwell on Wu's orders. Dunlop's working for Wu."

Towering buildings rose on either side of them as they made the slow climb up to the Pun Shan Kui—the mid-levels, as they were called—to the Happy Valley Sports Ground apartment complex. They veered right as they reached Wong Nai Chung Road, followed it south, and exited onto a side street just before the Aberdeen Tunnel. They got out of the car and walked the rest of the way to the apartment complex.

They entered the lobby and took the elevator to the seventh floor.

The corridor buzzed with police activity. Tony Mok lay facedown in the middle of the corridor in a meter-wide smear of blood, his hands at his sides, palms upward, his feet pigeon-toed, his head turned to the left, and his cheek speckled with blood. Gilbert and Lombardo looked at each other, then continued along the corridor past the open door of a tiny apartment where two detectives talked to a distraught young woman. They found Dunlop by the fire door at the end of the corridor conversing in fluent Cantonese with another detective. Spent shell casings circled in yellow chalk lay on the concrete floor of the stairwell landing. Dunlop nodded a greeting to Gilbert and Lombardo.

"I'm sorry this didn't turn out differently," he said.

"Is that Hsien's widow?" asked Gilbert, nodding back toward the apartment.

"That's her," said Dunlop. Dunlop shifted uncomfortably. He looked at Gilbert, slid his hands into his pockets as if he were trying to hide something. "Tragic, really. For Tony to end up like this. It doesn't seemed fair, does it? Oh, and by the way," he said, "I've just received word that Tony's blood phenotype and some other records have arrived from the Prince of Wales Hospital. Shall I have an officer bring them to your hotel? Are you still interested?"

Gilbert stared at Dunlop, disliking the man more than ever. "Yes," he said. "Have him bring it to our hotel."

"Right you are, then."

And that was that. He thought of Hoi Hsien, his purple velour nightclub jacket, his big ears, his pathetic attempt to play gangster; then he thought of Hoi's widow and her two little girls. He glanced at Tony one last time. He felt a presence in the air, that invisible monster at the center of it all, Bing Wu. There was no more to say. Tony lay dead on the floor, with corrupt police officers all around him. Gilbert turned to Lombardo.

"Let's get out of here," he said. He gave Dunlop one last look. "It smells in here."

The records from the Prince of Wales Hospital included not only the original of the blood phenotype on Tony but blood phenotypes on Foster Sung and May Lau.

"May Lau?" said Lombardo.

"I'm as surprised as you are," said Gilbert.

"Whatever prompted you to follow this up?" asked Lombardo.

"You know me, Joe," he said. "Desperate detectives always go for the long shot."

Gilbert phoned Dr. Blackstein in Toronto, and together they went over the results.

"Blood phenotype results are never a hundred percent accurate, Barry," said Dr. Blackstein when they were through. "But I'd say you've got a nine-out-of-ten chance that Foster Sung is Tony's father. And I would say that May Lau is his mother."

Gilbert hung up and told Lombardo the news.

"I still don't get it," said Lombardo. "Why would Foster and May deny their blood connection to Tony all these years?" He looked out the window, where Hong Kong glittered in the wet night. "Do you think Tony had any idea Foster and May were his parents?"

"No."

Lombardo frowned. "Why would they do something like that?" he said. "Why would they hide it from Tony? No wonder he turned out the way he did. I don't understand the way these people think, Barry, I really don't. This is almost as crazy as Edgar slashing Pearl's face, or Bing Wu hiring Tony to take the fall for Pearl's crime. How could May deny her own son? What is it with these people?"

Gilbert shook his head, as bewildered as Lombardo. "I wish I knew, Joe," he said.

BACK IN TORONTO, GILBERT AND Lombardo went to see Pearl Wu in her detention cell. Gilbert knew that holding her on a gun charge could be only a temporary measure, that they couldn't expect to hold her more than another two or three days before the Red Pole got her out on bail. But he hoped by then he would have affidavits from May Lau and Foster Sung to confirm her guilt in Edgar's murder.

Pearl smiled when she saw them, but her smile was wistful, and she looked infected—infected the way killers looked after they killed someone, afflicted with a brooding and persistent introspection; with guilt, fear, and, worst of all, with apathy. She looked at Lombardo. Her eyes widened.

"You a handsome guy," she said.

Lombardo grinned, but he wasn't taken in. Gilbert knew Lombardo felt the murder-rot coming off her. Yes, Gilbert wanted it arraigned as a manslaughter, she had suffered a lot, she was a victim, but, as Mok told it, her face still had gone blank at the penultimate moment. Her face went blank and she fired the gun. Blank with that blankness killers sometimes got. Her fervent love had been matched by an equally fervent hatred. And she deserved at least some time behind bars for that.

"And you're a beautiful woman," said Lombardo, because Lombardo couldn't stop being Lombardo, no matter what the circumstances.

She turned to Gilbert. "Hi you, there again," she said.

"Hi," he said. "I hope they're keeping you comfortable."

"No room service," she said. "And no complimentary towels."

"Pearl . . ." he said, his eyes narrowing. "Pearl, we know you killed Edgar. I spoke to Tony Mok in Hong Kong. He told me everything. And we have it all on tape." He had to make his try again. "The tape suggests you may have killed Edgar in defense of Tony Mok. You'd make this a lot easier if you'd just sign a confession to that effect."

Her beautiful Chinese eyes misted over with tears. "I not kill Edgar," she said. "You talk to my lawyer. I never kill Edgar." He saw she wasn't going to bite. "I love Edgar."

With that she began to weep. Her weeping reminded Gilbert of the way May Lau played the Chinese violin. Gilbert and Lombardo looked at each other. A woman weeping was a woman weeping, and what could you do about it? She had a lot to weep about. She was bursting at the seams with sorrow, and nothing they could do could fix that. Here was her grief, finally finding its full force. Here in this detention cell, Edgar's ghost haunted her. Here was her life, her sacrifice, and all the cruelty she had endured. She was a ruin, beyond redemption, any happiness fading right out of her, any hope long since departed. And so she wept.

There wasn't much left for her to do.

*   *   *

He went to see May Lau.

The day was windless, full of rain, with the drops coming straight down in thick silver streaks. May Lau wore black again. He had to look at her in a new light. She was Tony's mother. As on the previous occasion, she poured tea.

She dropped the teapot when Gilbert told her Tony was dead. Dropped it as if by accident. Her face showed no change. The hot green liquid dripped off the edge of the table to the floor. Her calico cat raised its head in momentary interest, then grew drowsy again and went back to sleep. Tendrils of steam rose from the cheap throw rug beneath the coffee table.

"These hands of mine," she said. She stooped to pick up the dropped teapot.

"Here, let me take that," said Gilbert.

He lifted the teapot and set it on the table. May Lau walked to the kitchen, came back with a towel, and wiped up the mess.

"How did he die?" she asked, her voice soft, resigned.

"He was shot."

May nodded, continued to wipe the tea from the floor, as if she always knew Tony would die that way. She was performing, he could see that. But her performance was a weak one, strained and unconvincing. As the dish towel grew dark with tea, she looked as if she were struggling for something appropriate to say.

"He was too young," she said at last.

Her words were anything but heartfelt. Her strain passed, and it now seemed to Gilbert that the death of Tony Mok meant nothing to her.

"I talked to him the night before he died," said Gilbert. "We talked about Edgar's murder." The same sad theme, played in a hundred different ways. Gilbert recounted Tony Mok's version of Edgar's murder to May Lau, how May had come up seconds after the shooting and found Pearl with a gun in her hand. He told her of Foster Sung's arrival.

"While Edgar lived, you all went with the unknown-assailant story," he said. "You knew Edgar would be questioned by police. He was going to tell them he had no idea who his attacker was. You were trying to protect Pearl. As a way to spare yourselves trouble from Bing Wu. But when he died . . . well, you all just waited to see what would happen. I'm sorry he died. And I'm sorry Tony died. You have my condolences."

He waited. Still no acknowledgment of Tony. He told her that her hearing was fine, that they had a report from Dr. Tse; he wanted to get under her skin for not acknowledging Tony. She made a face, but otherwise steadfastly denied Tony with her silence. He mentioned Rosalyn Surrey. He mentioned Garth Surrey. He told her how Edgar had broken Pearl's heart.

"I wouldn't know anything about that," she said.

"I've got the whole thing written out here," he said. "I'd like you to sign. Pearl has to do some time for this." He made his try yet again. "Even though we think she might have killed Edgar in defense of Tony, she still has to go behind bars for a while. It's only fair to Edgar."

May stared at a shredded spot in the sofa upholstery. The fabric looked as if it had been scratched to bits by her cat. The rain splashed against the window. She glanced at him through her big square glasses. She looked as if she had removed herself, as if she sat on top of a tall lonely mountain and didn't want anybody to bother her ever again. She ignored the defense-of-Tony theory. She was digging in her heels. She was going to deny. She looked afraid—afraid that if she were to say one word against Pearl, she might fall from the top of her mountain and never be able to climb back up again.

"Can we not forget this?" she said, her voice as soft as a wind chime. She gazed across the room, where her *erhu,* her Chinese violin, sat in the corner, its bamboo bow hanging over one of its two tuning pegs. Her eyes filled with sudden distress. "Why do you want to hurt me? Why do you want to hurt all of us? If I implicate Pearl, I put myself at risk. Why don't you let me be?"

"Because I clear murders," he said, apologetically. "That's what I do."

She continued to stare at her *erhu*. She was still on top of her mountain. Gilbert glanced at the instrument, the drum-like mahogany sound box, the snake-skin covering, the two cat-gut strings stretched along its ungainly neck, and wondered how such a primitive and ancient-looking instrument could make such sad music.

"I'm sorry," said May. "But I can't help you. Please go now. Please leave me alone. I've endured enough already."

Nothing about Tony. Nothing at all. Not even a tear. Her own son. He was perplexed. Lombardo was right. How could she deny her own son? What was it with these people?

AS GILBERT TOOK THE ELEVATOR to the twenty-fifth floor of Doncliffe Tower, he again wondered how May Lau, after her initial reaction of dropping the teapot, could so easily turn to stone about someone she had raised as a child, someone who was in fact her own son. The elevator doors opened on the marble-and-teak offices of New Asian Solutions. In sticking to her original story, she undermined Tony's story. Whether that would have an impact on Pearl's trial remained to be seen. He wondered if he should try again with her at a later date. If she would sign the statement, if she would take the stand, then even a mediocre defense attorney might reasonably offer her the homicide-in-defense-of-Mok theory as a way to pull herself free from any possible 14K reprisal. Pearl would have her mercy. May could go back up to the top of her mountain. And Gilbert would have his murder cleared.

Foster Sung sat forward in his chair, hands folded on his

desk, his face showing nothing, his eyes wide, unblinking, as Gilbert sat down.

"I'm afraid Tony Mok is dead," said Gilbert.

Foster Sung remained still. But then he leaned back in his chair and the strength ebbed from his body. He rested an elbow on an armrest, rubbed his nose, and narrowed his eyes. Sung's eyes momentarily clouded with tears. Gilbert could expect nothing less. Yet Sung kept himself admirably controlled, considering his blood connection to Tony, as if he, too, like May Lau, had distanced himself from Tony.

"He was gunned down in Hong Kong while trying to give money to the widow of a man he killed," said Gilbert. "We have reason to believe that Bing Wu ordered the killing."

Sung's face went stony. Gilbert kept talking; he wanted to give Sung time to recover. He told Sung of the events leading up to Mok's murder. He told him of his evening out in the boat with Mok, recounted Mok's story of the murder—how Sung had examined Edgar's wound, considered it survivable, then pressed the dish towel to Edgar's abdomen; how Sung, Mok, Pearl and May believed they could avoid a lot of police and 14K trouble if they told officers the shooter was an unknown assailant; and how they then had to abandon their unknown-assailant story because of Edgar's unexpected death.

"I've spoken to May Lau," said Gilbert. "She's sticking to her story." Gilbert couldn't help showing his perplexity, even though he had no intention, at least for the time being, of revealing to Foster Sung exactly what he knew about Tony. "She didn't seem particularly affected by Tony's death."

Sung looked up. "She didn't?" he said. "She wasn't sad?"

"No," said Gilbert.

Sung scanned his desk. His lips tightened. He grew still, calmer, seemed to retreat, folded his hands on top of his desk, took a deep breath, and looked out the window.

"Did she have any kind words for him at all?" he asked.

Gilbert saw this was important to Sung. He wished he could offer the suspected Kung Lok leader something that might make his pain easier. But he couldn't.

"She just wants to be left alone," said Gilbert. "She doesn't want to be bothered with Tony anymore. She's not going to help at all. That's why I'm here. I know Tony was your ward. I know he means something to you." Gilbert prowled around the edges of the truth. "You're distressed by his murder. I can see that. If his memory means anything to you," said Gilbert, "then here's your chance to clear his name and corroborate his story."

Sung paused for a long time. Gilbert saw the calculations, the tactical considerations—an examination of all the various scenarios and possibilities—flicker behind Sung's eyes.

"He deserves to at least be exonerated," Sung said at last. He raised his eyebrows, his resignation plainly evident. "I will help you, Detective Gilbert." His lips came together in an expression of resolve. "I will honor Tony's memory." He looked at Gilbert, his eyes clearing, the mist of emotion lifting from them. "But please first understand my intentions, why I did what I did on the night Edgar was murdered." Gilbert saw what Sung was doing—he was setting the ground rules, constructing a safety net before proceeding over dangerous territory. "I wished to save trouble," he said, "that's all. I wished to prevent harm. I never had anything but the best intentions." Sung glanced away. A hard look came to his face. "Pearl Wu did indeed shoot Edgar." He looked out the window. The drizzle was constant, thin, particulated, each droplet no bigger than a grain of sand. "What I told you before was true. I was on my way up to ask them to join me and my guests at my table downstairs." He paused, recollecting events. "When I got there, the door was ajar and I could hear May and Pearl crying."

"So everything you told me before about Pearl and Edgar having an argument when you went up, that's not true?"

Sung looked dismayed. "I'm afraid not," he said. "I was trying to protect Tony. You said you were looking for Tony. I thought if I could steer your suspicion, at least to a modest degree, in Pearl's direction, it might confuse your investigation enough to protect Tony."

Gilbert nodded. "Okay," he said. "So what you're telling me now is the truth?"

"Yes."

"So what happened?"

"I pushed my way in," said Sung. "Pearl stood by the door with a gun in her hand. May knelt next to Edgar. Edgar was lying on the floor by the table with what I saw was a minor gunshot wound to his abdomen. Tony was standing over by the bookcase trying to get some blood off his jacket with a piece of newspaper."

Here was the corroboration Gilbert needed. Regardless of the ultimate charge against Pearl, she was the instigator, the shooter, the wacky impulsive woman who carried around a Derringer, a gunhappy Gucci Chinese whose sense of right and wrong, life and death, love and hate had been hopelessly marred by her tragic bond to Bing Wu. Corroboration, yes. But now it was time for reasons. If anybody had any idea about the reasons, Foster Sung would.

"We found twenty-four hundred grams of heroin in Edgar's attic," said Gilbert.

Sung nodded, willing to concede the point, seemingly not

bothered by the personal legal risk it presented, holding up well despite the news of Tony's death. "Pearl and Tony went up to Edgar's apartment to recover property that didn't belong to him." He shook his head. "That's beside the point." Sung sat up straighter, lifted his chin, and took a deep breath, marshaling his thoughts, preparing himself for Gilbert's questions.

"Tony told me Edgar pulled a gun on him," said Gilbert. "That the reason Pearl shot Edgar was to stop Edgar from shooting Tony." Yes, he had to try for the poor woman. Despite the blank look in her eyes. The cage door had closed on her once again that night up in Edgar's apartment, and she'd only been trying to claw her way free. "Tony told me Edgar's move came unexpectedly, that he was just standing there doing nothing, waiting for Pearl and Edgar to finish arguing. Do you have any idea why Edgar might want to kill Tony?" Yes, he had to build it up, really try hard to convince Sung that it was all just a matter of defense so that when Sung took the stand he might face the Hukowich and Paulsen prosecutors with some ammunition. "Why would Edgar want to kill Tony?"

Of course the reason Edgar pulled the gun was obvious: Tony came in the back door unannounced looking for twenty-four hundred grams of heroin; but if Gilbert was going to make this work in court, he was going to have to sharpen and focus Edgar's murderous intent.

Sung looked at Gilbert speculatively. He showed no surprise. He appeared fully conversant with this particular aspect of the crime. But then Sung said, "Edgar had his reasons for killing Tony," and in that instant yet another complication was added to what was already a complicated murder.

"He did?" said Gilbert, feeling suddenly out of his depth, as if he were a caveman trying to understand rocket science. "Why would he want to kill Tony? We *do* have information that suggests Tony might have shot Edgar in Vancouver last August, but that was never corroborated, and we're beginning to discount that."

"Tony had nothing to do with that," said Sung. So much for Jeremy Austin's informant, thought Gilbert. And so much for Murphy's ballistics—a seventy-percent match was really no match at all.

"Then why did Edgar want to kill Tony?"

"In order to understand that," Sung said, "you have to understand what Tony and Edgar are to each other." He looked at Gilbert with appraising eyes—the man was trying to gauge the depth of Gilbert's understanding.

Gilbert decided to give him a break. "I know what they are to each other," he said.

Sung's eyebrows rose. "You do?" he said, with sudden emotion, as if he were actually relieved to hear this.

"I tracked down some blood phenotypes while I was in Hong Kong," he said. "They're half-brothers." He paused, looked out the window at the rain, endless rain, oppressive rain, rain all winter, and decided to open the bomb-bay doors. "You and May are Tony's parents."

Sung stared at Gilbert, as still as a deer in a forest, his eyes unblinking, the corners of his lips pulled down. He held this pose for several seconds, as if he had just witnessed an exceptional and perhaps paranormal demonstration of uncanny investigative skill and intuition. But then his shoulders sagged. He seemed to acknowledge Gilbert's words with this sag of his shoulders.

"This is so, Detective Gilbert," he said. And left it at that.

Outside, a DeHavilland commuter four-prop airplane angled down through the clouds toward the Island Airport.

"Why would Edgar pull a gun on his own brother?" asked Gilbert, wanting to get on with it.

"He had his reasons," said Sung, now sounding defeated.

"And if May Lau is Tony Mok's mother . . . she has no feeling for him. None whatsoever."

Foster Sung looked at him as if this were a point in which they might find common ground. "You find it incomprehensible that a mother can't love her own son?" said Sung.

"Yes." He loved his own children so much.

"Why Edgar pulled his gun on Tony, and why May has no motherly feeling toward Tony . . . you can't look at one without looking at the other. These are circumstances in a chain of circumstances that reach back a long way."

Gilbert leaned forward, rested his elbows on his knees, and gazed at Sung earnestly. "I have all afternoon," he said.

Sung's eyes narrowed. His face flickered with grief once more. He hesitated, as if he were trying to solve a complex puzzle, going over the same convoluted string of logic again and again but always winding up at the same dead end. "It happened nearly twenty-five years ago," he said.

His voice sounded thin, dry, as if the aperture of his throat had been squeezed. He looked overcome by everything, his eyes once again misting over with tears, his mouth opening as he took a small difficult breath, his lips stiffening into a rictus of remorse. Sung looked away.

"When we were forced to flee Vietnam," he said, "when we were forced to leave our country . . . a few years after the Communists took power . . . I offered passage on my freighter to May Lau, her husband, and Edgar. You know this . . . May's told you this." He seemed to struggle for the proper words. "To be honest, I wished I could have left May's husband behind. I loved May, and for that reason alone I wished I could have left Ying Lau behind. But May loved her husband, and I . . . I allowed him to come for her sake."

As Foster found his voice, he seemed to regain some of his composure, was able to continue with fewer moments of introspection and grief. He shifted in his chair, settled in.

"Ying insulted me constantly while we were on the boat," he said. He nodded at the memory. "He had a big mouth. He was a troublemaker. I never knew why May couldn't see this. He stole food while he was on the boat." Sung smiled at this, seemingly amazed by Ying's gall. "He wouldn't take any of the watches. He wouldn't even care for the children. He was always playing cards or dice." Sung looked at Gilbert. "Finally I thought I had to teach him a lesson. I thought I better force him to do his watches and take his fair share of the work. He was such a lazy man. So I had my men beat him. This might sound barbarous to you, detective, but in our various societies, secret or otherwise, it's believed that some men can learn a lesson only through their hide. Ying Lau was such a man. I had my men take him to the engine room and beat him. Not only wouldn't he do any of the work while on board, he owed me money, a lot, and he refused to pay. He was insolent. He was a fool. An oaf. He constantly dishonored me in front of May, in front of my crew, and in front of the other refugees. Dishonored me even though I'd saved his family from destitution and worse. I had many reasons for having him beaten. But the main reason was because of the way he mistreated May." Sung shook his head. "He mistreated her badly, detective." He shook his head as his eyes grew wistful with regret.

"Unfortunately, my men . . . my men went too far . . . they kept at him until . . . I'm sorry to report, but they kept at him until they beat him to death. They didn't mean to. They just went too far. We were all brutes back then. We'd just lived through a war. Human life meant little to us. We were all half crazy on that boat, frightened for our lives, hungry as could be, and thirsty, so miserably thirsty. In hindsight, it doesn't surprise me that they killed him. No one much liked him. He wouldn't lift a finger, even when the boat needed bailing."

"You told me he bailed so hard he worked himself to death," said Gilbert.

"That's just a story May and I concocted for Edgar's sake," he said. "So Edgar would remember his father as a hero." Sung's voice had taken on a brittle tone. Yet within that tone there was also defiance. "When he died," he continued, "when my men beat Ying Lau to death, I took May." His eyes focused more keenly. "Do you know what I mean when I say I took her, Detective Gilbert?" His face reddened. "I took her." He looked away. "I felt it was my due." He paused, leaned back in his chair. Gilbert waited. In a more reflective tone Sung said, "Way back when, I bought her gifts." He said this as if he thought it might mitigate the enormity of his admission. A melancholy grin came to his face. "Long before she knew Ying, I came to her with jewelry and flowers. I wanted her to love me. I wanted her to marry me. But she wouldn't. Or she couldn't. I was in a position to help her family. I was kind to her. But she refused me. I didn't understand."

Gilbert contemplated Sung. He again thought of the parallel between Sung and Bing Wu. Two men driven by women who didn't love them. Could there be anything more tragic? Unrequited love could at times be a dangerous force.

"The wrong sort of men always get power into their hands, Detective Gilbert," he said. "When she married Ying, I used my power. Power was the lesson of the day. I used indebtedness as a tool of bondage against May." Another parallel, thought Gilbert. "And when they had Edgar, when they had a son to look after, that just strengthened my resolve. I made them think they needed me. I made May think she needed me. And she did. Ying was bad with money." Sung shook his head. "I made loans to Ying. He welshed on every one of them. He was a gambler, spent everything at the gaming tables. I gave grocery money to May. At times she was grateful. At times she refused my generosity. But I persisted. I helped her with Edgar any way I could. I made her see that I could provide for her. I made her see that her husband was undependable, and that if she would only reconsider, she would have a much better life, or at least a much more comfortable life with me."

Sung was silent for several seconds.

"Well . . ." he said, casting about for more details. "Living conditions finally got so bad near the end of the war that even I found myself in dire financial straits. I did what I could for May, but we had a lot of shortages." Sung took off his glasses. Murder, war, mistrust, love, and hatred played behind his eyes in a dim kaleidoscope of emotion. "I had to go to great lengths to secure even the barest necessities for May, Edgar, and Ying. I risked my life several times for them." He covered his mouth with his hand, rubbed his lips with his fingers, and looked out the window at the overcast day. "May thanked me." He put his glasses back on. "But Ying took everything for granted, even during those hard times. You think he would show some respect for me. But he insulted me repeatedly. He took May for granted too. He knew how I felt about his wife and he thought I was a fool. He didn't even thank me when I offered them a spot on my boat." Sung leaned forward and looked at Gilbert more closely. "I wanted her so badly, detective. I needed her. So when Ying died, I took her. War can burn the conscience right out of a man. I wanted her and I was going to have her. I had my men bring her to my cabin. The ship was sinking. I was convinced none of us were going to get off that boat before it went down. What difference did it make if I finally got what I wanted? I'd fed her, I'd cared for her, I'd cared for her son, I'd even cared for her wretched husband. Now it was time to take my due."

Gilbert didn't see the point of trying to refute Sung's flawed logic, his justification for rape, and his futile attempt to convince away his actions by explaining them as something he believed he deserved. But he was at least beginning to see why May insisted on denying Tony. Sung grew still again, looked pale in the wan light coming from the sky.

"When we reached Hong Kong," said Sung, "we knew May was pregnant. By our second or third month in the refugee camp, she started having morning sickness. She wanted to report to the authorities what I had done to her, what I had done to her husband, but she knew she had to count on me. Who else was she going to count on? She was a refugee. She had to take what help she could get. You see? She needed me. She hated me but she needed me. That's what power is, detective. Her main concern was Edgar. Without me, she knew Edgar would have a tough time. If she jeopardized my freedom, she would have no one to support her. I had many contacts in Hong Kong. I had contacts everywhere. She knew I could arrange early release from the refugee camp for her. So we came to an agreement." A weak smile appeared on Sung's face. "We sold our souls, Detective Gilbert, each to the other. We made up a story for the authorities. We told them Ying died working himself to death bailing the boat. Then I got May and Edgar released from the camp. I squirreled May away in the New Territories during the last three months of her pregnancy and put Edgar in a boarding school. When the child was born, May refused to acknowledge it. She didn't want Edgar to know. She had a difficult labor. She was in the hospital for a whole week. When she finally came out of her confinement she insisted on a blood test to make sure of the child's paternity." Sung looked at Gilbert steadily. "The child, of course, turned out to be mine. The child, of course, was Tony." He shook his head, rubbed his brow, and sighed. "May and Edgar went to Canada three years later. I stayed with Tony in Hong Kong for the next five years after that. But I finally sent Tony to Canada as well."

Gilbert wasn't sure what this had to do with Edgar's reasons for pulling a gun on Tony, but he thought he'd better let Sung continue in his own way.

"May hated Tony from birth," said Sung. "He was a child of . . . of rape. She never told Edgar. I'm the one who finally told Edgar. I told him last November." He shook his head. "I wanted him to like Tony. I wanted to end all the secrecy." Sung looked at the diamond signet ring on his right hand. "I wanted them to really feel like brothers to each other. I've struggled for years trying to make a family out of the four of us. It's all I've ever wanted, but I've never succeeded. So I finally told Edgar. I never got around to telling Tony. I left Tony thinking he was an orphan. I didn't see the point of stirring up too much trouble at first. But near the end of November I told Edgar the whole story. The same one I'm telling you now. And something changed in Edgar after that. He couldn't stand the thought of what I had done to his mother. Or what I had done to his father. I wanted to be truthful. I was sick of all the lies. I wanted to build my family on a foundation of truth. I tried to give him the context, the war and so forth, the desperate times we were living in, his father's poor character, how his father's beating got out of hand . . . I thought he would understand . . . but he didn't. He hated me more than ever. He hated Tony more than ever. He changed. He said he hated everybody from Vietnam, and everybody from Hong Kong. He said he just wanted to start over fresh somewhere."

The end of November. The picture grew clearer. Something happened to Edgar at the end of November. A change. A darkness. Such as Rosalyn Surrey had said. Such as Tony Mok had said. Edgar just wanted to get away from it all. The Kung Lok. The 14K. Even Pearl. Just wanted to get away from it all and start a new life—with Rosalyn Surrey?—in San Francisco.

"I told him everything about Tony's conception," said Sung. "I thought I was doing the right thing. I thought if I did this, told the truth once and for all, I might finally have some luck turning the four of us into a family. I told Edgar that his mother and I were at peace with each other now. I thought he would accept that. I thought he would understand it. But telling Edgar the truth about Tony turned out to be the biggest mistake I ever made. Is it any wonder he pulled a gun on Tony? He felt he had to avenge his mother. And his father."

The rain outside came down harder. Through the tall dark buildings Gilbert caught a glimpse of the gray lake. Here were the reasons behind Edgar's actions, behind his decision to pull a gun on Mok, triggering Pearl's subsequent decision, prompting her to murder—a chain of circumstances that stretched all the way back to that boat in the South China Sea, to Sung's futile attempts to make May love him, and ultimately, to the Vietnam War. A love that had finally turned him into a brute. Just as Bing Wu's love for Pearl had turned Bing Wu into a brute. True, Sung was a man who had helped many escape from Vietnam. He was a man who had assisted dozens of orphans to make their way to the more prosperous shores of the Western democratic nations. But in the end, his love for May had defeated him. Love was so often blind and dumb and hurtful.

Gilbert still wanted to save what he could from all this.

"If you testify," said Gilbert, "if you tell the jury you believe Edgar pulled a gun on Tony . . . because of all this . . . because of what you told me . . ." Gilbert looked away. "And that Pearl shot Edgar to save Tony's life . . . well . . . she'll get a few years. And I think that's fair. She's a perpetrator, after all. But she's also a victim. She's suffered a lot at the hands of Bing Wu, but she also shot Edgar, and I think she should do some time for that. But I don't think it's right we should put a coffin lid on the rest of her life. If we can convince a jury that she fired in Tony's defense . . . well, they might show mercy."

Sung looked up, his face hardening. "Mercy?" he said. He shook his head, a deep woe coming to his face. "No. Forget mercy. I can only testify to what I saw." He took a deep breath and stared at Gilbert with clear steady eyes. "Pearl Wu standing there with a gun in her hand and Edgar lying on the floor bleeding to death. How you decide to proceed with those facts is entirely up to you, detective. Bing Wu killed Tony Mok. Tony Mok was my son. I loved Tony Mok, even if May didn't. I'm sorry if my testimony puts Bing

Wu's wife in prison for much of the remainder of her life. But I think Bing Wu will learn a valuable lesson from that. He will now know what it feels like to have his loved ones taken away from him. He will now know that pain. He will now know that grief. Just as I do."

CHAPTER
TWENTY-SIX

A TWENTY-ONE-YEAR-OLD POLICE volunteer named John Lotze found locker 43 in the Glengrove Shopping Mall, a mall of Chinese shops, restaurants, and boutiques in the suburban municipality of Agincourt. Inside the locker, constables of 42 Division discovered a briefcase—fake alligator leather, brass snaps with combination locks, and a New Asian Solutions travel tag tied to the handle. They delivered the briefcase to Toronto Police Headquarters, where it was X-rayed and examined by the Bomb Squad, then pried open by a remote-control robot. No bang. No explosion. Just three audiocassettes and a videotape.

The duty clerk brought the video and cassette tapes up to the Homicide office prior to their release to the Special Investigations Unit so Gilbert and Lombardo could review them for possible evidence in the Edgar Lau murder case. Gilbert requisitioned a TV and VCR from the Audio-Visual Department, but before the equipment could arrive, Lombardo, fulfilling his duties as the week's primary-detective-on-rotation, was called away to investigate a suspicious death near Grenadier Pond in High Park. Gilbert watched the videotape by himself. He played it again once Lombardo got back.

"Watch this part here," said Gilbert. "This has good footage of Donald Kennedy."

The videotape showed Constable Donald Kennedy accepting payments from Leslie Lee, a Kung Lok member—an odd-angled shot in a hotel room taken from a concealed-briefcase camcorder.

"And this next part here has Paul Szoldra in it," said Gilbert.

The tape showed Paul Szoldra out of uniform beating up an elderly Chinese fruit-store owner, presumably in an act of extortion, in a back alley just off Chestnut Street in Chinatown.

"Then there's these other guys," said Gilbert. "Nothing we can use in the Edgar Lau case, but certainly enough for the SIU to make some decent arrests down at 52."

The last part of the tape showed three 52 Division constables out of uniform accepting payoffs from Sid Yuen Pan and Leslie Lee.

"What about the audiocassettes?" asked Lombardo.

"They contain conversations of Donald Kennedy talking to Danny Leung," said Gilbert.

"Danny Leung?" said Lombardo, surprised. "You mean the *pai-gow* parlor owner I talked to over in Chinatown East about Tony Mok?"

"That's the one. The tape has Kennedy selling stolen cars to Danny Leung. Edgar Lau is there acting as a go-between. The Auto Squad confirmed that Danny Leung is under investigation for the exportation of stolen vehicles to Zimbabwe, Kenya, and Uganda. The evidence is all on tape—a list of business fronts, drop boxes, and contacts not only in Toronto but in Vancouver and New York as well—everything the Auto Squad needs to write viable warrants on Danny Leung, Donald Kennedy, and all the rest of those guys. Donald Kennedy's going down. And he's going down hard. I'm glad. After what he did to Regina, I'm really glad."

One of the first people Gilbert told about Donald Kennedy's arrest was Rosalyn Surrey.

"That's wonderful news," she said. But she sounded flat, uninterested, as if she really didn't care one way or the other. "I'm glad you got him," she said. "Edgar would have been . . . happy."

"And we've all but concluded our murder investigation," he said. He looked at her more closely. She seemed at loose ends, sat there in her chair as if she had nothing to do, appeared immobilized by everything that had happened to her in the last six weeks. "We may have to ask your husband to testify," he said. She looked fragile. He had to tread softly here. "How's Garth doing, anyway?"

She took a moment to answer. "Garth and I are getting a divorce," she said. "I tried." She smiled wistfully. "I really tried. But as far as our marriage is concerned . . . well . . . the grass just won't grow there anymore."

The next person he told about the Donald Kennedy arrest was Constable Jeremy Austin. Austin was jubilant.

"If you want me to testify, I'll be there," he said. "And thank you. My family's going to be able to sleep for the first time in a year."

"We want you to write a first-degree murder warrant on Pearl Wu," said Frank Hukowich. Hukowich was smiling, barely able to suppress his glee. "You did good work, Barry." Gilbert glanced at Ross Paulsen. Paulsen's gray hair had been freshly barbered, shaved close, looked more than ever like the nap of a tennis ball. "We're really happy with what you did for us," said Hukowich.

Gilbert looked at Tim Nowak. His staff inspector wouldn't meet his eyes.

"Tim, this isn't first-degree," said Gilbert. "Why would we want to ruin a young woman's life like this? I'll go with manslaughter or second-degree—she should do some time—but I don't think she planned to murder Edgar. There's no premeditation here. She just lost her head and winged a cap at him. You know the circumstances. You know what he did to her. The way he broke her heart."

Gilbert saw his words meant nothing to Nowak.

"Barry," said Paulsen, "we really have to insist on murder-one. It's the only way we're going to get any leverage out of her."

"Leverage?" said Gilbert.

"If you write a manslaughter or a second-degree, she's going to walk," said Paulsen. "Her lawyers will tell the jury she shot Edgar to save Tony's life, and that'll be it. They'll play the tape from your night out on the boat. Damn, I wish you hadn't mentioned the self-defense angle to Tony. The judge will throw it out as justifiable homicide. And then how will we ever use it as leverage against Bing Wu? We don't care if Pearl shot Edgar in defense of Tony. We just want her convicted. And that means murder-one."

"But that's not the way it happened," said Gilbert, hunkering down for Pearl's sake. "It wasn't murder-one."

"That might be true," said Paulsen, "but our lawyers are going to make it murder-one by going with the robbery theory. The slashed futons, the books pulled from the bookcase, and so forth. That way, we get a conviction no matter what."

So. They were going to use the robbery strategy after all. He had to fight it.

"I already told you, Donald Kennedy did that," he said. "Take a look at the time lines in my report."

"Pearl slashed the futons," said Paulsen, brooking no argument. "Pearl took the books down from the shelves. She committed robbery, and shot Edgar in the act of a felony. That's murder-one."

"But that's not the way it happened," insisted Gilbert.

"We've got a big budget for this, Barry," said Paulsen. "There's no point in fighting us."

"Barry," said Nowak, as unflappable as ever, "Ross and Frank have spoken to their respective legal departments. Donald Kennedy will have no place in this prosecution. Your twenty-four-hour report describing the condition of the apartment will. The two will never intersect. That's the way it's got to be."

"But that's not the way it happened," Gilbert said again.

Frank Hukowich frowned. "Why don't you let a jury decide how it happened?"

"If you have the Crown argue first-degree murder, she'll go to jail for twenty-five years," said Gilbert. "And that's not fair, not after seven years with Bing Wu. Hasn't she suffered enough?"

Paulsen smiled a grim little smile. "She can deal her way down," he said. "What better way to make Bing Wu suffer? We can use Pearl to chisel away at the old man." Paulsen took a deep breath, his smile intensifying. "You did good work, detective. We're all proud of you. You're a real hero."

"So you're going to throw Pearl's life away just so you can hurt Bing Wu?"

"We've got her, we're going to use her," said Paulsen. "We're going to squeeze every drop we can out of her. We want to inflict as much psychological damage on Wu as we can."

"I'll go for manslaughter," said Gilbert. "But murder-one's cruel and unusual as far as I'm concerned."

"Barry," said Nowak. "There's more at stake here. Really there is. I've reviewed the facts of the case with our own Trials Preparation section. They agree with Frank and Ross. On a manslaughter or second-degree charge, she walks, with the charges argued down to justifiable homicide because of Tony Mok. With a murder-one, backed by the slashed futons and the unshelved books, she's convicted. And if she's convicted, she becomes useful to Frank and Ross. Which is the whole point of this. Look at the facts, Barry. Pearl Wu in a ransacked apartment standing over a dead Edgar Lau with a smoking gun in her hand. We can go somewhere with that. Ross and Frank can finally make some headway against the old man."

"So you're going to ruin her life," said Gilbert.

"Criminals ruin their own lives," said Hukowich.

"I'm going to have to ask you to cooperate with us, Barry," said Nowak. "Without funding from Ross and Frank, you never would have gotten as far as you did." Nowak paused. "We want you to write a murder-one warrant on Pearl. There's no other way."

Gilbert gazed at Nowak. Then at Hukowich and Paulsen. He thought of the scar on Pearl's face. He thought of her weird clothes and her crazy addiction to candy. He thought of her harrowing and strange journey through the Chinese gang underworld, of her tragic bond to Wu, of San Francisco, her destroyed escape plan, and her love for Edgar. He thought of the way these three men were commandeering his evidence and turning it upside down. He couldn't do this. He *wouldn't* do this.

"I'm sorry, Tim," he said. "I can't write your warrant."

Gilbert lifted his chin, squared his shoulders, and looked past Nowak at the rain outside.

"Then I'm sorry, Barry," said Nowak; "you're off the case." Nowak glanced at Paulsen and Hukowich, then back at Gilbert.

"Have Carol gather it up for me. I'll be handling it from here on in. I'm sorry you can't see it our way. But Frank and Ross have to hurt Bing Wu any way they can."

"Even if they have to ruin Pearl's life?" said Gilbert.

"We do what we have to, Barry," said Paulsen. "We do what we have to."

Gilbert went to Donald Kennedy's arraignment. Though he had no absolute proof, he still believed Kennedy was the one who had beaten Regina. He kept on thinking of the nine stitches in Regina's head. Of her swollen left eye. And of the angry bruise on her cheek. He wanted to see Kennedy go down. He wasn't a vengeful man, but when it came to his wife . . . well . . . he wasn't that different from Bing Wu—those who would hurt his wife had to be punished.

Lombardo came with him.

Kennedy's arraignment was held in a modern, efficient-looking courtroom in Osgoode Hall. Gilbert was surprised to find Rosalyn Surrey there.

"Julie Winslow has just stepped down as Chair of the Police Services Board," she told Gilbert. "She felt she had to resign over this. She felt she wasn't vigilant enough, considering my persistence. I'm the acting chair right now, and this is important to me. This was my ball of yarn right from the start."

She looked better. She looked revived. Now that she had a cause, now that she was acting chair of the Police Services Board, she looked . . . resuscitated. Gilbert was happy for her. Lombardo stared at Rosalyn in a soft romantic way during much of the arraignment.

The arraignment was short. The Justice listed nine felonious

charges against Kennedy, charges that could put him in jail for fifteen years, then set bail at ten thousand dollars.

Lombardo stared at Rosalyn Surrey even when the judge
whacked his gavel down.

"You should ask her out," said Gilbert, once they were standing out on the courthouse steps.

"Really?" said Lombardo.

"Go on. Ask her. Before she gets in that taxi. A young detective and the acting chair of the Police Services Board. It couldn't be
better. Go on. Ask her. Before she gets away."

Lombardo hurried across the broad open space in front of the
courthouse and caught Rosalyn just as her taxi was pulling up to
the curb.

While Lombardo spoke to Rosalyn, Donald Kennedy came out
of the courthouse with his lawyer. Gilbert looked at the man. Big
beefy face, with that perpetually contemptuous expression on his
brow, as if he believed the world were full of idiots. Those small blue
eyes of his must have looked particularly terrifying staring out of
the eyeholes of a black ski mask. Gilbert's anger flared. He thought
of Regina getting pushed on the icy parking lot behind the school.
He thought of big fists smashing into her face, of her head hitting
the rearview mirror, and of her blood dripping darkly all over the ice
as Kennedy whispered the warning into her ear, thought of her nine
stitches and how stoically she had endured the whole frightening
episode. That was his wife, and no one was going to do that to his
wife. *No* one. Before he could stop himself, he marched toward
Kennedy, his jaw set and his fists clenched.

He grabbed Kennedy by the front of his coat and shook him. "I
bet you beat your own wife too," he said. "I bet wife-beating is your
specialty."

Kennedy gazed in alarm at Gilbert, recoiling from the attack, and turned to his lawyer. "Billy, for Christ's sake, help me, will you?" he said.

The man sounded pathetic. Gilbert felt his anger draining away. He stared at Kennedy in a new light. He saw that Kennedy was scared. That Kennedy was a coward. His strategy for dealing with the world was to cheat, steal, and victimize. Gilbert couldn't prove anything. Had he taken the towel away? And was he the reason Edgar had bled to death? Had he ransacked the apartment? And what about the Chinese man? Had Dock Wen originally seen Tony Mok and later on confused him with Garth Surrey, whom he might have also seen? Had Kennedy really brutalized Regina? Maybe. Gilbert couldn't prove any of it. But he thought he saw a cold and helpless guilt lying like a curse in the man's eyes. He could have trashed Kennedy right then and there. But he realized he didn't have to. Kennedy had already trashed himself. Kennedy would never be the same again. His job, his pension, his reputation, and his freedom were gone. He gave Kennedy a shove, then turned to Kennedy's lawyer.

"Good luck," he told the lawyer. "You're going to need it."

Kennedy and his lawyer moved off. Gilbert let them go. Kennedy was ruined. That was enough. He took a deep breath. He pitied the man. He looked up at the sky. The sky was blue. For the first time all winter there wasn't a single cloud in the sky. The city felt buoyant around him. He could feel its three million inhabitants coming alive in the sunshine. January, the beginning of a new year. He would forget about Kennedy. To Kennedy, this blue sky meant nothing. To Kennedy, January and a new year wouldn't amount to much.

He watched Lombardo talking to Rosalyn.

He watched Rosalyn shrug, then shake her head. She gave Joe

the smile all women gave potential suitors when they were turning them down. Lombardo accepted the rejection gracefully. He turned to go. He walked toward Gilbert, a distressed expression on his handsome Mediterranean face. Gilbert thought he'd never seen the man look so defeated. For the first time in living memory, Detective Giovanni Lombardo, the Don Juan of the Homicide Squad, was having a hard time getting a date, hadn't had one in over four and a half months now. At least not a real date. Gilbert discounted his dates with Jennifer. Could it be true? Was the playboy of the Western world really losing his touch? Would celibacy indeed become a habit for Lombardo?

Gilbert was just beginning to give up hope entirely when Rosalyn reached out and grasped Lombardo by the sleeve. A relinquishing grin came to her face. Joe turned around, surprised. She opened her purse, took out her card, and handed it to Lombardo. She said a few more words, then got into her taxi and drove away.

Lombardo stood there for a moment, looking at the card, perplexed. Then he turned around and came Gilbert's way. He was now smiling like a boy.

"Well?" asked Gilbert, when Lombardo reached him.

"She didn't want to at first," said Lombardo.

"But . . ."

"But I got her card."

"I saw that."

"She says I should call her in a few months. She wants to have a few months to get over things. She says wait until spring."

Gilbert nodded. "Spring's a good time," he said. "A great time to fall in love."

Lombardo's smile broadened. "Yeah," he said. "That's what I thought. And you know what else?"

"What?"

"I think I'm getting my touch back."

"I think you are too. I was worried about you. I thought we'd seen the last of the man with all the moves."

"No," said Joe. "No, I'm still here. And I think I'll be here for a long time." He stared longingly after the taxi. "Unless of course Rosalyn Surrey turns out to be the one."

Gilbert left work early that day. He just wanted to go home. Jennifer was still home but would be leaving to go back to school in the next couple of days, had taken an extra week off to pull herself together. She was feeling better. *They* were feeling better. He just wanted to put Pearl and Edgar behind him, put Kennedy behind him, move on, recharge himself for the next difficult and complicated homicide that would inevitably come his way. Nothing could revive his spirits better than some time spent with his daughter. He wanted to be with Jennifer. Regina was at work, Nina was at school, and Jennifer, with a longer Christmas break, was the only one home. As he got out of his Windstar, he waved at the two plainclothes officers parked in the unmarked Caprice across the street. His security detail. To protect him and his family from triad reprisals. Bing Wu would no doubt be furious about the part he had played in Pearl's arrest.

The television was on in the den. The sound of ocean waves came from the television. He shook his head, smiled. Jennifer was watching her videotape again. He put his briefcase on the floor, took off his coat, and walked to the den. The door was ajar. He pushed it open.

Jennifer was sprawled on the couch drinking 7-Up and eating ketchup-flavored potato chips. A kid again. His daughter again.

"Can I come in?" he asked.

She looked up, grinned. "Sure," she said. She sat up, made room for him on the couch.

He sat next to her and turned his eyes to the television. The video, shot on consumer-quality camcorder stock, showed twenty-foot waves, gray and cold, rolling to shore at Lockeport, Nova Scotia. Winter on the North Atlantic. Far in the distance, Gilbert spotted two icebergs. Jennifer was standing on the beach watching the waves, her dark hair flicking in the wind. A bereft scene, a stark and frigid seascape that made Gilbert want to shiver. But then suddenly, out on the waves, a figure emerged, dressed in a wet suit, riding the crest of the tallest wave on a surfboard. The man riding the surfboard through the sub-freezing water was Karl Randall. Patchy gray clouds roved southward, pushed like a pack of marauders by the relentless north wind. The morning sun rose to the left of the screen, backlighting the waves, making their crests translucent. Karl Randall did a lot of crazy things—stealing his friend's car, using heart medication as a recreational drug, driving drunk—but surfing the North Atlantic in the middle of winter, when the waves were at their biggest and the temperatures at their coldest, had to be one of the craziest. Yet Gilbert had to admire it. He glanced at his daughter.

"You loved him, didn't you?" he said.

She looked at him, surprised. Perhaps she heard the acceptance in his voice. Or the fatherly tenderness. Or the unspoken apology. Or the sorrow he felt for Pearl. She moved closer. He put his arm around her. She nodded.

"Yeah, dad," she said. "I did."

They sat there and watched Karl Randall surf the winter sea.

And as they watched, Gilbert couldn't help thinking of Pearl again. He wondered where Pearl's father might be. Whether he was grateful for the sacrifices Pearl had made for him. Whether he loved his daughter the way he loved Jennifer. And whether he would ever see Pearl again. Gilbert realized he was lucky. He had his daughter. He would always have his daughter. No matter what happened out there . . . out on the street . . . she would always be here.

And that made him feel like just about the luckiest man alive.

UPPER MERION TOWNSHIP LIBRARY
175 WEST VALLEY FORGE ROAD
KING OF PRUSSIA, PA 19406

ADULT DEPT. - (610) 265-4805
CHILDREN'S DEPT. - (610) 265-4806

1-02